To Steph Harbyon

Santa 6/12/2007

Preseli Jack

Richard Alderman

Published by
Terrace Books
Box 522
Swansea
SA1 9DE
e-mail: terracebooks@hotmail.co.uk

First published in Great Britain 2006

Richard Alderman

Published by Terrace Books
Box 522
Swansea SA1 9DE

ISBN 10 0-9554030-0-6
ISBN 13 978-0-9554030-0-2

Publisher prefix 0-9554030

Printed by Gwasg Gomer Press, Llandysul, Wales

Cover design and painting by Christine Eynon

No character in this book is related to any person living or dead.

The geographical background to this story is that part of Wales which I have known. Historically, I have had to do my own research. The public libraries of Swansea and Llanelli have been particularly helpful. Should any reader find fault with any of the historical or geographical facts in this book then only I can be blamed..

I particularly have to thank Lynne Smith and Christine Eynon, without whose assistance this book would not have been written.

To Vicki and Rachel

Preseli Jack

Chapter 1

It was nearing dusk on the first Tuesday in November 1858. The Cardigan hiring fair had been held the previous day. A mile outside Newcastle-Emlyn, on the coach road leading to Carmarthen, was a man walking very briskly. He had a grey military cape over his head and shoulders to protect him from the driving rain which came from his right hand side. Keeping to the hedge, he only felt the full force of the rain when he passed a gateway. Then he pulled the cape further over his face. Looking neither to right nor left and only occasionally ahead, Preseli Jack was a man in a hurry.

The light was failing; he was wet through and knew he would have to find somewhere to sleep within the next hour or two. The grey wool cape was now completely soaked and clung to him like a second skin, giving him no protection against the unrelenting downpour. It was an uphill trail and he continued to climb for another two miles. Now looking around him, he hoped to see a track and hopefully a light from a farm where he could shelter. His pace did not slacken as he wished to get as far away from Cardigan as possible.

There was a track to his left, which looked as though it was used regularly. Turning into it, his pace immediately slowed down. Water was gushing from it but as there was no grass growing in the trackway, there seemed every chance of it leading to a habitation. At last he felt less conspicuous and became aware he was quite out of breath. It was now almost dark. His eyes gradually adjusted to the failing light and he continued to walk, but without seeing any sign of life. This went on for some time and he had almost given up hope when two faint lights appeared, one near the other. Walking on for a further half-mile, the lights grew larger. The water that continued to gush down the track had moved stones which he tripped over. Now shivering all over, he drew nearer to a farmhouse which was double-fronted with a cowshed attached at the side. One light came from the cowshed and the other from the window of the house which partially lit the hall as the door was open.

The cowshed door was also open and steam was visible inside. He walked towards it, removing the cape from his head. As he entered, the six heavily-horned welsh cows glanced towards him and then returned to eating their hay. Over the noise of this came the bish-bish-bish of someone milking. This continued for some seconds. Jack coughed. The milker continued to press his head into the side of the cow, intent on what he was doing. He was a man of about sixty with a head of thinning white hair, short in stature and with a florid face, all the more so now because of the effort he was making. Jack coughed again, only louder. It gave the milker a start. Gripping the bucket, he looked around at this visitor. Not having good sight, he could not initially focus on this man. The milker rose, stool in one hand and bucket in another then turned around to face him. What he saw before him was a man, maybe in his early twenties, with a face made bright red by the rain and cold.

Jack was broad and his good head of fair, curly hair was flattened by the rain. Gradually Ieaun focused on his visitor, looking into his eyes which filled him with a momentary paralysis. The eyes were blue and had a piercing quality which made him feel defenceless.

'I'm lost,' said the visitor in a soft tone which gave his face a milder aspect. 'Where am I?' His words and manner had a pacifying effect on the milker.

'You're a long way from the road. Where're you going?'

'Carmarthen. I can't go any further, can I sleep in the barn?'

'Man, you're wet.'

6

Ieaun drew breath, hung up the stool and put the bucket on the windowsill. It gave him a moment to think. Fearful, he didn't want to agree to Jack's request but felt he could not refuse. As always he left these decisions to his wife, Mair.

'I'll see the missus.' He grasped the milk pail and, as he passed his visitor, he was again aware of his very powerful presence. Just under six feet tall, he was quite broad and exuded power and a capacity for violence. He walked back quickly to the house with the milking pail and put it on the table.

'Mair, there's a man in the cowshed, says he's lost and wants to sleep in the barn. What do you think?'

'In this weather?'

'Yes. He's soaked through.'

'Is he a tramp? Funny to be here in this weather.'

'Not this one, there's plenty of work in him.'

She was curious as they had few visitors this far off the road. 'Well, bring him in.'

'You sure?'

'Yes, of course. Couldn't leave the devil out in this weather.'

Mair was a cheerful woman whose four children had all left home. She was curious about the visitor.

Ieaun went back to the byre. 'Come on, the missus'll give you something.' They walked to the front door. 'Go on in, you.'

Mair faced the visitor. He looked at her directly. She could feel her face go red all over. Men and Mair had always got on well but never had she felt like this in the last thirty years. Her heart beat faster and she was quite overcome by him. This feeling was only momentary but Jack was aware of the effect he had on her and gave a very slight smile. He knew he would have a warm bed and something to eat. He was shivering badly which immediately brought out the mother in her.

'What's your name?'

'Jack.'

'Jack what?'

'They call me Preseli Jack.'

'Travelling far?'

'Carmarthen.'

'Have you eaten today?'

'No.'

'Get those wet clothes off, Jack or you'll catch your death, man. You're shivering all over.'

Being made aware of his shivering reminded him of his predicament. 'And your cape first,' she said as she pushed him towards the fire. It put new life into him. Going downstairs, she returned with a large blanket and some of Ieaun's clothes. 'There, go in the next room and change.' The clothes were too small but they were dry and warmed his chilled body.

'Cavalry boots and a cavalry cape. Been a soldier, have you?' she asked.

'Yes.'

'Crimea?'

'Yes.'

'Wounded?'

'Slightly.'

He was missing a finger on his left hand and had a nasty gash higher up. Mair fussed around her visitor as the evening wore on. In his youth he had been without a mother and her attentions were as welcome as they were unexpected. Slowly he relaxed.

Two hours later a meal of salt bacon, swede and potatoes was on the table, also a jug of cider. He hadn't eaten for twenty-four hours but gulped his cider down and immediately felt the effect. Then he reflected and felt he had been discourteous. The meal eaten, Jack pondered on the past and the future and his present position. Mair became curious.

'Been working on a farm?'

'Yes.'

'Nearby?'

'Near Cardigan.'

'No work at the fair?'

'None.'

'Big man like you should get work.'

'Getting it's easy, keeping it is the problem.'

'A few quarrels?'

'More than a few.'

'Punch up?'

'A few.'

Mair smiled at him. He smiled back, looking straight at her. They really did have an understanding.

'Move on then, there's plenty of work in the iron works and the mines.' He nodded. She had touched on the matter that was going through his head. What trouble he had been in she had no idea but she was sure it was serious and he was anxious to put as much distance between himself and Cardigan as possible.

'I was at Waterloo,' said Ieaun. 'A long time ago.'

'Wounded?'

'Came out without a scratch, but left too many friends behind. Wouldn't want to do it again.' Mair was surprised. He hadn't mentioned this in years. 'We got rid of Bony.'

Jack became interested in trying to picture this short and very mild old man
in military uniform, facing the army of Napoleon.

'At the front.?' he asked.

'All day.'

' Infantry?'

'Yes, in the squares.'

'Lucky to be alive?'

'A miracle. God was on my side that day. Not many made it.'

'A long day?'

'Longest day of my life. Don't know why I'm alive. Still, saw the Old Guard retreat. Biggest cheer I ever heard in my life. Thought I might see tomorrow. Never want to see a day like that again. Death everywhere.'

Mair had never before heard Ieaun speak of his time in the army in such detail and she saw him now in a different light. She wanted to hear Jack's story.

'You were a soldier in the Crimea, then?' There was a

9

brief pause. He didn't feel inclined to reply but felt he had too.

'Yes, I was.'

Ieaun was interested in Jack's story. 'Cavalry or infantry?'

'Commissariat, you know the waggoners, suppliers, transport.'

'Why not the sabre regiments?'

'Got recruited on the docks. We'd taken a hundred and forty drove of cattle to the docks to be killed and salted for the navy and I got caught. Just like that. There's no future in droving. Took the first offer.'

'If you got the sabre units you might have bought it?'

'For sure. A lot of blood got spilt out there. We didn't have such big losses. It was getting in and out with the supplies when we lost a few.'

'More fun than droving?'

'For sure. Seen the world. Come out alive. Trouble is you can't put the clock back. The railways will put an end to the droving. Being a farm servant doesn't suit me. Got to move on.'

'Quite right.'

The conversation dried up. In the forefront of everyone's mind was Jack's future but they all remained silent. It was getting late and the heat from the fire made them drowsy, the two men falling briefly asleep. Seeing this she said,   'Time you two went to bed.'

The couple retired to bed and left their visitor to sleep by the fire. Mair and Ieuan lay awake in bed together. Ieaun reverted to his old mild and cautious self, no longer the survivor of Waterloo. 'Jack's in trouble and I don't want to be dragged into it,' he said. 'Back from the war, can't settle, handy with his fists, that's why he can't settle.'

'Don't worry, go to sleep,' She was twenty again and tingling all over at the thought of being with Jack. She would have made a farmer out of him, he'd never have got away from me, she thought. 'You were a soldier once, who looked after you when you came back from Waterloo?' She reminded her husband. She smiled to herself. They went to sleep.

Jack awoke before dawn and immediately checked that he had the three sovereigns which were all that had been due to him from the last year on Willie James's Dyffryn farm. He was relieved. It would be difficult for him if he lost that. Sitting up, he considered his options: go back to the army; go to sea, emigrate; go to South Wales and become a miner or iron worker. He couldn't make up his mind but felt an opportunity would present itself.

His clothes were now dry. After washing his face in the spring outside, he waited for Ieaun and Mair to get up which they soon did. It occurred to him to take some food and leave before they appeared, but he dismissed this from his mind. Rarely in his life had anyone been kind to him, rarely had he been able to trust anyone. Mair was an exception. The thought went through his head, 'I could stay and work here.' It was a momentary thought, he knew that the farm was too small to support a servant and it was also too near Cardigan. He shrugged his shoulders and smiled a cynical smile to himself. 'There are not going to be any easy options for me. Have there ever been?'

Mair prepared the breakfast while Ieaun fed the cattle and counted the sheep. Jack stood awkwardly in the kitchen with nothing to do and wanting to be off.

'Want anything done Mair?'

'No, sit down you.'

He didn't sit down. She crossed the kitchen, looked him directly in the eye and took hold of his scarred left arm which was covered in thick fair hair.

'Are you going to be alright?'

'Don't worry, I'll get by.' Her concern touched him.

They all had breakfast together in a heavy silence. He was anxious to go. She gave him a loaf of bread and almost a pound of cheese, wrapped up. She took his arm and squeezed it once more.

'Look after yourself.' There were tears in her eyes. She released his arm. He took hold of her by each wrist for no more than a second. 'I will.'

11

He walked towards the road without looking back. Had she been able to see his face as he walked away she would have seen tears also. Reflecting on when he had last shed tears, he could not remember.

The rain had passed and it was blowing a cold dry southwest wind, which caught him on the right hand side of his face and sharpened his mind. Underfoot it was still wet but the water flowing down the track was reduced to a trickle. Stones had been displaced in the downpour and he had to keep his eyes on the track.

Reaching the main road, he turned toward Cynwyl Elfed, reaching it by midday. Not stopping or slackening his pace, he walked through the village and continued on the coach road to Carmarthen which adjoins the Afon Gwili. The river was in spate. He found the increased sound of the water pleasantly distracting. By nightfall he wanted to be beyond Carmarthen, so that he would be within striking distance of Swansea and a new life whatever that had in store for him. Cardigan was the past; he had no wish ever to see it again. No more a farm servant or a drover.

There were a few signs of life in the villages he passed through, people carrying water, driving a few cows and clearing up some of the damage done by the torrential rain. Slowly Carmarthen came into view. The road moved away from the Gwili and towards the town.

He would like to have avoided the town but the bridge over the Twyi was the only route available. As he approached the town he knew it was market day as the streets were full. Most of the trading had by this time been done and the life of the market was now in the streets and taverns. Looking down and not slackening his pace, he walked through the town. Briefly looking up, he saw a figure he had known more than ten years before: Eddie, the drover's mate. That day he had obviously had a great deal to drink and was looking very shabby. They looked one another in the eye and established mutual recognition.

He put his arm around Jack's shoulder and grinned in a

childish way. 'Jack, bach, how are you? How many years is it? You're a big lad now. Come and have a drink with Eddie.'

'No, I've got to get on.'

'Come on boy, have a drink with me for old times sake.'

'No I've got to get on. What you doing Eddie?'

'Things have gone bad. Lost the job with Tommy. Only doing the odd bit of droving, it's bad, bad.' He became reflective and maudlin. 'Next stop the workhouse.'

'Eddie, I've got to get on.' He broke away from the grasp on his shoulder and continued his brisk walk, with Eddie shouting incoherently after him.

Walking over Carmarthen Bridge and out of town, he got to the top of Nantycaws just before dusk. As he walked up the hill, he looked for any isolated barns well away from the farmhouses, where he could spend the night. Around half a mile from the top he saw one on the right. He slackened his pace, awaiting the approaching darkness which would allow him to enter the barn without being seen. Climbing over the gate at the side of the road, he walked across two small fields and, opening a large wooden oak door, entered the barn which was half filled with sheaves of oats. Pulling the door shut, he climbed up onto the sheaves. It was dark in the barn and he was only very dimly aware of his surroundings. Making a trench to lie in amongst the oats, he spread his cape over himself and settled down to sleep. It was at that moment that he realised how hungry he was. In his anxiety to cover such a distance, he had forgotten to eat and, remembering the food he had been given, ate about half of it. He then fell into a deep sleep.

During the course of the night he heard a rustling noise near him, not loud but very close, and the unmistakable sound of straw being moved. He was in no doubt what it was. 'Bloody rats!!!' he muttered to himself. From that moment he slept only fitfully and lashed out blindly when he heard them nearby. They had been just as bold in the Crimea and their targets had frequently been human. It sent a shiver down his spine. Before the sun came up over the eastern horizon, he was fully awake. He jumped down to the ground holding his bundle of food. Walking round to the back of the barn which had a hedge adjoining, he cleaned his cape of all signs of the oat straw, did the same with his trousers and then combed his hair. He took the bread and cheese out and noticed the rats had eaten just a little of the cheese. Eating half what was left, he then walked quickly to the road and resumed his journey to Swansea.

The weather continued cold and windy, the views were extensive. Feeling a real change in his life, the fear diminished with the time and distance from Cardigan and his expectations for the future increased with every mile. He gradually became more hopeful.

Shortly before nightfall he arrived at the top of Mayhill, overlooking the town. Nothing prepared him for the frenzied and polluted scene of industrial activity. The docks were full of ships and there was not a glimpse of water between them. Above the docks and adjoining the river Tawe were the copper smelting works surrounded by waste heaps and discharging smoke of a colour all its own. Work at a large imposing iron foundry stopped for not one minute in the entire year. Railway trucks constantly came and went. Lights from the furnaces were always visible. Raw materials going in. Iron products coming out. All the while, men were working without respite. Surrounding this industrial activity were rows and rows of terraced houses built one near another, with hardly any streets visible between them.

He looked at the scene in fascination. The gaslights were now being lit which gave the whole scene an eerie, manic quality. As a background to the frenzied human activity was the constant hum of noise which was interspersed with the steam blasts from the railways, change of shift hooters and the foghorns of ships in the bay. He knew there was no going back now. Standing for a time in the darkness, he appeared mesmerised by the scene below. Always at his best in the morning, he decided to find a hedge to sleep under and face the town afresh the following day. Finishing the remains of his bread and cheese, he slept fitfully for the rest of the night thinking of the past eighteen years, what had happened to him and why he was alone under the hedge. What would the future hold?

Chapter Two

It was early in the winter of 1840. Around fifty people were crowded into the Tabernacle Chapel that was built right under the Preseli Hills. It was cold, wet and windy outside and almost as cold and wet inside. The misty breath of the mourners hung over the congregation, several of whom were audibly sobbing. The roughly made coffin lay in front of the altar. The congregation, all from the immediate vicinity, were farming people dressed in their Sunday best, paying their last respects to a mother for whom the struggle to rear a family had proved too much. No one was talking and the only sound was a muffled one of damp clothes moving as the mourners stirred in the pews. Everyone's gaze was directed toward Meg, a sixteen year old who was now head of the family. She was crying uncontrollably and continuously. Annie, aged thirteen and Mary, aged ten were crying but not with the intensity of their eldest sister. Further along sat Jack, only five years old and somehow unaware of the enormity of the tragedy. Though of the family, he seemed not to be part of it.

In the pew behind were the deceased's two brothers; weak, ineffectual men who somehow held down work and supported their families but who both spent too much time in the local tavern. They were going through the motions of grief but were sharp and observant as to what was going on.

The service began and hymns were sung. Picton Jenkins, the minister, dressed all in black and much loved by his parishioners, preached for more than half an hour. Repeating again and again how good the mother, Maud, had been and how, with all the

16

difficulties ahead, God would provide. Meg, Annie and Mary again sobbed without restraint. There was hardly a dry eye in the chapel apart from Jack who seemed quite unaware of the proceedings. Even the brothers Eddie and Jim were visibly upset. The preacher had no more to say, the final hymn was sung and the service came to an end.

Four men (two workers from a nearby farm and two decrepit old men hired by the undertaker) lifted the coffin onto their shoulders and walked towards the grave. It was obvious to everyone, even Jack, that the coffin was painfully light. Slowly the mourners followed. It had been wet for some days and even now the rain was coming in with the driving south-west wind. Everyone was wet through and, in spite of the occasion, wanting to be home as soon as possible. The recently dug grave had at least two feet of water in it which made the atmosphere even more despairing. Prayers were said. 'Ashes to ashes, dust to dust.' Meg threw a handful of earth in the grave and also a bunch of snowdrops. The grave-digger shovelled the first earth onto the coffin which gave a hollow thud. Jack listened to that sound and for the first time the full tragedy of the death hit him and tears came into his eyes. Never would he forget that moment till his dying day. The sisters hugged one another and continued to cry. Jack stood by, overlooked by all. Excluded, he felt unable to show any emotion and stood back like an observer.

Slowly the family, now only four, walked back to their home with a dozen close friends who included their two uncles and the minister. The rain continued without respite as they walked. It was a two-roomed cottage called Ty-owen. The family lived in one room and slept in the other. It was now full. On the table were welsh cakes and tea as well as bread and cheese.

On everyone's mind was, 'How will this family survive?' It had to be discussed. The elder uncle, who had drunk a good deal before the funeral and was now in need of more, said to Meg, 'Any beer?' Through her tears she glared at him 'No.' It would be no good pursuing this request. Dismissing from his mind what he had just said and trying to appear concerned, he said 'What's going to happen to the family now?' She glared at him with even more intensity. 'It will be kept together. I'll see to that. Don't you worry, good boy, we shan't trouble you.' He backed away; the whole room had heard their conversation. In a moment he became sober and reflected on what he had said, looking and feeling ashamed. He wanted to go as soon as possible.

Picton Jenkins had overheard this exchange and came over to speak to Meg. He was a kindly man of more than seventy, quite bent with thin white hair and not carrying his age very well. 'It won't be easy. How are you going to manage?'

'They are going to the workhouse over my dead body.' She looked him straight in the face. He had known families stay together after a very significant death but rarely had he seen a family face such a bleak future. 'It'll be hard, very hard, but we'll manage somehow.'

'You don't have family nearby?'

'No, apart from my uncles and they'll be no help.'

'What about your father's family, they were from Devon weren't they? Could they help? What about Jack's father, does he keep in touch?'

'No, he left before Jack was born. Don't know where he is. Wouldn't want him around. I hated that man. Real trouble.'

'You're going to have your hands full, Meg. I'll call in again soon.'

The house was starting to empty now. Many left money in the bowl on the table. The uncles had delayed going. They had wanted to go for some time but it felt more awkward to go than to stay. They wanted to appear responsible but were unsure what to do next. The elder one said, 'Well Jack, you're the man of the house now. You'll have to look after your sisters, won't you?' Not thinking he had got through to him, he repeated himself. Jack looked at him without saying anything but felt very annoyed by the remark. He had never liked his uncle and now he didn't trust him. The uncles left without leaving any money on the table. The elder said, 'Call us if you want anything.'

The minister took his leave of them. 'I'm coming back very

soon.' He left five sovereigns in the bowl. Meg noticed.

'You're too good minister, you shouldn't do that.'

'That won't last long with all your mouths to feed.'

The whole family were devastated by the tragedy but only Meg realised the implications and the superhuman effort which would be required to keep them together. They were all asleep under two blankets in the bedroom. The fire had gone out and the house got slowly colder as the night wore on. This made sleep more fitful and they needed to huddle closer together. That is, except for Meg. She hardly slept, but just lay on her back staring at the ceiling. Her thoughts were of what would happen in the next days and weeks. She wasn't even sure what they would have for breakfast because there were only the remains of the funeral meal and little of that. At the back of her mind was the prospect of the workhouse with all the shame and despair that accompanied it.

The minister's gift would pay the undertaker and keep them in food for a fortnight. How would they survive after that? It would no doubt be a constant struggle. She had grown up quickly, left school at thirteen, run the house and looked after her mother while she was dying and been entirely responsible for the family for the last year. While her mother was still alive, she felt she had some emotional support though no practical assistance. Now she felt totally alone. Almost overnight she became even more single minded and determined. She also became visibly older.

The dreaded dawn came. Meg got up. 'All of you out of bed,' she shouted. They rose, rubbing their eyes, knowing that getting up immediately was preferable to the venom of a second call. Somehow they all knew that life was not going to be the same again. They ate the remains of the funeral fare.

'Annie, there'll be no more school for you.'

'Why, Meg?'

'You must work now. We need money, my girl. We've four mouths to feed. With you in work there'll only be three.'

'Work where?'

'Wherever I find you a job.'

'But I like school. Why?'

'Like school or not, it's work for you.'

Annie cried quietly for some minutes.

'Girl, you're going to work, like it or not and soon too. You're not going to school again. Stay in and look after Jack.'

'Where you going, Meg?'

'To look for work for you.'

Never putting off till tomorrow what could be done today, Meg put on her only coat to make a tour of the farms and houses to look for work.

'Annie, mind Jack. Don't know when I'll be back.' Annie nodded, knowing that she didn't have a choice.

Walking down the track and the mile to the village, Meg's first call was to the carpenter's shop which she entered, seeing the owner at the bench working on another coffin. Looking at it, she was reminded of what had happened but steeled herself to the day ahead and what had to be done.

'The funeral cost, Billy?'

Billy, a good natured man who had inherited the shop from his father, stood up, surprised by the visit and the request. He did not want to charge the family but also did not want to offer charity.

'I'll give you the bill in time.'

'I want it now.'

She heard someone coming into the workshop behind her but did not turn round. She was aware of a presence behind her, taking everything in.

'Meg, I haven't made it out. You'll have it in time.'

'Billy, I want to pay it now.' She was becoming irritated, pulling the five sovereigns from her pocket.

'Come in the back,' he said, taking her into the kitchen of his house which adjoined his business and closed the door. 'Sit down, Meg. I am not going to charge you.' She protested that the last thing she wanted was charity, but he could not be persuaded to take her money. 'Did you see who came in behind you?' She

shook her head. 'Your uncle. Watch him and those sovereigns.'
He looked her directly in the eye. She understood. She also felt
she was no longer entirely on her own.

'I will,' she responded gratefully.

She had to go through the workshop to get out and saw that
her uncle was still there. 'Managing alright, Meg?'

'Yes,' she replied slowly, looking him straight in the eye.
She felt strength within herself as he was unable to meet her
gaze.

Looking away from her he said, 'Come over any time.'

'What for?'

'Perhaps we could help you.'

'What help have you given so far?' He didn't know how to
reply.

In his mind was the problem of how he could get through
the day without work and how he could raise money to go to the
tavern as soon as possible. Meg had money.

'You know Meg, I'm off work because of a cough and we
need money for the house. Could you lend your old uncle one of
those sovereigns? The family badly needs money.' During this
request she was walking away from him and he following her.
Though smiling inside, she kept a straight face. At that instant
she could not resist turning around and savouring the moment.
She looked him straight in the eye, relishing a sense of power,
knowing she had seen through his ploy and that he was aware of
the fact.

'No, good boy, try someone else.'

A look of shame and defeat crossed his face. It was the gesture
of the drunk humiliating himself for one more drink. He knew
his request was hopeless but couldn't help making one last try.
'We got no food in the house.'

'Get to work then,' was her reply and she walked away
down the road and over the bridge. It had been a good day so far.
Would her luck continue?

She knew the smaller farms would not give Annie work, but
she tried the three larger ones without success. They were all

sympathetic, knew what a desperate position she was in but could not give a girl work, even a very young one. They had trouble enough paying the wages of the farm servants they had, but employing a domestic servant was out of the question. The last farm she visited suggested she ask at the Hall. Admiral Sir George owned the only place in the neighbourhood where they employed domestic staff. It hadn't occurred to her before but it was her last hope.

It was now raining again and she was starting to get wet through. It was a mile and a half to the Hall and as she continued to walk she became progressively wetter. Though near despair, she had not run out of courage.

The Hall was the estate of Admiral Sir George. Walking up the drive, she was fearful in the extreme. Though she had never met him she had heard of him by reputation and he was regarded by all as a near god-like figure. Indeed he also owned the last three farms she had visited. Walking up the last quarter of a mile through an avenue of oaks she saw the Hall in front of her. Never had a walk lasted so long though it only took five minutes. She had never been near the Hall before and was quite overcome by the size: feeling full of apprehension she nonetheless carried on. Walking to the back door, she knocked. It was opened by a scullery maid younger than herself.

She gave Meg a mocking laugh in response to her dishevelled appearance and lack of confidence.

'I'm looking for work for my sister.'

The maid laughed and sneered with even more zeal. She would not give Meg a reply. The housekeeper, a large woman with a firm mouth and eyes of authority looked toward the door. 'Who is it, Bessie?'

'A woman wants work,' she replied in a loud voice, still giggling and not taking her eyes off the caller.

'I'll deal with this. You go back to work.' She didn't encourage humour amongst her staff.   Returning to work, the maid ensured she was within sight and earshot of the caller.

'Yes?' questioned the housekeeper.

Bessie continued to look, listen and mock. Meg was aware of this even though she did not return the stare.

'You see, I'm looking for work for my sister.'

'There's no work here.'

Meg's eyes filled with tears which she wiped away with the back of her hand.   Then a flash of recognition came over the housekeeper's face. 'You're the eldest Lloyd girl aren't you?'

'Yes.'

'Sorry to hear about your mother but we don't have anything here.'

The door closed behind her as she walked down the drive, beyond tears and beyond despair. It seemed that determination was not enough.

'Have you got me a job Meg?' asked Annie when she returned.

'No.'

'I can go back to school then.'

'I'm getting you a job if it kills me.'

That night they ate potato and swede.

Though Meg had been unaware of it, Lady Jane had seen her from the drawing room window. 'There's a dreadful looking woman coming up the drive.'

'Mmmm,' replied Admiral Sir George who was dozing in a comfortable armchair in front of the fire. He didn't want to be disturbed. It was a large room in semi-darkness, lighted only by the fire and the failing light coming from outside at the end of this cold damp winter day.

'Why on earth is she coming here? She looks like a roadster.'

'Mmmm…. staff will deal with her.'

Meg walked towards the back door. Lady Jane returned to her letter writing. Ten minutes later she saw the same person walking down the drive to leave.

The housekeeper knocked at the drawing room door some time later. 'Yes?' called out Lady Jane. Walking in confidently, holding a notebook, the housekeeper gave a small curtsey.

'Lady Jane. The arrangements for dinner tonight, I believe there are eight.'

'That's right Emily. Soup followed by pheasant. How long have they hung?'   'Five days m'lady.'

'Who on earth was that bedraggled figure who called earlier?'

'Meg Lloyd, m'lady. Wanted work for her sister Annie. I told her there was nothing available. We're full at the moment.'

'Who is she?'

'She lives at Ty Owen on the hill. Her mother died recently and the father was drowned in the 1833 storm. You remember the November storm.'

'Will I ever forget it.?'

'Meg is sixteen, Annie must be thirteen and there is a younger girl and also a boy.'

'How old?'

'Perhaps five or six, he has another father. All the girls are slim and dark, but he is fair and well built like the father.'

'What happened to the father?'

'Disappeared. It wasn't the only bit of trouble he left behind. Went back to sea and hasn't been seen since.'

'What was his name?'

'They called him Lefty. No one knew his proper name. He worked on the farms in the summer. Came from nowhere and went back where he came from. Was only over here a short while. One summer, possibly two. From the West Country, I believe. He was a drinker and handy with his fists.'

'And something else!' Lady Jane said, making Emily blush. 'How are they managing?' she continued.

'As best they can. You know folks like that get by.'

'She wanted work for her sister, did she?'

'Yes, ma'am.'

The Admiral had now woken up and was listening to the conversation. The topic changed to the evening's guests and their needs. The matter of the destitute family was put to the back of their minds. However the Admiral, ever the man of action, pulled himself up in his chair and in his bluff manner said, 'Emily, send the girl here and we'll find a place for her.'

Emily, not wanting to take on any more staff and certainly not this rough child, braved the Admiral. 'But we're full in the kitchen, Sir George. We don't need any more help.' Knowing she would not be able to resist his direct order, she juggled in her mind with the difficulties she would face integrating this rough and raw girl into the household where appropriate behaviour was essential.

'In the kitchen or a job outside, send her here tomorrow,' he said, in a tone that brooked no argument.

The housekeeper left the room and returned to the kitchen, her mind full of the problems she would have moulding the girl to the needs of the Hall. Lady Jane sat back in the chair wondering if the right decision had been made to employ Annie. The more she pondered, the more she thought it was unwise and that even more burdens were being put on the housekeeper.

'George, do you think we are being wise to employ that girl? She will have a lot of rough edges to knock off and may not fit in with the other staff.'

'Of course she'll fit in. We'll find work to suit her.' Further comment would prove fruitless so she did not pursue the matter.

Later that night the Admiral's coachman called at Ty Owen to let Annie know she could start at the Hall the following Monday at eight o'clock. With great trepidation on that Monday morning Annie, with her few personal possessions, walked up the drive as her sister had done several days earlier and knocked at the back door. She knew life would never be the same again.

Chapter 3

Marie, wife of the Reverend Picton, was the sole teacher in the small hall attached to the Tabernacle Chapel. She received a small stipend for her efforts and had held the post for as long as she could remember. There were sometimes as many as thirty children in class, of mixed age and ability, but attendance was erratic.

Marie was as unpleasant and irritable as her husband was calm and good natured. Thin, with a slight stoop, she always wore glasses, behind which were a pair of steely blue eyes exercising constant surveillance for improper behaviour. She was constantly on the lookout for trouble and was rarely disappointed. Her thin, heavily veined hands gripped a short thick cane, which was always ready for action. She was known far and wide for her sharp tongue and rigid discipline.

The schoolroom was too hot in summer and too cold in winter. There was a small fire which was lit in winter and only generated enough heat to warm the teacher. In such cold weather the children moved and wriggled to keep warm.

Reading, writing and arithmetic were taught. Those who attended regularly left school literate and numerate. Many attended infrequently and left school no better educated than the day they started.

On this day in April 1842 there were maybe twenty-five children attending. Looking around the class with her sharp gaze she said, 'Write this sentence on your slates.' She wrote, "Thou shalt love thy neighbour as thyself." Jack wrote the sentence on the slate as best he could, copying what was on the board visually rather than having any knowledge of the words and letters. He couldn't read it, knew he would never be able to read and steeled himself for what was coming.

'Jack Lloyd, read it.'

He felt himself go mentally numb, but hoping by some magic means he could read the sentence. 'I can't miss.'

'Oh yes you can. What's the first word?'

He knew it was 'th' and said 'Th.'

The other children looked at him, two of the older girls with amusement and condescension, the boys with some degree of sympathy. They knew their turn was coming soon.

The cane came down on his knuckles. 'Th' what?'

'Don't know miss.'

'Th, now what's next?' The cane came down again. Over ten minutes this continued and resulted in him being able to repeat the quotation parrot fashion but not able to read and understand it.

She was acutely socially aware and those from deprived backgrounds were given more dismissive treatment than those of more gentle birth. The latter invariably received some educational assistance at home which reinforced her prejudices.

'Jack Lloyd, you have only been in for three days in the last month. Where have you been?' An answer she already knew. She missed nothing that went on in this community.

'Driving the cattle to Eglwyswrw for James, Miss.'

'Those drovers won't teach you to read and write, will they Lloyd?'

'No miss.'

'Why do you do it then?'

'Money, Miss. Meg needs it.'

'That's no excuse.'

'No miss.'

'Don't say, "No, miss". You'll probably be absent tomorrow.'

'Don't know, miss.'

The two older girls looked round in their usual amused and condescending manner. He thought there was nothing he would like better than to be droving cattle. In the back of his mind he knew the end of school would come eventually and possibly much sooner than anyone expected. It was a matter of suffering this school and all its humiliations for as short a time as possible.

'Read that from the board.' She pointed at each word in order. He repeated them from memory.

'What's that word?'

He counted the place where the word was in the sentence. One, two, three, four.

'Thy, Miss.'

She pointed to the last word in the sentence. He repeated the sentence checking that the last word was thyself.

'Thyself, Miss.'

'Do I have to beat every single word into you?'

'No miss'.

Thus his fragmented education continued till he was nine years old. He never did learn to read and write in spite of the heavy handed methods he suffered but he did have an ability with figures which he had picked up in spite of school rather than because of it. His calculations took place entirely in his head; he was able to store these figures away for months at a time.

His lack of literacy did not hold up his development in other directions. He was now bigger than any other boys of his own age and bigger than some boys three years older. Every day he grew more like his father, becoming more robustly built and having a good head of curly fair hair and a fresh complexion. In early April 1843, he went to school for the last time. Always an irregular attendee at school and always in near regular work, he knew on that spring day that his school years were coming to an end and also his childhood. His ability to get work even from a very early age was the subject of some comment in the village. Comparisons were made regarding his uncles' capacity for work and his own. 'Make a dozen of them,' was an aside frequently heard.

He remembered his first job scaring crows off a field of recently sown oats for which he earned a shilling for ten days work. Soon he was helping drive small numbers of cattle down to the holding fields to meet the big droves. Jack was always excited when he saw two or three hundred cattle being driven east by men on horses with dogs. He loved the shouting, the visible heat rising from the moving cattle and the noise of the dogs which accompanied their long journey to England. He knew one day he would be doing that.

Life at home was becoming more and more difficult. Always the odd one out in the family, he became quite isolated within his own home. His sisters made little effort at improving their relationship with him. Spending less and less time in the house and more and more working, he often did not sleep at home. This raised no comment from Meg. What he earned he gave to her, though it was little enough.

The family had three shillings a week outdoor relief from the Narberth workhouse coupled with what Jack made. There was rent of a shilling a week which bought flour. They grew potatoes, swedes and kept a pig. Somehow the family got by but it was a fight all the way and Meg never received the help she so clearly needed. In fact she repelled all help, seeming to be able to keep the family together in her own way. The poverty and self denial had taken its toll. Though still less than twenty, she now looked like a worn-out forty year old, had developed a cough and grown thinner. Jack, when he saw his sister that afternoon, was aware that she did not look well and had lost weight.

'Jack, you haven't been to school today.'

'No.'

'Marie called by today and said you won't learn. Why not?'

Jack didn't answer. 'Why not, I said?' She hit him round the ears with all her energy. It had little effect on him and he accepted it as he had accepted all the other blows and canings he had suffered in the past. He thought it was part of growing up which indeed it was. The blow he had just received was almost completely without pain. It had been delivered with all her strength and at that moment Jack knew she was sick.

'Can't understand the school work,' he explained.

'Can't? Won't, you mean.' She looked at him with as

much venom as her worn out frame could muster. 'You been with the drovers today?'

'Yes.'

'Earn anything?'

'Yes, thruppence.'

'That'll help with the rent.' She held her hand out and he gave the money over to her.

'We can all read and write. We all went to school,' she said, meaning herself and the other sisters, 'Like your father, you are. A real wrong'un.' There had been hints and asides before. Now he knew he was different, made of tougher material than his sisters, aware that he would always, under any circumstances, be a survivor. He was strangely reassured. Meg continued, 'A real wrong'un he was and back to Devon he went, no doubt with the law on his tail. Just like him you are, a great big lump with curly hair.'

He was curious but he knew it was no good asking any questions

'Mother was stupid about him.' A triumphant anger appeared on Meg's face. 'And glad I was to see him go. Mother brooded over him for months and then you were born. A right time she had, having you. It nearly killed her.'

These facts of his background swept over him. It made him even more determined to get away.

There was a pot on the stove with cawl in it, making him feel hungry even though he had been fed by Dewi's wife. He had a grudging feeling about giving the money over as he knew things would never get better.

'That's all there is,' said Meg, putting three bowls of thin cawl on the table. She burst into a fit of coughing again. In spite of his feelings of alienation, he was still the man of the household and wanted to say something or put his arm around his sister but did not do so from force of habit. Though he had experienced much pain and some joy he had been unable to ever express it. He wanted to help his sister, make life easier for her but he didn't know where to start. The call of the open road and travel with the drovers beckoned him and he knew he had no choice but to follow this path.

The opportunity to leave did not present itself for some time. He went to school irregularly, made no progress in learning to read and write and missed no chance to work for Dewi on his farm. The farm could not support a full-time servant but Jack was at least as good as any full-grown man. More and more he stayed overnight, never missing an opportunity to make himself useful. Soon he was spending more time with his new family than with his first family. When he did see his sisters, it was only to give them what money he had earned which was little enough but better than nothing. He made the visits also out of a sense of duty. With every visit the gulf got wider.

Meg got progressively thinner, coughed more frequently and became much more benign towards him. Often his uncle's words at the funeral came back to him. 'You're the man of the house, you'll have to look after your sisters now,' but he said to himself, 'I'm not the man of the house. I'm not even their brother. I can't do anything for them and they only cause me pain. Everything else I do except working on the farm is pointless.'

He came home for the last time in September. Meg was lying in the living room in front of the fire with a coat spread over her. Mary, always a quiet girl, saw Jack approaching some yards from the house. Quietly she said, 'Jack's coming.' Meg did not hear. Mary met her brother at the door and told him, 'Meg is very ill.' As they walked into the house Meg woke. She lifted herself up on her elbow and looked at them both. 'Well I don't know what will become of me.' She fell back with a fit of coughing which racked her whole frame. She managed to say, 'Doctor came yesterday, he gave me some medicine so I slept well, but there is nothing more he can do. Listen Jack, Dewi will have you.' He knew that was true, being virtually part of Dewi's family already. Feeling sorry for his sister, he nonetheless saw his old life virtually at an end and the new one beginning.

Looking at her younger brother and sister, Meg said in a practical and direct way 'I haven't got long.' Mary burst into tears, quite overcome by what was said. Jack had been aware of his sister's impending death and felt unable to cry. Mary clung to her dying sister and continued to do so for quite some time. Even to the end a practical woman, she said to Mary, 'You'll have to see Annie and get yourself a place at the Hall.' Mary gradually became calmer but would occasionally sob, only to be remonstrated with by Meg.

Jack put more wood on the fire and they all gradually dozed off only to be woken by the sound of a horse's hooves. Mary went to the door but before she could get there the doctor had walked in. He spoke to no one, but went straight to the patient, took her pulse and checked her heartbeat. He produced some white medicine in a bottle. 'Give her this, two teaspoons-full every two hours during her waking hours and again at night if she can't sleep or is coughing.' He gave the bottle to Mary and went to leave but turned. 'It's just you and the lad is it?' She nodded. They walked outside and Mary closed the door after them.

'Has Meg got long? Three months?'

'No, not three days.' What would happen to the children, he wondered. He would have to speak to someone.

'Have you any aunts or uncles?'

'We don't see them much,' Mary replied

'How long have you been on your own, the three of you?'

'Since mother died three years ago.'

God, how awful, he thought to himself. What can be done? Where are these two going to be in twelve months time or even twelve days?

A week later the funeral took place, Meg only being saved from a pauper's grave by the assistance of the Reverend Picton and Billy the undertaker. Jack and Annie were alone in the front left pew, having been ushered into place by Billy. The eyes of the congregation were on them continually. Behind them sat the two uncles who said not a word to them before or during the service. The preacher spoke for more than half an hour though to the children it seemed longer. He frequently repeated himself

32

and Jack constantly heard the words, 'Struck down by God and the little ones all alone'. He spoke of Meg's courage in the face of almost impossible difficulties and the words, 'Taken away in her prime,' were constantly ringing in Jack's ears.

After what seemed an age, the final hymn was sung and the coffin was carried out of the chapel by the same four pallbearers as had carried their Mother's coffin only a few years ago. Meg's grave was next to her mother's which made the funeral even more tragic. The mourners shuffled out, the coffin was lowered and again they heard the words, 'Ashes to ashes, dust to dust,' then the sound of the first shovel-full of earth and the hollow ring of the soil falling on the coffin. The grave was rapidly filled and the mourners returned to the chapel to talk. There was no hospitality and over the mourners hung a heavy silence. Here was a family at the moment of disintegration. On the outside of this group were the two uncles, making irrelevant conversation and hoping the subject of the future of the children would not involve them.

Jack knew where he would stay that night, as did Annie, even though they had not discussed it with one another. The Reverend Picton took Dewi aside but before he could speak to him, Dewi said, 'He's coming with me.'

'Thank God,' was the reply.

'He'll be alright with us.'

Picton, normally not a tactile man, took each of Dewi's hands in his own and shook them for several seconds. With tears in his eyes, he said 'Dewi, you're a real Christian.'

The uncles saw what was taking place but did not hear, each looking at one another with at least partial relief. Now they were almost certain they would not have to take their nephew in as an alternative to the shame of the workhouse. The uncles were further reassured when they heard the elder sister say to the younger, 'Got a place for you at the Hall. We'll share a bed.'

Mary thankfully replied, 'That's what I was hoping.' They stood close to one another, the younger looking intently and with relief at her sister.

It had now filtered through to everyone present that the immediate problem of finding a home for the children had been solved. The uncles were now convinced they would not be burdened with the children. Ned, the elder edged his way towards the two girls.

'Where you going tonight, Mary?'

'The Hall.'

'Permanent?'

'I think so.'

'That'll be nice, both together. Come to me if you need anything, won't you.' There was no answer. He gave them an insipid smile. 'You know we're always there to help you, don't you, there's nice you'll be together.' He was about to turn round and go when he was joined by Caleb, a quieter man than his brother. Hearing what his elder brother had said, he repeated, 'Always come over to us if you need any help.'

The uncles now moved slowly towards Jack who was standing by Dewi and clearly part of his family already. When they were within speaking distance they heard, 'The boy's coming with me.' A shiver of emotion went through Jack. He had been sure it was going to happen but it was reassuring to have it confirmed.

Ned, with his weak blue eyes and sickly smile, leant towards Jack and said, 'There's good of Dewi to have you.'

'Mmm,' he mumbled in reply and looked his uncle straight in the eye for a few seconds. Ned had been exposed for the devious and shallow character he was and his nephew was aware of this. He became awkward, rubbed his hands, mumbled, walked backwards and with his brother left the few that remained talking. It was the most awkward twenty seconds in his life. As he walked down the path away from the chapel, in his mind he could still see those eyes; all knowing, all powerful. That look was to stand Jack in good stead in future and it was the first time he had been aware of its power.

When he looked up, everyone had gone except his new father, the minister and his wife Marie. The uncles had left and

34

his sisters also, without saying goodbye

'I expect better attendance from you in your new family. There'll be no excuse in future, will there?' said Marie. The minister gave his wife a look which said, 'Not now,' but did not speak. She said nothing further but did fix Jack with a piercing look which said much but did not have the dominating effect upon him which she had wished. The preacher and his wife walked home and Jack and his new master made their way towards the farm.

'That boy'll do no good, he's a real wrong'un. You mark my words, Picton.'

'Give the boy a chance Marie, he's only nine. He's had a hard time. Mother dead, sister dead, never seen his father.'

'That's what I mean. Father was a real wrong'un and a vagrant.'

'Marie, be charitable. Give the lad a chance. He can work which is more than I can say about his uncles.'

'He's got bad blood in him; he'll never come to any good. Bad father and look at those uncles. Wasters. He won't learn and can't learn. Mark my words,
he won't come to any good.'

'Marie, don't condemn him. Not everyone needs schooling, Marie. We can't all be scholars, can we?'

Chapter 4

Jack had slept in the bed at the farm before but only with the knowledge that he had to return to Ty Owen from time to time. Now he knew this was his permanent home and it gave him relief to know he need not return to his old life. The bedroom was at the top of the house and right under the roof. It was hardly a bedroom and approached only by a ladder. The beams and slates were all visible. Any wind that blew went right through this loft. On the floor were half a dozen planks on which were several sacks of straw in the absence of a mattress and pillows. This improvisation was known as "sleeping on the donkey's breakfast". There were several old blankets and an old coat under which he could sleep. It was hot in summer, cold in winter and draughty all the year round.

It was just before dawn on the first morning with his new family. Hilda, Dewi's wife, called him. Getting up almost immediately, he put on his clothes more by feel than sight and climbed down the steps from the loft and then the stairs. Hearing him come down and not even turning round, she said, 'Wash your face and go and see Dewi.' He had to manipulate the pump with his right hand whilst washing his face with the left, then shake his hands free of moisture. Now wide awake, he went to join Dewi in the cowshed. Dewi was pushing one of the cows with his shoulder saying, 'Get over, you.' The cow moved over slightly, making milking it more comfortable. The family used only enough milk for their own needs, perhaps two gallons a day for tea, butter and cheese with any surplus fed to the pigs. They looked at one another.

'Can you milk?' Dewi asked him.

'No.' Though only nine, he was fearless of cattle.

'Come on, get down here.' Dewi thrust the bucket into his

36

hand, put him on the stool and instructed him in how to milk. .He did as he was told and made his first efforts. The cow, unaccustomed to being milked by Jack and looking round while eating the hay, kicked and the milk bucket and stool fell over, all the milk being spilt.

'Blast your bloody eyes,' said Dewi, 'Go on you, get back.' Again Jack went back to milk and again he was kicked but this time managed to hold on to the milk bucket. He managed to extract only two pints from the cow who would not let down any more. Knowing he could master this skill, given time, he felt strangely at home with these animals. Milking over, the cows were turned out to pasture.

'Jack, we're going to count the cattle. Come with me because you'll be doing this soon.' They walked up the cart track to the fields behind the house. They climbed over the gate, crossed the first field and reached the gate to the second. Leaning over the gate, they saw before them a herd of Welsh Blacks. 'Thirty two cows, thirty one calves.' Climbing into the field, they positioned themselves ten yards away from the hedge. Sending the dogs to herd the cattle slowly, so that they would walk between the two of them and the hedge, was the method of counting. The dogs, always eager, drove the cattle too fast and accurate counting was impossible. They had to repeat the exercise several times, calling out, 'Woo boy, woo,' to the dogs until the message got through.

'Jack, count cows and heifers first then the calves.'

Twice the animals went through the gap at a slow pace and twice they counted thirty-two. His schooling or perhaps the lack of it had made his mental arithmetic acute. It was never to let him down.

'How many?'

'Thirty-two.'

'Correct, now the calves.'

This was a more difficult task as calves could hide behind cows and it was essential they go through the gap even slower. They reduced the gap and the dogs were commanded to be virtually still.

'How many calves?'

'Thirty-one.'

'Correct first time.'

In the next field were ninety-four store cattle which were counted four times.

'How many?'

'Can't count that far.'

'You must learn.'

Jack knew he would have to make a great effort and soon too. He couldn't respond to Dewi in the way he had with Marie.

'Breakfast now,' said Dewi.

It was already half past nine and the girls had gone to school. They had bread, cheese, butter and red gooseberry jam.

'Davey and the others will be here by ten o'clock to cut the oats,' said Hilda.

'I know. Have you got food in?'

'No need to ask that.'

'It'll be hard work, the crop is down and the grass is growing through it. Should have been cut three weeks ago but the weather has been bad. Can you tie a sheaf, Jack?'

'No, but I seen it done.'

'Think you can do it?'

'Yes, sure.'

Before breakfast had finished, five men, all neighbours, arrived with their scythes over their shoulders and cylindrical sharpening stones in their pockets. Also with them were two women and two girls aged fifteen. Davey was the eldest and the leader.

'Top field first, Dewi?'

'No, start in the lower one. Take Jack with you and teach him how to tie a sheaf.' He nodded and made his way to the field of oats with his harvesters following; five reapers and five followers to tie sheaves.

They passed the two fields of pasture which contained the cattle and then into the first field of oats. It had been a damp summer and the soil was rich from the preceding crop of turnips which had been eaten off by the sheep. The crop had been a very good one at first. The weather in the latter part of summer had been wet and windy and the crop had gone down and in places grass had grown through and much of the crop of black oats was hardly visible. Even if it was possible to harvest it dry it would be little use thrashing it all, although some might be saved with the flail, so as to have oats for the horses in spring.

The mowing was an annual ritual. Holding the scythe upright at the joint between the handle and the blade, they sharpened their blades with a regular but unhurried motion. After a few minutes they stopped as one, tested the blades with their thumbs and nodded. First Davey started to cut, followed two or three yards behind by one then another till all were cutting in unison. Swish-swish-swish-swish, they cut the crop. Starting on the outside of the field and going round it in an anticlockwise direction, they cut the swathes perhaps four inches deep and three feet wide. The cut crop was laid out in rows eighteen inches apart, exposing the stubble. Woe betide anyone cutting an uneven stubble.

It was a matter of pride that you never got behind and that you never had to sharpen the blade before the leader. Even more important was it that you never dug your blade into the ground. Anyone doing so did not live it down for years.

Following behind were those tying the sheaves; two women, two girls and Jack. Davey's wife Maggie, well into middle age and long familiar with this work, showed Jack how to tie the sheaf. 'See.' She pulled a length of oat straw out with one hand, grasped enough for a sheaf, tied it with the straw, twisted it and tucked it under. 'Got it?' she asked.

He had been watching intently and had grasped the skill. It was not hard to pick up but keeping up the pace would be more difficult. Maggie was in the first swathe, followed by Jack and the three younger women. So it went on until the reapers stopped to sharpen their blades. They continued in this way all day, stopping only for the breaks for bait and to sharpen. The tying skill was easy and keeping up with the mowers not as difficult as he expected. Almost nothing was said. Anything that was said was initiated by Davey. It was expected that one man should cut one acre in a day. This field was slightly over five acres and there was no time to lose.

In addition to tying they also had to stook the sheaves, two leaning together upright in the centre and two leaning towards them on each side. By midday they had been round the field once. Bait arrived at one o'clock; bread, cheese, welsh cakes and tea which were eaten with very little being said and any conversation started by Davey..

'It's badly down. Same everywhere.'

'Mine's even worse.'

'Take a lot of drying.'

'Aye, be lucky to have a week of sun and the year's going on.'

'Well Jack, you can tie a sheaf.'

'He's done well,' said one of the younger women. He said nothing, hoping actions would speak louder than words.

'Finish tonight?' asked Hilda

'Should do unless the weather breaks. Sky looks clear.'

She picked up the remains of the meal and walked back to the house. It was half past one, the weather looked clear. It had been a good day so far. The mowers returned to their work; a substantial piece of the field was now cut, the stooks were in orderly rows and there was every hope that the field would be cut that night.

The work continued without respite for more than an hour, with nothing to distract their attention. But soon they became aware of the gentle clatter of horses' hooves. It sounded like quite a number of them. In a few minutes, they could see over the top of the hedges and coming up the track the heads of a troop of soldiers. Slowly they came up the lane. Davey returned to cutting and the others followed. The noise ceased, indicating that they must now be in the field. They continued cutting, aware of the presence of the cavalry getting nearer and nearer but unwilling to take notice of them until they had to. They were apprehensive of the reason for the visit. It could only mean trouble and these days that meant Becca. When the soldiers were about five yards away, Davey could continue working no longer. He looked up into the face of the leader who was towering over him and seated on a fine chestnut horse, on his headdress a white plume which made him look even taller than he was. He looked into the lieutenant's face and was surprised to see a man of extreme youth, hardly more than a schoolboy, with a smooth, pink complexion. He looked down at Davey with an air of mildly amused contempt which he made little attempt to conceal.

Some ten yards behind him were a sergeant and six troopers, all on horses much inferior to the chestnut. They now stopped and waited to hear what their leader had to say, which had already been said a dozen times that morning.

'Good morning to you all' he said in a patronising tone and with a supercilious smile on his face.

'Good day.' Davey returned the gaze without deference.

'Have you seen any large groups of men with or without horses today or within the last few days?'

Davey removed his cap. 'No we haven't, have we?' he said, addressing the officer and seeking to obtain the assent of the others, 'No, we haven't.'

'You sure?' Again he gave them his patronising and mildly amused smile.   'You are aware that you could be in trouble if you were found hiding them or shielding them in any way?'

'Oh yes.'

'There've been riots at the tollgates which you are all well aware of, aren't you?'   There was a long pause. 'Aren't you?' the officer repeated

'Oh yes, we know about that.'

'Have any of you been active in these riots?'

'No, none of us, all we want is peace and quiet.'

'So does Her Majesty Queen Victoria, so the sooner these men are arrested the sooner you will have peace and quiet here

41

and the sooner we will go. You understand this?'

'Oh yes.'

The troopers' horses were bored, stamped their feet and snorted. The riders by now were only half conscious of what was going on and perhaps even half asleep. One horse moved toward the stooks and started to eat the grain at the top of the sheaves. Now a second horse did the same. Then a third. No attempt was made to stop the horses and two stooks were knocked over.

'Well, if you do see anything you wish to report, I am stationed at Narberth and you could very well be given a substantial reward. You have everything to gain and nothing to lose by assisting to clear up this matter. These disturbances will cease, you can be sure of that. Again I would remind you that it is an offence to hide information from the authorities. I hope I have made myself clear.' The gleam of power, authority and his infinite superiority to all around became written across his face and obvious to all there. 'Have you any questions?'

Davey's son Willie, always at the centre of any humour asked, 'What did they charge you at the toll on the main road?'

The lieutenant was, for a moment, nonplussed by the remark. A very slight smile crossed his face. 'We have a joker among us, have we?' He rode towards him, looked him in the eye, made a special effort to identify him and lingered while doing so. 'I shall be keeping a lookout for you in future. You cross my path at your peril. Do you understand?' There was no reply. 'You should all know, even in this god-forsaken backwater that no one on the Queen's business ever pays tolls.' He turned to go, followed by his troops, saluting to everyone but no one in particular. 'Goodbye to you all.'

Out of earshot of the reapers, the sergeant reprimanded the troopers for allowing the horses to eat the sheaves Down the road the horses walked, the leader in front, the rest ten or fifteen yards behind. There would probably be two or three similar visits that day.

The reapers all breathed a sigh of relief, having felt very threatened by the Dragoons. The Rebecca rioters had been active for four years now, disrupting turnpikes, toll houses and workhouses. It was an unusually depressed time and these taxes made the inevitable poverty even more difficult to bear. The small farmers were the worst hit and nearly everyone had sympathy with them. Many families had members who were active and all knew, if only by rumour, those involved with Rebecca.

'Willie, you should have kept your mouth shut,' said his father, 'You're a marked man now. Stupid boy.'

'He was asking for it,' said another.

'Boy, you're asking for it now.'

'Bloody arrogant bastard,' said Willie.

'Willie, you've got to keep your head down now,' said his father. 'You're a marked man.'

The work had now been held up for nearly forty minutes so they returned to cutting the crop with more vigour to make up for lost time. The field was changing before their eyes. Every circumference of the field became smaller as they went round and round. The sun went down further, the day, though cooler, remaining dry. Hilda brought the final meal up in a great hurry accompanied by Jimmy, Davey's grandson.

'Davey, the Dragoons been to your place,' she told him.

'Jimmy, what happened?' he asked.

'The soldiers came up and asked about Owen. Mam said she didn't know where he was.'

Davey was worried and everyone knew it. 'Go home, Davey. We can finish here. It'll take no more than an hour.' Knowing the others understood his position, he left with his scythe over his shoulder and walked home at a fast pace with his grandson trotting at his side. They walked home without saying a word. There was nothing the remaining harvesters could do but carry on. The field was completed when dusk had just fallen. Jack fell asleep as soon as his head touched the pillow that night. It had been an eventful day.

The harvesting continued the next day. Davey and his son did not come, only the Thomases. The field took two days to cut rather than one. Jack resumed tying the sheaves. Initially he was aching all over, but this soon disappeared as the work got under way. He found it easier, probably because he knew what to do and because the reapers set a slower pace. On the following day by six o'clock the field was cut, the stooks in orderly rows, the supper eaten and the tea drunk. Throughout the two days they had all talked almost entirely about Owen.

'Haven't seen Davey.'

'Guess they're looking for Owen.'

'Poor Davey. I know he worries about Owen.'

'They know he's part of Becca.'

'Who are they?'

'Magistrates, constables, even the army.'

'How do they know? Who's the informer?'

'Secrets get out, don't they?'

'Anything we can do?'

'Not really.'

'That Dragoon Officer was cocky. Knew more than he said.'

'Can't be long before the Narberth Tollgate gets it.'

'Owen is away. Hasn't done a stroke of work on the farm for weeks, and at harvest time.'

'Must have been noticed.'

'Tidy boy but a bit of an idealist.'

The conversation drifted and they finally dispersed. The cutting was now completed. They had to hope for fine weather to dry the crop out.

Husband and wife talked for longer that night than they usually did.

'What'll happen if they catch Owen?'

'It'll be the assizes. He might face transportation, who knows.'

'Willie could go the same way.'

'He could that.'

'Young fool.'

'That family is marked now; you can take that from me.

44

They'll never leave them alone.' They were both tired and drifted off into drowsiness for some minutes. Then Hilda spoke again, 'Those store cattle must go and soon too. There's little more keep for them and you owe the bank money.'

'Within the next two weeks. Two droves are leaving by the end of the month. They need those cattle to make up the numbers. I'll get a good price.'

'I hope so. You're not the best of traders Dewi, are you?'

He did not reply. Soon they were in bed asleep.

Chapter 5

Jack was woken up at the usual time, washed himself outside and went into the kitchen to find Dewi finishing his breakfast but with a look of urgency on his face.

'You're not milking the cows today. Do you know Narberth?' he asked, without looking up.

'A bit.'

'It's not big. Do you know the Saddler's Arms?'

'No.'

'Well, find it, go there and ask for Tommy the drover. He's a big cattle drover and stays there when he's in town. Tommy hasn't got a proper home. If he's not there, ask for Nellie. Whoever you see, ask when the next big drove is leaving. Understand? If he isn't there, she will know. Tell him I have ninety-four four year olds at fifty-five to sixty stone. Have you got that?' Jack memorised the figures.

'Repeat back to me.' Jack did so, almost word perfect.

'Also look at the tollgate. See if it's manned and see if it's been damaged. If it is manned, who by? Got that? Keep your eyes open for anything else.'

'Yes, I will.'

'Have breakfast and go. It'll be a long day.'

He ate all that was in front of him, took some bait he was given which he put in his pocket, and started the long walk to Narberth. As he walked, he reflected on his present home and all the hard work he undertook, comparing it with life with his sisters and the drudgery of school. The way was downhill and would take him almost three hours. The harvest on some of the farms he passed was over but a few fields still had stooked oats unharvested. On two fields the stooks had been turned over and the sheaves were being forked onto two-wheeled horse-drawn carts. Welsh mountain sheep were grazing with their lambs on the higher ground and Welsh black cattle on the lower ground nearer the house. It occurred to him that Dewi had many more cattle than any of the farms he had passed but his farm was no bigger. Was that why he wanted to sell them so soon?

The track he was on became more level as he reached the bridge over the Cleddau and for some time he was within sight of the river till he reached the main Narberth road. Jack observed all that was happening on the way down but did not stop till he reached the tollgate. It had been completely burnt out. The roof had been set alight and had collapsed into the building. All the woodwork was charred and everything had been burnt which could be burnt. The tollgate had been pushed through the front door and also burnt. Inside, there were a few slightly smoking embers which showed the fire had been at its most intense some hours before.

The town was full of people who seemed to be quite animated and walking quickly to and fro though keeping away from the tollgate for fear of being identified with the incident. It was unmanned. As he walked towards the centre of the town he could hear the chanting and shouting. The nearer he got to the middle, the more he saw those moving in the side streets gravitating towards the centre. He now caught a glimpse of the square and saw a crowd of perhaps a thousand shouting and jeering at the constables and the same troop of dragoons which he had recently seen.

Those trying to control the crowd met with little success. The crowd was noisy but not violent and in many ways quite humorous. Staying to watch for perhaps ten minutes, he was stimulated by the number of young men taunting the keepers of law and order. The dragoons came in for particular attention with revellers, both drunk and sober, jostling the horses, as well as those of more serious intent shouting at them. Such was the mood of the crowd, that the troop felt no need to take direct action at that stage. The constables were also subjected to ridicule and named personally, but they did not show quite the calm of the cavalry. Jack did not linger but made his way to the

47

Saddler's Arms which was situated away from the centre of town.

He walked in the front door, finding the bar to be crowded with noisy men some of whom were joking about the Rebecca riots and others who were more interested in drinking. There was a buzz of animated conversation. Approaching a man sitting alone, while holding a pint pot and looking towards the floor, he asked, 'Is Tommy the drover here?' He said 'See her,' pointing to the large dark-haired woman of maybe thirty behind the bar. He shouted 'Nellie, little 'un wants you.' 'Yes?' she replied, giving him the remains of a smile caused by a funny remark heard moments before. He walked towards the bar keeping in sight of her though the bar was taller than he was. Always busy, she went on serving beer, keeping him waiting. Eventually, having a free moment, she said 'What do you want?'

'Is Tommy the drover here?'

'No, what you want him for?'

'Message from Dewi.'

'Which Dewi?'

'Maenclochog.'

'Yes, I know. Married to Hilda. Come over here. I can't hear you.' They moved towards the entrance to the living quarters. 'What you want?'

'Dewi wants to know when the next drove is going. He says to tell Tommy he has ninety-four to sell at fifty-five to sixty stone.'

She gave him a smile and looked him in the face. He smiled back and felt a funny feeling in him which was pleasurable but which he didn't understand   'You're a small boy for a big message aren't you?' He felt his face go warm and pink and knew Nellie had seen it.

'You should be in school.'

'Yeah' he muttered.

'Listen, it's Saturday today. Let me think. He's coming on Tuesday with one hundred and he has one hundred in the holding field. On Wednesday he goes east. Tommy will be up with Dewi early on Monday morning. Got that?'

'Yeah,' he replied.

'Off you go then.'

He turned to go, but she called after him, 'Mind to tell Dewi the Tollgate has been burnt down. Old Maggie won't go back. She is frightened out of her wits and is in hiding. Also tell him there is a crowd causing trouble on the cross here. They'll have gone by Wednesday and the drove will go. Got that?' He nodded. She pinched his cheek, ruffled his fair curly hair and gave him a push. 'On your way and keep away from the crowd.' Had he looked round, he would have seen a smile on her face. She had only daughters. He'll break a few hearts, she thought to herself.

He went past the square where the crowd had reduced in size and many of the hecklers were by now drunk. The forces of law and order were all visible but they were now more relaxed as the crowd began to disperse and the threat of trouble subsided. It was early afternoon and he had to get home. A thrill of adventure pulsed though him. This was better than school.

Walking home the way he had come, he noticed that most of the oats he had seen waiting to be carried had now been harvested and two round beehive-shaped ricks had been partially built. Around half way home he realised how hungry he was, climbed over a gate and sat behind the hedge eating his bait of bread and cheese. Hardly had he started to eat when he heard the brisk trot of a pony and the grating sound of cart wheels on the road. Nearer and nearer it came and louder and louder grew the sound of hooves and iron wheels. The obvious speed which the horse was travelling at made him curious. There was a sense of urgency about the pace and Jack had a premonition that something of significance was happening. It was now very near and he stood to look through the gap in the hedge to see what was passing.

He saw a pony and trap with a constable in the driving seat, leaning forward with the reins in one hand and a whip in the other. The pony was sweating with its mouth slightly open and there was a sense of extreme urgency about the vehicle and all connected with it. Behind him was a young man in his twenties facing backwards with his hands tied behind his back and that rope tied to a metal rail in the trap. The driver was overweight with a red, coarse and brutal face on which there was a look of great intensity. He looked neither to right nor left and appeared anxious to cover the ground to his destination as soon as was possible.

His passenger could hardly have been more dissimilar. Young, slim and with dark hair caught in the wind. He was bruised around the left eye and there was a cut on his face which was still bleeding. His eyes were turned in the direction of where he had come from, but didn't seem to be focused on anyone or anything. It was a look of resignation and also a look of reflection. The trap passed in seconds and when it had done so, he looked over the hedge after it. It passed out of sight with the passenger looking in his direction but not seeing him, his mind elsewhere. The sound gradually faded into the distance. So this is what happens when the law catches up with you, he thought.

He continued on his way, walking at a slower pace than he had all day, hardly seeing what was around and dwelling on what had happened, particularly the fate of the prisoner in the trap. Could he be Owen, Willie's brother and Davey's son? So this was part of being grown up, some of the time it was exciting, sometimes difficult and always part chance. What would happen to the man in the trap tonight? Would Jack ever suffer a similar fate? What control did you have over your own future?' Jack reflected that what happened to you was much about luck. Once you were dealt the hand of luck, bad or good, you could with quiet determination turn it to your own advantage. That constable wouldn't have me tied in the back of a trap, he vowed to himself.

Finding no one in the house, he went to the cowshed to find Dewi.

'You're back. See Tommy?'

'No, but I saw Nellie.'

Then he gave him all the news: the burnt tollgate and house; Maggie the gatekeeper in hiding; Tommy arriving on Monday to look at the cattle and going east on Wednesday; the large crowd in the square in Narberth and the Dragoons trying to control it. Finally he told him of the constable in the trap and the prisoner tied up in the back.

'What did he look like, colour of his hair?' Dewi asked.

'Dark hair.'

'Thin or fat, how old?'

'Thin and quite young.'

At this point they were joined by Hilda and the news repeated. 'That'll be Owen alright. Poor Owen and poor Davey. What will happen to the boy?'

'The magistrates for sure, perhaps the Assizes.'

'What does that mean?'

'Maybe transportation, twenty years in Tasmania.'

'Dewi, don't say that!'

'It's true. That's the price we have to pay, like it or not, and all we fight against is crippling toll charges. If we don't fight against them, things will only get worse for sure.'

Hilda's eyes filled with tears as she reflected on the tragedy which had befallen their neighbours.

'Jack, finish the milking.'

'Where you going, Dewi?'

'To see Davey. You both count the cattle. I'll be back later.'

He handed the stool and bucket to Jack and made his way to his neighbour's without another word. Hilda looked after him, watching him walk just up the track over the field to the brow of the hill and disappear out of sight. Would he return? Could he suffer a similar fate to Owen? Was this the beginning of a wave of trouble which would infect the whole area with hardly a family untouched? She walked towards the house deep in thought, her mood becoming blacker as she went. Jack followed minutes afterwards with the bucket.

Standing awkwardly in the kitchen, he wanted to speak but didn't choose to break her thoughts.

'We've got to count the cattle,' he said softly. She looked at him, hardly aware he had spoken but somehow knowing he had done so.

'Count the cattle, did you say? You do it, Jack.' He didn't know how to but was scared to say so. He remained in the same position without moving, his mind racing as to what he should do next. After a couple of minutes she looked up and said, 'Go on, count them.'

'Can't count to ninety-four,' he responded.

'What can you count to?' It felt like school again. The silence was more painful than any of Marie's canings.

'Fifty.'

'Fifty and forty-four are ninety-four. Count them in two blocks.' She did not have to repeat herself: it was a lesson he would never forget.

Jack pondered as he walked back up to the field. Challenges of a mainly physical nature he felt able to overcome with ease. The mental challenges were more difficult and uncertain. Counting to ninety-four was the most problematic which he had faced since leaving school. He remembered the impotent anger he had suffered at the hands of the schoolteacher. This was now starting to be left behind, but it had been replaced by a distrust and hatred of authority which became all the more intense with time. He resented the lieutenant of dragoons with his boyish face, cool assurance and knowledge that he would always have the power, the wealth and authority to do as he pleased. Born to this position, he had no conception what the lives of ordinary people were like. He felt that they were all low-lifes because of their own fecklessness. The constable with his fat, red brutalised face was another object of his hatred. He felt sure the world would bring him into contact with many more.

The counting proved to be an easier task than expected as the cattle were all lying down and chewing the cud. He counted them twice, walking down the way he had come at a slow pace becoming increasingly aware that he was very tired and very hungry.

Hilda was now busy in the house preparing a meal, with the girls seated at the table not very seriously doing some school work. The two girls had been a little condescending towards him to start with, but now largely ignored him as he was out working most of the daylight hours. They were also aware that their parents found him useful and so treated him like a rather rough, uncouth younger brother with whom they had little in common.

While the meal was cooking, Hilda got out pencil and paper and was doing rudimentary accounts which she pored over for perhaps half an hour. Going over one column then another, she became lost in the figures before her. Would they make a loss or a profit from the sale of the cattle and would they have enough to pay off the bank debt? Certainly they would not be able to keep any of them over the winter. They would only be able to keep the cows and calves if they harvested the oat crop without loss and that was entirely subject to some dry weather in the next three weeks.

Hilda also reflected on the fact that Dewi was not a good trader. Tommy's trading ability was legendary but she also knew that he needed that number to make up the drove and he wouldn't get them elsewhere. She would have to browbeat Dewi into trading hard and that would not be an easy task. She knew she could deal with the negotiation better than her husband but could never humiliate him in public. Only widows dealt directly with the drovers.

When Tommy had bought the herd as he surely would, there was the problem of getting them to the holding fields. Who would drive them to Narberth? Who would get them through the tollgate and pay the fees? There was also the problem of getting the money to the bank. Tommy always paid in the back room of the Saddler's and the bank was in Carmarthen. How would they get the money into safe-keeping? Dewi had never had such a big deal before and he would want to celebrate. Before they married and got the tenancy of the farm he had been a drinker. She was concerned.

Chapter 6

It was on the following Tuesday as they crossed the yard that they heard the gentle trot of hooves. The light quick ring left them in no doubt that it was the approach of ponies. In spite of what had happened in the last few days, Dewi did not show alarm. Their visitors' heads came into view over the hedge, one wearing a large felt hat and the other, slightly behind him, a cap. As they came into the yard, Tommy, a man well into middle age, was riding on a small pony which seemed hardly large enough to carry him. He was wearing a voluminous coat of indeterminate but dark colour which reached below the stirrups and ended perhaps a foot from the ground. A piece of cord was tied round his waist. In his hand was a short stick which he occasionally tapped the pony with, almost as a gesture of affection rather than of command.

Perhaps five yards behind him was his long time assistant Eddie. He lived in the shadow of Tommy, did anything he was asked and, when not droving cattle, in the pub or out of it, regaled anyone who would listen with the exploits of his master which were numerous, colourful and frequently amusing. Tommy was known in the cattle trade from St David's to Kent and the two were inseparable.

The older man, a little above medium height, was carrying a lot of weight, perhaps fifteen or sixteen stone. In a time when girth indicated wealth and leanness, poverty, his appearance and the aura of his presence made an impression on nearly everyone. Tommy, aware that he was a man of significance, played the part to the full and enjoyed the attention. Every aspect of his appearance, manner and lifestyle were the subject of much comment. Winter or summer he always wore the some coat and hat which had according to rumour never been washed. Gyp, the pony he had ridden for many years, was as well known to all as his assistant Eddie. They were master and servant but the relationship was really an ideal partnership. Never in all the years they had been together had they ever quarrelled, betrayed a confidence or done anything less than support one another. Neither had Gyp ever let her master down. She was a small pony but of sturdy welsh stock.

Dismounting from Gyp with an economy of effort and a movement you were hardly aware of, Tommy walked in a slow deliberate manner towards Dewi with whom he shook hands. He carried a great deal more weight than was apparent when riding but his clothes hung on him easily. The face, though pale, was wide and the jaw, which had four days' growth on it, unusually so. His eyes were deep brown, looked at you directly and missed nothing. Though close-fisted in matters of money, he always kept his word when a bargain was struck. A man of few words, he said 'Well, Dewi, you got cattle?'

'Yes.'

'Let's have a look. Where are they? In the top field?' He had seen where they were on the way up.

'Aye, that's right.'

'Eddie, tie the ponies and come up.'

He nodded. All four walked up towards the top field, Tommy and Dewi in front and Eddie and Jack behind. Rarely did Tommy give instructions, the raising of his hat, the flick of a stick or the movement of a shoulder and Eddie knew what to do. They rarely spoke to one another and anything that was said was done so within a sentence. In truth, Eddie worshipped his master and when in his cups wanted to talk about him to anyone who would listen as a form of release from the nearly monosyllabic communication they had when working.

Once started on the subject of Tommy he found it difficult to stop. He was the shrewdest cattle dealer and drover. Nobody had ever fooled him, not even other dealers or the naval contractors at the dockyards. Eddie's life was entirely devoted to Tommy and Tommy knew it. The only cloud that ever appeared on the horizon was that Tommy was well into his fifties and twenty five years older than himself. There were few if any drovers over sixty. The thought was only momentary. Tommy had almost god like characteristics. He would go on forever.

Eddie was aware how badly the cattle were needed to complete a full drove, not by word but by that slight look of anxiety on his master's face which only he recognised. He was also in no doubt that they would be bought within the hour but not by any expression, word or gesture would he give away his master's need. Even Tommy was unaware how accurately and perceptively he was understood. The dealer went into the field and looked at all the cattle, first as a group and then individually for signs of lameness and of any that were in poor condition and would not make the journey east. He made each beast walk in front of him, using his stick to hurry one up and slow down another. This continued for an hour till he had seen every animal on its own twice without saying a word to anyone. He walked towards Dewi, juggling weights, numbers and prices in his head and considering what his margin of profit would be at the point of sale. He already knew what price had been paid several weeks before and the amount of interest owed for he knew that Dewi could never have had the resources to have paid cash for them.

Dewi knew he could not keep any of the store cattle over the winter because there was not enough hay, straw or oats. He needed all the fodder he had including the unharvested oats to keep the cows and calves. Aware that Tommy knew this fact, he felt at a disadvantage. What put him at a further disadvantage was his being unaware how badly Tommy needed the cattle.

'Well Dewi, what you asking?'

He did not answer but he thought of the bank loan which would have to be repaid, the interest owed and what would become of him if he could not make the payment. His very thoughts became apparent on his face. His companion knew the deal was sealed. Almost as a gesture of impossible hope Dewi quoted, 'Fourteen guineas.'

Tommy looked him in the face and could see him weaken visibly before his eyes. 'The naval contractors two hundred miles up the road won't give me that price.' This was true enough.

'They're fifty-five, sixty stone; they must be worth nearly that.'

'Dewi, fifty-two, fifty-three average, no more.'

'What you offering then?'

'Ten guineas.'

'No, no! Starvation price. I'd sooner keep them through the winter.' He knew he couldn't do this, so did Tommy and he regretted saying it the moment he heard himself. He didn't know how badly the cattle were needed to fill the drove to go east.

'What price d' you want then?' responded Tommy.

Dewi knew he couldn't get the margin of profit he had hoped for and he again juggled with prices and the outstanding loan. It was now not whether he could make a profit but whether he could pay off the loan.

'Twelve.'

'Can't make it.'

Tommy knew he had him in the palm of his hand but did not want to humiliate him, however he needed to have the animals at eleven guineas a head. He wanted to keep Dewi's goodwill and already knew, through his many contacts and the information they had given him, that he would still make a small profit.

'What's your price then?'

'Eleven guineas, that's my last offer.' Looking him in the face, he knew he would accept. His last offer was always final. Never had he been known to increase a last offer. This was known far and wide and was one of the ingredients of the aura which surrounded him.

Again Dewi undertook more mental arithmetic. Ninety-four times eleven guineas. Would that make a thousand pounds? He knew it would but couldn't calculate the surplus. 'Alright Tommy, but you're robbing me.' Tommy reached for his hand which was accepted with less vigour than it was offered. Dewi knew he would now have to deal with Hilda.

'Listen Dewi, that offer is conditional on you delivering them to the holding field outside Narberth by first light tomorrow, all correct.' Tommy was trading hard. It was a distance of eight miles and a tollgate had to be passed and possibly a shilling a head paid. Also the Becca crowd were in town which could create untold difficulties or might prove an advantage.

Dewi tried to protest, 'Tommy, there's the boy and me and ninety four cattle and the boy's only nine.' The problems of taking them seemed overwhelming. He was no longer juggling with money but with names of those who would help him drive the cattle. 'Me and the lad can't do it, I'll need Eddie.'

'You can have Eddie. Shouldn't take longer than three hours and you have the rest of the day. Drive them in the daylight if I were you. No good at night, you might lose some.'

'Not even on a clear night?'

'No. Deliver 'em correct and I'll pay you by cheque or sovereigns.'

'Sovereigns, Tommy.' The thought of all that gold in his hands filled him with a sense of worth and pride he had never experienced before.

'Sure,' replied Tommy, 'but be careful with the money, you could be robbed.'

'Safe with me, sure, safe with me.'

'Sovereigns it is then.'

Dewi's thoughts returned to the matter of the drive. 'Was the tollgate manned?'

'No, burnt out and Maggie nowhere to be seen. The Becca crowd won't let anyone come just now. You're safe.'

Tommy walked towards Gyp, mounted with the same ease of movement as he had dismounted and also took the reins of his assistant's pony. 'Get them down as soon as you can, should be before dark. You'll be in good hands with Eddie.' Then he rode away without looking back.

Dewi questioned Eddie about the Becca crowd. 'How many of them about?'

'Hundred or two only. They won't trouble you, they're all in the middle. Turn right at the tollgate, half a mile further and you're there.'

Dewi reflected again about ninety four beasts and a crowd of rioters, some of them drunk. Could he lose some of the animals, broken legs maybe?

'Don't worry, good boy, they're all on your side. Been doing this for twenty years,' reassured Eddie. He felt more confident, the sooner they were on their way the better. 'We'll get through alright, on a drove it's a hundred cattle to one man you know.'

It was now almost eleven o'clock and he had the bit between his teeth. They would be on the road by noon and there was no reason that they shouldn't be driven fast. Three hours it would take at the most.

Now it was having to deal with Hilda that would be the hardest part of the day. He made sure all three of them went into the house together. His wife would never bring up matters of money in front of others. Finishing breakfast together, they discussed what had to be done. Eddie cautioned against too much speed. The long droves to London and the south coast were only two miles an hour. No good having cattle excited and steaming; that could lead to trouble, perhaps even a stampede. He'd only seen it once and didn't want to see it again. Cattle broke legs and had to be killed. A lot of money was lost. They all moved to the door to start when Dewi was called back by Hilda.

'What price you get?'

A troubled look came over his face. 'Eleven guineas.'

'You were talking about fourteen.'

'Said they wouldn't make that from the naval contractors on the dockside.'

'Believe a cattle dealer, would you?' He didn't answer but could feel his face go red and he looked at the floor. She continued, 'You're soft, you are. He runs rings round you, he does. Eleven guineas won't pay the bank off.'

'Yes it will, just.' He looked even more troubled. There was no way out if she started questioning him. Could he have got more from Tommy? Would Hilda have done any better?

'Why isn't Tommy taking them down?' she demanded, 'You've never done this before.'

'Got other things to do, anyway he left Eddie to help.'

'Who pays the toll? That'll be ninety-four shillings. Suppose you want the cash for that now?'

'Yes, just in case. Don't think we'll have to pay. They've burnt it down.'

'It'd be your luck to have it re-opened ten minutes before you got there. You're a fool, Dewi. You need a wife like me or God knows where you'd be.'

The other two were waiting out of earshot. 'She's giving him a hard time. Look at his face when he comes out. Avoid women, boy; they nail your feet to the floor. I never bothered. I'm a free man .They're trouble, boy, real trouble,' said the elder. Jack looked at Dewi as he left the house and had to agree with what was said.

Dewi had a face full of concern. At least he had got away from Hilda for the time being, now came the journey to Narberth. Eddie reassured him that a slow drive down, taking perhaps four or five hours, would have them all at their destination before dark. 'Don't lose a wink; we'll get them down alright. Let's go.'

'What about the Becca crowd. Will they be alright?'

'Don't worry about them; they're on our side. I never seen a hundred beasts take notice of a couple of drunks.'

'Sure.'

'We get down correct and you can give me a guinea. A bargain?'

'A bargain,' Dewi agreed. They shook hands on it. It made him feel better and Eddie knew he would not be short of beer money that night.

'Lad, here, shut all the gates on either side of the lane, then do the same on the main road. Don't want the cattle straying. Stop at the tollgate. Quickly, you'll have to run. Away now.'

The cattle were herded by the two dogs, out of the field, down the lane and towards the main road.

60

'Easy now, easy,' called Eddie.

This was a remark directed towards Dewi as much as the dogs. The beasts must be kept to a slow walk.

Running down the road, Jack closed the gates on either side. Dewi knew that some of the farm entrances did not have gates and they would have to run down the fields on the other side of the hedge to stand in the driveways. This left Eddie to drive the animals at his own pace. Gradually the animals covered the distance. The track led to the bridge over the Cleddau and on to the main road to their final destination.

The journey was a slow and noisy one with many of the farmers coming to the roadside to talk. This did not delay the journey as they walked along with them. It was just an excuse to gossip, keep up with the news and if possible find out the price paid. They were curious about the Becca crowd, the broken tollgates on the way to the town and who had done what. It was communication of hope rather than despair and a cause for some jollity.

The other farmers could tell that the price Dewi had received was not high from the look on his face. For weeks it had been known he would have to sell them. There were jocular remarks about making his fortune in response to which he gave a bleak smile. The task in hand took all his attention. Had an observer been a few hundred feet above the ground he would have seen a long black caterpillar wending its way down the track, between hedges, with dogs barking at their heels and one or two cattle making their way through un-gated entrances only to be driven back to the main body of the caterpillar which was all the while moving at a slow and even pace. They continued without incident till they reached the outskirts of the town.

'Half a mile to the tollgate. Hold'em here. I'll see what's happened,' called Eddie.

The dogs were ordered back; they retreated twenty yards but continued to bark.

'When I come back, you drive the cattle on, me in front, you behind.'

61

The barking continued, the animals were standing against one another and there was a restlessness about them. Some of them lowed.

Eddie returned to the head of the herd, leaving Jack by the tollgate. With a wave of his stick he indicated that they could move. 'Slowly,' he shouted, and for perhaps fifteen minutes the journey continued. At this time human voices could be heard above the animals. Men were loitering on the side of the road and some were obviously drunk. They shouted incoherent words of encouragement. The tollgate came in sight, there were perhaps a hundred revellers there, not in a riotous frame of mind but looking for some excitement with their inhibitions let off the leash by alcohol. Cheering started. They walked into the road and the cattle became frightened. Their pace turned to a run and soon a run was a gallop. This alarmed the revellers and temporarily sobered them up as they clung to the side of the road while the herd rushed past. The cattle having passed, they gave out a large cheer which made everyone feel better and relieved the tension, with no more harm done than a few trodden feet and hearts beating a little faster. The last they saw was Dewi with a dog on either side and the herd retreating almost as fast as it had come. Fortunately the side roads were blocked due to Jack's efforts and they moved in the correct direction. Having left the crowd behind, they moderated their speed. The holding field came into sight and within minutes they were at the end of their journey, breathless, steaming and thirsty.

Tommy was there to receive them, his pony tied up in the corner of the field. Thirsty after the drive, the cattle drank long and hard and it was perhaps half an hour before they left the stream. 'Let'em cool down a spell, then we'll count them.' Rarely in a hurry, they made small talk till the animals cooled down and settled.

Eddie, with beer and a sovereign uppermost in his mind, was gauging the time and the manner to strike. There was a lull in the conversation. 'Well, Dewi, I think I've earned my sovereign.' Without looking round, Dewi thrust his hand into his pocket and gave him one of the coins which had been reserved for the tolls. Eddie took the coin, wondering how long he would have to stay before he could depart for an evening of good cheer. It had been a hard day and he could already taste the beer in his mouth. His mind was on anything but the matter of the count.

The herd was counted, recounted, examined for lameness and the delivery pronounced correct. 'Ninety- four, correct.'

'Dewi, you want sovereigns, why? My cheque is as good as sovereigns in the bank. You know that.'

'I know that, Tommy, but I want it in sovereigns.'

'Where d'you bank?'

'Carmarthen.'

'Pity. If it was here you could pay it in at once. It would be safer than keeping it overnight.'

'The money will be safe with me, Tommy.'

Slowly they walked towards the Saddlers. They entered the bar which was full of men over which hung a hum of conversation, an atmosphere of elation and the smell of beer. Without a word to anyone they walked through the bar and into the back room which was not open to the public but was known as a place where private business was transacted. It was a dark room, perhaps twelve feet square and much in need of a coat of paint. Across the window, partially drawn, was a pair of shabby curtains which made the naturally dark room even darker. It looked out into a backyard and no-one could be observed within. In the middle of the room were four chairs and a table.

'Sit down.' They did so while Tommy left the room, returning with a small hessian bag tied with a cord. As he sat down he said, 'Well Dewi, that's ninety four times eleven guineas. How much do I owe you my boy?' Tommy could work these figures out in his head as well as any school teacher and perhaps a bit quicker. Dewi couldn't work out the sum without a pencil and paper and thought he might have difficulty if he did. Knowing he could trust Tommy, whose honesty was legendary he said, 'You work it out Tommy.'

Tommy brought out a note book and, turning to a fresh page,

went through the figures in a slow and simplistic manner for the benefit of his audience. Jack was mesmerised at the way the arithmetic was done. Slowly Tommy undertook the calculation. 'Dewi, one guinea is a pound and a shilling. Ninety-four times eleven shillings. That's fifty- one pounds and fourteen shillings.' He put the figure down. 'Ninety-four times eleven pounds. That's one thousand and thirty-four pounds.' He put the figures down and added them up 'That's one thousand and eighty-five pounds and fourteen shillings. Give me the fourteen shillings for luck. I owe you one thousand and eighty-five pounds. Right?'

'Yes, that's right.' Dewi was relieved that the figure would cover the bank loan and the interest but it would leave hardly anything over.

The money was counted out in piles of fifty, which Jack understood. He had never seen so much money before. While his family was scratching around for pennies and shillings, here was over a thousand pounds and all in gold. The glint of the metal, the tinkle of its sound, the feel of the wealth mesmerised him for the moment. Whilst thrilled by the amount, he was attempting to calculate the figures. Tommy had proved a more impressive teacher of arithmetic than Marie.

'There, that's yours,' said Tommy, scooping the money into the bag, tying it up by the neck and handing it to him. 'One more thing. I want a receipt.' Going out of the room, he returned with a piece of paper, pen and ink. He slowly and deliberately wrote out the transaction, which Dewi signed without comment. They shook hands and parted.

Chapter 7

Dewi had never known such elation. More than a thousand sovereigns in his hand from a profitable deal. Next year he could borrow double the amount, buy two hundred cattle and drive them to the English markets himself and make a fortune. This was the way to live.

The remaining sovereigns were returned to the safe and Tommy re-appeared in the back room.

'I'll have two hundred for you next year,' said Dewi.

'Anything over fifty stone and I'll take them, Dewi,' Tommy replied. He was apprehensive as to what would happen to the gold over the next few hours. He thought he should have insisted on giving him a cheque but said no more about it.

'Tommy, have a drink,' Dewi offered.

'Just a small one.'

'Two pints and a small one for the little'un,' Dewi commanded Nellie.

'The little'un won't get one here.'

'Won't do him any harm.'

She looked him straight in the eye and he knew it was no good pursuing the matter. Tommy gave her a two index finger cross-sign which she responded to by giving him a half pint only. 'Tommy, have a pint.' He shook his head. Dewi's pint tankard was now in his hand which was emptied in two rapid mouthfuls. This was followed by another pint which was consumed almost as quickly. The successful deal, the cash in his hand, and the fact that he hadn't drunk for two years had an immediate effect on his behaviour

'That's better,' he slurred.

Tommy couldn't stay any longer but whispered in his ear, 'Watch all that money.' He also warned Nellie to get him up to bed as soon as possible and to persuade him to lock the money away in the safe.

'I'll be alright,' Dewi shouted after Tommy as he left the bar. 'Another one, Nellie.' She served him another pint but from then on kept him under observation.

Jack saw a change in him he had not seen before. He had never seen him drink, never seen him so relaxed, unobservant and good humoured. He gave Jack his tankard and said, 'Try it boy.' He did and found the taste unpleasant, giving the tankard back immediately. 'Good stuff, lad, you'll come to like it.'

Nellie leaned over the counter, grasped his wrist and said to him, 'Dewi, give that cash to me. You could lose it in your state. Don't be a fool, give it to me.'

'It'll be safe with me Nellie, don't you worry.'

Tommy came back to the door beckoning Nellie. 'Have you got the money from him?'

She shook her head. 'He's getting more drunk all the time but he won't let the money go.'

'Get it off him and in the safe as soon as you can. Put him up here tonight, he can never go home in that state,' Tommy said quietly. 'Trouble is, he's a fool and he doesn't know it. If that money gets stolen it will affect us all. There's a few bad eggs in the Becca crowd who'll stop at nothing. These aren't normal times.'

'I've dealt with much worse than him. Trust Nellie.' She was becoming irritated by his anxiety and his lack of confidence in her ability 'No drunk has ever got the better of me yet. Dewi was a drinker before he married, but once Hilda got hold of him, he stopped. Trust Nellie.'

Tommy finally departed, feeling he could trust her to keep the gold in safekeeping. It would be a busy day for him tomorrow, going east with three hundred head of cattle.

Dewi was now drinking his third pint and talking to anyone who would listen. Feeling full of goodwill and success he talked about his recent deal. 'How much do you think is in this bag?' he would ask, giving it a shake and then allowing a glimpse of the contents. By now there was quite a crowd round him. No one gave a figure but everyone became more curious. 'Go on, guess.'

'Don't know,' answered one man.

'What's your name?'

'Willie.'

'I'm Dewi.' He offered his hand which was reluctantly taken. 'Have a drink, what you having?'

'Beer.'

'Nellie, a beer for Willie.' She gave him a searching look and continued to do so as she poured the drink, placing it in front of Willie.

'Dewi, how long since you've had a drink?'

'Long time Nellie. Very, very long time Nellie.' He looked at her in an appreciative manner. She was a good looking, confident woman and no stranger to compliments from men whose needs were more ardent than hers.

'Dewi, how you going home tonight?'

'I'll walk.'

'With all that money?'

'I'll be alright.'

'You sure?' She tentatively flirted with him.

'Yes, I'll be alright. Jack'll be with me, won't you Jack?'

'Yes,' he said, not knowing what else to say. Realising that there were going to be difficulties, he had no idea how the night would end.

'Dewi, you're going to stay here. I don't want you on the road with all that money. You'll be robbed. The whole of Narberth knows you have this money.'

'Nellie, I can look after myself.'

'Not with all that beer in you. You're staying here.' Her tone didn't allow for any argument.

'Alright Nellie, if you say so.' Through a haze of alcohol he now warmed to her. 'I'll stay here Nellie. You'll look after me. I'd like that Nellie.' He gave her an amorous smile. 'I want another beer, Nellie.'

'I'll get you another beer but I want that money in the safe.'

'No, Nellie, it'll be alright with me. It's mine, see.' The pride of having such a large sum in his hand thrilled him. It did not occur to him that nearly all of it was owed to the bank and should be in their hands next morning. He felt he had come a long way since he was a farm servant earning six pounds a year and sleeping in the barn.

Nellie added a generous measure of whisky to his beer, hoping he would get drunk enough for her to be able to get the cash from him.

'That's better, I'll be alright Nellie.'

'Get that down you,' she said, almost throwing the glass at him.

Again he shook the bag, looked inside and said, 'It'll be alright with me.'

He was now the centre of attention in the bar but unaware of the fact. Nellie noticed that the bar had filled up with many she did not know. The Becca crowd were, by and large, a law abiding crowd but it always attracted an unruly element.

She had to do something and quickly. One more doctored pint and she would hustle him upstairs. If the money were stolen it would affect her, the tenancy of her tavern, Tommy, not to mention the bank who had forwarded the money. A cloud would hang over the whole town. Dewi was a fool but those involved with him had allowed him to be a fool.

By this time his head was hanging on his chest and he was mumbling to himself. She moved rapidly to the other side of the bar, grabbed him round the waist and with a mixture of lifting, dragging and pushing from Jack she got him into the living quarters and sat him on a chair. 'You're going to bed now.'

'I'm alright, Nellie,' Dewi protested.

'Come on, bed!' she commanded.

He now stood up a little unsteadily still hanging on to the bag, making attempts at sobriety. Slowly, she persuaded him to go to bed in a room at the back of the house. She removed his boots but left his other clothes on. He flopped on the bed.

'Dewi, I want that bag.'

'No, it's mine!'

In spite of his condition, his grip on the bag remained one of iron. She could not understand how a man so drunk could hold out so long or muster such strength. He was now in bed with Jack beside him and her mind eased a little. She had to get back to the bar.

As she went she told Jack, 'I'll leave a candle on the landing. Back in half an hour. Get hold of the bag if you can. Shout if there's trouble and keep Dewi's stick by you.'

'Yes Nellie.'

'Remember, call if you need me. There's no lock on the door. I'll leave it ajar so you can just see out. I'll be back in half an hour.' Reluctantly she went downstairs and served continuously for nearly half an hour. 'The banker's asleep.' 'Midas upstairs.' 'Golden Dewi,' were all remarks she heard but did not respond to. They made her uneasy. By implication rather than by direct word, she let her customers know the money was in the safe. Whether they believed her she wasn't sure. The bar was now very full and the noise was considerable.

Dewi was, by now, fast asleep and snoring, having relaxed his grip on the money. Jack remained awake, took the money from his grip and placed it in the bottom drawer of the wardrobe. The candle flickered more violently than usual and he could feel a draught come through the door. The conversation in the bar sounded as a distant hum which he found reassuring.

There was a creak on the stairs and then another. The candle flickered even more violently. He shuddered, the shiver going down his back. Shaking Dewi lightly without result, he was uncertain what to do. There were more creaks followed by a slight muttering. He shook Dewi again but all he did was groan. Suddenly the candle went out, there was a rush into the room and the sound of a man's voice; strong, commanding and very aggressive. He could feel the two men in the room rather than see them as the head of the bed was against the window.

'Get the kid; put your hand over his mouth. I'll deal with him.' Jack grabbed the stick but, before he could use it, felt a hand grasp his chest and rapidly move to his mouth which was held with great force. 'You make a sound and I'll tear your eyes out, you little rat. Understand?' It was obvious that the man threatening him was not the one who held his mouth. His mouth was not released for him to reply but he gave a nod of his head. Dewi's mouth was now grasped by the man doing the talking which roused him out of his stupor. 'Where's the bag?' demanded the intruder. Dewi gave no reply as he was still half drunk and couldn't understand what was happening.

'Where's the bag? I'll twist your bloody head off if you don't tell me. Where is it?' Dewi quickly sobered up. He reached out to where it had been when he remembered it last without success. Not knowing where it was, he tried to shout out but the words would not come.

The men were adjusting gradually to the dark, searching the room with one hand whilst the other still held on to their victims. Jack felt the grasp on his mouth slacken as their search became more desperate. The more forceful of the two robbers threatened him, 'Where's the bag, little 'un. If you don't tell me I'll tear your guts out, you little rat.' The voice this time was of even more uncompromising aggression. When he didn't immediately reply, Jack found himself gripped round the neck from behind with such pressure that he truly feared for his life. Should he tell them, should he say he didn't know or should he try to make a run for it? These thoughts went through his mind in a flash. By now he had become accustomed to the darkness and could make the two figures out. They still searched the room while holding onto their captives. As the man tightened his grip on Jack's mouth, he managed to bite his thumb with all his strength. The robber let out a loud scream which was heard all over the building. Jack then rushed through the door and toward the stairs, screaming himself.

While this took place, the more desperate of the two men knew he only had a few seconds to make one last effort to find the bag. He searched under the bed and in the wardrobe, finding the bag at last. Knowing the stairs would be blocked, he put his hand through the window to break the glass and jumped down to the back yard, still holding the bag. Now he had to get over a nine foot wall. He was followed by his partner, who cut himself badly on the glass on the way down.

Meanwhile, everyone in the bar had become aware of some trouble upstairs. Nellie was the first to reach the room, followed by Jack and several men anxious to satisfy their curiosity and perhaps be of assistance. Dewi was, by now, standing and shouting as he looked out of the window. Nellie and three others peered out, seeing the men trying to climb the wall without success.

Trying to think logically, Nellie asked Jack, 'Where's the bag?'

'Wardrobe drawer,' he replied, going to look. 'My God, it's gone. Get after them. They've got the money.'

No one would jump out of the window, which was covered in blood, but they rushed downstairs and through the back door. By this time the active robber was on top of the wall, having dropped the bag on the jump up. It now lay on the floor with the contents nearly all spilled out. 'Throw it up,' he yelled to his companion, who was successful at the second attempt. The bulk of the gold was now scattered around in the public house back yard. On top of the wall, he gave his accomplice his hand and lifted him out of the yard. The hand he grasped was streaming with blood. They jumped to the ground on the other side of the wall. 'Now cut and run. Every man for himself. You're on your own now, boy.' They ran to the corner and stopped.

'We got to share the money.'

'There ain't that much money to share, boy. We'll meet at Pembroke. Then we'll share the money, see.'

'That's not fair though,' replied the younger man.

'It's not fair we didn't get all the money. Trust me, good boy. I'll see you all right in Pembroke. Now we're going our own way boy. Understand?'

'It's not fair,' he muttered again, his voice tapering off. He knew he had lost. The two robbers ran off in different directions.

The bedroom and yard were both now full of people. Dewi was told what a fool he had been by nearly everyone. He stood in the middle of the room, not knowing what to say. In the yard half a dozen people were picking up the sovereigns by the light of candles. Nellie joined them and supervised the operation, not wanting any more to be stolen than had been already. Spending almost an hour there and searching every inch of the area they managed to retrieve eight hundred and fifty-five coins. The money was immediately put in the safe. Tommy, hearing the news, had returned to the pub.

The initial excitement over, they now discussed what to do. Nellie left her sister, Matty, in charge of the bar and joined the others in the backroom. Tommy proceeded to question Dewi briefly, in a dismissive manner. 'You were bloody drunk, you damn fool. You might just as well have given the coins to them yourself.' Dewi didn't know what to say but was thinking of ways to avoid the consequences. Jack was questioned. Would he know them again? Would he recognise their voices? How long were they in the room? Were they told where the bag was?

'Why did one of them shout out and alert everyone?' asked Tommy

'Cos I bit him on the hand.'

'Good for you, boy.'

Dewi felt out of it and wanted to be heard, after all it was only an hour or two since he had been a bar-room Midas. 'They must have found the money as soon as they got in the room.'

'What? In the room ten minutes and knew where the bag was all the time? Stupid fool! As soon as they got the money they would have run.'

'I only thought…' Dewi began.

Tommy interrupted him, 'Think before you make stupid remarks again. I've been a fool to give you cash for you to show the town.'

Tommy pondered. Normally a man of few words, he was now a man of many.   'It's to the magistrate's in the morning.'

'We haven't got to do that, have we?' said a worried Dewi.

72

How his world had fallen apart in an hour or two.

'Too right we have, and it ought to be done tonight, though it's too late at this time. He probably knows by now. Sooner there's a search party out the better. The weather's dry and there may be a trail of blood. They'll probably put the dragoons after them. It's about time they did something useful. They won't want them getting away. They might even recover the money.'

'Do you think they would?' asked Dewi.

'It'd be your luck. They say the Good Lord looks after fools, drunks and children and you're all three.' This was as bad as getting a hard time from Hilda.

The full reality of what had happened was beginning to dawn on Dewi. The coins that had been saved would not pay off the loan. What would he say to the bank? Would they give him time to pay off the remainder over a year or two or would they insist on selling the rest of his stock to repay the loan. That would leave him with insufficient cattle and sheep to make a living enough to pay the rent. What would Hilda say? That is what really worried him. Certainly, news of the crime committed tonight would be all over the area within a day. It would be back to being a farm servant again, perhaps he would have to face court proceedings, who knew what the outcome would be. His only hope was the recovery of the money or if not an arrangement with the bank. Was it just possible?

There was nothing more to be said. 'The pair of you go to bed now; you're not going to be robbed again tonight.' They made their way upstairs and got into bed. Dewi remained awake till the very first signs of dawn and slept for perhaps an hour. Jack remained awake for a while also, his head filled with thoughts of what had happened. The excitement and his role in it had thrilled him but he knew Dewi was in trouble. Somehow he knew his stay with him would not be a long one. Would he have to move on? When it would happen he did not know but happen it would.

Chapter 8

The grey dawn was just emerging on the eastern horizon and the drovers had been busy for some time. The cattle were starting to leave the field with drovers in front and men and dogs behind. The occasional lowing of cattle was heard but the air was dominated by the barking of dogs and the shouting of the drovers. They moved at a steady two miles an hour eastwards, a thick black ribbon flowing between the hedges, perhaps three or four hundred yards long. By nine they were clear of the town and by half-past out of hearing. They would stop for water before Whitland, around midday, and be near St Clears by nightfall. Along the way, six tollgates would have to be passed and the tolls paid. Going by alternative routes with so many animals would be difficult, if not impossible. The day was clear and no obvious problems had been encountered so far. Fortunately there were no other droves using the road. Bringing up the rear was Tommy, the only rider, on his pony Gyp.

He'd spent many years in his present trade and was beginning to feel his age. There was a shortness of breath and he had not the energy he'd had two years before. He hadn't the enthusiasm either and the responsibility of it all weighed on him more heavily. The robbery last night passed through his mind. What a fool he had been to give Dewi cash. Never in the past would he have made such a mistake. A feeling of depression passed over him. How many more years would he be able to work at this demanding trade? Not many, he thought. How many more times would he be wet through? If he gave it up, what would he do? He had no family apart from his married brother and no home apart from the Saddler's.

Sharp though he was, perhaps a quarter of his droves made losses. Gone were the days when he would drive four hundred to London. His current herd would be sold whenever he could get a pound a head profit and that would probably be before he got over the English border. Problems which had been relatively easy to solve when he was young, were now a burden which had to be borne. He had no wife, no children to hand the business on to and none of his drovers had the ability to run the financial side. Eddie would fail on the first drove; he was too fond of beer and would drink even more if Tommy wasn't breathing down his neck. He had no leadership or trading qualities.

Tommy wondered what he would do if he retired. Farming was out of the question. His brother would only have him under sufferance. Nellie would take him in permanently but what would he do except serve in the bar? Again he dwelt on the time he was living in: the Becca riots, the presence of the army, not to mention the grinding poverty everyone suffered. It was only a question of time before the railways came and that would be the end of hundreds of years of this trade. These thoughts passed through his mind but, he reflected, it was a fine day, he hadn't overpaid for the cattle and the herd was moving. It could be worse.

Meanwhile, as dawn was breaking, Nellie was cleaning the bar and kitchen which, in view of the robbery, had not been done last night. She was doing this almost automatically. The justices would have to be told and soon, early that morning. She climbed the stairs, entering the bedroom. 'Get up, you two,' she shouted, which woke Jack from a deep sleep. Dewi was already awake, dreading having to face the day ahead.

'We're going to be at the magistrates at nine,' Nellie told them.

'Which one?'

'Colonel Herbert, he's the nearest. All of them will know by now.'

'We don't all have to go, do we?' asked Dewi.

'Yes, all of us. The crime was committed in my tavern and you two saw what happened. Don't argue. You're going!' Keeping quiet, Dewi knew he had to go. 'Wash yourselves and get ready to see him.' They did so. No breakfast was given to them and by half past eight they were on their way. 'Listen you two. No lies. You won't fool this man. He'll tear you to pieces if he catches you out.'

Walking at a quick pace, they soon entered the drive and walked up to the house which was surrounded by trees. It was perhaps two hundred yards but to Dewi the journey seemed all too short. Nellie did not know whether to knock at the front or back door. Matters concerning the servants went to the back. Matters relating to the Colonel and his wife went to the front door. Plucking up all her courage, but not slackening her pace, she went to the front door and knocked. It was some time before the door was answered by a stout middle-aged housekeeper dressed in quite formal black. Nellie, who stood in front of the other two, was dressed in her best clothes, a grey hat, black tweed overcoat and brown shoes. She felt nervous.

'Yes?' said the housekeeper in a condescending manner not attempting in any way to put the caller at ease. In fact, quite the reverse.

'I need to speak to Colonel Herbert.' Nellie gained some confidence as she started to speak. The housekeeper wanted to know what she needed the colonel for but did not ask directly, leaving a long silence which lasted several seconds.

'Something happened?'

'Yes,' answered Nellie. Again there was a silence during which the housekeeper hoped her curiosity was to be satisfied. Nellie realised this, saying 'I need to see a magistrate.'

'Come in, stand there. I'll speak to Colonel Herbert.'

The hall was large, dimly lit, and there were half a dozen portraits on the walls of men in military uniforms who all seemed middle aged or older. There was also a large picture of a battle scene. The cannons were smoking and lines of troops were facing one another, who all seemed to be dressed in red. In the foreground was a man on a horse, obviously the Duke of Wellington many years before, possibly at the Battle of Waterloo.

After what seemed to them all a very long time the housekeeper returned. 'He'll see you one at a time. You go first,' she said, indicating Nellie.

She entered the room and the Colonel was sitting at his desk. He didn't ask her to sit and looked at her directly. 'I hear there was a robbery at your tavern last night. What happened?'

'Well, sir, Dewi had sold some cattle yesterday. He went to bed with the money and some of it got stolen.'

'Went to bed with the money? Why wasn't it put in the bank?'

'Don't know. His bank is in Carmarthen.'

'How much money?'

'Over a thousand.'

'You have a safe. Why wasn't it put in there?'

'It was his money, you see.'

'Doesn't seem to be his any longer. How much was stolen?'

'About two hundred sovereigns.'

'Where's the money you still have?'

'In the safe now.'

'Pity it wasn't there in the first place. Did you see the men who were involved?'

'No-one saw them. There were quite a few strangers in the bar.'

'Where was the money taken? How did they get away?'

'Dewi and the lad, Jack, were sleeping in the bedroom when the money got took. Then they jumped through the window. One got cut very bad. A lot of blood everywhere.'

'Did you see them?'

'No.'

'Wait outside and send Dewi in.'

She walked outside, relieved the ordeal was over but feeling very drained. Without looking at Dewi, she said, 'You next.' He tried to enquire what she had been asked, what mood he was in but she ignored this. Again she said, 'You next.'

He walked in.

'You've made a right fool of yourself,' said the magistrate,

'What time did you go to bed?'

'Early, sir.'

'How much had you drunk? Don't tell me any lies.'

'Sir, about two pints, sir.'

The Colonel raised his voice and venomously said, 'Don't tell me lies. How much did you drink?' fixing him with a penetrating glare.

'Sir, perhaps one or two more, sir.' His tone became more timid.

'You were drunk, you damned fool.' This was now heard by the two waiting outside and the housekeeper, who with impeccable timing was in the right place at the right time. A self satisfied smile came over her face as she looked at Nellie and Jack. What can you expect from such people, she thought. Neither woman nor boy could miss her thoughts.

The Colonel continued, 'You went to bed drunk with over a thousand pounds on you.' He became progressively more irritated. 'What did the robbers look like?'

'Sir, I don't know, it was dark.'

'Too drunk to see them. You're a damned fool. There is a deficiency of two hundred pounds, I hear. How much do you owe the bank?'

'Sir, a thousand?'

'Plus the interest.'

'Yes sir.'

'How will you pay this two hundred pounds?'

'Sir, give me time and I'll pay it, give me time.'

'I can't give you time. I'm not the bank director. Banks are not fools and they will want their money now. How much stock have you got? Will that cover the two hundred pounds?'

'Sir, I think so.' He now saw the folly of his behaviour and its full implications. The stock would pay off the loan but he would be left with only a few head of cattle which would never give him the living he needed to pay the rent.

'Send the boy in,' demanded the Colonel. Dewi walked out in a virtual daze.

'You next,' he said to Jack automatically. He walked in.

'I don't know what you can say that will help but I'd better hear from you?' He looked the boy in the face and was surprised by the direct, unflinching look which was returned. 'Well, lad, tell me what happened from when you went into the bedroom until the time the robbers jumped out of the window.' Jack went through the details: Dewi getting into bed, not releasing the sovereigns initially, but eventually Jack prising them from him and putting them in the wardrobe drawer. He recalled the creaking noises on the stairs and the candle going out, the rush into the bedroom and the hand over his mouth.

'Sir, only one spoke and he didn't sound local.'

'What accent?'

'Sir, don't know.'

'Then what happened?'

'Sir, then the one who was holding my mouth released his grip and I bit into his hand. I think it was his thumb and he shouted out and I ran downstairs then they all came up.'

'At last, some commonsense. Did you go up again?'

'Yes sir.'

'What did you see?'

'They'd left the room and there was blood on the window. Suppose they jumped out.'

'Did you see them again?'

'No sir.'

'You've done well, lad. Is Dewi your father?'

'No sir. I don't have a father. He took me in when my mother died.'

'Do you have a family?'

'Two sisters working at the Hall sir, that's all'

'You've done well, lad. Leave now and tell them they can all go home.'

He waited till he could see the three figures walking down the drive then rang the bell. The housekeeper knocked and entered. 'Send Jessop to town and ask the dragoon captain or lieutenant to come and see me as soon as possible.'

79

'Very well, sir.'

As the three of them walked silently back to the town, Dewi felt even more depressed than he had on arrival at the house. Though a reasonably fine day, it was autumn and getting cooler, which they hardly noticed. Slowly they walked back to the tavern, lost in their own particular thoughts, Dewi's of financial ruin and Jack's of an uncertain future. Darkness came over them both. After what seemed an age, they found themselves in the kitchen. 'You get what's left of that money back to the bank today,' advised Nellie.

No longer feeling he had a mind of his own, he was prepared to accept orders from anyone. 'Suppose I've got to walk to Carmarthen.'

'Too right, you have. Start now and you'll get there tonight and pay it in tomorrow.'

'Where'll I sleep?'

'You're a big boy. Find somewhere.'

Nellie walked to the safe, extracted the bag and gave it to him. 'For God's sake, don't go drinking tonight. Don't be a fool all your life.' He wanted to delay the journey till tomorrow but knew he could not resist the pressure.

Knowing Tommy would be taking the drove through Llanddewi Velfrey, he took the road south through Lampeter Velfrey, walking very fast. Though the drovers had a start of an hour he knew that he could be in Whitland before them, being able to walk at more then twice their pace.

'Leave the boy with me,' Nellie had said, 'You don't want him giving Hilda the bad news do you?' He didn't answer. Would the humiliation never end?

'No,' he muttered to himself, 'but she probably knows by now.'

He left on the route he had decided. At least alone he would suffer no more public degradation against which he could muster no defence. Lost in his own thoughts, he walked through Whitland, Saint Clears, Bancyfelin and the outskirts of Carmarthen by nightfall. Depressed by his own thoughts and

80

what had happened to him within the last twenty-four hours, he reflected on the future. Finding shelter in a disused barn beginning to fall into ruin, he sat on the floor with his back against the wall and tried to make up his mind what he would tell the bank in the morning. They would probably know already but would they give him time? Where would he be in a year? Where would he be in a week or perhaps even a couple of days? Banks looked after their own interests, everyone knew that. Just before dawn, probably from mental and physical exhaustion, he managed to sleep for a while still sitting against the wall.

Hardly had an hour passed since their return from the magistrate's, when the sound of horses was heard outside the inn. A dragoon sergeant and four troopers were outside. The leader did not dismount but waited for someone to come out. When no-one did, he shouted. Nellie came out with Jack behind her, and looked up at the sergeant. Jack saw the five men dressed in their uniforms and a certain thrill went through him which was quite at odds with his response to the dragoon officer in the field where he had seen him last..

'The robbery?' He addressed Nellie.

'Yes?'

'Someone cut badly?'

'That's right.'

'Better have a look.'

'Come in, then.'

He dismounted, gave the reins of his horse to the nearest trooper and followed Nellie upstairs. She showed him the broken window, the blood stains and where they had got over the wall.

'How many?' asked the officer.

'Two,' she replied.

'Better try and find them then. What did they look like?'

'No-one knows,' she admitted.

'Anything else about them?'

'The lad bit one of them in the hand or thumb.'

'The lad downstairs?'

'Yes.'

81

'Your son, the rabid dog?' he joked, giving her an engaging smile. She smiled for the first time in hours.

'Not my lad, more's the pity.' He turned to walk down the stairs giving Jack's head a rough rub as he went out saying, 'Mad dog,' with a smile.

'We'll try and follow the blood stains,' was his parting remark. He remounted his horse and departed.

All five soldiers had had an exhausting and frustrating few weeks. Long rides during the night and day looking for Becca rioters and toll-gate breakers without any success. No information was forthcoming. They and their horses were exhausted. Controlling the protestors was a frustrating task when even the school boys jeered at their impotence. Though they'd had a busy day yesterday, their evening had been spent in a tavern where they all drank a great deal, getting into bed drunk with one exception and he was in the arms of his girlfriend. They all had matters other than the task in hand to focus on, be it headaches or emotional needs.

Clip-clop, clip-clop, the horses and riders set off through the town on their mission, the finery of their uniforms giving no indication of the lethargy and lack of commitment within. Slowly they travelled south towards Narberth Bridge, following the blood stains, which was a reasonably easy job. Jack, quite mesmerised by the troopers, followed at a distance of fifty yards which was not hard in view of the slow pace of the horses. At the bridge the blood stains ceased. Like all good cavalry men, they would not dismount but looked over each side of the bridge and along the stream a short way without success. They had lost the trail and rode on, no more committed to finding the robbers than they had been when first given orders that morning. On they rode, clip-clop, clip-clop, for the next two hours enquiring here and there without purpose or direction, staying on the roads where they would be unlikely to find their quarry. They went through the motions of looking but hoped they would not find them and looked forward to the time when they could return to their lodgings in the workhouse that night and matters more pressing than riding around the country on this hopeless errand.

Jack did not follow them beyond the bridge although he was fascinated by them. The slow pace of the horses, the humped shoulders of the troopers and the drowsiness of their expressions confirmed to him that they would have no success today. Onwards the troop walked, up the hill until they disappeared into the distance, unaware that he had followed them, even less aware that he had left them. On they travelled looking neither to right nor left, kept awake only by the sound of the horses' hooves on the road.

Jack peered over the bridge, into the water and to either side of the stream. With his youthful good sight and clear head, he detected a footprint some eight yards away. Climbing down to the side of the stream, he saw that the tracks in the mud were fresh. Walking on a few more yards, he saw blood again but not in the quantity it had been on the road. He looked ahead. Never again did he want to be held in that grip. 'Is this the man I bit?' he said to himself and felt a mixture of thrill and fear in his stomach. On he walked, his gaze looking at the tracks then returning ahead. Rapidly he came to the wood where his pace became even slower, his boots making more noise. He was able to follow the footprints, but with more difficulty as the woodland floor was rougher. The occasional spot of blood still appeared. The wood became darker and colder; he was more fearful. His assailant might not be far away. Looking up once more, he saw one leg then another lying on the ground with the body leaning against the trunk of a tree. There was no movement.

Walking backwards and keeping the legs in view, he continued till he was out of earshot. Then, running as fast as he could along the bank, onto the bridge, up to the town and back to the Saddler's he arrived breathless. 'Nellie, found one of the men.'

Recounting what had happened, pausing briefly only to get his breath back, he told her everything. Nellie felt some degree of relief, rather than excitement. It looked as though one of the men would be caught. Walking immediately to where the dragoon officer lodged, she learned that he was with the troopers outside the workhouse. Attempting to gain his attention, she eventually did. It was the same officer who had spoken to them in the field of oats.

Riding up in ten or twelve yards, in a languid manner, he said, 'Yes.'

'He's found one of the robbers,' reported Nellie.

'Really, where?'

'In the wood by the bridge. Narberth Bridge.'

'Who found him?'

'He did,' she said, pointing to Jack.

'Well, well, well,' he replied in mocking disbelief. 'We'd better pick him up. Something positive is happening at last.'

Within half an hour the robber had been taken, none too gently, to the court cells and his wounds attended to as a prisoner.

Chapter 9

The autumn had come and it was a cold one. It was now some hours after dark and the sisters, Mary and Annie, had got into their bed, right under the roof of the Hall, after a long, hard day's work. The wind was whistling through the slates and the temperature was very cold. It had been Mary's bedroom for almost three years and Annie's for less than a year. Their life followed a pattern even when they were in bed alone. The subject was invariably the same: Dilys.

'Annie, are you awake?'

'Yes.'

'That Dilys has been at me again.'

'Oh,' replied Annie more inaudibly.

'She's been sucking up to Admiral Sir George again.'

'He likes all the young girls.'

'She pushed into me when I was taking the silver into the dining room, then gave me one of her sneering laughs. If it had been china, I would have dropped the plates. Then what would have happened to me?' complained Mary.

'The plates would have smashed and you'd have had to tell the housekeeper.'

'She wouldn't have believed me.'

'She might do. Dilys don't give me no trouble.'

Annie recollected the confrontation she had had with Dilys soon after she arrived. As a scullery maid and perhaps the most lowly person working in the house, she was doing the washing up one day when from behind her she heard Dilys's voice command, 'I want all those plates in the next ten minutes. Do you hear?' Up to her elbows in soap suds, she looked round to see Dilys's eyes which were aggressive and confident. She didn't answer. 'Did you hear? Those plates in ten minutes.' Still no reply and Annie looking at her directly eventually saying, 'No,' with all the confidence she could muster.

'They're needed in the Admiral's dining room,' said Dilys.

The housekeeper heard the end of this conversation. 'Dilys, what's this?'

'I want the plates for the dining room, madam. I need to lay the table.'

'Not at this time of day you don't, they'll all be covered in dust by tonight.'

'Yes, madam.'

'Get on with what you are supposed to do. You only come in here twice a day. You should know that by now.'

'Yes, madam.'

Annie told Mary this story, ending with, 'She hasn't troubled me since.'

Despite what Annie said, Mary went on, 'She never stops going on at me.' During this conversation Mary was in tears as she had been for the last thousand nights. She didn't seem to appreciate the support her younger sister gave her. Every night Annie listened to what jibes her sister had received. Every night she tried to reassure her. Every night the elder sister wanted to talk and the younger one to sleep. So it had been since Annie's arrival.

Annie snuggled down under the feather quilt, going to sleep in seconds. Mary thought about her problems for perhaps half an hour. Whatever she did, her adversary was always one step ahead. Soon however, tiredness took over and even she was asleep.

Mary was small, painfully thin and black under the eyes from worrying about everything. How she stood up to Dilys, she did not know. Almost nightly she had fantasised about what harm she could do her but in the morning the fantasies were gone and she had to face the problem once more.

The next morning, Dilys was initially pleasant. 'Going to the fair?'

'Don't know. May stay here with my sister. She hasn't done a year so she can't go.'

'It's a good laugh at the fair. You should come.' Mary became suspicious at all this.

'You didn't go last year did you?' continued Dilys.

'No, I stayed here.' She was still wary of this apparent friendly attitude. Was she hatching something? Of course she was.

'Leave at midday and be back by dusk the next day.'

'Sounds alright.'

'Got a place to sleep?'

'No.'

'What about the workhouse. They'd put you up.' A gleam of pleasure came over Dilys's face. Yet another arrow had gone home. 'That's your home, the workhouse.' Though wounded, Mary did not shed tears but the hurt showed in her eyes and they both knew it. 'Once a workhouse brat, always a workhouse brat.' Yet again the smile of power and sadistic triumph came over Dilys's face and she made it linger. It seemed one humiliation after another against which Mary seemed to have no defence. Would she ever get out of this? Was life like this all the time? No other person seemed to endure such unrelenting unhappiness.

Annie was much lower in the Hall hierarchy. In fact she was the lowest person indoors. The only person lower was Dolly who did the milking, looked after the poultry and worked in the garden. Why, when they were in a lower position did they not suffer such distress? Her sister, three years her junior, had dealt with Dilys quite quickly. Why do I lack such a life force, she thought? Why do I feel I have to be so controlled? I'm sure if got in a fight with her I wouldn't come off badly. This job, this house is so stifling.

Meanwhile, Dolly came to the back door and was soon let in with a basket of produce: vegetables, eggs and two plucked birds. She was a breath of fresh air. Not yet eighteen, she was of medium height, had a robust build and a fresh complexion made all the more so by a life lived outdoors, frequently in wet, windy conditions. But what impressed all who met her was her vitality. Always walking quickly, she had a ready smile and a face that, when amused, would become creased with humour. Most liked her, a few were wary of her and any number of young men and some older ones lusted after her. Dolly lived with her father who worked on the estate. She had strong fair hair, the palms of her hands were as tough as cow hide and she was as strong as an ox. Many men had pursued her without success but it was only a question of time before someone was successful.

'Going to the fair, Annie?'

'No, haven't been here a year.'

'I forgot. They don't break the rules here.'

'Next year maybe. Think my sister's going.'

'She needs something to cheer her up. She looks miserable.'

'Too true.'

'What's wrong?'

'It's that bloody Dilys, it is.'

'That stuck-up little Duchess. I'd see her off in one minute flat.'

Annie smiled to herself. 'I'm sure you would.'

'Tell your sister and Dilys the Duchess they can come down with me. My father always goes in the trap. Think he can take us all. We'll have some fun. Dad has business to do, so he says. Pub business is what it usually is.' Again Dolly smiled and then left to continue her chores.

Annie returned to the task in hand but more slowly, reflecting on her recent visitor. What was it about her? Her strength? Her infectious gaiety? She was on the lowest rung of the employment ladder, she couldn't read or write and only count to perhaps thirty or forty, yet she bowed to no one. Half the young men in the parish wanted to marry her yet she repelled their advances, but still keeping their goodwill. Formality went over her head and that confident smile infected anyone who came within its orbit. What was it about her? How did she do it? She was Dolly. Just Dolly.

Mary came into the kitchen having a minute or two to spare

and spoke to her sister. 'You know we get paid the week before the fair?'

'How many days before?'

'Two or three I think.'

'What you going to do with yours? Spend it?'

'Some of it, not all though.'

'How much will you get?'

'Two pounds I think. That Dilys gets two pounds ten shillings?'

'Don't know what I'll get. I haven't done a year. What do you think?'

'Twenty five shillings I should think.'

'Be good to go down. Still, I'll go next year. Going down with Dolly?'

'Yes. She'll be good fun. I like her dad too. He'll have a few but Dolly can drive us back.'

'The same night?'

'Yes. Pony knows its own way home.'

'Can't get back in the Hall at that time.'

'No, we can sleep at her place.'

'Could you get me something if I give you the money?'

'Yes, what?'

'You know the dress that Dolly wears on Sundays?'

'Yes.'

'One like that. You know, the red and white stripes?'

'Yes I know. You'll have to give me the money.' She nodded.

'Seen Jack lately? Any news?'

'Not really. He's still up with Dewi. Think he's alright?'

'Course he's alright.'

'He's only nine or ten, you know.'

'He'll be alright as long as there's no more school. Only thing he don't like is Marie.'

'True enough. He's a tough one. He can look after himself. Pity you ain't as tough, Mary.'

The housekeeper's walk was heard in the passage. It had the

even, firm clip of authority. They stopped talking, waiting for her arrival. Looking at the two sisters, she exclaimed, 'Mary you should be at work. Have you nothing to do?'

'Yes, madam.' She wasn't a woman hungry for authority but she couldn't let standards slip.

'Then get back to work.'

'Yes madam.' She did as she was told.

'And you get back to the washing up, Annie.' She didn't reply.

As Mary went back to her work, she passed Dilys who gave her the usual unpleasant and knowing glint. 'Housekeeper caught you out, has she? She's got her eye on you.'

Two days went by in the usual manner, the servants' main topic of conversation being pay-day. It was never announced till the day and it always occurred around eleven o'clock a day or two before the fair. The air was always rife with speculation and when it finally did happen, the routine was always the same. They would be called one by one to the housekeeper's office which was little more than a cupboard. Each would go in for a minute or two, learn their fate then walk out and call the next one. One by one they would go in, close the door behind them, sign for their annual pay, be told how they had performed that year and what they would be paid the following. It lasted perhaps three-quarters of an hour and was the subject of gossip, guesswork, disappointment and joy for weeks to come.

Several entered, leaving in the same frame of mind. Dilys was called.

'Well Dilys, sign for the two pounds and ten shillings here.' The housekeeper turned the tick account book round for her to sign. 'You've done quite well this year. The Admiral is particularly impressed with you. He has specially asked that you have an increase in pay. Next year you will have five shillings extra. Are you happy with that?'

'Oh yes.' A smile came over her face.

'Do you get on with Mary?'

'She's alright.'

'She doesn't look very happy to me. Does she?'

'I don't bother with her much.'

'Don't bother with her. You work with her every day.' Dilys's face became red. She could feel the embarrassment. 'Don't bother with her. Honest.' Her eyes could not meet the housekeeper's.

'Just let me say I've got my eye on you.' She looked at her intently. Dilys could only return the gaze fleetingly. Her face became even more flushed. 'You can leave now. Send Mary in.' Her gaze continued till she had turned her back on her and left the room. Dilys left the room flushed with pride. So the Admiral took enough notice of me to give me a rise, she thought to herself. 'He'll see a lot more of me.'

Mary took her turn in the housekeeper's room. 'Sit down Mary. We owe you two pounds.' She signed. 'You've done alright in the past year but your pay will remain the same. Do you understand that?'

'Yes.'

'You never smile Mary. You seem unhappy. What's wrong?'

'I'm alright,' she replied, not looking the housekeeper in the face. What would be the good of telling her; she could do nothing. She couldn't be hovering over Dilys all day. 'I'm alright, honest.' she replied.

'Annie seems happy, why not you?'

'Different I suppose.'

'What are you going to do with your money?'

'Don't have family to give it to. Spend some I suppose.'

'Alright, you can go. Send your sister in.' Mary left the room, wondering whether she had missed an opportunity to solve her problems.

Annie knocked and then walked in, drying her hands on a towel as she did so. She had not removed her apron or combed her hair. Annie was as relaxed as her sister was anxious, already starting to put on some weight in the months she had been at the Hall on the improved diet. Not only did she eat better meals but, when no one was looking, she ate any morsel which presented itself. She had languid eyes, moved and thought slowly. Living in the present, she hardly thought of the past and never the future. Whatever will be, will be, was her philosophy. Her real friend was Dolly and on many occasions she said to herself, 'I want to be like her.'

'Sit down Annie,' said the housekeeper. She did so. There was a brief silence. 'Well Annie you haven't been with us a year yet. Have you enjoyed it?'

'Alright, madam.'

'When we took you in you had a lot of progress to make, hadn't you?'

'Suppose so.'

'Some of that roughness has gone but I expect more progress in the coming year. You do understand we did you a favour by taking you in. We weren't obliged to do so. You do understand, don't you?'

'Yes madam.'

Annie did what was asked of her but she would never be deferential. Never ever. Dolly wasn't, she certainly wouldn't be and would sooner go to the workhouse than ingratiate herself with others.

'You'll get twenty five-shillings and the same annual rate next year.'

'Yes madam.'

'Sign here.' She did so. 'And remember we all expect a little more respect from you in the coming year or your present rate of pay will not be maintained. Do you understand?'

'Yes madam.' There was a silence for some seconds. 'Can I go now?'

There was again a silence. 'Yes and remember what I have said.' She left. The housekeeper felt she had made no progress with her.

Some days passed. The subject of the annual pay and what the housekeeper had to say had now drifted into the distance. The younger members of staff talked about nothing but the fair, what they had done in previous years and how they were going to get there. This problem was solved for some by Dolly's father, Percy who, around midday on fair day, found himself driving the trap to town with his daughter, Dilys and Mary on board. They drove at speed down the drive passing the Admiral returning home after a walk. The driver, with his whip in his right hand, touched his cap to the Admiral and the girls, almost in unison, said, 'Morning, Admiral.' A look of good cheer came over his face. Raising his stick, he almost shouted, 'Hello there, hello Dolly.' Dolly blushed as the trap passed him and after travelling perhaps a further thirty yards said, 'Bloody old ram.'

Mary replied, 'How do you know?'

'Chases me, of course,' said Dolly, with a knowing laugh.

Percy listened to this conversation and a slight smile crossed his face. Dolly could hold her own.

'How d'you deal with him?'

'Easy. Laugh and then run. He never gives up, but as I say you can out run the old'uns and outwit the young ones. It's the ones in between you have to watch.' Everyone laughed.

Dilys and Mary were strangely silent. They hardly looked at one another and hardly spoke. Dilys felt awkward and ill at ease in this environment; the rawness of the company, the roughness of the transport and being so exposed to the elements. Above all she felt ill at ease with the tough, direct attitude of Dolly and even more the attraction of the admiral to her. He hadn't even noticed Dilys. Two days before he had granted her a pay rise but now he ignored her. Should she have come? She looked to her own side of the road and had the others seen her eyes they would have noticed tears. As the journey continued, Mary felt less constrained the further away from the hall they travelled. The wind blew into her face and it became rosy once more, the speed was exhilarating and her sense of expectation increased. She relished this break from the monotony of being an under parlour maid. They arrived in a couple of hours, the pony being quite exhausted by the end of the journey. A stable was found, the pony unharnessed, groomed and fed within twenty minutes. All now went their own way, Percy to the tavern and the girls, initially together, to look around the town.

The streets were awash with people: stall holders, fortune tellers, farm servants on their annual visit to town, crippled soldiers begging, and people leading horses. There was a restless movement of the crowd, all searching for something at this once a year event. The two girls stayed close to Dolly as she spoke to one person after another. She knew everybody. Everybody knew her. They hardly knew a soul.

'Dilys, I'm going to go.'

'Where?'

'Shopping.'

'What for?'

'A dress for my sister.'

'I'll come with you. Dolly won't miss us.'

'I know. What you buying, Dilys?'

'Nothing. Got to give it all to my mother.'

'All of it? That's a bit hard.'

'That's the way it is.' For the first time, Mary felt some sympathy towards her.

'Mother and father are very poor,' continued Dilys. 'Got to go home for half an hour to give them the money. Then I'll be back. Meet you back here.'

'Don't be long.'

Mary searched the stalls, looking for the dress her sister wanted. Every conceivable trinket was sold. There were china dogs, ornaments of metal, cheap jewellery and even cheaper watches, bedclothes, fabrics and hand tools of every description. Card sharps lingered on corners, playing "Find the Lady". All the salesmen were competing with one another for the attention of the crowd. Some salesman were more colourful than others, mesmerising the crowd with their sales pitch and their humour

Eventually Mary found the dress she wanted which cost five shillings and which she was clutching when Dilys returned.

'Got the dress for Annie?'

'Yes.'

'Let's have a look.' She opened the brown paper.

'There's nice,' Dilys exclaimed but Mary detected a look of envy on her face.

She wrapped it up again. 'Let's go and hear the hucksters. They're great.' They drifted towards them. Mary clutched the parcel. Her sister's five shillings had been spent but she still had the two pounds. She wondered whether she should spend it or not.

A drunken farm-worker tried to get them into conversation without success. How would Dolly have dealt with him? They walked to the edge of the stalls then, returning to the salesmen to laugh at their line of patter. Once they had a mark, the salesmen worked on them and few could resist such pressure. It was like watching a cobra with a rat. It was the greatest show they had ever seen. Mary laughed, clutching the dress to her, seeming quite overcome with the show. With every sale she became more mesmerised. Her laughter now completely controlled her; it was almost like being in a fit as the salesman's patter became more outrageous. At this moment Dilys put her hand into Mary's coat pocket and removed the two pounds, her year's wages.

They walked off together, Dilys stopping a moment to slip the two sovereigns into her stocking while Mary went on. Walking away from the stalls, Mary felt she had had a good day. It was well after dark and before too long, she would be going home in the trap with Dolly and her father, leaving Dilys with her parents to make her own way home the next day. There was an hour or two to go yet. There was a warm glow within Mary. Never had she felt as cheerful as this before. Life at home then at the Hall had all been rather grey and at times hellish. She became reflective. Could it last?

Dilys wanted to be parted from Mary but she wondered how soon she could do it without arousing suspicion. She had never stolen before. She knew the consequences if she was caught. If she left now, she knew her manner would be awkward. Mary would pick it up. She was less confident in this environment than at the Hall. She began to regret her actions. Her face became red and she knew she would show embarrassment if confronted now. Pull yourself together, she said to herself, knowing that at that moment she couldn't.

Mary continued walking, still filled with contentment and oblivious to her surroundings. It had been a good day, the best ever. A very small gust of rain refreshed her and woke her up from her thoughts. Putting her hand in her pocket to check her pay she found it gone. 'Dilys, my money's gone!'

'Gone? It can't have.' She did not look Mary in the eye.

'Yes, gone.'

'Pick-pockets I suppose.' Still she could not meet her gaze.

'It's gone.' Tears welled up in Mary's eyes. The parcel fell on the ground as she searched her pockets. 'Who's got it? The bastard.'

'You've dropped it somewhere I expect,' Dilys said.

Mary looked at her and saw the uneasy, shifty look on her face. It lasted less than a second as Dilys looked away. Mary knew she need look no further for the thief. Dilys could tell she'd been found out. They now faced one another eye to eye.

'You little bastard,' Mary yelled, facing up to her. She grabbed Dilys by her hair and pulled it with all her might. 'Give me that money back, you little bastard.' By now her own hair was being pulled as they rolled on the ground. A murderous rage, built up over three years of humiliations, gripped her. She pulled and kicked and would not let go. Dilys fought back, knowing the consequences of being caught, which would mean perhaps imprisonment, losing her job and shame in the community.

By now a small crowd had gathered and were cheering, kicking whichever one was on the floor at the time. It grew larger by the moment. On they fought, kicking, scratching and pulling hair. Dilys was getting the worst of it. It continued for a minute a two more then finally Dilys was kicked in the mouth twice, which knocked out several of her front teeth. They were now exhausted with the unexpected effort of the struggle. No money had been found. Indeed it was not on their minds at that moment. They looked at one another and snarled.

Dilys retrieved her shoes and walked the short distance to her parents' home, searching in her mouth for how much damage had been done, the two pounds still in her stockings. Mary felt she was the victor but, realising the money had not been found, shouted incoherently after her retreating foe. Mary reflected that three years of humiliations had now been erased but it seemed something of an anticlimax.

Dolly came running towards her, having just arrived as the fight was ending. Mary told her what had happened. Picking up the parcel, Dolly said, 'This yours?' She nodded, exhausted and not knowing what to do next. 'We'll have to get you washed and find some clean clothes. Got till tomorrow afternoon, haven't we?' Again Mary nodded. Half carrying, half supporting her, Dolly took her to the tavern her father was drinking in to clean her up. Her hair was a mess and she had lost some of it. Fortunately her face only had a slight bruise or two. She would be more or less presentable to return to the Hall the following afternoon.

Dilys returned a week later, a much chastened person, no longer in possession of six front teeth or much of her hair, but with the bruising no longer visible.

Chapter 10

Dewi had made the walk to Carmarthen at great speed along the main roads, arriving some time after dark. He was exhausted and found a bed at a pub he had drunk in many years before. He ate but did not drink, using the change from the only sovereign he had managed to rescue. The journey and his surroundings had kept his mind off the difficulties ahead for some of the time. Now, alone in his room with only himself for company, he thought of nothing else. Was he at fault? Of course he was, and must take some of the blame but it was catastrophic bad luck. What was he to say at the bank tomorrow? Would they give him time to pay? If they knew what happened, whose version of events would they have heard? He hoped that he and Hilda would somehow survive this experience and continue to farm.

Since the robbery, he seemed to have aged. He noticed a few more grey hairs and he could feel the furrows deepen on his forehead and worry lines grow round his eyes. He knew he looked depressed and felt it. When he walked into that bank, could he put on a cheerful face? Doubt flooded his mind.

He hardly slept all night but finally did so for half an hour before day break. Waking up as dawn appeared, the problems overwhelmed him again. The bank opened at nine thirty. It was now around eight. He got up, washed, dressed, ate a meagre breakfast and walked around town. Carmarthen and District Drover's Bank was only five minutes walk away. Wandering the streets, he hoped to freshen up before the fateful call. He contemplated making a run for it with the remaining sovereigns. He could go to London, even America. He could make a new life for himself, set up in business, live happily ever after. The thought of Hilda and his two daughters passed through his mind and he knew he would have to face the bank and soon. As the clock struck half-past nine, all thoughts of escape deserted him and he propelled himself along the last two hundred yards to the bank, entering with an almost confident air.

No sooner had he presented himself at the counter than the bank clerk said to him. 'The director wants to see you.' He went by an internal door to inform the director of his arrival. Dewi was commanded to enter. 'In here.' The director sat down but did not offer a chair to his customer. 'I hear there's been trouble.'

'Yes.'

'How much money is missing?'

'I've got eight hundred and fifty-four.'

'Give it to me.' He grabbed the bag from Dewi. Ringing the bell for the clerk, he commanded, 'Drop everything and count that.'

Going back to his desk, he opened the thick account book directly at the appropriate page. 'We forwarded you one thousand pounds, plus interest. One thousand and eighty four pounds. That makes a deficiency of two hundred and thirty pounds. What arrangements are you making to pay off this outstanding amount?'

'Give me time and I'll pay it all. Just give me some time. That's all.'

The director was not unduly concerned about the non-payment. He was much more relishing the dressing-down he was giving Dewi, and was only just warming up.

'Why were you paid in sovereigns?' Dewi didn't immediately reply. 'Why were you paid in sovereigns, man?'

Dewi was a little dazed by this quick line in questioning. 'Answer man, answer.'

'Well, it seemed more like proper money.'

'Proper money. What do you mean, proper money? Are you suggesting this bank's notes are not legal tender?'

'No.'

'This bank's notes are accepted from Milford Haven to London yet you suggest they are not proper money.' There was no defence against this onslaught.

'We're going to start from the beginning, from the moment

you were paid. Let me also tell you that I have had three versions of this incident and all of them show you as a fool.'

Dewi told him the truth apart from the amount he had drunk.

'In a bar full of Becca rioters, drunk and exhibiting a thousand sovereigns to the entire world and his wife!' The director was really warming to his assault on Dewi. He became louder and needless to say the clerk now ceased to work, listening to every word.

'I'd never had so much money before.'

'Or ever will again,' replied the director.' It was like being in a boxing ring with your hands tied behind your back. 'Then you went upstairs, full of beer, with all the money?'

'Yes'.

'Nothing had been stolen at that time?'

'No.'

'Anyone with you?'

'My lad, Jack.'

'Jack was drunk also, I suppose?'

'No he's only ten.'

'One in the party sober. At least all your family are not fools. Why did you take the money upstairs with you?'

'For safety.'

'For safety! Why was it stolen then?'

'Bad luck, I suppose.'

'Bad luck? You fool.' He now wanted to explode with invective but felt he had to calm down for the good of his health. There's a safe in the Saddler's, why not use that?'

'Thought it would be safe with me.'

'You have made every mistake possible.'

'I know.' Dewi conceded.

The director calmed down and now the talk was of how the money was to be paid.

'This outstanding amount will have to be paid and within the next twenty-one days or we will foreclose on the farm.' He now felt a certain sympathy for Dewi. His anger had exhausted him. In the past he had done foolish things but had never had to

100

encounter so much bad luck. Had I found myself in this position at this man's age my father would have helped me out, he thought. This man has no such safety net. It is the bank's money and I have to do what is expected of me. My own money is invested in this bank.

'Twenty one days it is. The proceeds of any sale must go to pay this debt. You do understand don't you?' The interview was at an end. 'Pick up the receipt as you go out.' Dewi nodded and went to leave. 'One more matter. When you make any sales in future, accept this bank's notes. I think you've learnt a valuable lesson today don't you?'

Walking out of the office in a daze, through the town and on the road west towards home, Dewi was in no hurry to get to his destination. Thankful the confrontation with the bank was over, he nonetheless felt much chastened by the experience and reflected whether life could ever be the same again. Half the cows and calves would have to go and would that leave enough income to pay the rent and keep the family? He knew Hilda was strong, and would stick by the girls come hell or high water, but would she put up with a fool of a husband? Was he to live in the shadows in future, living in the family under sufferance, at best tolerated and at worst despised? It was cold but dry and he felt drained as the walk continued. There was hardly any traffic on the road so he got to Whitland by dusk. With the last few shillings in his pocket he got a bed for the night, making his way by side roads the following morning back to his family.

Slowly and with a heavy heart, he walked the ten or so miles home along rough roads and tracks which became progressively more familiar as he got nearer home. The individual fields, farm buildings and now and then the people came and went till he passed his immediate neighbours and then arrived home, walking in through his own back door. Entering the kitchen, he found Hilda sitting at the table with eyes red from crying and numb with grief. They looked at one another without saying a word. Looking down at the table in a gesture of near despair for a moment, she resumed her gaze at him. What it said he did not

101

know. He had expected to be vilified, the silence was infinitely worse. She looked almost in a trance. It continued for minutes but seemed like hours to Dewi. He had to break the silence, but how?

'Hilda, we're in trouble' She didn't reply and her gaze continued, unblinking, He became more alarmed 'Hilda, we've got to talk'. He reached to touch her hand.

She repelled this contact with alarming speed. 'Don't touch me.'

He withdrew his hand, frightened of alarming her further. Gradually, her catatonic demeanour became less rigid. The look in her eyes became more focused as some movement in her shoulders became visible. It was like she was unwinding. Dewi waited and waited. He felt easier as she returned to the present time, bit by bit. After some moments, she shook her head and as if by magic, she returned to her usual self

'Well Dewi, what's happened this time?' It was the old Hilda. 'I've heard a dozen different stories. No one gives me the true facts. Dewi, tell me the truth.' He did so.

'Well, Dewi boy, we're in trouble for sure. What are we going to do?'

'I asked the bank for time to pay but they wouldn't consider it. It's only twenty days now.'

'First of all, I'm taking charge of the farm and the money,' she declared. Dewi was shocked by this, but knew he had to accept the inevitable. By his immediate but reluctant acceptance, she knew the first hurdle had been jumped successfully.

'We'll have to draw our horns in, you know. Cut our living expenses.'

'Of course. The girls may have to go out to work.'

'That they won't. If anyone's going out to work, it's you Dewi, make no mistake.' He felt and looked ashamed as she drove the point home.

'Who can I work for?' he asked.

'We'll see. If you have to go out to work, I'll find you a job.' He'd rarely been able to argue with Hilda, even less so at

102

this time. Would he ever be able to make a decision again?

'First of all, this debt. I'll have to go and see the director,' Hilda told him.

'You won't change his mind. He tore me to pieces.'

'We'll see,' she replied. They discussed the numbers of cows and calves they had, what prices they would make and whether they could keep them through the winter. She now felt, in spite of the problems, like a new woman. She was in charge of her own destiny and would stand or fall by her own decisions. Hilda knew that her husband, though a hard worker, had a weak, feckless side to him with a liking for drink. Living with this since they had married, she had always felt uneasy in matters of money where he was concerned. Now a cloud had lifted and she welcomed the new challenges.

'Where's Jack then?'

'Still at the Saddlers.'

'Didn't come back through Narberth?'

'No, cross country from Whitland.'

'Jack costs nothing except food and he can be around the farm if you have to go out to work.' This remark was meant to hurt and it did so. 'I hear he helped find one of the thieves. We could do with help like that here.' She looked at him and saw the defeated and wounded look on his face. More of these remarks would have to be aimed at him if she were to remain in charge. 'We've got to get him back here before someone else gives him a home.'

'Who'll get him back'? Now he seemed unable to make any personal decision himself.

'Not you. You've caused enough trouble in Narberth already. Stay here and look after the farm and the girls while I go to the bank.'

'You're going to the bank. What for?'

'To get more time.'

'They won't give it to us.'

'You mean they won't give it to you.'

Dewi shrugged his shoulders in resignation, was there no end to it?

'When are you going'?

'Tomorrow morning early. I'll be away a couple of days. In the meantime, when someone goes to Narberth, send for Jack. We need him.'

'Yes.'

'Don't go yourself. I don't want you getting in any more trouble there. Send someone else.' Could he take any more of her barbs?

The girls came in from school, knew something had happened but didn't know what. They had heard about a robbery but were relieved to see their father safe. They accepted that Hilda would be away for the rest of the week, and ignored the altered relationship between their parents, returning to their own interests.

Hilda set off for Carmarthen, leaving Dewi at home. He contemplated his future. Would he ever leave the farm again, have a drink, talk to his friends on equal terms or even make a decision for himself again? Would his daughters despise him and order him about? Was life now one long humiliation? It took a long time to come so far, but such a short time to fall.

It was a strenuous two day journey but Hilda reached the bank before closing. Exhausted and quite red in the face, she had blistered feet after the unaccustomed walk. Her future lay in the next fifteen minutes. With almost superhuman effort she calmed down, drawing on reserves of confidence she was unaware she possessed. Introducing herself to the clerk, she asked for the director. Shown in, she was offered a seat which had been denied to her husband.

'Your husband came in earlier in the week.'

'I know.'

'What can I do for you?'

'I want to discuss the loan.'

'Yes.'

'I am now in charge of the farm, I handle all the money and make all the decisions,' she told him. 'I am now responsible for the loan and I want extra time to pay it off.'

'Has your husband discussed this matter with you?'

'Yes.'

He mentioned the amount outstanding. Only eighteen days left to pay the debt. 'Whether you are in charge of the debt or your husband, the circumstances are the same. Why should the bank change its mind? Tell me that. Its money is at risk.' His manner was a good deal more courteous than when dealing with the husband, but his mind at this stage was set.

'But I'm in charge now. I'm in total charge.'

'Pity you didn't have some positive control over him during this recent unfortunate transaction. A great pity.'

She felt she was getting nowhere. Her world was slipping away. She mustn't let this happen. She burst into tears, wiping her face on the shawl which she wore. It was for no more than a moment or two. Looking at her directly, he felt pain at the hurt he had caused. He too had been brought up by a widowed mother in impoverished circumstances who had struggled to give her children the best she could.

'Let's go over this again. You say you are now responsible for everything.'

'Yes, that's right,' she replied.

'Being responsible for this debt means your husband no longer has access to this bank account.'

'That's what I want.'

'In which case, the bank may be able to help you.' She smiled to herself and knew she'd won. 'How long do you want this loan to run?'

'Pay half of it off in one year and the rest the second.'

'Are you sure you can manage that?'

'Yes, I'm quite sure.'

'In which case I want you to come back in half an hour, sign some documents and the account will be in your name.'

'Thank you,' she said with relief.

The arrangements made, she set off towards home. She became aware how exhausted and hungry she was. Her stomach had become concave and she was breathless. None of this seemed to matter, compared to her new-found sense of pride and purpose. She followed in the steps Dewi had taken several days before, but in a very different frame of mind.

Chapter 11

The prisoner, Bertie, had been in the cell all night, was shivering from head to foot and hungry. The wound had been attended to and had stopped bleeding. Occasionally he touched the dressing and wondered if it would be alright? He was reassured, but in every other aspect of his life the prospect was grim. Sitting on the bench in the cell, he felt the cold, damp wind blow past the iron bars. There was no way of escape. He continued to shiver as he again reflected on why he had found himself in this position and what his immediate prospects were.

There was an occasional hum of voices just within range. He could identify the sound but not the words. It continued for a short while then ceased. Then the sounds of everyday life began: the shouting of children, the clip-clop of the horses' hooves and the grinding of the iron cartwheels on the road. The town was waking up. Gradually the cold lost its paralysing grasp on him. Familiar smells of everyday life came and went. It was strangely reassuring after the cold, silent and lonely night.

Reared in a large family and used to working in the company of others, he had never felt so alone. He would do anything to get out of this predicament. Anyway, when would he get out? What would they do when they did open the door? He had never been in trouble before. This was a whole new hell. You stupid fool, he told himself, to get involved with Leftie after a few beers and less than an hour's acquaintance. Why, why, why? He'd got trouble written all over him. The more he reflected the more depressed he became. This, of course, was the frame of mind the constables wanted him to be in and why they had left him as long as possible alone.

Eventually he heard the sound of boots in the passage, the grind of the lock and then the door opened to reveal two constables well into middle age, a little overweight and with rather red faces. The leading one had a gleam of satisfaction on his face, clearly trying to assess the effect the time alone had had on the prisoner. He was reassured by the prisoner's defeated expression. 'Sleep well?' he asked in an attitude of mock concern which was not lost on Bertie.

'No. A bit cold.'

'This isn't a hotel, you know.' He nodded in agreement. 'Going to ask you a few questions.'

Bertie was slim, dark, perhaps twenty five and appeared almost in rags. His normally poor clothes had been further damaged by the robbery and the rough handling he had received at the hands of the dragoons. In addition they were still wet. He started to shiver again; defeat saturated every cell of his being and was evident in his eyes.

'Here.' They each grabbed an arm and hustled him along the passage to a room at the end where there was a desk and four chairs. The constable who had spoken deliberately grasped him hard on the forearm where the wound was dressed which made him wince. He gripped the arm even harder, looked him in the face and smiled. Bertie was pushed into the chair.

'Listen you, there's two ways to do this, the easy way and the hard way. Which way do you want'? The words were spoken by the same constable.

'What do you mean?'

'What I say. The easy way or the hard way? It's your choice.' It was a deliberate method of making the prisoner uneasy and establishing dominance. He was also to trying to assess his likely degree of co-operation.

'Are you hungry?'

'Yes.'

'Are you cold?'

'Yes.'

'You answer our questions and you won't be hungry or cold. Right?'

'Right,' Bertie responded.

'Get the man breakfast,' he directed the silent constable. 'You see, we're trying to help you. Aren't we?' Bertie nodded. 'We're trying to help you, but you've got to help us. You see?' Again Bertie nodded. The breakfast arrived which he ate with gusto. He felt better already. The shivering had ceased though he was hardly warm. What do they want, he thought. 'You help us and we'll put in a good word for you. If you don't, we can be really nasty. Understand?' Again he nodded

The one constable had done all the talking. The other remained silent as he had only been sworn in earlier in the week in response to the Becca riots. He was fascinated by this new world.

'Right. You were not alone. Who was the other man?'

'Leftie.'

'Leftie who?'

'He was just Leftie.'

'Listen good boy. Leftie who? Tell us or we'll give you a leftie and a rightie.'

'Honest, I only knew him as Leftie.' They didn't hit him.

'Where'd you meet him?'

'Tavern in Haverfordwest.'

'You come from there?'

'No, I'm from Castlemartin.'

'How long you known Leftie?'

'That day. About midday.'

'Never seen him before?'

'Never.'

'What did he look like?'

'Big strong man. Red face, curly fair hair.'

'Sure you never seen him before?'

'Never.'

'Where's he from?'

'Not local. Talks different.'

'Where from, d'you think?'

'West Country. Maybe Ireland.' The constables whispered to one another.

'How'd you get from Haverfordwest to Narberth?'

'Walked.'

"Saddler's the first tavern you drank at?'

'Yes.'

'How much did you drink?'

'A few pints.'

'How did you know about the money?'

'He was flashing it for everyone to see. Leftie said to me "We're in luck tonight boy." I said "Don't be a fool, we'll be caught with this crowd." "No, we won't," he said. There was no stopping him.'

'You went along with it?'

'I couldn't say no to him.'

'How'd you do it?'

'Him with the money went to bed with the lad. Drunk as a lord he was. Leftie went out and saw which bedroom they went into. The candle was in the passage and he saw it out of the window. Leftie said "They've as good as invited us up there. They're asking for it to be pinched and we're not going to disappoint them are we?" I couldn't say no to him.'

'How'd you get upstairs?'

'Easy, through the back door and up.'

'Who found the money?'

'Leftie. I never seen a sovereign of it.'

'Sure?'

'Honest. Not a sovereign.' They did not pursue this line of questioning as they felt he was telling the truth.

'Then what happened?'

'Well, the lad bit me and I shouted out. Then we jumped out of the window. That's when I cut myself.'

'When did Leftie find the money'?

'Don't know.'

'Sure?'

'Honest. First I saw was when he dropped the money jumping over the wall. He was over first. Then me.'

'He was holding the money?'

110

'All the time.'

'How long did you stay together?'

'We ran to the corner. I was bleeding. He said, "Each man for himself now." I said, "What about the money?" and he said, "It's safer with me. We can meet in Pembroke. I'll see you alright when we get there." I haven't seen him since.'

'Sure? Said he was going to Pembroke?'

'Yes.'

'What sort of man was he?'

'He was tough alright. Nobody messed with him. Too true, nobody messed with Leftie.'

The constables left the room, whispered in the corridor and returned after only a minute or two.

'Listen Bertie, you've been very helpful and we're going to keep our word and get you some dry clothes.' He nodded in appreciation. 'You understand we're not obliged to do this but we're doing it because we want to help you.' They escorted him back to his cell, locked the door and walked out into the fresh air. The constable who, at this stage, had not opened his mouth asked, 'What do we do now?'

'Tell the magistrates.'

'When?'

'Now.'

'Why so quick?'

'Get the other man.' It was beginning to dawn on the recent recruit how the system worked.

'How will they do that?'

'I'll bet you they have the dragoons after him in half an hour.'

Two magistrates were found, evidence was heard from the one constable as to what the arrested man had said and particularly whether any money was found upon him. A warrant was issued for Leftie's arrest. The lieutenant of dragoons was called, given the warrant and instructed to try and execute it. Information the constables were unaware of was the outstanding amount of money. The Justices were so informed and instructed the troop leader that it was an appropriate task for him and his men and not the local constables.

After the court business, the officer spoke to the constables to extract what further information he could. 'What else did the prisoner say? How old is this Leftie? What does he look like? He talked, did he?'

'Yes he talked. We couldn't stop him talking,' replied the constable in a tone of self congratulation. 'Yes, he talked alright.' He went over what had been said.

'You've been most helpful,' replied the officer in a condescending manner as he mounted his horse and led off at a gentle trot in the direction of the nearest port, Pembroke.

They would be lucky to catch him. He had an eighteen hour start and sounded a very tough, resourceful character. So far as they knew, he had no wounds and nothing to impede his progress. He also had more than two hundred sovereigns on him. They would be very lucky to get him.

The constables, flushed with pleasure after such a successful morning, felt the day was over and so went into the Saddlers' Tavern. They might be able to pick up some more information, they told themselves. One pint led to more. Morning became afternoon and afternoon became dusk. Their tongues became loose. They started to go into detail, giving all who would listen, a blow by blow account as to what had happened. Then the name 'Leftie' was heard.

One drinker said to another, 'I bet it was that Leftie who was up towards Preseli back in the thirties.' This was not heard by the constables, who by this time were only responsive to their thirst.

'Yes, I remember him, a real wild man.'

'You can say that again.'

'He wasn't a Welsh boy, was he?'

'No, Irish he was. I know that.'

'Those two fools would never catch him.'

'Too right, they wouldn't.'

'I could never forget him. That mop of curly hair. He could drink and fight.'

112

'And shag!'

'So I heard.'

'You know that lad with Dewi when the money got robbed?'

'Yes.

'His son.'

'Father robbing son. In the same room they were when they robbed the money.'

'That's a turn up.'

'These two don't know.'

'Course they don't, they don't know anything.'

'You know that lad's living here in the Saddler's?'

'Sure, spit of his father he is.'

'He's been here since the robbery. It's him who bit the robber the constables have got. They'd have got away but for him. When he bit him, he shouted out. Then everyone ran up the stairs and the robbers had to run for it.'

'A chip off the old block.'

'The little'un has got guts.'

'We'll see him here tonight.'

The constables became progressively drunker. They no longer had anything of interest to say and, running out of money, would accept a drink from anyone prepared to pay. They talked to one another in a progressively more incoherent manner and became a source of amusement as they slapped one another on the back in mutual congratulation. The beer they drank was now called "Constables' bank account" and it was a matter of speculation as to how long it would be before they walked, staggered, crawled or fell out of the bar.

'Those two fools, drunk as owls, and Leftie escaped with all the money.'

'I don't think they want to know where he is. They've got someone for the crime.'

'They're bound to have heard of Leftie. He was here a year or two. Everyone knew him.'

'Why'd he leave?'

'Trouble for sure. Don't know what though.'

The evening continued. The constables had run out of offers of beer and they staggered out with their arms round one another and endeavouring to speak sensibly. Most of the bar laughed or smiled as they went.

The dragoon lieutenant and his troopers made the journey to Pembroke at a fast trot on the main coach road. Enquiries were made as they went, without result. They reached the dock by nightfall, where they learned that the packet had left earlier in the day. The ticket seller was found and questioned.

'Where do you sell the tickets from?'

'Bottom of the gangway.'

'How many passengers?'

'Very few. They're all coming this way.'

'Was there a man in a hurry? Breathless, looking as though he had slept out?'

'Yes, there was one like that. Big rough fella. Curly hair. Very wet.'

'You sure?'

'Sure. Soaking wet he was, looked as though he'd been out for weeks.'

'Did he have any luggage?'

'No, nothing, just what he stood up in.'

'How'd he pay?'

'Gave me a sovereign and I gave him the change.'

'Did you get his name?'

'No.'

'What sort of an accent?'

'Accent? What does that mean?'

'Where's he from?'

'Irish. Not strong though.'

'Wasn't Devon?'

'Not Devon, I know that. My father's from Devon.'

'How many hours ago did the boat leave?'

'Four.'

'If you see this man again, contact the local magistrates. He's wanted for a very serious matter. If he's arrested, you might get a reward.'

'Yes. I'll keep a look out.'

The lieutenant turned and, when out of earshot of anyone but his troop, said to himself for them to hear, 'Another fool's errand. Our man has slipped through the net with the gold.'

Their return to base in the morning was at a slow pace and the memory of a wasted journey hung over them.

Two days passed and Bertie was still held in the makeshift cell awaiting an appearance before the magistrates. Still cold, frequently hungry and almost always lonely, he awaited his fate. The constables no longer had any interest in him and he hardly saw them.

Around midday on that second day in custody, the key in the door was turned, the door creaked open and the more vociferous constable filled the doorway. 'Got a visitor for you,' he beamed. He stepped to one side to reveal Bertie's brother, Sammy who had heard the day before of his brother's difficulties. He walked in and sat by Bertie on the wooden bench which doubled as a bed at night. Everything about the cell was depressing. The mortar on the walls had never been painted and more than half of it had fallen off. The window sill was about seven feet high and it was impossible to see outside. There was no glass in the window which had a southwest aspect and was a sponge for any rain that fell or wind that blew. There was little light and an atmosphere of foreboding. Graffiti was over the walls and spelt out the impending fate of many of its previous occupants.

'What's happened Bertie?' He told him the whole story. 'Drinking again, Bertie. You're in real trouble this time. You know that.' He nodded.

'I've been a fool. I know that now. Only with him a few hours and I end up here.'

'You'll have to get a lawyer.'

'Don't need that, do I?'

'Course you do. I saw Waterloo Jones on the way up. He says you need one badly.'

'That'll cost money though.'

'I know. It'll have to come from somewhere. The Becca man does it for nothing. He'll not do this for you though.'

'Who can pay then?'

'We'll find it from somewhere. You've been a fool but you are our brother. You're in real trouble, you know. If it's robbery it could be the gallows.'

'No, not that.' The frightening prospect went through Bertie's mind and he remained silent. Sammy could see his brother almost disintegrate before his eyes. There was nothing he could do but look at him and grasp his forearm, which continued for several minutes while the full implications sank in. 'Bertie, that's why you need a lawyer.' He nodded. Gradually his mind absorbed what might happen and gradually he seemed to recover from this poleaxe blow. 'What else did he say?'

'It could be transportation. You know, Tasmania.' He contemplated this alarming prospect, remembering all the stories he had heard.

'What else did he say?'

'You need representation, even in the magistrates' court and definitely at the assize court.'

'Why two courts?'

'The magistrates' court sends you to the assize court.'

'When'll I go to the magistrates' court?'

'Soon. I got to get back to see the lawyer today. Anything you want?'

'Yes, a warm coat.'

'I'll bring it into court.'

He returned home via the lawyer's office.

The appearance was on the Friday. Earlier in the day, Waterloo Jones spoke to the prisoner and went through what had happened and what he had told the police.

'You're in trouble, real trouble but it could be a lot worse. You've been a damn fool but at least you haven't used firearms, otherwise almighty God wouldn't save you from a short walk soon after dawn. You haven't benefited from the robbery. Also, you were influenced by a more purposeful accomplice. In view of what you have said to the police and what you have told me, you will have to offer a guilty plea. However, though you apparently have no monies from the robbery on you, a large sum still remains outstanding. Are you sure you know nothing about this matter?'

'I never even touched the money. Honest.'

'I believe you. In view of all these facts in your favour, I think I can say I am going to save you from the gallows. What else fate has in store for you, I cannot even begin to speculate.'

The threat of the gallows had been lifted from him. Waterloo Jones had such confidence and assurance that some of it brushed off on him. Almost like a father figure, Bertie placed himself entirely in his hands.

'The court will commence at ten o'clock but we shan't be heard until after eleven. They will go through what the constables will have to say and perhaps some other evidence. Then you will be committed to the Carmarthen Assizes.'

The minor business of the magistrates' court over, Bertie stood in the dock and the constables at the back of the court. The fittings were all of oak with several panels cracked with age. The court was not well lit and an atmosphere of gloom overhung it.

Four magistrates sat on the bench with Admiral Sir George as chairman. The justice's clerk, a small thin man of indeterminate age, hawkish appearance and wearing pince-nez glasses rose to address the prisoner. He was a humourless man with a sharp, commanding voice who took himself and his position very seriously. 'Prisoner at the bar,' he began, asking his name, address, age and occupation. With some prompting, Bertie responded.

'Prisoner at the bar, you are charged that on the night of the sixteenth of November you, with an un-named other, in the back bedroom of the Saddler's Tavern, Narberth, did rob one Dewi Richards of the sum of two hundred and thirty gold sovereigns, these being the property of the said Dewi Richards. Contrary to common law. The learned justices will hear the evidence and decide whether there is a case to answer. If there is a case to

117

answer then you will be remanded on bail or in custody to Carmarthen Assizes as this court has no jurisdiction to deal with matters of robbery. If the justices decide there is no case to answer then you will leave the court a free man.'

The constables went through the evidence. Nellie was questioned briefly. The case went on into the afternoon and the bench adjourned to make a decision. The result wasn't in doubt and they found that there was a case to answer. Waterloo Jones made an application that Bertie be allowed to return to his own home in Castlemartin on his brother's recognisance which was refused.

Next day he was in a wagon on the way to the jail in Carmarthen along with several prisoners who had been involved in the Becca disturbances.

Chapter 12

It had been the best harvest for many years. The hay and oats had been harvested in generous quantities, then dried, and there was sufficient to feed all the animals through the winter. The small flock of Welsh mountain sheep would have to come onto enclosed land shortly, the lambs having been sold earlier in the season for low prices. Jack had returned to live with his honorary parents, continuing to make himself useful. The only apparent cloud over the family was the debt to the Drovers' Bank in Carmarthen which Hilda hoped would be paid off in two years. On the surface, matters seemed to have returned to what they had been before the robbery.

However in this community there were no secrets. Dewi's folly in the matter of the robbery which had been fuelled by drunkenness, together with Hilda now holding the purse strings, were the subject of local knowledge, comment and frequently black humour.

On one occasion Dewi had returned to the Saddler's Tavern only to be taunted with such remarks as, 'Hilda got the purse strings now?', 'Petticoat government' and 'She let you have the price of a pint?' Such was the intensity of these remarks and so badly was he hurt by them that he never returned to the town.

He spoke less and less to Hilda and, even when he did, she was dismissive in the extreme. Now no more than a labouring child in the household, he spent more and more time with Swni Hopkins, a man who had been a part time labourer all his life, had never married and survived by growing his own food, doing some hedging in the winter and harvesting in the summer. Much older than Dewi, he was known for his reluctance to hold down regular work, his meanness and his low cunning. He was also well known for his homebrewed beer of which he was inordinately fond.

It was around dusk when he made his way to Swni's hovel which was no more than one room with a fire at one end. Swni always welcomed him. He was glad of the company as he was frequently lonely. The conversation almost always reverted to the same subject: Hilda. 'I can't do anything right with that woman,' Dewi complained.

'Women are like that, Dewi.'

'Don't have a penny to myself.'

'Don't trust'em Dewi. Look at me, free as the birds. Answer to know one.'

'I know'.

'I wouldn't want to be you.'

'I don't want to be me either.'

'No money! Man, you've a right to a bit of money.' He gave him a smile and a devious wink. 'You'll have to do something about that.'

'I will, but how? If I ask her she'll refuse, saying, "We're still paying for your drunken stupidity." How can I raise some money?'

'Well, you'll have to do something,' Swni insisted. 'Even this home brew costs money, you know, the hops and that.' He nodded in reply.

'She's even put the girls against me,' Dewi continued. 'They hardly speak to me any more. It's the look on their faces. It's awful.'

Swni nodded, 'Yes.' He had no idea.

Dewi became maudlin and lost in his own troubles. Silently looking into the fire and sipping his beer, becoming progressively drunker. Was this the way things would be for the rest of his life? Even Jack, the orphan boy, was treated with more respect than him.

Conversation had ceased. He would have to go home. Drunkenly, he walked across the field and up the lane. It was by now late and the lights were out. The front and back door were locked so he hammered hard on each but without success. Hilda eventually came to the window when he was about to find somewhere else to sleep. 'What you hammering for? Drunk again?'

'Let me in, woman, I want to sleep.'

'So do I. You're drunk and you can sleep it off in the barn.'

'Let me in, it's my house.'

'It's not your house, it's mine. You're not coming in, in that state.' She slammed the window shut and the noise jarred him all over. He wondered what to do next. Should he get the axe and knock the door down, keep shouting all night or go back to Swni's. He took the easy option, opening the barn door, climbing up on the stack of oats and immediately falling asleep.

Waking soon after dawn, he was cold and his head ached. His immediate actions were to get up, brush the oat straw off his hair and clothes and wash quickly under the tap in the yard. He returned to the farm and heard the sound of milking. Going into the cowshed, he saw the back of Jack milking the house cow. Jack was unaware that Dewi was near and continued with his task. Dewi stood there awkwardly for a minute then ventured, 'Well Jack, you're doing a fine job.'

Jack turned round replying, 'Yes,' but not stopping.

'Didn't get in last night. How's Hilda?' he asked in expectation. He received a grunt in reply. 'In a bad mood, is she?' Jack didn't reply. Even at this age, he knew never to take sides in a husband and wife quarrel.

'I couldn't make it home last night, you know. Expect she'll be mad.' When Jack remained silent, Dewi continued, 'Seen her this morning?'

'Yes, she told me to do the milking,' Jack eventually had to respond.

Knowing he would get no further with Jack, he entered the house through the back door and, hearing noise from the kitchen, ventured in. At the table were his two daughters, getting ready for school with Hilda fussing around them. He felt an outsider among them. 'Anything I can do?'

'Yes, clean yourself up. You look as though you have slept in a hedge.'

The girls looked at one another and gave a just audible giggle. Dewi hung around the kitchen, not knowing what to do. He felt awkward, embarrassed and beaten. Whatever he did was wrong. Whatever he said was wrong.

As Hilda took the girls to the front door to see them off to school, she said to him, 'Stay there. I want a word with you.' He obeyed.

She returned to say, 'Drunk again last night?' The remark cut into him. He was used to it but every onslaught always hit the target.

'I had a few.'

'A few! You could hardly speak last night, you were so drunk.'

'I'm alright now. I want to get the work done.'

'You aren't alright. You're a mess.'

'Hilda, be fair. Give me a chance.'

'You've had twelve years of chances. Look where it got us.'

'I made one mistake. Don't go on about it, woman.'

'Go on about it? One drunken night and we're two years in debt.'

'What can I do then?' At this moment he would do anything to stop the constant onslaught. 'Give me a break. I'm sorry.'

'When you've got over your drunken spree with Swni, you can get all the cows and calves in for the winter. That should occupy you for the day. Jack can help you. That boy seems to have more sense than you do and he is only a third your age, a school boy.'

'I'm worse than a school boy, am I?' She didn't answer. 'What about some food before I start?'

'Clean yourself up, then you can eat with Jack.' He walked towards the back door but was called back by her voice, 'One more thing. I have moved a bed into Jack's room. You can sleep there as from tonight.' How many more shocks were in store for him? Now he was truly no more than an unpaid labourer.

Half an hour later, Dewi and Jack were in the top field bringing the cows and calves down for wintering in. One by one, they were tied up for the winter; the older ones going to the stalls quietly but the heifers, unfamiliar with the routine, having to be pushed, sometimes quite forcefully. It was not a long task and by midday they were all tied up and the calves in a loose pen. All had been fed. Dewi felt at last he was making himself useful with the physical effort dispersing the hangover. He felt better but for how long would it last?

He hung about the yard in the cold not wanting to go into the house to face her tongue and not knowing what to do outside. Cold and getting colder he slapped his arms against his body to keep warm.

Jack kept himself busy feeding the cows and heifers and then the calves. He had a natural feel for animals and farm work, knowing what had to be done and what could be left undone. Always busy, he nailed up planks which prevented a draught blowing at the rear of the tied up animals, saw there was enough straw to keep them comfortable and looked out for scouring in any of his charges. Dewi no longer took any interest in his farm and Jack, young as he was, felt responsible for the welfare of the stock.

Twice daily they were unchained to go to the trough to drink then tied up again. There was little trouble getting them back in again as, during their time in the yard, hay and unthreshed oats had been put in the troughs for them. So the routine went on through the winter months. Feed, water and clean out the cattle, count the sheep and look forward to the lengthening days.

Dewi played a progressively more passive role as Jack did more and more. He spent his time with Swni Hopkins, drinking, on one occasion not returning for two days. Hilda, though in some respects glad to be rid of him, knew that in the spring she would need him for the tilling of their few ploughed acres, even more for the haymaking. Jack was a gem but he couldn't manage all that. The neighbours would help but she would have to reciprocate. She would have to humour him and try to get him back to regular work.

At the end of one February day Dewi was in the yard, doing

nothing in particular, when Hilda approached him. 'I want to see you,' she said in a conciliatory tone. He hadn't received a civil word from her in three months and he could hardly believe his ears. She moved towards the house and he followed. 'Sit down Dewi. We've got something to talk about.' He didn't answer but waited for her to speak.

'We've got the spring work shortly; ploughing, sowing and getting the muck out. We can't do it the way we are.'

'Why not? I'm alright. We've got Jack. We've got the neighbours.'

'You're not alright Dewi. You haven't done even half a day's work in three months. You spend all your time drinking with Swni Hopkins. You look like a drunk and you smell like one. In six months you'll be as hopeless as him.'

'I can do it.'

'You prove it to me then. Work from dawn till dusk for the next six days getting the muck out on the fields without having a drink and you and me will get together again.'

'You're on. That's a bargain.'

'Dewi, I've given you a hard time since November and you deserved it. We've got to keep this farm together. There's a lot of work to be done these next ten weeks. You know it and I know it. Remember, six days work and no beer.'

'I know I can do it. Trust me.'

Dewi felt a new lease of life come over him almost immediately. He found himself more gainfully occupied around the farm. Tasks that he had ignored or even been unaware of in recent months now became obvious to him. Making plans, he decided which horse to use, where he would start the work and in what order to undertake the jobs. Beer, he could well do without that, he thought. Why was he wasting time with Swni? He talked to Jack much more and more positively. Gone were the fearful inquiries about Hilda's mood. He spoke of his hopes for the future, a tidier farm, well laid hedges and animals that were well cared for. Certainly the farm of late had developed that shabby, untidy look.

124

He was in bed early that night, going to sleep with true hope in his heart. Rising before first light, he and Jack fed and watered the animals, ate breakfast with gusto and had the horse and cart harnessed in record speed. They spread load after load on one of the fields due for next year's hay crop. Jack did his best to keep up with Dewi's manic pace but was unable to do so. Dewi worked at a speed and generated a level of energy which can only be produced by one who is trying to prove himself after months of idleness.

After the fourth load, Dewi became breathless, was sweating profusely and had to rest, leaning against the shafts of the cart. The cold weather and the sweat made him cold and he began to shiver. Eventually his breathlessness had largely gone and, feeling he had made an impressive start, he continued at a slower pace.

Monday completed, he slept well having been given some encouragement from Hilda. Tuesday was much the same. They did a similar amount of work, broken for half an hour during the afternoon by a call from Davey on his way across country to the Carmarthen Assizes where his son Owen was appearing shortly.

'Poor Owen,' Dewi sympathised. What will happen to him?'

Davey shook his head. 'Don't know. Only God knows.' His eyes became moist. 'Silly boy wants to put the world right.'

'Good scholar too.'

'I know, but it won't do him any good in court.'

'Got a lawyer?'

'Yes, Waterloo Jones.'

'A good man. Not afraid to speak his mind to anyone.'

'Yes, we couldn't do better.'

Davey looked at him searchingly. 'Things alright now, Dewi?'

'Yes, I'm alright Davey. Hasn't been a good few months but everything's alright now. I'll be thinking about you and Owen.'

Davey walked back to the track and onto Whitland and Carmarthen by the back roads.

Dewi didn't resume work immediately but reflected to himself, then Jack. 'Poor Davey, his son is in real trouble. Might be transported. Never see him again.'

'What's transported?'

'You commit a crime and they send you abroad. Tasmania. Meant to be for seven years but no-one's ever come home and they've sent a few.'

'Tasmania, where's that?'

'Australia. As far as you can get from here. Some die on the journey.'

'Will the robbers of your gold get transportation?'

'Yes I hope so. They've caused me a lot of grief'.'

Wednesday came and went, the piles of muck reduced in size, the collars on the horses became a looser fit and gradually Dewi settled into the rhythm of the farm. Hilda had a more constructive relationship with him, giving him gentle but not gushing encouragement. He responded to it. Dewi could see the end of this work and the ploughing starting possibly by Wednesday of the following week. Mentioning it to Hilda, she was more cautious. 'Let's get this job done first. We're ahead of any of the neighbours. You've done well so far. Keep it up.'

He didn't agree with her caution and said so as he set off for the afternoon's work. As he was coming in from the final load, he said to Jack, 'Can you take the mare in, unharness her and groom her?'

'You'll have to help me with the shafts,' Jack replied. He did so, leaving the cart in the yard. Jack led the horse to the stable for grooming. Dewi, with a furtive look at the house, walked down the lane and within twenty minutes was drinking a pint of Swni Hopkins's beer.

Drinking the first pint in two gulps, he wiped his mouth. 'That's better Swni, I needed that. Haven't had a drink for nearly a week.'

Swni looked at him with his cunning smile 'Knew you'd be back, Dewi. Nothing like a pint after a day's work.'

With the empty glass in one hand and a look of expectation in his eyes, Dewi lingered for a few seconds. A smile came on both their faces. 'Want another I suppose?'

'You can say that again.' He sat down, sipping the beer. 'Swni, I been working this week. Real work.'

'I can see. You're ahead of everyone.' Swni appreciated the company but reflected on how much the beer cost him to make. He thought it was not the correct time to make a financial request. He guessed correctly that Hilda had put pressure on Dewi to work and give up beer. 'Hilda alright?' he asked in a cunning aside.

Dewi didn't answer immediately but eventually said 'She won't like me being down here.'

'Better have another and be killed for a sheep and not a lamb.'

'Go on then'. Another pint was poured and drunk and then another. He now felt extremely drowsy with this strong beer on an empty stomach. Too drunk to go home, he slept where he was.

As the working day ended, Jack went back to the house. Hilda asked him as he entered, 'Where's Dewi?'

'He walked down the road almost an hour ago.'

'Seen him since?'

'No.'

Hilda gave a sigh that said more than a thousand words.

Chapter 13

It was around five o'clock in the morning on the first day of the Carmarthen Assizes. The prisoners had been fed and were awaiting shackling in readiness for the journey to the Guildhall. Bertie and Owen found themselves in the same cell, having been arrested by the same constable and committed by the same court. Becoming friends over the preceding weeks they had their innocent former lives and uncertain futures in common. They were nervous and spoke to one another in short bursts, followed by reflective silences. Pale after so long in prison, they had both lost weight on the prison diet and because of the stress of their predicament. Neither had been in trouble before, everything was new. Their fate would be decided that week.

'It's cold,' said Owen in the absence of anything else to say, visibly shivering.'

'Say that again,' was Bertie's reply.

'Hope my father'll be there. I want a change of clothes.'

'I hear my brother'll be there. Got Waterloo Jones for me.'

'He's the best, so they say. I've got him too.'

'Afraid of no-one they say.'

'I hope so. We can't speak for ourselves, you know.'

'I know.'

'Waterloo says I'll have to plead guilty,' said Owen. 'They caught me at the riot. Couldn't run fast enough.'

'Told me I'd have to plead guilty too,' agreed Bertie. 'Cut myself on the window and admitted it to the constables. Didn't make a penny. Leftie got all the sovereigns. Lawyer says he can save me from the gallows.' A shiver went down his spine as he reflected what might have been his fate. 'Dear Lord I hope so. I'm only twenty-two. I've been a real fool you know. A bloody fool.'

Owen hardly heard what Bertie said and was thinking of his own fate. Waterloo Jones had given him no idea what the sentence might be. The uncertainty of it all overcame him. The only reassurance was that there were others in a similar position to him in the prison; rioters who had never been in trouble before and from respectable farming backgrounds. At least he would know his fate by the end of the week.

'I've been stupid too. But, you know, those toll gates were ruining the farmers. You paid for everything. Any animals, lime or carts going through. It was ruination. The magistrates never paid when they went through. One law for the poor, another for the rich.'

'That's life, isn't it?'

By seven o'clock the prisoners were shackled in readiness for the short journey to the cells under the Guildhall, even though they would not leave for some time. The prison was now dominated by the sound of iron clanking against iron as men tried to keep warm, which discouraged conversation except for some gallows humour heard above the clamour, spoken to try and relieve boredom and encourage a heroic spirit in a desperate situation. At nine o'clock the prisoners were transported the short distance to the Guildhall.

At around ten thirty Mr Justice Bannerton left the judge's lodgings in the carriage especially made for that purpose. With him was the High Sheriff. Clad in ermine and red he made the journey slowly through the town, observed by many onlookers who had turned out for the occasion. The power he possessed was awe-inspiring. Hardly regarded as human, he was a superior being whose look could paralyse, whose word was unquestionable and who had the power of life and death. The Assizes were a spectacle for all to see. Slowly they proceeded through the town. Mounted Dragoons and footmen at the front and rear, escorted the carriage. Alongside the steps of the Guildhall, the carriage stopped. A footman opened the door and the judge stepped up the stone steps followed by the High Sheriff. Trumpeters signalled his arrival and the opening of the

Assizes. He looked casually to right and left as he walked up the few steps, but acknowledged no-one as he made his way to his chambers.

In the cells down below, Waterloo Jones was taking final instructions from Bertie. 'Right, my boy. You plead guilty and I'll do my best to save you from the gallows.'

'Yes, sir.'

'There's a lot I can say in your favour. What was Leftie's surname?'

'I don't know. Only met him that day. Leftie might not even have been his name.'

'I shouldn't think so either. Are you sure you haven't got any of those sovereigns?'

'Sure, I got nothing.'

'I thought so but I've just got to make sure.'

'You can go back to your cell. Your brother's outside.'

'Can I see him?'

'Ask the constable there,' he said, pointing to one several yards away. Bertie was taken away again.

Waterloo Jones stated that he wanted Owen next, who arrived very shortly. Owen was now almost skeletal and black under the eyes. Even the lawyer was shocked by his appearance.

'Have you been eating?'

'Not much lately.'

'Why not?'

'Been getting me down here.'

'You must eat, you know,' he said sympathetically, then, more briskly, 'Right laddie. The evidence is overwhelming against you. You know that?'

'Yes I know.'

'You must plead guilty. You know that, don't you?'

'Yes I know that.'

'You've got a lot going for you. Good character. Good scholar. Want to be a preacher, don't you?'

'Yes.'

'You plead guilty and I'll do my best.'

'What will I get?'

'I don't know. But I have to tell you that this judge is a hard sentencer. For all that, I'll do my best. Right, your father's outside, I'll get him sent in.'

'Thank you.'

The court was full of barristers, court staff and onlookers as well as those who had played an active role in the recent arrests. All were facing the bench with their eyes on the door leading to the judge's chambers including the court clerk. He became aware they were on their way. In a loud voice he said, 'Be upstanding in court'. Mr Justice Bannerton and the High Sheriff entered and stood behind their seats. Those assembled bowed to the bench. The Judge sat down beneath a royal coat of arms, the High Sheriff on his far right. Those assembled sat down, the court clerk remaining standing. Again he spoke, louder than you would have thought possible for a man so thin and weedy. 'Oyez, Oyez. All persons having any business before My Lords, the Queens' Justices, draw near and give your attendance.' He sat down.

The clerk asked the Judge in which order he wanted the cases heard.

'The robbery first.'

'Yes, your Lordship.'

Again in a loud voice, the clerk directed 'Put up Bertie Howell.' The command was repeated till it was out of earshot of the court. Slowly the prisoner made his way along the passage and up the stairs, the noise of the manacles becoming louder as he got nearer. As he entered the dock, everyone looked at him, much of it out of a mawkish curiosity. His arm was in a sling and bandage, seen by all.

'Stand up and face the bench,' said the constable in a stage whisper. Bertie did so. He confirmed his name.

The clerk addressed him directly. 'Prisoner at the bar. You are charged on one indictment in that you, with an un-named other, some time on the evening of the twenty-seventh of October last, did rob one Dewi Richards, lodging at the Saddler's Arms, Narberth, of the sum of two hundred and thirty sovereigns, the property of the said Dewi Richards, contrary to Common law. How do you plead?' Bertie seemed quite dazed by what was said and did not reply. Some moments passed. 'Prisoner at the bar, how do you plead?'

At this moment Waterloo Jones looked round and caught the prisoner's eye. As quietly as he could, he said, 'Guilty my Lord,' and nodded.

'Guilty my Lord,' answered Bertie still in a daze, having repeated his plea almost parrot fashion.

Sir Toby Guy QC, prosecuting for the crown, went through the circumstances of the offence. His address cast the defendant in a foolish rather than villainous light. He went through his disastrous role in this crime highlighting his cut arm, loss of blood, failure to gain from robbery, disappearance of his partner and his final arrest under a tree less than a quarter of a mile from the robbery, on the information of an eleven year old boy. 'Never in all my years at the bar have I seen such an ineffectual and doomed participant in a robbery. Never have I seen a man more ill-fitted for crime. His partner has all the money and gets away. This man is wounded, gains nothing and gets caught. To his credit he has helped the constables and pleaded guilty.'

A wave of humour flowed through the court. Even the judge briefly showed a wintry smile. The constables and the public could hardly contain their laughter. Waterloo Jones stood up and addressed the bench, thanking the prosecution for presenting a full and fair picture of what had occurred. He went into some detail about his client's shortcomings, painting him as a fool rather than a committed criminal. 'A man of former good character, he has been influenced by a more purposeful drinking companion who he had known for only a matter of hours and whose true name never became known to him.' Much of what the prosecutor had said, he repeated in mitigation adding that he was a man of good family.

'Your Lordship, on the matter of sentence, I ask you not to impose the ultimate sanction upon this man. You have the powers to do so in cases of robbery but I would ask that this man's weak and ineffectual role in this matter make you consider an alternative.'

The judge looked at the defence counsel, heard every word that was said, but remained impassive. Eventually Jones sat down. Hardly had he become seated when the judge addressed the prisoner.

'Prisoner at the bar, you have been a foolish man and you have also been prepared to follow a path of violence for personal gain. You will not be dealt with until tomorrow morning at which time I will have come to my decision. Go down.'

The judge muttered quietly and very briefly to the Court Clerk, out of everyone's earshot. The clerk looked at the court register and in his usual loud voice said, 'Put up the prisoner Owen Price.'

Again the name was repeated till it was out of earshot. In a minute or two the prisoner was produced, finding himself in the dock. As he did so he looked around to see his father with other members of the public. They exchanged greetings which were no more than a raising of their hands. 'Face the judge,' he was directed by a person he neither saw nor recognised by the voice. He did so.

The clerk, looking directly at the prisoner, confirmed his name, age and place of abode. 'Owen Price you are charged that, on the evening of the ninth of September of this year in the County of Pembrokeshire, you did with numerous un-named others unlawfully, riotously assemble to the disturbance of the peace. Prisoner at the bar, how do you plead? Guilty or not guilty?' Remembering what Waterloo Jones had said, he made his plea looking the judge straight in the face. The look which was returned by the judge alarmed every ounce of his being. Till this moment he had lived in a mood of mild hope but more frequently despair. Now he knew he was being carried along on a tide over which he had no control. It caused him some terror but soon he subsided into a mood of fatalism. Everything was in the hands of others.

Prosecuting counsel rose. 'My Lord, in view of this plea, I

am prepared to offer no evidence on the second indictment of damage to the tollgate and ask that it be struck out.'

'Very well.'

He went through the evidence, stating that there were a large number assembled at the tollgate, some in women's dress. There had been a considerable confrontation and the riot had lasted for more than an hour. Dragoons and constables had been at the scene but they were far outnumbered by the rioters. The gate had been damaged during the disturbance.

The judge interrupted his evidence. 'He pleaded not guilty to the damage to the gate. The court wishes to hear nothing about that matter.'

'As Your Lordship pleases,' he replied, feeling more than mildly rebuked by this intervention. He continued his speech. 'The crowd became more aggressive and the police were unable to make any arrests. The crowd finally dispersed at which time the dragoons tried to arrest a straggler but without success. In the struggle, the female mask of the defendant slipped. As a result one of the constables recognised him and made an arrest some days later. He subsequently made a full and frank admission of his involvement in this matter.'

Prosecuting Counsel sat down. The judge addressed him and he rose again.

'Is there any indication that this man was a leader in these disturbances?'

'No, Your Lordship.'

Waterloo Jones indicated his desire to speak.

'Yes, Mr Waterloo Jones?' responded the Judge.

'My client is a young man of former good character.' He looked towards the prosecutor who nodded in agreement. 'A young man of good family, a young man of intelligence who has ambitions to become a minister in the Methodist Church. A young man who has not embarked on this crime for personal gain but as a political action against a system which has impoverished his community. However misguided you feel this man's actions are, they were certainly not for personal gain. This young man

134

has, during the instructions I have taken from him, shown every indication that he is contrite and wishes to embark on a law-abiding way of life in future. He played a lesser role in this disturbance and no part whatever in the damage and destruction of the gate. This young man is a follower and not a leader. I ask your Lordship to deal with him as leniently as you feel able.' He sat down.

Hardly had the defence sat down than the judge addressed the defendant, setting on him his steely gaze.

'Young man, you have quite rightly entered a guilty plea in this matter and the bench takes this into account. The bench also takes into account the fact that you were a follower and not a leader. Nonetheless, you have embarked with numerous others on a riot which is unlawful in the extreme even testing the political stability of this country. The court therefore cannot overlook this when passing sentence. These riots are widespread, and though you have only admitted to one offence of this nature you will have to be made an example of in order to discourage others who may consider acting in a similar manner This court could impose a sentence of transportation which means that you would be taken from here and be unlikely ever to see your family again. The least sentence this court can impose will be one of imprisonment for six months. I do not expect to see you here again and if I do then do not expect the court to be so lenient in future. Go down.'

Owen turned to walk down the steps, catching his father's eye. They exchanged a weak smile as he clanked his way down. The court would have to end before father and son were able to meet. Back in the cells he expressed relief to Bertie.

'I'll be out by haymaking. June I'll be out.'

'You're lucky, out by June. June eighteen-eighty I'll probably be out.'

Owen then settled down and neither spoke. The final result seemed an anti- climax. Suddenly he felt cold. Prisoners came and went. The cells were rarely quiet. Time passed. Then they learned that the court had risen.

Davey was allowed to speak to his son. Shocked but relieved the sentence had not been harsher.

'Well father, I'll be out by haymaking. June the tenth.'

'Owen, I don't want to go through this again.'

'Neither do I. Honest father, I've had my last of this.'

'Your mother and I have cried blood over you. You know that.'

'I do. Waterloo was good.'

'He was. I don't know where you'd be without him.'

'Neither do I,' Owen agreed. 'Thank him for me.'

'I have done already.'

'What will he charge?'

'Never mind that, you're safe or you will be in six months.'

'Don't worry about me in there. I'll be alright. It could be worse. I'll be out for haymaking.'

'Haymaking and not rioting, mind.'

'Yes.' They both smiled. Davey then had to leave.

The following morning the routine was the same. Shackled early then taken to the court around an hour before it started. There was no ceremony on this second day and by half past ten the first prisoner had been called. Bertie made his way up the stairs, now knowing the way up and the need to face the judge without prompting.

'Have you anything more to add, Mr Waterloo Jones?' Sure that the judge had already made up his mind and that he was known for becoming acutely annoyed when listening to legal windbags, he replied, 'No Your Lordship.'

'Very well. Albert Howell, you stand before the court having pleaded guilty to an offence of robbery. A man of former good character and good family, you now stand before the court a convicted felon. The evidence the court has heard was that you were not the leader in this matter and that you made a full and frank confession. Nonetheless you, with another, committed a robbery during the hours of darkness for nothing more nor less than personal gain. That your accomplice got away and took all the money, which was substantial, does not lessen your role in this matter. You embarked on this felony with evil intent and you must not expect mercy from the court.'

Bertie's eyes glanced for one moment to the left of the books in front of the judge and saw a black piece of cloth. A shiver went down his back.

'Had you used firearms then this court would have had no option but to impose the death penalty. However, bearing in mind all the matters told in your favour by your counsel, then this court can only follow the other alternative sentence, one of transportation. This court is of the opinion that the minimum length of time that you be transported for is a period of ten years. May this sentence be a lesson to you and a warning to others. Go down.' A hushed silence hung over the court as sentence was passed which was only lifted as the prisoner went down the steps. Then it became a gentle hum before the court resumed as another prisoner was called.

Bertie sat alone, not wanting to talk to anyone. Would he ever see his home again? He thought what a fool he had been, all caused by a drunken evening and a bar-room acquaintance he had known for only a few hours. He felt numb and was glad the other prisoners did not try to speak to him but left him alone with his thoughts.

The court rose. Relations were allowed to see the sentenced prisoners. Sammy, as he entered the room, immediately felt the oppressive atmosphere and was wary of putting one foot in front of another. Eventually he saw his brother seated on a bench, looking at the floor and hardly aware what was going on around him.

'Bertie.' He looked up. 'Well Bertie, it wasn't the gallows.' He didn't seem to know what was said to him, looked at his brother but his eyes did not focus on him. 'Bertie, are you alright?'

He seemed to become conscious again. 'I'm alright. As alright as you can be with ten years transportation.'

'Waterloo's coming to see you.' They heard the lawyer's voice nearby.

He addressed Bertie. 'Well Bertie, ten years transportation was quite a reasonable sentence given all the circumstances. It could have been the gallows or twenty years. You've done quite well.'

'Have I?'

'You could make representations to the Crown but you can take it from me that will get you nowhere. There's nothing more I can do.'

'Nothing?' Bertie asked despondently.

'Nothing. I'd better go.' They shook hands and he left.

Bertie and Sammy talked till the prisoners were due to return to the prison.

Three months later, early one cold misty morning in March, Bertie and six others, shackled and guarded, were rowed out into Carmarthen bay to board a steamer on the first step of their long journey to Tasmania, going via Bristol and then Millbank. The journey would take six months. Not all would survive.

Chapter 14

It was September 1848. The Rebecca Riots had ceased and were only occasionally mentioned. The tollgates had been drastically reduced in number and the drain on limited incomes was lessened. Owen had completed his six month sentence and was nearing the end of his training at the Bible College at Lampeter. In retrospect his sentence seemed to have been a rite of passage and more of an asset then a handicap, giving him considerable kudos in the eyes of his fellow students.

On the lips of many was talk of the famine in Ireland, made visible by the numbers of destitute men, women and children that were to be seen, prepared to do any work just for food and shelter.

Hilda had paid off the loan to the bank and was very much in charge of the farm. Dewi had become a very heavy drinker, most days finding him drunk in the afternoon and sometimes earlier. He now hardly ever did any farm work at all, made no decisions and husband and wife rarely spoke. He slept in a room no bigger than a cupboard at the back of the house. Their girls had left home, one to become a schoolteacher, the other to marry.

Jack had now grown out of all recognition and did most of the farm work. He had a confidence about him out of all proportion to his age, looking more like an eighteen year old and in most respects treated like one. His height was around five feet nine, he had a ruddy complexion and was becoming quite robust in build. Though a man of few words, neighbours were beginning to show some deference towards him. Though aware of changes in himself and others' attitudes towards him, it made him neither boastful nor arrogant. He never supposed he would develop any other way. Jack was also receiving the attention of women, not all of them single.

Hilda had a small surplus of cash in the bank and she felt comfortable and confident. There really wasn't a problem on the horizon. She smiled to herself with some satisfaction at the progress she had made. Dewi was no more than a nuisance now and funding his drinking as modestly as she was able, at least kept him in his twilight world of inactivity where he could not interfere with the farm. Jack she took for granted but she did occasionally look at him and, perhaps more frequently, think about him as a man. For a man he certainly was now. Quickly she put the matter out of her mind knowing that these thoughts, if acted upon, might get her into a position she would have difficulty extracting herself from. She took trouble not to let Jack know how she felt. Caution dominated her emotions.

The harvest was in and, though not a good one, it had been enough to see the animals through the winter. There was still plenty of grazing for at least another month. The sheep had been shorn, most of the lambs and cull ewes sold and the more idle time of winter was approaching.

Jack had other thoughts in mind. He had been with the family nearly eight years; almost one of the family yet not fully so. He was not complaining because it suited him. He had always been something of an outsider. Family life held no attractions for him. What he really liked was work as it gave him an outlet for his truly formidable physical energy. He had a natural grasp of agricultural skills. This ability gave him satisfaction along with the knowledge that others held him in high regard.

What had come into his mind was that in all these years he had never been paid a penny and hardly knew what having money felt like. These thoughts came more frequently now that the hiring fair was no more than six weeks away. If Hilda would not pay him any wages in cash, then he would have to find alternative work and the hiring fair was the place to attend. In the back of his mind were the drovers. Would he have a chance of joining them? He felt it was time to leave and move on. Nonetheless he was going to ask Hilda for wages before he made

140

his final decision.

September came to an end and October was half over. The days were closing in earlier and the weather grew colder. The rain lingered in a way it did not during the summer. The final harvesting was of potatoes and now that was almost concluded. It was a poor crop but would see them through the winter. He sat in the kitchen with the day's work done, supper eaten and a chance to sit by the fire before going to bed. There was only Hilda and himself in. Dewi, as usual, was elsewhere.

She smiled towards Jack in a slight but appreciative manner. 'You've worked hard this summer Jack. Done well.' Praise was something she rarely gave but when he did hear it, he appreciated it all the more.

'Glad of that Hilda.' he replied. 'I do my best, you know.'

'Don't know what I'd have done without you,' she continued.

Was this the time to strike?

'Dewi's not much use any more.' He nodded in agreement. 'Don't know what'll become of him.' Again he nodded. 'Didn't do a stroke at harvest this year, did he? Drinking all day and every day he is. Costing me a fortune.'

'It's home brew with Swni, isn't it?'

'Even home brew isn't cheap you know.'

'Cheaper than the tavern though.'

'Wouldn't be here if he drank tavern beer. Hasn't been to the tavern since the robbery.'

'No he hasn't, has he?'

'Swni's looking bad, you know. Old man now and lives on beer. He don't have long. Dewi ain't looking well either. Face all red and purple. You know he hardly eats now.'

'I know,' he replied.

She relapsed into silence for several minutes, lost in her own thoughts. It seemed to her a time to talk though she didn't know what to say, remaining silent for a few minutes more. 'Jack, see your sisters at all? How they doing at the Hall?'

'Only seen 'em twice since I been here. They're alright. So

they say.'

'Would you like to see them more?'

'No. I can't help'em. I don't have any money.' His remark gave Hilda a jolt Jack wanted to say more but didn't. They went to their beds shortly.

The routine on the farm continued, however the all too brief mention of money had brought an awkwardness between them. Hilda knew that Jack, sooner rather than later, would bring up the matter of wages. By now quite successful, she had become somewhat avaricious and did not want to pay him. He was family wasn't he? She had rescued him from the fate of the workhouse. Where would he be now without her? She knew she should really pay him and it made her feel awkward not doing so. She also knew that many Irish families had come over escaping the famine who would work for food only. Why should she pay? She wasn't yet fully aware how dependant she was on him. She took him for granted. Jack knew this but Hilda didn't.

The month of October was drawing to a close. All the harvesting was now completed. Routine had set in. In a fortnight the cattle would be indoors and tied up for the winter with only a brief break for watering twice a day. The sheep were on lower ground and needed to be counted once a day. Jack was asked to take the horse to town to do some shopping. It was the first time he had held money in months.

'Be back by nightfall,' was her final remark as he rode away.

Riding at a good pace, he got to town in two hours. Running the errands quickly, he then called at the back door of the Saddler's.

Nellie greeted him with, 'You're a big lad now.' He blushed and laughed.   'Come in then, you. Sit down.' He felt immediately at home in a way that he had never felt with Hilda. 'What you doing, Jack?' He looked a man now and she treated him like one. 'No catching robbers up there then?'

'No.'

'How long since I seen you?'

'More than a year, Nellie.'

'Jack you've grown. My, you've grown.' Again he smiled and felt warm inside in a way he had rarely felt before.

'What you doing then, Jack?'

'The farm work, you know.'

'Dewi has gone downhill, we hear.' He nodded, feeling it would be disloyal to say anything.

'You doing it all now?' Again he nodded.

'How much you getting, then?'

'Nothing.'

'Nothing? Don't let that go on too long. Boy like you'll always get work.'

'Will I? I know the hiring fair is in two weeks.'

'Boy like you won't have to go to the hiring fair.'

His horizons had suddenly expanded. There was paid work to be had out there. Nellie knew everybody and everybody knew Nellie. Not only was he reassured that work was available but that Nellie would help him to find it.

'What sort of work, Nellie? The drovers?'

'A bit late in the year for that now, but from the spring onwards, they're busy.'

Jack again reflected on his prospects. One thing was certain; Nellie was his ally. He fantasised about driving cattle to London, sleeping in a different place each night and meeting different people. Better than being wedded to the farm. He knew that he would have to ask Hilda for a wage but he almost hoped that she would refuse. She had been good to him but he had repaid her in full measure. He had done his duty by her.

'Tommy's the big drover around here, isn't he, Nellie? Does he still live here at the tavern?'

'During the winter but he's away now.'

'Eddie's his partner, isn't he?'

'Eddie's not as young as he was but he's a good deal thirstier.'

'Would Tommy give me a chance?'

'I'll speak to him, you leave him to me. No promises though.' She looked him straight in the face saying, 'Not a word to a soul,' putting her forefinger to her lips.

He drove back almost in a daze with plans for the future and the prospect of adventure. The pony was hot and sweating by the time he arrived at the farm. Getting out of the trap, he unharnessed the pony, took her to the stable, groomed, fed and watered her, closing the door as he left. Lifting the shafts of the trap, he pushed and guided it till it was under cover then walked to the house. Hilda met him at the door.

'You've been a long time.'

'Yes, I know.'

'What you been doing? It didn't take all this time to do those errands.'

Never one to tell a lie, he replied, 'Talking to Nellie.'

'You shouldn't be in a tavern at your age. You're too young to drink.'

'Haven't been drinking. Just talking.'

'You shouldn't be talking to her.' He shrugged his shoulders. 'Not at your age.'

Why the hell not, he thought to himself, hoping his thoughts were not revealed on his face. 'Haven't been off the farm in twelve months. Just talked to her.'

'You're giving me cheek after all I've done for you,' she said angrily. She wanted to hit him but knew he was far too big and strong. Prior to the first signs of the breach in their relationship the previous evening, she regarded him as no more than a very useful and obedient cart horse; a man to be fed, watered and harnessed to any task at hand. Now she knew matters had changed for ever and that Jack also knew. At this moment Hilda at last realised how dependant she had become upon his abilities. He was everything that Dewi wasn't. Above all he wasn't a drinker, in fact he didn't like it. The fact crossed her mind that he would go but it only lasted fleetingly. Where could he go without any money? She would do her best to keep him dependant.

'There's the work to be done before dark. Get on with it.' He did the dreary tasks automatically, not thinking of the matter

144

in hand but only of the future. What would happen when he walked down the road to town? What opportunities would present themselves in the future? One thing was certain, Nellie would be his first call when he left. Would he ask Hilda for wages or would he just walk out. It was a challenge and he felt he had to ask her. He hadn't many possessions and decided he would pack them that night.

Going into the house after all the work was completed, they looked one another in the face and both knew that the breach between them was widening. In spite of this change, they came to understand one another more, she realising he was quite a determined young man who would go his own way and he knowing how vulnerable she was having to run a farm on her own with a hopeless husband. He softened toward her but only briefly, knowing ultimately he was on his own.

In the minute or two that these thoughts were going through their minds, Jack had failed to notice that Dewi was slumped in a chair in the corner, obviously drunk. He hadn't been near him for some days now, only having seen him at a distance. His face had become more dissipated and he was thinner. In his drunken sleep he seemed almost corpse-like with hardly a movement visible. Hilda looked at Dewi and then Jack. The awkwardness briefly vanished as Jack said, 'Let's get him into bed.' They both moved towards his chair, taking an arm each round their shoulders and carrying him to his bed. Easing him down, they covered him in blankets then returned to the kitchen.

'See what I have to put up with?' she said.

He nodded sympathetically, saying, 'Yes, Dewi looks bad.'

'Drunk you mean,' she responded aggressively.

'Sad,' he replied softly.

'No good giving him any sympathy. He's a drunk and he'll never be anything else.' Jack didn't reply.

He went to bed reassured that his bag was packed, ready to move on. It was only a few days to the hiring fair. For two more days life went on as before but with the awkwardness still existing between them and hardly a word spoken, each one waiting for the other to speak. The rain fell, the yard was never dry and the cattle no sooner unchained and watered than they wanted to get back indoors again. The following week, the rams would be put in the field with the ewes, but they were currently huddled under the thorn hedge, sheltering from the driving rain. In every direction the aspect looked dark, damp and depressing.

Jack knew he was running out of time. He would have to act quickly. After the morning work was done he walked into the house and looked Hilda in the eyes, saying,

'Hilda, I shall have to work for wages this year.'

Even though she was expecting such a request she was briefly at a loss for an answer, eventually saying 'There's no money here for wages, boy.' She had never called him boy before. Even she was surprised by the reply she gave. 'You're family, you know.'

'Am I?'

'Didn't we take you in when you were an orphan? You could have gone to the workhouse.'

'I know, but haven't I worked every day since I've been here?'

'You ungrateful boy. We took you in when you needed a home and you've been here ever since. The Irish will work for no wages, just keep. They're grateful for a home. You aren't.'

He remained silent for perhaps a minute but which seemed very much longer. Again he looked her in the face. 'No wages then this year, Hilda?'

'I've told you no and I mean no. That's final. You can do what you like'.

'I will, I'll leave.'

'Leave. Leave when?'

'I'm going now. Right now.'

She couldn't believe her ears. For nearly eight years she had taken him for granted. Day in, day out, he had made himself useful till it had got to the point that he was essential to the running of the farm. She could feel him slipping away but pride would not let her bargain with him and possibly pay wages.

146

Looking up, she realised he was no longer in the room. Jack returned with the jute sack over his shoulder and Hilda knew he was really going. He walked towards the door without looking round, never to cross the threshold again. Walking towards the town, within sixty yards he had disappeared into the mist. Hilda's eyes filled with tears. She had had no idea until this moment how attached she was to him.

Chapter 15

It was the spring of 1849. Hilda had a dozen or more heifers and bullocks to sell. The winter feed had lasted well and they were in good condition. Tommy had been summoned and was riding up some time in the middle of the morning with Eddie to make a deal. The ponies were walking and in no great hurry. Both the men were older and a little more inactive with Eddie still drinking more than was good for him. Tommy had warned him about it but still he was always up on time and ready to work, though frequently suffering from the night before.

They arrived in the yard and remained mounted until someone became aware of their arrival. Eventually Hilda came out, at which point both men dismounted. They shook hands, she wiping her hands on her apron before doing so. Tommy became aware that there was a worried and rather harassed look on her face. In the three years that she had been in charge of the farm, he knew that she had become increasingly confident, but she no longer appeared so. There was a darkness under her eyes and the lines on her forehead had deepened. She had also lost weight.

'Good to see you, Hilda. Got some stock for me?'

'Yes.'

'How many?'

'Fourteen.'

He could see that she wanted to talk and he was too well-mannered to be offensive. 'Been a hard year Tommy,' she volunteered as they walked towards the pens. The cattle had been put in fresh straw, awaiting Tommy's arrival. Wanting to listen to her as little as possible, he leaned over the gate and with his stick made them walk around the pen.

'They look good, Hilda. Have to get them out to see how they are on their feet.'

'Things have been tough recently Tommy,' she persisted. She had hardly left the farm in twelve months. He knew he would have to listen and he was fairly certain what she would say. 'Haven't been right since Jack went. The workers I've got now are terrible.'

'So I hear,' Tommy replied.'

'Said they'd come for bed and board. Now it's just money they want.'

'Can't keep a family without money. The famine has driven them over here to work.'

'I shouldn't have let Jack go.'

'No you shouldn't. He was a good boy.'

'A good boy alright.'

'Where's he now?'

'The Forge.'

He didn't let Hilda know in any way that he intended to employ him. A blacksmith would be worth his weight in gold on any drove and save a good deal of expense. Might make all the difference between a profit and a loss.

'Think he'd come back Tommy?'

'What're you going to do with the people here? Getting rid of them's not going to be easy. What about Dewi. Can't he help?'

'He's worse than useless now. Drinking with Swni and now Paddy. It's hopeless here.'

'You'll have to handle it as best you can.' Tommy had no help to give her.

While this conversation was going on, some thirty yards away and out of earshot Eddie was talking to Paddy. Paddy was doing most of the talking. 'A great woman she is taking us in, but she has a powerful grasp on the money.' Eddie gave monosyllabic replies and periodic furtive looks at the other two. 'Haven't a rag to our backs. She's got to keep a lighter grasp on the money.'

'Yes'. Again he glanced across at Hilda and Tommy, thinking to himself, this woman has got into deep water. How's

149

she going to get out?

Hilda continued to complain, 'This is as bad as the time Dewi had the money stolen. Worse even.'

Tommy nodded. 'Can't you do anything with Dewi? He's not old you know.'

'I've shouted and screamed at him but nothing works. He's lost weight and hasn't done a day's work in a year or two. Don't know whether he'll be alive for long. Swni's on his last legs. Now Paddy's drinking with them too.' Tears came into her eyes. He found it awkward but patted her arm in a gesture of sympathy. One foolish and hasty decision and she had an insoluble problem.

'I don't know what to do'. Again she cried, putting her face into his shoulder. He found this awkward in the extreme having never had anything to do with women. Better get out of here quickly, he said to himself.

When Hilda had ceased giving vent to her feelings for a moment he said, 'Let's get the cattle and see how they walk'. He beckoned Eddie over. He walked towards them, followed by Paddy.

'Close the yard gates Paddy,' Hilda said looking directly at him. Her tears had disappeared but her eyes were still red. Each of them knew there would be confrontation ahead.

Paddy felt he could control the situation. He went to close the gates but failed to notice one, which remained open. Everyone watched him as he did so. 'He ain't no farmer's son, Hilda,' Tommy commented. They weren't well-hung gates and had to be lifted which he did with a maximum of effort and a minimum of skill. Paddy returned to the group.

'Paddy, the third gate,' Hilda directed him.

He walked towards it slowly and reluctantly, clearly having his pride hurt by taking orders from a woman. Whilst they were checking the cattle, Paddy felt it appropriate to shout at the animals, wave the stick at them and hit them if they were within reach. 'Less of that Paddy,' said Hilda.

Tommy finished his inspection and motioned Hilda towards

him. 'In the house,' he said. He indicated to Eddie without speaking to get the cattle penned up again.

They sat either side of the kitchen table. A figure of nine pounds was quickly agreed upon. She wanted to talk and Tommy knew he had to listen.

'I'd sooner be without anyone than keep him. He's no farmer's son.'

'I know that. I saw him handle the gate and the cattle.'

'What can I do?'

'Has he given any real trouble yet?'

'Not real trouble. His wife's alright, but he gives her a hard time.'

'What you going to do when the spring and summer come? He can't plough a field or use a scythe. What's he like with the horses?'

'Alright with the horses but he does drive'em hard. I don't know what to do.'

'He'll have to go you know. Farm'll go to pieces with him here. Nothing'll get done. Tell him to go and if he don't, go to the magistrates,' advised Tommy.

'How long will that take?'

'They can act quickly you know.'

'Can they?' asked Hilda.

'They'll get a constable round straight away. Might take more than a constable to get them away. Say two or three. I've done it myself twice. That's what they are there for.'

She seemed relieved after this conversation, seeing a solution to the problem she had faced almost from the day they had arrived. Now she thought of the future.

'Think I could get Jack back?'

'He's making himself useful at the forge you know.' He didn't tell her that Jack spent at least two nights a week at the Saddler's.

'You know he asked for money and I said no.'

'Wasn't he worth it?'

'Yes.' She now realised her mistake. 'Do you think he

151

would come back? I'd pay him the same as the forge. Perhaps a pound more.'

'I think he's gone for good, Hilda. This farm is too small for him. I think Narberth is too small for him too.'

'I see what you mean.' The matter was closed. Tommy wanted to go.

'Hilda, Eddie will come tomorrow with one of my other boys. I don't want Paddy doing anything with the cattle. Mid-morning. Alright?' She nodded. Tommy left the house, glad to be gone.

The two men rode off down the lane as they had done in the preceding years. Tommy was more talkative than usual. 'She's got a problem, Eddie. Wonder where it will end? Husband a drunk. Farm servant hopeless. Doesn't know how she'll get the spring and summer work done.'

'She misses Jack?' Eddie asked.

'Yes, she does that.' Eddie felt sure Tommy would employ Jack for the coming season although nothing had been said between them. Knowing he was not as active as he had been, Eddie felt a certain jealousy towards Jack. He knew he had been placed at the forge to gain shoeing skills which would be invaluable to Tommy; skills which Eddie did not have.

The following morning Dewi got up in his usual dishevelled condition. Hilda confronted him. 'Sit down. We've got to talk.' He did as he was told.

'What is it, Hilda?'

'Things can't go on as they have done. Paddy's got to go. You've got to stop drinking and get down to the farm work.'

'Alright Hilda.'

'You've got to do it now, and Paddy's going to go today.'

'And his wife and the child?'

'Yes, all of them,' Hilda replied.

'What if he won't go?'

'We'll cross that bridge when we come to it. He will leave even if you have to go to the magistrates.'

'Magistrates?' Dewi said in a surprised voice. 'We

152

shouldn't have got Paddy here in the first place'.

'If you weren't a drunk, he wouldn't be here.' He knew there was no answer and he had to get Paddy to leave. They had become drinking cronies which made it all the more difficult. After a cup of tea and breakfast he then washed, trying to make himself feel as confident as possible. He walked to the back of the house where Paddy lived with his family. Half expecting him, they met at the door.

'Top of the morning to you Dewi,' Paddy greeted him in his usual manner.

Dewi had only one thing in mind. Get rid of him as soon as possible; get rid of all of them.

'Paddy you've got to leave the farm. Got to go now.'

'What d'you mean? Paddy seemed shocked. 'I'm not going.'

'Yes you are and now.' Dewi went into the living space with the intention of throwing them out but was barred.

'Sure, we're not man. Not escaping the famine to be treated like this,' declared Paddy.

Dewi made another attempt to get in and again was blocked by Paddy, this time more roughly, receiving a slight blow to the side of the face. This did not deter him. He walked back two paces and then made a rush to get through the door. In this contest there was no doubt who would win in the short term. Paddy overpowered his adversary with an ease of effort and a confidence in his physical superiority. At this moment Hilda appeared at the door, shouting, 'Get out of here. We don't want you.'

Paddy was now starting to lose his temper. 'If you come in here again I'll have you.' Yet again Dewi confronted him, receiving three more blows to the head. Paddy went indoors, shutting the door behind him. 'That'll keep'em off, mark my words,' he said to his wife who was cowering in the corner.

Dewi knew he was hurt and bleeding as he and Hilda retreated to their own kitchen. 'Got to clean myself up, Hilda.'

'No you haven't. You go down straight away to the

magistrate and make a complaint. I want him to see you with all the blood on you. Make no mistake about that good boy.'

'I see.'

'You tell the magistrate he can't do the work on the farm so he was ordered to leave. He refused and then hit you. Remember, don't wash your face. Dewi, for once do this properly, boy.' They looked at one another for a moment before parting. 'Dewi, don't have a drink.'

'I won't. Rely on me.'

'He walked down the road at a fast pace, passing the lane to Swni Hopkins' hovel without a glance. Within two hours he was in town, calling first at the Clerk to the Justices' office, being directed from there to Colonel Herbert's.

He walked up the gravelled drive at a much reduced pace and by now quite breathless. Knocking on the front door, he asked for Colonel Herbert. Within minutes, he was directed to go to his study but was not asked to sit down. Without looking up, the magistrate barked, 'Yes, what do you want?'

'Make a complaint Sir.' The Colonel looked up.

'Who has hit you? What's happened to you, man?'

'Paddy, the Irishman. He's up on the farm. No good at the farm work. Told him to go. He hit me.'

'When did this happen?'

'This morning, Sir.'

'You always seem to be in trouble, don't you? Last time it was the stolen sovereigns, wasn't it?' It was painful to be reminded of that.

'Yes Sir.'

'What do you want us to do about this matter?'

'Get him out Sir.'

'Shouldn't have employed him in the first place, it seems to me. Why did you?'

'Needed someone in a hurry, Sir. Our son left home, Sir.'

'Left home, has he? Where is he now?'

'The forge, Sir.'

'Good trade. Right. Wait in the hall while I make out a

154

warrant which you can give to the Clerk to the Justices. Did you see any constables in town as you came through?'

'No Sir.'

'In the meantime, go round to the back of the house and wash your face.'

'Yes Sir.'

Within twenty minutes he was back in town presenting the warrant to the Clerk to the Justices. Waiting there a further twenty minutes, he was eventually called into the office.

'How many are there in this family?'

'Three, Sir. Husband, wife and a young child. She's pregnant too.'

'Know where the constables' office is?'

Dewi went as directed and was told the constables were probably in the Saddler's which proved correct. He managed to extract them from there without attracting Nellie's attention He didn't want to face her.

They entered the Clerk's office smelling strongly of beer which did not escape his notice. Keeping as far away as possible from them, he gave them the warrant. 'What about the wife and child?' they asked.

'The warrant is for him but they won't want to stay there without him. Bring them down if they ask, but remember they are not on the warrant.'

'Yes Sir.'

Little more than an hour later, the trap, pulled by a breathless pony, arrived in the farmyard with the constables and Dewi on board.

'Leave this to us,' said the older of the constables to Dewi. 'We'll manage this. You keep out of the way.' They walked towards the door of Paddy's section of the house. They knocked and the door was opened almost immediately.

'Paddy, we've got a warrant for you.'

'What in heaven's name is this for?'

'The assault on Dewi.'

'I hardly touched him.'

155

'Listen, you can do it the easy way or you can do it the hard way. Which way do you want?'

'Why should I leave here, I only gave him a clip. All this fuss.'

'Listen Paddy, we won't shackle you if you behave yourself.'

'Alright. I'll be a good boy but where's the missus and the little one going to rest their heads to night?'

'We'll see when we get to town. Got some friends from home there, haven't you?'

'If they haven't moved on.'

By dusk Paddy was in the cells and his wife and child were with their Irish friends, making their overcrowded accommodation even more so.

'I knew it was too good to last at the farm,' Paddy's wife, Siobhan told them.

'Good as that was it?'

'Paddy's no farmer's boy and they caught on to it. Lucky to be there as long as we were.'

Paddy spent the night in the cells and was called before a specially convened court in the morning. He was charged and asked to plead to breach of the peace. He rambled on, 'Sure I gave him a clip. He was trying to put me and the missus and the little one on the road. Wouldn't you? And the missus expecting as well. Just barged in the house and tried to throw us out. Well wouldn't you, if he did that to you, I ask you? Sure I gave him a clip.' The magistrates could not suppress a smile.

'Do you plead guilty to this matter?' asked the Clerk to the Court, feeling it was an opportune moment and beginning to feel impatient.

'Sure, I gave him a clip.'

'Is the bench prepared to accept that as a not guilty?'

'Yes' agreed the chairman. The bench wouldn't have minded the interaction continuing. The clerk thought otherwise. No real evidence was presented, apart from the information on the warrant. Paddy was allowed to continue to speak on his own

156

behalf which he did with increased gusto. Eventually, even he ran out of words. The bench retired to consider the sentence. When they returned, Paddy was bound over to keep the peace for the next twelve months. The clerk spelt it out in detail and in words of one syllable. He left the court and as he did so was given, at the request of the bench, ten shillings from the court poor box.

'The court has given you this sum from the court poor box to be spent on your family, not on beer.'

'Tis very good of you, Sir. If I get short in the future, I'll be looking to get in trouble again.' He winked at the humourless clerk who was clearly against such gifts being given.

Chapter 16

Jack had been at the forge for six months, making himself useful far beyond any initial hopes that he had when he arrived six months before. His employer, known to all, was Evan Black not because that was his surname but because it was his trade. His father had been a smith and his grandfather before him. Having only daughters, the trade line would cease with his generation. Apprentices came and went, some doing well and others not, but none of them stayed. Jack had been different. Strong, willing and skilled, he was a natural at the trade.

During the dark days of winter they had spent most of their time making the shoes. Over the last three months much more time was spent shoeing. Evan, a skilled man rather than a strong one, had had difficulty casting the animals even with the assistance of his apprentices. Jack seemed to have the knack of throwing them over with the minimum of effort and no harm to the beast. Never had a leg been broken and rarely a horn broken off.

Jack and Evan got on well but talked little. In the back of Jack's mind he wanted to join the drovers and knew it was only a question of time before he did so. Everything was unsaid. Both knew the fateful day would come when he responded to the call. It was like standing on the banks of a fast moving river waiting to jump. The water would be cold and the current strong but it would carry him away to whatever fate awaited him. Many times a day he saw the stream only yards away knowing it would be days and at most weeks till the call came. He knew it as surely as he was standing beside it.

Evan took to Jack in a way he never expected. He became the son he had never had. Thoughts frequently went through his mind as to the possibilities. The business could go on and the forge still prosper if Jack continued to work there. Occasionally he mentioned it to his wife Edith.

'Edie. Wonder if Jack would stay. Be a good living for him.'

'He's a good lad, Evan. We've never had better. But he's his own man and will go his own way.'

'Do you think so Edie?'

'Sure as eggs is eggs.'

'I'll miss him.'

'So will I. He'll go, mark my words, and soon too.'

'We could have given him a permanent home, Edie.'

'Evan, he don't want a permanent home. Not him. Mother died. Never known his father. Hardly been to school. Look at him, he's tough and independent.'

'You don't have to tell me that. I know he's more like a man. But he's still a fifteen year old.'

'Evan, he's like a twenty year old man in every way and what's he getting here? Sixpence a day. He's going to move on.'

'I can't afford more than sixpence a day.'

'That's why he'll move on. He's going to spread his wings. He's got things to do.'

'I suppose you're right,' he reluctantly conceded.

'He'll join Tommy the drover's gang. He wants to see the world. Ain't going to see it here.'

'Never thought of that, Edie.'

'Evan, you don't know what's going on around you. Get to sleep now. Jack's going to make his own life, whatever you do.'

Next morning, as arranged, Tommy and Eddie brought up thirty-five heifers and bullocks for shoeing. This arrangement was repeated till more than two hundred had been shod. Even Tommy was surprised at how skilfully the beasts were cast and shod by Jack.

On the third day, during a lull in the work, Tommy was standing by Evan.

'Evan. You know Jack'll be leaving you and coming with me.'

Evan resigned himself to the inevitable almost as soon as the words were spoken. A mood of dejection overcame him and was evident in his reply. 'It was too good to last. He's a good lad. The best. When do you want him?'

'Sunday night for Monday morning,' Tommy answered. Evan drew in on himself, feeling his eyes become moist. Tommy always felt awkward in matters of emotion and looked away.

'He's been a great help to me. I was talking to Edie about him last night. But if he's got to go, he's got to go.' Again he reflected on his loss, thinking of all their time together in the last six months. 'Edie said he'd go to you, Tommy. You've got a good'un there.'

Tommy tried to steer the conversation onto more practical matters. 'I'll need sixty shoes in some grease.'

'You can have them and a good smith to go with them,' replied Evan.

Tommy thought he may as well make arrangements immediately. 'Jack, you're starting with me on Monday morning. Be at The Saddler's on Sunday night. Bring the shoes with you.'

'Me'. His face lit up briefly. 'Got to tell Evan, then.'

'I told him,' said Tommy. Feeling there was nothing more to be gained by staying, he returned to the town leaving Eddie behind.

Eddie had heard nothing of the conversation but was aware that Jack would be taken on. He was rarely wrong and felt able to ask Jack when he was alone as to whether he would start on Monday. 'Yes, Monday.' was the reply. Eddie felt jealous, his position threatened and aware of his physical resources which he knew to be past their best. He also reflected on Tommy's warnings to him regarding drink. Jack immediately detected Eddie's feelings of envy and insecurity. Whilst not wanting to upset him, he felt some pride that someone as experienced as Eddie should feel jealous of him. Jack knew that his blacksmith skills would be a great asset and that his fellow employee did not possess the same advantage.

'It's tough on the road, Jack. Very tough. Think you can handle it?' He was in no doubt about it. Of course he could do it

160

and he didn't have to brag about it.

'Have to see,' was all he said.

He was beginning to see that Eddie was a weak, rather vulnerable man who felt his position had become threatened by Jack's arrival. Not wanting to crush him, he nevertheless wanted to have little to do with him. Having seen the trouble that drink could cause, he was keen to avoid it. To him, heavy drinking went with stupidity and chaos. He knew that Eddie spent every spare moment in the taverns. Tommy didn't drink and neither did Evan or Davey. They led active lives. It seemed as though men were either drinkers or non-drinkers. Strange that no-one was a modest drinker. He knew it would never be a problem with him.

Soon after Tommy went, he walked straight over to Evan to give his notice but before being able to speak he heard him say, 'Well Jack, you're off on Sunday. Me and Edie will both miss you.'

'Yes. I liked it here, you know.'

'Setting out into the big cold world you are then?'

'That's right.'

'Don't forget you've got two months' wages to come.'

'How much?'

'Twenty-two shillings. What'll you do with it? Have a drink?'

'I don't drink.'

'That's wise.'

There was nothing more to say, so Jack went back to work.

Eddie was left with nothing to do and felt awkward, standing around. He became cold, stamped his feet to get them warm, slapped his arms around his body and reflected on his own position and how vulnerable he was. He was no match for Jack in any way even though his adversary was no more than a schoolboy in age. What would he do if he lost his job? He had no home, his relations would have him under sufferance only and he no longer had the physical resources of a young man. He felt he was facing a brick wall. Without a penny to his name, how would he survive? He knew he drank too much and in the last

161

year or two had found the droves hard. He had trouble getting up in the morning and by nightfall he was exhausted. One thing was sure, nothing would stop Jack. He could do anything.

Jack, for his part, found Eddie a rather sad and lonely character. Like all young people he felt anyone over thirty was quite old. Eddie didn't escape this observation. Such was Jack's confidence that he did not feel in competition with him, but rather his attitude was one of sympathy. Eddie always started any conversation they had and, once started, he found it difficult to stop. Much of it was boasting about his many years on the road, what had happened in that time and above all his hero worship of Tommy.

That night, Jack said goodbye to Evan, his first real employer. He gave Jack a handful of silver. 'Twenty-two shillings, lad. That's two months pay.'

'Well Jack, you're leaving us then' said Edie. From the beginning she had guessed he would be off sooner rather than later. She could have become very attached to him but knew it would be better not to. 'Carmarthen, Gloucester and London now. Come and see us when you get back.'

He nodded. There was no more to be said.

'Don't forget us, we're always here.'

He gave a faint smile, 'Thanks.'

With two bags over his right shoulder, one containing his possessions and the other sixty spare shoes for the journey east on Monday, he walked behind the cattle he had shod earlier in the day.

Saturday night passed into Sunday, during which time he became irritable and bored with the lack of activity. What kept him going was the prospect of Monday's drove. During this time he hardly spoke to a soul and time hung heavily. Twice he went to the holding field with Tommy to count the cattle and, more particularly, to check how they walked. Tommy then seemed to disappear, where he didn't know. Whenever he put his head round the door of the bar Eddie seemed to be drinking pint after pint and talking to anyone who would listen to him.

The waiting over, before dawn on Monday there was a barking of dogs, lowing of cattle with steam coming off them and the shouting of the drovers. Getting them out of the field quickly, they were very close together and becoming more so as they were driven out. Most of the beasts in the middle had to raise their heads in the crush. Tommy and Eddie were on horseback, Jack and another man on foot. The herd appeared as a black mass, broken up only by the pale horns with white tips. Half a mile along the way the noise lessened as they became more spread out and all that could be heard was the constant barking of the Corgi dogs. Ned, the recently engaged drover, walked in front of the riders and Jack behind. In this way they covered perhaps two and a half miles per hour. For three days they continued without problems; mile after mile for up to ten hours a day. First stopping outside Saint Clears overnight, then Carmathen and Llandeilo. The routine was always the same: count them morning and night, feed and water them and every third night sleep out with them. The beasts came first, the drovers second. Little was said and communication was almost monosyllabic.

At Llandeilo there was some talk of tomorrow's journey.

'Got to make a good start tomorrow.'

'Up all the way,' moaned Eddie, having been to Llanduesant many times before which the two others hadn't. 'Yes, up all the way.'

'We'll stay there a day or two,' put in Tommy. 'It's early and we're in no hurry. A rest'll do them the world of good.'

'Where you selling 'em, Tommy?' asked Eddie.

'Hereford, maybe Gloucester. See what I hear. Trade isn't good anywhere.'   'Haven't seen anybody coming back,' put in Eddie.

'Never failed to see someone yet.'

It was a habit going back centuries to talk to any returning drovers coming back west and even in the middle of the day they would stop for half an hour. The conversation was always about markets, prices, personalities, the weather, the level of the river

163

crossings, the amount of keep available and who was doing what. Sometimes there were messages to be taken to girlfriends along the route and, less frequently, gifts for them. There was a tradition of honest dealing and, though tight-fisted, they always kept their word. Failure to keep these rules would ostracize a man immediately, such knowledge spreading like wild fire.

It was a long day and uphill all the way but by four o'clock they were in the village and shortly afterwards lodged in the Drovers' Arms. There was an abundance of grass and plenty of water so within an hour or two the animals were all lying down. All felt they could now sit down and rest.

Eddie wanted to start drinking but thought better of it, knowing Tommy would disapprove at this time of day. They were sitting down outside in their heavy coats enjoying the remains of the warm part of the day.

The next day passed. Again the animals were counted and two shoes replaced. Tommy was impressed by the skill of his young drover. That was money saved. Jack was working for two shillings a day but, while they were alone, Tommy offered him fifteen pence which he immediately accepted with enthusiasm.

'Jack,' Tommy said softly. 'Go to my saddle bag and get a package out. Done up in red paper.'

Tommy had no great liking for women, thought they were trouble and was always awkward in their company. They embarrassed him and even now, in his early fifties, could feel his face go red when even the mildest piece of emotional attention was addressed to him. Not that he received too much attention of that sort. His whole persona repelled it. He never put himself in a position where he would be vulnerable and made great efforts to avoid such encounters.

Jack returned with the small package, offering it to Tommy who would not touch it and made great efforts not to do so, almost jumping back as you would to avoid a snake bite. Hoping the others would not hear, he said softly, 'Down the road,' he pointed, 'first house on the right. Give her that. Go now.'

'Who's it for?'

'A woman. Off you go.' He wanted to get rid of the package.

Eddie had overheard this exchange. 'Rosie-Drove. You want to watch her.' Eddie was almost as innocent as Tommy but lived vicariously in these matters, sometimes indulging in impotent bragging which fooled nobody. 'She'll eat you alive.' Tommy gave him one of his disapproving looks and he shut up. Jack walked towards the house and knocked.

'Come in,' a woman shouted over the noise of two children.

He walked in feeling a little excited and apprehensive. What was in store for him? Rosie did not look up for some seconds but, when she did, looked him straight in the eye. Her look had only one meaning in any language in the world. He felt his face grow intensely warm. It was normally ruddy but now it was scarlet. Not knowing what to say, he couldn't look her straight in the face and felt he was on the verge of wetting himself. 'Here, for you.'

She looked at the package extremely briefly and threw it behind her. 'Who are you, big boy?' she demanded with a slight smile on her face, maintaining her bold predatory gaze on him. He didn't answer immediately, first looking at her then having to look away, his face still bright red and his heart beating faster than it had ever done.

He had experienced rumblings before, felt sexually attracted to women but never pursued them. Rosie was perhaps a little below medium height, had dark hair and a figure which could best be described as well-nourished, curvy in all the right places. She had a fresh complexion but above all it was her bold brown eyes which mesmerised him. Whenever he looked at her she met his gaze. There was no escaping it. Not knowing whether to run for the door or put his arms around her and kiss her, he didn't know how to act. In fact he did nothing. This immobility lasted only briefly but it seemed to him an age.

'Well, who are you, my lad?'

'I'm Jack.'

165

Maintaining her bold gaze, she said 'Jack who?'

'Jack Lloyd.'

She stepped nearer to him until they were just an inch or two apart but not touching. Putting the index finger of her right hand inside the belt of his trousers, she gave him a slight shake before releasing it. He never dreamed it would be like this. Moving her hands lightly from his upper chest to below his waist and back again, she made him tingle from head to toe. In a low husky voice she said, 'Jack, I like you.' Still her gaze never left him. He felt hypnotised by her, unable to move but with an erection which he thought would burst.

Rosie loved every moment of it. This boy was a bit special, she thought, I'm going to make a man of him. Very lightly she frisked him from the waist down. Again she looked him in the face and laughed a warm inviting smile, followed by a look of mock outrage. 'You naughty boy. You've got something big and strong down there for Rosie.' He laughed at this remark, partly from embarrassment, part amusement. It released the intensity and he put his arms around her. He loved the feel of her breasts against him but above all the smell of her. The smell of her hair, the smell of her neck, the smell of all of her. He didn't want to let go. Never had he felt anything like this before. Rarely before had he touched anyone, or been touched in any affectionate way. It was like finding an unexpected oasis after a life of brackish water. He didn't want to let go.

She put a hand between his legs and gave him one quick firm shake. 'That'll have to wait'. Then she released herself firmly from his grasp. 'You're with those bloody drovers aren't you?'

'Yes.'

'Where you going?'

'Hereford, maybe Gloucester.'

'What's that, four or five days away?'

'Don't know.'

'Never been on a drove before?'

'No.'

'How you coming back? Like the rest, lodge and make your own way?'

'Two are on horses. We won't come with them.'

'You come back on your own through here, and remember Rosie wants a present.'

'A present?'

'Yes a present. A dress, a brooch or a necklace.' They smiled at one another. There was a mutual understanding in their smile. She held him close again for a while then pushed him away. 'Get back to those bloody drovers.'

He hadn't been gone more than twenty minutes. No one commented on the length of his absence. Eddie wanted to but knew it would irritate Tommy. Everyone knew something had happened. The silence was heavy with unspoken thoughts. Tommy wouldn't have it any other way.

Chapter 17

Jack had left the farm the previous November. He was now rarely thought about and even more rarely mentioned. He had become the past. Dewi hadn't had a drink for a similar period and was knuckling down to regular work. The limited amount of arable land had been sown with black oats and a small area with turnips. He now looked well, his skin was clear and he had put on weight. Hilda, though still in charge of the finances, left the everyday running of the farm to Dewi. At least outwardly, her former criticism followed by her silent disparagement had now become a thing of the past. Inwardly she was not so sure but went to great trouble to hide her doubts.

Dewi was unrealistically hopeful, sure he had beaten the urge and when the subject was brought up, would say, 'See, I don't need a drink.' What really concerned Hilda was Swni Hopkins. No more than a short walk down the road and still drinking. The mystery was that he had lasted so long. Dewi never went in his hovel these days but always spoke to him if he saw him on the road. Swni was lonely so would hail anyone going past his house and attempt to engage them in conversation.

Being well known for his drunken habits, the young men viewed Swni with amusement and did not want to stop, the older ones spoke for as short a period as possible, feeling sorry for him. The few women who passed him were more dismissive. Hilda had a particular dislike for him. Thin, bent and with a lined face, he could only walk with the aid of two sticks. Never of a sturdy build, he was now positively emaciated. What everyone noticed was his sharp eyes which missed nothing, in spite of having the typical bloodshot appearance of the hardened alcoholic. Between them was his thin nose, heavily veined. He had the look of an aged hawk. He hadn't got long and everyone knew it.

Most tolerated him, although he was held up as an example not to be followed. Hilda had good reason to dislike him as he was the one person who could start Dewi drinking again. She was frightened of him, feeling a shiver run down her back when she was forced to pass him. When near him, she saw him as a snake in the grass and a poisonous one, at that. Had he lunged ten feet at her, bitten and poisoned her, she would not have been surprised. She knew deep down that it was quite irrational and when she reflected on her feelings towards him, she knew he was only a drunken old man near to death. Still, she tried to avoid going down the lane at times when she thought he would be there. However, he seemed to have an uncanny knack of always being there, almost as though he could read her thoughts.

Swni was aware of the effect he had on her, giving her his sly and knowing smile as she passed. 'In a hurry today Hilda?' he would volunteer to which she would mutter an inaudible reply. If she had looked round she would have seen a laugh of triumph on his face which had more than a touch of evil in it. Whenever Dewi had to pass near the lane to his cottage, she dreaded his return expecting the old problems to recur. Swni knew this and never missed a chance to offer Dewi a drink. Hilda lived in fear of him, secretly wishing he were dead. Surely in his condition it couldn't be long.

'No sign of Swni this week,' Dewi told her one day when he came home.

'Good,' was her response.

'Don't be like that, Hilda, he's a harmless old drunk.'

'Drunk but not harmless,' she said. 'He didn't do you much good.'

'Hilda, that's in the past.'

'A bad past.'

'Don't bring it up again. We're alright now. Aren't we?'

'Now, yes.' She didn't want to mention the drinking again.

Dewi had an hour to spare and, without Hilda seeing him, walked down the lane and towards the hovel. Opening the door, he saw several rats run away. Partly wrapped up in a blanket, was Swni, who must have been dead some time, the rats having eaten into his dead body. Dewi was sick on the spot. Recovering himself after a time, he looked at the body again, repelled yet fascinated. He did not know what to do. Almost without thinking, he ran for the door and then ran home as fast as he could.

'Swni's dead! He's dead!'

'You sure?' replied Hilda

'Yes sure, the rats have got him.'

A shudder went down Hilda's back as she imagined the scene. Even in death, Swni was still haunting her. Clutching onto her husband, she felt waves of irrational fear flow over her.

'We'll have to do something, you know,' he said.

'What?' She clung on to him even more tightly.

'You know. Fetch the doctor, get him buried.'

'Let the rats have him.'

'Don't be like that, Hilda.'

'I mean it. Will he haunt us forever?'

'He was alright.'

'No he wasn't, he was evil.'

'I've got to go.'

'Alright but come back quickly. You will, won't you?'

'I will. Don't worry.'

'Dewi, promise you won't have a drink.'

'Sure, I promise.'

'Get off then and be home tonight.' He nodded. In ten minutes the pony was harnessed into the trap and he was off at a trot for the town.

Five days later the farm cart was drawn up the lane towards the Tabernacle Chapel. The weather was fine and dry. The iron-wheeled cart grated over the stones as it was pulled by the old black horse, specially chosen for its slowness. There were about thirty mourners in the chapel, much less than the usual crowd at funerals. The coffin was brought in and the service commenced. Hymns were sung and the preacher spoke of Swni, dwelling briefly on his eccentric and feckless way of life. 'We all knew

Swni. He had his funny ways. Swni liked a glass too.' A smile went through the mourners. The final hymn was sung and the coffin buried around ten yards from Jack's mother's grave. Dewi attended. Hilda did not.

There wasn't a tear shed at the funeral. Swni's relations had long ceased to have anything to do with him but felt obligated to attend. For perhaps twenty minutes they remained in the grave yard, remembering details of his feckless life and idiosyncratic ways but ultimate harmlessness. Hilda would not have agreed.

The funeral cart had departed and perhaps seven or eight remained to talk, having nothing more pressing to do. Many had not seen one another for a month or two and they had matters to catch up on. The sun declined and the temperature fell.

'Don't want to stay here. Let's go to the Cross,' said one of them.

'Aye, only one way to see Swni off.'

Dewi knew he shouldn't go in and drink but the temptation was strong. He didn't have any money but he thought he'd have one and then go. Just one, that was all. They walked the short distance to the Cross, Dewi keeping behind as they walked and particularly as they entered the bar. Standing back, he waited to be asked. 'A pint?' He nodded in acceptance.

Grasping the glass, he drank more than half of it with one gulp which was noticed by the purchaser. 'Needed that one bad, Dewi.' He wiped his mouth with the sleeve of his jacket, smiling in agreement. 'Drink up and have another.'

'First since last year,' he almost gasped in relief as he downed the remainder at one gulp.

'Same again,' said his beneficiary to the landlady. He would not get drunk, he thought. These two pints would be all he would have. Lingering over this glass he thought to himself, that's better. I can handle a pint or two and I'm here with friends. Why shouldn't I be here? Aren't I entitled to a pint or two at the weekend and a chat with friends? A third pint was placed in front of him and was consumed. The pleasure of the first two pints had turned into a knowledge that he was not in control of himself.

171

The glasses kept coming and he kept drinking.

So drunk was he that he had to be taken home in a trap. It was only nine o'clock as the pony trotted into the yard, getting as near as possible to the back door in the approaching dusk. Opening the back door of the cart, his far from sober comrades-in-alcohol got out and lifted Dewi, an arm round the shoulder of each, with a look of drunken amusement on their faces as they carried their burden. Staggering as they went, they arrived slightly out of breath at the back door. Dewi drifted in and out of consciousness and, when he did try to speak, could only manage inebriated gibberish. They knocked at the door, losing hold of Dewi then having to grab him to prevent him falling over.

The door was opened almost immediately by Hilda who lost her temper in a manner which none but Dewi had seen before and he only rarely.

'You damned fools, getting him drunk. Bloody stupid fools.' This immediately sobered up his companions. Their tipsy grins vanished from their faces in a flash as they looked at her for her next reaction.

'Getting him drunk!' She hit one hard with the palm of her hand and then repeated, 'getting him drunk,' in a voice filled with fury. Her temper grew even more ferocious. 'Getting him bloody drunk. What do you mean by it?'

The two inebriates were by now quite sober and rational. Dewi sobered up as far as he was able, making efforts to stand up, but when his supporters released their hold on him, he fell to the ground. They were prevented from picking him up by the rain of hysterical kicking which Hilda directed towards her husband on the floor. The men tried to prevent her from doing so without success and were rewarded for their efforts by having the blows directed towards them. She kicked and hit out at them as they retreated from her and Dewi, who was now making unsuccessful efforts to stand.

The two men were sober and active enough to get out of her range to which she responded by redirecting her blows towards her husband. They advanced again, trying to protect Dewi, by

172

which time her anger had become largely spent. The blows and the anger in Hilda's voice had now made him aware what was going on. He eventually succeeded in getting to his feet, but was still swaying badly.

His friends didn't desert him, saying, 'We got to get him in bed missus.'

'In there,' she directed them.

In the kitchen, still holding him, they asked, 'Where now?' Walking towards the cupboard under the stairs, Hilda opened the door and pointed inside. The blankets were still in it from the previous time he had been made to sleep there. Never again would he be allowed to return to her bed. It was a large cupboard and they put him in gently, making efforts to tuck him in and make him comfortable. Hilda interrupted them, 'None of that. Just put him in.' They obeyed her instruction. 'Now go. You've done a good day's work for this family!'

They walked to the back door saying, 'Goodbye Hilda,' as they went, to which she responded by slamming the door behind them. They got in the cart stone cold sober and drove home. Hardly out of the yard, one said to another, 'We've put our foot in it,' to which the other responded, 'I think we have.'

'A man's got to have a drink now and then. He hadn't had a drink since last year.'

'I know.'

'Why shouldn't he get drunk now and then? I do.'

'And me.'

'Course Dewi makes a fool of himself when he has a drink.'

'Does he?'

'Lost all that money when he was robbed. Drunk then.'

'Just unlucky.'

'He was getting drunk with Swni you know. Didn't do a stroke for years.'

'Swni's dead now. Won't have any more temptation. We were only saying goodbye to him.'

'Dewi'll be alright now.'

173

'I hope so. It's petticoat rule there you know. I wouldn't want to be him.'

'Nor me.'

They drove the rest of the way home silently and reflectively and went straight to bed, never mentioning to anyone what had occurred to them all that night.

Like many a drunk before him, Dewi did not lie in bed but got up before his wife. Going outside he washed his face and drank some cold water. Walking around in the approaching dawn, stamping his feet and getting fresh air into his lungs, he felt the headache begin to disperse. Vague recollections about what had happened the previous evening drifted into his mind, as well as the pain from the numerous kicks Hilda had given him. He wasn't clear what had happened but it was coming into his mind bit by bit. Yes, she had shouted. Yes, she had kicked him. It was beginning to come back.

He heard the back door open. 'Here, I want to see you,' she commanded. There was no alternative, he had to go. Get it over with as soon as possible. She looked at him in a direct and demanding manner. 'What have you got to say for yourself?'

'I had a drink.'

'A drink! You were roaring drunk.'

'Haven't had a drink since last year. A man's got to have a drink.'

'Drink? You must have drunk the pub dry.'

'Saying goodbye to Swni.'

'Don't mention that man to me. Evil old devil. Glad he's dead.'

'Don't say that Hilda. He was alright. Decent old boy.'

'He never did us any good. He's dead and still haunting us.'

'Don't be like that about him.'

'I will be like that about him. He kept you drunk for years and you're drunk again.'

'Just once in six months. A man's got to have a drink.'

'When you drink you make a fool of yourself. Lost the

gold, remember? Didn't do a stroke for years. Always drinking with Swni.'

'You were nagging me all the time.'

'I haven't been nagging you for six months and you're drunk again.'

'It won't happen again, Hilda. Promise.'

'You've run out of chances, good boy. Back in the cupboard it is for you,' she answered with relish. He knew he couldn't argue.

Life reverted to the old state of open hostility, though on this occasion he did not drink regularly and did his best on the farm. It was difficult in the extreme. She did not want to lose control of the farm and therefore controlled him with a degree of rigidity which verged on the obsessional. Dewi felt he was no more than a horse brought out to work at the mistress's bidding. When she looked at him it was with a cold disapproving look and more often than not only to issue orders. No mutual communication now ever took place between them. He almost never left the farm and hardly talked to a soul. When anyone passed by, he almost fell upon them like a thirsty man offered a drink of water. If Hilda saw this taking place, she would shout from the house that he was needed for some pointless task. Always obeying, he was now a quite beaten man. This was well known to his neighbours, some of whom were amused, others feeling pity. All said he would have to stand up to her. He never did.

Stealing money one day from the house, Dewi went to the Cross on a busy day and met some of his old friends. Able to buy at least one round of drinks, and feeling like a man once again, he revelled in the talk. He had to put up with a certain amount of gentle teasing from some of the young men. 'Got away from the foreman.' and similar remarks were directed at him, to which he returned a weak smile. These were soon forgotten as the talk changed direction. With two pints inside him he became gregarious, discussed old times and times not so old, enjoying himself as he had not done in years. Swni had been a drinking mate but he had always been repeating himself and was tedious

175

company. This was different. I must do this more often, he thought. Trying to moderate his intake, he knew that he would have to walk home and face Hilda eventually. He prolonged his stay to avoid the confrontation and, by the time he left the bar, his friends doubted his ability to make it home.

'You alright Dewi?' he heard from several directions as he staggered out. Waving an impotent hand, he signalled his capability of walking. 'Alright,' he mumbled.

As he departed, someone chirped up, 'He'll be in trouble at home.' Everyone agreed.

Staggering over the road, he looked for somewhere to lie down. It was now dark. Finding a shed with little in it, he lay down on the floor. Hard and cold, it was initially uncomfortable but drink-induced sleep soon took over.

Hilda had been unaware of his absence, thinking he was working on the farm. The light failed, she noticed her money missing and knew he was drinking. By now she didn't care and waited for his return, whenever that would be.

He did return next morning, soon after dawn, looking ill and shivering with cold. No verbal criticism was offered, only cold rejection which seemed worse than the quarrels. Cold hate and disapproval administered with a silent relish. Breakfast given to him silently and coldly. He didn't speak, knowing she would not reply. Working on the farm that day he was overcome with a degree of depression he had never known before. Not returning for the midday meal, he worked on, lost in his black thoughts. Just before dusk he returned to the farm building, entered the lavatory and hung himself. Hilda found him next morning.

Chapter 18

At around seven o'clock in the morning the drove was on the move from Llandeusant. They had all had a full day's rest in preparation for the journey to Hereford or Gloucester. All except Jack who hadn't had a moment's peace and thought constantly of Rosie. He fantasised about the smell, the look, the sensuality of their time together. Nothing tactile had ever been a part of his life before. Once he had got up in the middle of the night, walked to her house, knocked, received no reply and walked in to find it empty. Had she disappeared? Was she with someone else? Did she no longer want him? He went back to bed remaining awake for some hours with these thoughts going through his mind. Towards dawn he fell into a deep sleep and for the first time in years had to be roused to get up. The thoughts of Rosie came back to him and remained with him all day. He felt awkward, knowing he was not giving the drove the attention he should and heard Tommy say, 'You're not with us today.'

'Just thinking,' was his reply. Giving his attention to his work for some time, his far away look returned and he was lost in thoughts of the future. How soon would these cattle be sold and how soon could he get back to Rosie? It was a day without problems. The stock moved as a black mass and at a constant speed filling the roads as they moved along them. The decision would have to be made today. Gloucester or Hereford? No returning drovers had passed them so far. By midday that had changed and they passed three, two on horseback and one walking. Tommy knew them all. Letting the drove go on, he stopped to talk to them.

They greeted one another in a formal and quite cautious manner. 'Sell them all?' volunteered Tommy.

'Yes, all.'

'What's the trade like?'

'Not good. Not good at all.'

'Hereford or Gloucester?' Tommy enquired.

'Gloucester.'

'Sell outside or in the market?'

'Outside. Poor trade though, we'll make no money on this drove. Where you taking yours?'

'Hereford probably.' The drove was by now two hundred yards on. They waved their sticks at one another and moved on.

The drovers were all in competition with one another. No one wanted to lie but they certainly did not tell one another the full facts. If the beasts had been sold outside the market they certainly would not have made a loss; probably a good profit. No one sold outside at a loss, knowing they might get more in the market. He thought Gloucester presented the best prices, but over the years he had done better in Hereford. Where would he go?

Jack, anxious to know where they were going, asked Tommy. 'The first man to show me a pound a head profit, lad.' Jack hadn't got cattle in mind, only Rosie, and he knew by now that Hereford would be a shorter journey and therefore pay less but he would make any sacrifice for her. In two or three days he would have been paid off and making his way back to her. He couldn't wait but knew he had to. Once the money was in his hand, he would buy her present and be off like the wind. He was in no doubt he would be able to find his own way back.

The night was spent outside Brecon. Eddie was certain they were going to Hereford and mentioned this as an aside to Jack. He was only guessing but for years he had thought he could read Tommy's mind and frequently did. Tommy had given it a great deal of thought. Common sense told him to go to Gloucester. The trade sounded good and profits would be made. However, trade could change in the course of an hour and change drastically in that time. He thought prices would be high there but it was a matter of luck. He had had most luck over the years in Hereford and felt more comfortable there. There was no news from that market and no reason why he should go there, but he was working from intuition. Hereford it would be, he decided.

Rising early, they soon reached the outskirts of Hereford. Two other droves were in sight, all black and from central Wales. Perhaps they numbered seven hundred in all. Not liking this, he knew he would have to accept the first offer which returned a decent profit. The last thing he wanted was for his cattle to remain unsold and have to find keep for them for several weeks. Within two miles of the city, buyers came out on horseback, two of which he knew. There was hope. He wanted a sale quickly, not wanting to spend tomorrow in the market.

The two buyers rode towards him and exchanged formal pleasantries. Riding each side of him they carried on for perhaps fifty yards not wanting to start the conversation which each thought would put them at a disadvantage. The younger one was impatient and could wait no longer.

'For sale, Tommy?'

'Of course.'

The young man already thought he was being made to look too eager but couldn't stop. 'How many?'

'Two hundred and twelve. All sound.'

They continued riding in silence for a further few minutes. Each was weighing the other up. The two buyers, though trading independently, had a mutual understanding that they would not tread on one another's toes. Eager to buy and impatient at the prospect of the deal, he said, 'What you asking?'

'What'll you give me?'

'What you asking?' the buyer tried again. Tommy did not reply. Always a man of few words, he knew silence was a good ploy in trading with an eager youngster.

The young man was getting impatient and the older buyer became an observer in the trade, smiling to himself. This man will learn, he thought, if he doesn't go bust in the process. Tommy made sure his own amusement did not become apparent. The young man was becoming slightly flustered, feeling his face go red, which made him all the more impatient and anxious to complete the deal. The older buyer, seeing that the other droves

179

had dealers approaching them, knew they would have to act quickly and said, 'Well Tommy, what's the price?'

'Eleven pounds.'

'You can do better than that Tommy.'

'What you offering?'

'Ten pounds.' The younger man now felt out of it which made him annoyed. He wanted to bid over his fellow dealer's head but knew he couldn't. He became impatient inside and frustrated at being sidelined. Tommy gave a look of shocked amusement at the offer. 'They cost me that in Pembrokeshire good boy. Drive'em up here for charity!' he declared, which of course was not true.

'Guineas then,' the dealer replied.

Tommy ran through the figures in his head. He would make a good profit but not a pound a head. Could he try for more? 'And two more shillings?'

There was a short silence while the other dealer considered the offer. Could he give him the final challenge? Yes he could. 'That's my last offer.' Again there was a short silence while the dealer considered the proposition, eventually putting his hand out to shake on the deal. Anxious to be on the way home, Tommy said, 'Will you take them now?' The dealer nodded in agreement, adding, 'I want the boy to stay with the drove till we get them penned.'

'How long for?'

'Half a day.' Tommy nodded without even looking at Jack.

The men dismounted to bring the transaction to a close; the animals were counted, the arithmetic completed and the cheque was signed leaning on the saddle of Tommy's pony. Before remounting he motioned to Jack.

'Six days at one and thruppence and that includes today when you'll be with them. If they want you for more you'll have to get them to pay you. Make your own way home in four days and there's sixpence a day for lodgings. Nine shillings and sixpence. Be home in a week and there'll be more work going.'

Never before had Jack heard Tommy say so much.

Tommy had done well but not as well as he had hoped. He was very tired and anxious to get a rest. Reflecting on what had happened, he was relieved that his demand for the last two shillings had been met. Had they refused to pay this last addition, he might still be with the drove, searching for a deal. Such ploys didn't always work. Briefly he thought of Jack and felt a little guilty at leaving him to get home alone, but he knew that he was tough and resourceful enough to make it on his own. Tommy rode off to find a bed somewhere.

Jack remained with the drove for two more hours, getting them through a built-up area and into pens for whatever fate awaited them. Leaving them, he wandered round the city with more than a pound and ten shillings on him and with Rosie now constantly on his mind. The shops were closed and he would have to stay overnight but he didn't know where. He went window shopping, never having been to a city before and never having seen such a range of goods on sale. Men's clothes, women's clothes, ironmongers, butchers, bakers and offices whose names he could not read.

He was fascinated by all the well dressed people and also by what looked like tramps begging on the street, some without a leg or an arm. Who were these people? They looked more depressed and dirty than anyone he had ever seen before. All of them were painfully thin with a hangdog look on their faces, pleading for a penny. Where had they come from? There were none in Narberth. Even Swni who was pitifully thin had a better life than these people. They had a look of hopeless, ground-down lethargy. How did they get in this condition? The Irish from the famine in Narberth did not look this bad.

He walked on, fascinated by all that was new. Dusk was approaching and he knew he had to find a lodging house. Going into one of the taverns, he looked around. Listening for a welsh accent, he failed to hear one. A man with an empty glass and slightly unsteady on his feet moved towards him.

'From Wales, Taff?'

'Yes.' How did he know he was from Wales?

'Which part'?

'Pembroke.'

'Lots of rain there.' Jack didn't answer. The man sidled up to him and lowered his voice, saying, 'Got a spare copper or two. Get me a beer?'

Jack felt in his pocket for his hard-earned money, all in silver. He didn't want to reply and certainly didn't want to buy beer for a drunk. He had met many in his life and had come to despise them. However he wanted to know how the man knew he was a Welsh drover, even before he had spoken to him.

'How d'you know I'm Welsh?'

The drinker laughed into his empty glass. 'Boy, you look like one, smell like one and dress like one.'

Jack made for the door, then continued walking down the street, taking in the remarks he had just heard. He decided to look for a Welsh drover and wasn't long in finding one, not much older than himself. Walking up to him, he didn't know quite what to say but volunteered, 'You with the cattle trade?'

'Of course,' he replied, through a haze of beer fumes. 'Where you drinking?'

'I'm not,' replied Jack.

'Come with me,' the Welshman replied, grabbing his arm and propelling him along.

'Where you staying?' Jack asked him.

'Where we're going.' His pace became faster. 'All Taffs there. Good crowd.'

They walked to a less crowded part of town, coming eventually to a tavern with a name he was unable to read but knew was Welsh.

His new found companion immediately bought him a drink which he sipped, moving away from him at the same time. He searched the room for someone to question, finding a man not much younger than Tommy. The man was not talking to anyone and looked as though he didn't want to, appearing vaguely ill at ease in this gregarious company. He held his glass but didn't sip from it. From his appearance he was a drover. 'Is there a place to stay tonight?' Jack enquired of him.

The older man looked at him for a second or two, picking up on the fact that here was a drover new to Hereford, 'Stay here for fivepence or two doors down for fourpence.' He paused before adding, 'In town for the first time?'

'Yes,' Jack said, thinking, is it that obvious?

'Stay here. You could get robbed down the street. Worth the extra penny here.'

'Who do I see?'

'Missus in the back.'

'Which way?' He was shown where.

'Safer here. Not often you get thieving. They're all Welsh boys in the cattle trade. A good crowd really. They drink a bit though.'

'When can you go up? Anytime?' The man nodded in reply.

Looking around the bar, Jack found he didn't know a soul but could see that they were dressed differently from the others in Hereford. Some wore the large felt hats, others had taken them off. Yes, there was a smell about them which he had never noticed before. Was that why Rosie had said to him, 'Get back to those bloody cattle drovers?' Once Rosie had come into his mind, he couldn't stop thinking about her. Could he buy her a brooch and get to Llandeusant by the following night? He would try.

He was in bed by nine, taking his boots off and sleeping in all his clothes with his hands in his pockets to safeguard his money. Woken several times by noisy drunks getting into bed, he slept in a room which accommodated eight. Up at first light and before anyone else, he knew he had a vigorous day ahead which his fellow sleepers would not face. Walking through the town, he looked into the shop windows for a gift for Rosie. He wanted a brooch and a brightly coloured one. At last he found what he wanted but had to wait till the shop opened. Impatient at this unnecessary delay, he walked to and fro along the street till nine

183

o'clock, sometimes looking at himself in the shop windows and smiling.

After what seemed an age the shop opened. He walked straight in, waiting for the girl to take her place behind the counter. 'That brooch,' he pointed, 'How much?'

She picked it up and showed it to him. He held it in his large, rough and far from clean hand, covered in calluses from the hard manual work he did. He was mesmerised and looked at it for several minutes. It was a silver metal with a red and a yellow stone mounted in it. The girl serving him was curious and wanted to know who it was for.

'For your girl friend?' she asked gently.

Looking up as though roused from sleep, he said, 'Yes,' giving her a wan smile.

'How much?' he asked.

'Seven and six. Do you want it?'

'Yes.'

'Do you want it wrapped?'

'Yes, please.'

Giving him the package she said, 'That'll be seven and six.' He fumbled and gave her eight shillings. In order to delay matters, she counted the change slowly.

'What's her name?'

'Rosie.'

'That's a nice name. When you going to give it her?'

'Tonight.'

'Think she'll like it?'

'I hope so.'

'If she doesn't, come back and give it to me.' First love, she thought to herself. Lucky girl with that great big rough drover. I hope she appreciates him.

By ten minutes past nine he had set off almost at a run. Within an hour he had started to pace himself, walking about four miles an hour. With one object in mind, he had tunnel vision. Rosie was uppermost in his mind; she was a goal to be reached as fast as possible. Clyro by early afternoon, Brecon by

184

late afternoon, Rosie by night fall. He pressed on, not slackening his pace. Not aware that he hadn't eaten that day, thinking only of his destination and how soon he could get there.

Arriving at the village at dusk, he knocked on her door. She answered, giving him a warm and sensual smile. 'You've been quick, big boy.' He stood on the doorstep. Having felt full of expectation all day, he now felt awkward, gauche and blushed slightly. Rosie gave him her all too familiar searching look and he blushed even more. How long could she go on teasing him? It was such fun, she thought, and wasn't he handsome?

Jack tried to speak but the words would not come out. Rosie was more confident. 'Well big boy, come in. Shut the door behind you. The neighbours might talk.'

The children were in the back room making a noise. He stood there, still unable to talk, only being able to hold her amorous glances for a moment. Almost without knowing what was happening, he felt the brooch in his pocket. Taking it out, he gave it to her. 'For you, Rosie.'

Taking the wrapped parcel from him, she could tell it was a brooch and gave it back to him with both hands lingering as she touched his own hand. A shiver of erotic excitement went down his spine. He made a move to put his arms around her which she repelled at lightning speed, whilst also giving him another of her inviting glances. The brooch had dropped to the floor. 'Jack ....patience...Give me that tonight.'

He picked the packet up and resumed his original stance, feeling awkward once more. She gave him a softer look now and he noticed a tear run down each cheek.

Feeling suddenly maternal towards him, she asked, 'Have you eaten?'

'No. Not just now.'

'When did you eat last?'

'Not had anything for a while.'

'When was that?'

'Last night.'

'Man, you must be starving. Sit down,' she said, pointing

to an upright chair.

He sat down. There was a pot of cawl heating over the fire. When it came to simmer she ladled a steaming plateful into a bowl and said, 'Get that down you.' He wolfed it down like a starving man. Without asking she gave him another bowlful which was consumed a little more slowly. 'Another?' she asked. He shook his head as he now felt satisfied.

'That's better,' he managed to say, with a smile.

'Who do you live with, Jack?'

'At Tommy's place.'

'Where's that?'

'Narberth. You know, West Wales.'

'Not with your mother?'

'Don't have a mother.'

'Dead?'

'Yes, died when I was six.'

'No father?'

'Never seen him.'

'Who brought you up?'

'Dewi and Hilda took me in. Left there a while back. With Tommy now.'

'Tommy have a wife?'

'No, he lives in the Saddler's.'

'Any family of your own?'

'Two sisters in service. See them maybe once a year.'

She thought to herself, this lad is all on his own and making a good job of it. Fifteen, all alone in the world and walked forty miles to see Rosie. He even brought a present.

'Go to the tavern, Jack?'

'Only when I have to.'

'Do you like beer?'

'No not at all.'

'Not many like you. I'll get the children to bed in a short while.'

She busied herself with the children, feeding them and getting them to bed. Jack was on her mind all the while. On the one

186

hand, she felt maternal but also admired his toughness of spirit and was excited by him as a man. She was quite confused in the knowledge she had gained about him, wishing she had not asked so many questions. One thing was sure; he was an innocent where women were concerned. Whether it was to be her or another, he wouldn't remain so for long. She sat down saying, 'They'll be fast asleep in half an hour.'

He moved to put his arms around her. Without looking, she resisted him. 'Wait,' he heard her say almost aggressively. He could smell the scent of her hair which aroused him even more than he was already. She continued to look away from him, appearing almost annoyed but in fact listening for the children. They did nothing for what seemed an age. Getting up finally, she walked to where the children were sleeping to satisfy herself that they were soundly asleep.

When she returned, she gave him a smile that he would never forget as long as he lived. 'You can give me that present now,' she murmured. He did so, then hurriedly and rather clumsily put his arms around her, kissing her on the cheek, the mouth and then burying himself in her neck. Again she pushed him back, but with a smile. She looked into his eyes, commanding his attention, 'Jack. Listen to Rosie. If you want to make Rosie happy, take your time. We have all the time in the world.'

Quite overcome by what had happened, he heard the words come out, 'Rosie I love you,' not knowing where they had come from.

'Jack, don't say that to me.' She looked at him, with tears in her eyes, hugging him tightly; burying herself in his arms. This went on for some minutes. She shook with emotion when she eventually released him and, through even more tears, said, 'You lovely boy,' then kissed him long and hard. 'Let's have a look at this present.' She opened the package and stared at the brooch for a few seconds before pinning it onto her dress and asking, 'Does it look good?'

'Very good.'

'Looks better than that. It's wonderful.'

'Wonderful,' he repeated to himself.

Again she hugged him, feeling his erection against her. She wanted this to go on but knew she would not be able to hold him off for long. Looking him in the face, she again kissed him. Quickly she frisked him between the legs, gave him a knowing smile and pointed to the bedroom with a movement of her head. 'That's what you want,' she whispered. Leading him in by the hand, they were naked and in one another's arms in a flash.

She took hold of his right hand, kissed it and said 'Jack…..
listen to Rosie…slowly.' She released his hand and took hold of him between the legs again. 'All for Rosie.' She remained smiling in her warm knowing way. 'You're as stiff as a poker and nearly as big.'

He became eager and tried to mount her. After some inexperienced fumbling, he managed to penetrate her in a clumsy and awkward manner made all the more difficult by his impatience. He started to move but in a second or two it was all over. He knew it was not right, but she had never expected anything else. 'You naughty boy, you'll give me a baby,' she said teasingly. He let out a large moan followed by a soft whimper and sobbing. She held him tightly while he continued to cry. It was the first and last time in his life he would ever do so. 'You're in Rosie's arms. You'll be alright.' She repeated it several times until he calmed down. 'No more crying now Jack. No more crying.' He lay in her arms, wanting to say sorry but didn't. Never in his life had he ever felt more comfortable, more secure or closer to anyone. Half awake, half asleep, he had no idea how long it went on. She whispered in his ear, 'Turn over.' He did so. She put her arm around him, holding him between the legs all night, feeling his erection wax and wane till the all too brief night slipped into dawn. She nudged him awake.

He turned towards her, she continuing to hold him. 'Move further down the bed. That's right. Your feet against the footboard.'

She slipped him into her. 'Jack, slowly. Use the foot board.

188

Slowly.' He did as he was told. 'That's better. Slowly…..Slowly.' They started to thrust in unison with one another. He started to speed up. Again she said, 'Slow down….that's right. You're making Rosie very happy. Slowly.' He continued to thrust into her, feeling the power and sensuality of his movements which were in harmony with hers. How long this lasted he had no idea.

The children were starting to stir. 'Quickly now,' she urged him. A second or two more and it was all over. So different from last night. He felt he had made amends. She grabbed him for the few remaining seconds, hugging him hard. 'Get up now,' she commanded.

They were up only seconds before the children appeared. Again he hung about the kitchen, feeling awkward. They all had breakfast. He washed and got ready for work as he had done every day of his life. Why should this day be any different? Sending the children out on a trivial errand, she held him by the elbows, 'Jack, I know you've got to get back to those bloody drovers, but remember when you come this way, you always come and see Rosie. Understand?' He smiled in a boyish way and went red again. 'I'll come to see you always. Always, Rosie.' She smiled back at him.

'Now go away before I break down and cry. Go on, get out quick.' He kissed her once more and walked away towards Llandeilo without looking back. She watched him go with her eyes moist. When he was out of sight, she returned indoors and looked at the brooch.

In the village the tongues were wagging. At it again and him so young!

Chapter 19

It was the spring of 1852; a time of change for the drovers. All the talk was of the railway to Carmarthen. How would it change their lives? Would the long droves continue or would they just drive the cattle to Carmarthen, load them and return? One thing was sure; change would occur. The old were apprehensive, the young more welcoming. Fewer men would be employed if the transition to the railways was totally taken up. In other parts of the country this change had been slow and the old ways had continued alongside it. Tommy was worried but went to great pains to hide the fact. Would this drove be his last? His needs were limited and always had been but would he have enough to survive? The possibility of the workhouse loomed up before him. He wouldn't be the first cattle drover to end his days in such a place. He became depressed. A long life of trading, much of it in public, had taught him to keep his feelings to himself. An inscrutable exterior hid a mind always active, juggling with prices, numbers, places, fellow traders, farmers and their personalities. He feared above all failure and penury. Margins were always tight, the edge of the abyss never far away. A man of few words, which was part of his defence. Now that the end of his droving life was in sight, he felt able to talk to Jack who was by his side waiting for the last journey out.

Jack was now much taller than when he had first engaged him. Manhood had arrived. His mop of curly fair hair, atop his fine physique and above average height was unusual in a land of shorter stature and darker features. He stood out. He made many a heart flutter, but remained loyal to Rosie, in spite of her wandering affections of which he seemed to be totally unaware. Whenever he was near, she seemed to have a sixth sense and repelled all other advances. Those wishing to lay claim to her affections always kept well clear of Jack, being no match for his aggression. He seemed mesmerised by Rosie, possibly loving her more for the streak of mother in her, to which he responded so eagerly. They understood one another. In spite of his worldly exterior there was more than a touch of innocence about him. Only Rosie knew this and kept it to herself. That was part of his charm. Her shabby cottage, which was little more than a hovel, was his real home, where he felt comfortable, where he was loved. Loving Rosie, her easy manner and their ability to communicate with one another, made him feel understood in a way he had never felt before. He also supported her with what limited money he had.

'Well Jack. The end's in sight for our trade,' Tommy remarked.

'Don't say that.'

'It's true. True.'

'Why, Tommy?'

'Railways'll change every thing.'

'Not straight away, surely?' asked jack

'Could be. We don't know yet. Railways could be a lot cheaper.'

'Not cheaper than us driving them along the roads? Never!'

'Railway can take'em to London in half a day and we take ten, twelve days. They're clever, those men. They haven't spent all this money for nothing. It's the new thing. Be all over the country soon.' Tommy was sounding despondent.

'Never.'

'Not in my lifetime but in yours.'

Tommy's remarks were beginning to sink in. Jack had seen the railways but never thought how they would affect his life.

'For hundreds of years, perhaps a thousand, we've been droving cattle east. The end's in sight, boy. The end's in sight.'

'You sure?'

'Sure lad. You've got to move on. In ten days you won't have a job with me. I'm too old to change. You aren't. You've got to move on and now.'

It was beginning to dawn on Jack that he would have to find another life but where? His mind ranged over all the places he had been. He didn't like the built up areas; at heart he was a country boy. He hoped an opportunity would present itself.

'When we sell the cattle in the holding field I won't have a job with you?'

'Correct,' said Tommy, 'but you're young and strong. You'll get work alright.'

'What'll you do, Tommy?' asked Jack

'Sit back here and live on my pennies.'

'You've got plenty of those.'

'Not as much as you think.'

'You're the richest drover in Pembrokeshire.'

He shook his head 'Margins have always been small and on one in four droves I take a loss.' He paused for a moment. Jack felt Tommy was being more revealing than he had ever been before. Perhaps he was lowering his guard at the end of his trading life. 'I'm not rich. Few drovers are. They handle a lot of money but the margins are small. It's an overcrowded profession. Cut-throat. You've seen that.'

Jack agreed and thought of the tactics employed by the drovers. Each one was always trying to get an advantage over another; trying to sell a lame animal, passing on information of low prices ahead in order to buy cheap now. Everything that was heard had to be taken with a pinch of salt. Constant alertness was part of the trade. Perhaps Tommy wasn't as well off as everyone said.

'Will you miss the droving, Tommy?'

'No, not really. Beginning to feel my age. Getting a bit breathless now.'

'Stay on the pony then.'

'You still have to walk. The weather gets me too. Just don't want another soaking.'

Jack was beginning to get some idea of ageing. He couldn't contemplate it happening to him. Tommy was speaking out in a way he had never done before and he was beginning to feel some sympathy for him. It felt almost as though they were father and son which was an unaccustomed situation. Previously there had been an understanding and a silent mutual regard and trust but communication was by gesture and look rather than by word. Speaking in depth like this seemed to bring them closer.

'What will Eddie do, Tommy?'

'He'll have to take his chance like us all.'

'Farm servant, maybe?'

'Too old for that. Can't keep up with the younger men any more.'

'What'll he do?'

'He'll find something.'

'But what?'

Tommy didn't reply. He knew there was no answer. Jack had come to the same conclusion. They remained silent for perhaps a quarter of an hour. Jack wanted the conversation to go on but didn't know when to break the silence. Eventually and hardly realising he had spoken, he said, 'Eddie's going to miss his beer.'

'If he doesn't watch it, drink'll be his downfall.' Jack didn't know how to respond to this and remained silent. 'More men have been ruined by beer than anything else.' Jack nodded his agreement. 'It's been the ruination of hundreds, thousands perhaps,' Tommy continued. He was vehement on this point. He had never expressed this view so strongly before, but it was quite obvious that he despised and dismissed drinkers. Why had he employed Eddie so long? One thing was sure; he would not be giving Eddie handouts when they parted company. He had known that Tommy didn't like Eddie's drinking but had never realised he felt so strongly about it. It was part of Tommy's secretive personality. 'See you don't drink, lad.'

'I don't like it much. The taste or the effect,' Jack reassured him.

'Good for you, keep it up. Never get anywhere if you drink.'

They relapsed into silence for a while. Jack was curious about Tommy's life. Tommy was a non drinker yet he lived in a tavern. He had never married; always felt awkward in emotional matters;

193

liked his own company.

'Tommy. You live in a tavern and yet you don't drink.'

'Right. Been there for years. Saddler's is a good place to do business. Good as any market. Nellie's my agent and unpaid.'

'Nellie's good.'

'The best. Absolutely reliable.'

Jack thought of the way she had acted during Dewi's robbery and had to agree.

'If you're in business you have to have one or two people you can trust. You're one of them and they're not very thick on the ground.'

Never before had Jack received such a compliment. Such praise came to him like a bolt from the blue. Lost for words, he said nothing but thought to himself that all the cold, wet, long days, lost animals to be found, conflict with other drovers and sleepless nights had not been in vain. So Tommy thinks that much of me?

His mind returned to the immediate future. He knew he would be looking for work in ten days. They didn't yet know where the drove was going. Tommy would try and make it a good one as it was his last. Jack was anxious to get moving. If he had to make another life the sooner he faced the challenge the better. 'When you leaving Tommy?'

'In two or three days. I'd like another fifty before I leave'.'

'Got your eye on any?'

'Some, but not that number. May have to leave with what I've got. One hundred and ninety is a small drove.'

'Does Eddie know it's the last?'

'Not yet. I'll tell him on the way.'

The last drove left with the addition of no more animals. No one else knew it was the last but many suspected. Eddie thought they would go on for ever.

At the end of the first day, everyone was glad of a rest. The beasts were fed, watered and lying down. The men settled down for the night. Outwardly everyone seemed at peace. Jack thought about Rosie and Eddie about drink. Tommy was sitting alone

194

outside his lodgings when Eddie passed.

'Here, Eddie,' he called out. Eddie walked towards his master.

'Sit down. I've got something to tell you.' There was something ominous about the way Tommy addressed him. He'd never been asked to sit down by Tommy to hear what he had to say. Tommy almost always communicated by gesture and perhaps a word or two. Sometimes he spoke less than half a dozen words a day. Eddie could tell what Tommy had in mind by looking at him. Words were largely unnecessary.

'Sit down boy.' He was hardly a boy having been with him more than twenty years. There was an awkward silence between them which lasted a minute or two. 'Eddie, this is the last drove. There'll be no more after this.'

'I don't believe it! You won't have another?'

'No this is the last.'

'I can't believe it.'

'I'm getting old. Get breathless. Don't want another soaking; I've had too many of those.'

'You're not old Tommy.'

'Fifty three is old in this trade. I'm going for sure. What'll you do Eddie?'

'Don't know. Have to find something. Stay droving I suppose. Does Jack know?'

'Yes.'

'What's he going to do?'

'Ask Jack. Moving on I suppose.'

'Will he stay with the drovers?'

'Not if he's got any sense and he's got plenty of that.' Eddie felt he was being made to look inferior by his, soon to be, former employer.

'Why d'you say that?'

'The drovers are finished. The railways are the future.' It had never occurred to Eddie that the railways would undermine his employment. Tommy had magical powers. Tommy could overcome anything. Then he realised Tommy would soon no longer be his guardian angel. He wouldn't meet another Tommy and he knew it.

It took some time for it to sink into Eddie's mind that he would have to find an alternative employer. For the rest of the night he seemed to be in a daze, looking ahead but not seeing what was in front of him. On one occasion he walked into an animal without knowing it was there. Eventually he spoke to Jack.

'Tommy's finishing. When did he tell you?'

'Just now.'

'What you going to do Jack, stay in Narberth?'

'No. Move on to wherever I can get work.'

'England or Wales?'

'I'll start looking when this drove is sold.'

'Will you go droving again?'

'No. It's finished. Tommy says so.'

'What'll you do?'

'Find work,' he replied impatiently, signalling the end of the conversation.

The drove went well for the next two days in good weather. They were now travelling between Llandeilo and Llandeusant. The three of them had different expectations. For Tommy, a days rest; for Eddie, beer and, for Jack, Rosie. They made an early start but the weather turned wet, driving in behind them from the south west. It came down in sheets, drenching them from head to foot. Their heads were bowed as they walked on. The cattle seemed to be in the same frame of mind, putting one foot in front of another looking neither to right nor left, their heads as bowed as their drivers. For seven hours it continued almost without respite as they walked along the tracks running in water, tripping over the stones which had been dislodged. They had no choice but to continue. One thing was certain; when the cattle were driven into the holding field they would not stray far.

Few words were spoken. They had made the journey many times before. Words were unnecessary. Tommy seemed to be in a world of his own, oblivious to all around him. The journey could not be hurried; it was a matter of covering the miles and enduring the rain. Their pace slowed as they reached the higher ground. Had it been a fine day, they would by now have seen the Carmarthen Vans rising before them. The rain prevented this and all they could see was the head of the drove and that not very clearly. The noise from the rain falling and the tramp of feet over the rough road was all that could be heard. Gradually the landmarks of the journey came and went. Their capes and hats clung to them even more closely as the rain soaked through them and onto the ground. It was not possible to become wetter. After what seemed an age, the Drovers' Arms came in sight at which time the rain eased, a patch of sunlight appearing intermittently through fast moving cloud.

Tommy was, by now, shivering. He had dreaded being caught in another rainstorm and now it had happened again. Giving the reins of his pony to Eddie, he walked into the tavern without saying a word to either of them.

'Got to get to bed,' he called to the landlady as he entered the main room, his cape still on him and spreading water all over the floor.

'Get that cape off,' she said, helping him to remove it, 'and sit near the fire.' The fire rarely went out. She threw more wood onto it. Slowly it gave out more heat as the logs started to burn more vigorously. With a blanket round him, Tommy removed his other clothes. His inhibited personality made him look to the wall as he did so. Eventually, after sitting by the fireside for a while, he slowly warmed up and dried out. Still shivering however, he felt himself becoming more and more breathless. Everything was now dry except his hair so he called out.

'Bed, missus.'

He stood up, almost stumbling as he did so. The landlady put her arm right round him, almost carrying him up the stairs. He could only just put one foot in front of another but it made him breathless. Slowly he got into the cold bedroom and then the bed. His breathing was still shallow and he found it impossible to take a deep breath. Always a man whose mind was active, he reflected on his own position. The drove would have to be sold for whatever it could make, hopefully in excess of eleven pounds. Jack could do that. It was Tommy's last drove and he would not be able to finish it. What he had dreaded was another soaking and he was now paying a heavy price. His breathing had suffered and he knew he would not get better. What would he do now? Sit in the back of the Saddlers and wait for the end, a breathless old man with a stick? His reason for living had been rooted in his reputation for shrewdness and honesty and the power that gave him. That time was over. He was now yesterday's man. He had no home, except a room in a tavern. No wife or children. He was grateful at least to Nellie who he knew would always look after him as she had done for years. He had a reasonable bank balance but not a large one. Had it been worth it? He didn't know.

'Drop of whisky Tommy?'

'No, tea. Send the boys in will you, missus?'

Even sitting up to drink the tea made him breathless. Lying back, he waited for Jack and Eddie.

'Boys, I shan't be with you now.'

'Why not, Tommy?' enquired Eddie.

'I've had a pull.'

'You're not that bad.'

'Listen, will you,' he said shutting Eddie up. 'You drive these to Hereford and sell to the first man who offers eleven pounds.' He became breathless again and signalled to them to be quiet. Tommy waited till his breath came back, then whispered, 'You act together.'

'Yes, Tommy,' they both replied.

'Make sure of that. Don't tell them I'm ill.'

'What about expenses on the way?'

'See me tomorrow morning. You'll get costs and wages. Now let me sleep.'

Eddie went no further than downstairs and the bar. Jack made his way to the arms of Rosie.

The rain hammered against the window of Tommy's bedroom as he lay awake all night reflecting on the future. Any movement made him breathless.

Eddie, without the silently disapproving presence of Tommy, drank more than usual.

Jack, with his arms around Rosie, discussed the change in his circumstances.

'It's the end with Tommy. He won't even finish the drove.'

'When did he tell you this?'

'Two days ago. Said it was the last.'

'Just like that?'

'He's very fair you know. Didn't keep me in the dark. He's ill now. Got a soaking today. Told me he dreaded another soaking. Then he got it.'

'He won't get better you know.'

'How d'you know?'

'Women know these things,' she said, giving him a gentle poke in the ribs.

'Wonder what'll happen to him?'

'He could die.'

'Don't say that.'

'It's true, and what's going to happen to you?' Again she gave him a gentle dig in the ribs.

Chapter 20

Plymouth May 1855

Dear Rosie,

Sorry I haven't been in touch over all this time. You know I can't read and write. Now I've got this friend Ned who can and he's helped me write this letter.

I'd better start from the beginning. It's three years since I left the drovers. Haven't been back to Wales since. I heard Tommy died a week or two after I got to Hereford. I suppose it was only a few days after I left. Did he die at the Drovers? Was he buried in Narberth? He would want that. I liked Tommy. He taught me a lot. What has happened to Eddie? Has he got a job? I hope so. He did like his beer.

I've been here and there but haven't had a job that lasted. The longest, I think, was twelve months. I didn't stay in Hereford long and went to Gloucester for a while. I tried to get a job with the drovers again but it was all short drives for a few days and then they came to an end. Me being Welsh didn't help, made me an odd man out in England and made getting work more difficult. Also I got in a few fights and had to move on. I didn't get any second prizes but got labelled a trouble maker. Had to move further away where they didn't know my reputation. For twelve months I was on a farm in Suffolk. The work was hard which I didn't mind but the pay was poor and I moved on after a year.

When I was in Suffolk I met Ned. He's from the farms but it's mostly ploughed round there and a lot of work with horses. We sort of got on and have been together more or less ever since. He's a better scholar than I am and writes this letter from what I say. Ned's strong in the head and I'm strong in the arm. Ha ha. We've tried a few things but nothing lasts. Mostly we have worked together coming down the Essex coast on a barge with a

200

grain cargo. That's how we got to London. For a few months we sailed up and down the coast and got to know London when we were ashore. The pay was poor and we got restless so we didn't rejoin when it was due to sail. This was in the spring of this year.

Anyway, we were walking round London and along Waterloo Road. You know I don't drink much. Ned does but he's not a drunk. Walking along Waterloo Road we passed the Wellington Arms and we heard the shouting and listened to this recruiting sergeant. They were wanting men for the Crimea. We stopped and listened to him. He was better than any Narberth Fair huckster. You had to listen to him. On and on he went. I don't know where all the words came from. He seemed to bewitch us. All the time he couldn't take his eyes off me and Ned. Then he came up to us. He couldn't stop talking. Fighting for Queen and country. Doing your duty. He had this loud voice and smart uniform, you had to listen to him. There was no getting away. Anyway, we went inside and spoke to this captain. The sergeant was breathing down our neck. There was no getting away from them. The captain looked straight at the sergeant who was behind us. Didn't say a word to him but his look said shut up. He discussed joining up and said they were paying half a crown a day. Well, I'd never had that sort of money in my life before. He also said we might be sergeants within a few months. So I signed and he gave me the Queen's shilling.

As soon as we signed the sergeant started shouting at us and ordered us to this small holding depot. We were like cattle being penned in the market ready for sale and slaughter. I never seen such a crowd of weedy looking men. Most of them looked a bit frightened but I suppose they were attracted by the money. It was good.

Me and Ned were the only two farmers' boys there. The rest looked pale and thin. We talked to a few of them. One had worked in a draper's shop and another as a domestic servant, they were sad really and wouldn't have a chance on a battlefield. There was one real rogue in the bunch. You could tell he fancied his chances with me and Ned but he kept his head down. The

201

next day we got marched to the railway and sent to Bristol, then marched on to Horfield Barracks. We were the first levy. We didn't stay in Bristol long. The barracks were overcrowded. Some were lodged outside. It was chaos really. The thieving was almost out of control and you had to have your things with you all the time. We were issued with boots in Bristol and more uniform in Plymouth where we went in a couple of days. We leave for the Crimea tomorrow. The boat is already in dock. I'm looking forward to it.

Sorry for not writing before. I didn't have Ned then. Will write again

Hope the two children are alright.

Love Jack

****

Balaclava June 1855

Dear Rosie

Hope you got my last letter. Two days ago we landed at Balaclava in the Crimea. I'd better start from where I left off last time.

We weren't long in Plymouth, sailing out here in two days. Sailing is really the wrong word, the ship is steam driven. We had to take turns stoking the boilers, it was very hard work and we were stripped to the waist. Four hours on four off. Then it was rest. There's been a lot of thieving on board and when you go on deck you have to wear all your clothes. You've got to have a friend here. Thankfully I've still got Ned, I couldn't wish for anyone better. I'm very lucky. When I'm stoking he looks after my things and I do the same for him. It's hot in the hold and now we're in the Meddie hot in the day on deck and also down below. One or two of the boys have got quite burnt staying out on deck.

A man was caught thieving last night so we gave him a

202

hammering. I hope this stops it from happening again. It's terrible if you can't go anywhere without taking all your stuff with you. Different from Tommy and the drovers, they were an honest crowd. There was a lot of thieving in London but not as bad as this. We didn't report him to the sergeants in charge here. If we had he'd have been flogged for certain. He hasn't got up today and they haven't asked for him. If they do he'll have to say he fell down the gangway.

We haven't had any training so far. It's been a bit too cramped on board for that. I suppose the stoking keeps me fit. What they have done is give us some idea what we have to do. Taking supplies here and there particularly to the front. Ammunition, food, water, medical supplies to the front and wounded coming back. The commissariat have been blamed for a lot during this war. Supplies not getting through. They're civilians and some have been bloody minded. That's what they say anyway. We are soldiers and they expect better. I'm looking forward to it, don't know about some of the others. A few of them are in a very poor way. I don't think they'll ever make front line soldiers or be able to control a horse or a mule. They've never lived in the country or known anything about horses. I pity some of them.

We're in what they call the Sea of Marmora. The Meddie and Dardanelles are behind us and before nightfall we'll be through the Bosphorous and into the Black Sea. Then in two days it's Balaclava where we unload. The weather's getting hotter and I can't wait to get off this ship.

Balaclava is in sight now. It is very full. There's a lot going on, even a railway. Everyone is looking not knowing what to expect. Will write more later.

We've docked now and got off the boat almost immediately. They started straight away to order us around. Given uniform and arms, a bayonet and carbine. Then away to our billets. Training is very short and they shout at you all the time. The sergeant never speaks a word, always shouting. He's been in the artillery. I got immediately chosen to be the senior soldier in the troop and

203

must keep them in order when he is not around. They chose me because I am bigger than the rest and have been a blacksmith, know horses and living with animals. I wanted to be a farrier but the sergeant and the captain said, 'You'll do what you're bloody well told and be a senior soldier. Understand?'

We've been here a week. One of my troop has gone to hospital. He was in a poor way and I don't know what will happen to him. Should never have been brought out here. I think he weighs less than seven stone. Tomorrow our troop goes to the supply depot which goes direct to the front two or three times a day.

You can't believe the animals they use here. As well as horses and mules they have oxen, camels, and buffalo. The place is full of Turks, Spanish, Italians, Sardinians and Croats and of course the French. A real mixture. All we have to do is win the siege of Sevastopol. Most of the time there is shelling sometimes day and night. All the talk is when will the infantry go in and finish it off?

Tomorrow I go to the front with the first lot of supplies. It will be ammunition in my case. Three of my troop will be there. I tried to choose the best of them. We're only a mile or two away and perhaps we will make three journeys a day. I must have a good night's rest before I start at dawn tomorrow. It will be a 5am start and may go on till midnight. Got to get to bed.

Hope you and the children are alright
Love Jack.

****

Sevastopol July 1855

Dear Rosie
    A lot has happened since I wrote last. As I told you we were

going to the front shortly. There was a big artillery bombardment of the Russians. How they stuck it I don't know. It was very heavy indeed. Even those who had been out here some time said it was the heaviest yet. Generally it's one day at the front and one behind. Those few days it was going to the front two, three, four and sometimes five times a day. No rest at all. We go up in troops and I, together with a corporal and a sergeant supervise the men and mules. I don't know what's more difficult, the men or the mules. The mules I think. You can threaten the men but the mules really are stubborn. If they think they will stop they stop and there's no shifting them. Some of them don't even move when you give them a good thrashing. Somehow or other we get the loads to the front. Give me horses anytime. During those busy few days it was ammunition we were taking up and just a few wounded coming back.

Then came the big infantry push in the early hours long before daylight. First the French went in then ourselves. It was a clear night and you could see them going in. Then the Russians opened fire with musket and artillery and soon much of it was out of sight in the smoke. You got occasional glimpses at what was going on. I particularly remember a ladder party trying to scale the walls only to be shot down. They hadn't a chance. Soon they were all in retreat. Not that we had much time to see.

It was now all out to take the wounded back. For two days and two nights we never stopped. Taking moaning, thirsty and sometimes dying men back behind the lines. I wouldn't want to spend another few days like that. I saw Lord Raglan on the day of the retreat. He looked exhausted. Ten days later he was dead. We all loved and respected him. He was the General but he was also a father to us all.

He's not the only one who is dead. One of our troop died in hospital. He should really never have come out here. He was small and pale and not up to the long hours and exhausting demands that were placed on him. What he died of I don't know. He was only in hospital one day and that was it. Working from five o'clock in the morning till midnight exhausts me. It killed him. Another was killed by enemy fire during the push on Sevastopol. I wonder how many more will go.

We don't know where we're going from here. They say if Sevastopol falls to us we will win the war, if it doesn't we will lose. How the Russians soak up all this artillery fire I don't know. They are a tough lot and very good shots. The losses we and the French had they say are five thousand. How many of those I took back, I don't know. In those two days I didn't know whether I was awake or asleep, mad or sane.

It's a bit easier now. One day at the front, one day at base. The artillery is still firing at the Russians. Their losses must be very heavy.

There is a lot of drunkenness here. The navvies particularly who are digging the trenches are rarely sober and get a lot more money than we do. They are a surly lot and now and then you get fights. Most of it is about the big money they get and also they don't like taking orders from engineer officers.

The military men drink a lot too. Almost everyone drinks themselves stupid if they get a chance. I still hardly drink. Don't want to end up like Eddie, Dewi or Swni. You haven't met the last two but I think I told you about them.

I had a day off today and looked around here. This place is packed with military equipment and soldiers. There are a lot of Turkish troops attached to us here. They work the oxen, buffalo and camels. Their carts are the strangest things you've ever seen in your life. Only they could work them. They don't do the amount of work that we do but do their bit behind the lines. There's a lot of stuff to be moved. Tents, cookers, food for the military and of course fodder for the animals. A man can work on an empty stomach, not these animals.

They're talking about a big push soon to enter Sevastopol before the winter. I haven't been here in winter but they say it is very cold. Last winter it was in tents, this time it will be in huts if we have to stay.

The weather here is hot and may get hotter. I don't do much but work and sleep. Have I ever done anything else? It's new out here and I'm enjoying it. That is apart from having to deal with those bloody mules. You just can't persuade them if they don't want to move. Suppose they are a bit like women.

How are you and the children?
    Love Jack.

****

Sevastopol September 1855

Dear Rosie
    A lot has happened since I wrote last. Sevastopol has fallen and they say the war is over. I'll believe that when I get on the boat home. It's getting a bit cold at night.
    Since I wrote last we've been directing the fire against the Russians almost continually. That means ammunition being carried up day after day. A long day at that. It exhausts me and there is no respite. Most days are eighteen hours. There was firing at their defences. The naval gunners have been giving it to them also. Then there was a terrific barrage and we knew this would be followed by an attack. The noise was continuous and you could see them fall beyond their defences. The Russian casualties must have been enormous. You could see the French digging trenches nearer the Russian defences, as the bombardment continued. Then around midday the French infantry went in and within a very short while they had put up the tricolour. Then we went in and it was touch and go for some time but they did gain ground. Eventually getting on the ramparts and looking down from Great Redan which had cost so many British lives. The French taking of Malakov sealed the day and the Russians were in retreat over the pontoon bridge to the northern part of the city. We were taking the British wounded back. It was an impossible job and we couldn't take them all back. Had to do

207

the best we could. It was non stop day and night. The worst sight of all was inside Sevastopol. There were Russian dead and dying everywhere. No one remained behind to look after them. There was shrieking, moaning and the crying of the dying everywhere. Shouting for water, for brandy, for death, for God, for their mothers. They were everywhere. Sometimes two and three deep. You couldn't get away from them. There was smoke from the buildings on fire but above all it was the smell. The smell of rotting flesh. Some must have been there for days. No-one to look after them. The best thing to do seemed to be to shoot them. Death would be a release.

Our own dead and dying were lying everywhere. Everyone was exhausted. I think we fought to a standstill. The Russians the same. Our drivers were in very poor shape and two more have died. One in action with enemy shrapnel and another with exhaustion. I think he had dysentery as well.

At the end of June I lost a finger from enemy artillery but I was only in hospital a day and they sent me back. I'm one of the lucky ones. I could have been killed. If I'd been a foot nearer it would have had me in the chest and I wouldn't be writing this letter. Thank God Ned is alright too, he hasn't had a scratch.

Three days after the battle things have eased up a bit. We won the battle but the Russians are still over the river in the other part of the city. Everyone says we've won. I hope so.

There's been a lot of bad feeling between us on the first levy and the second one which came out a week or two back. The trouble is money. We signed on for half a crown a day and they for one and sixpence. There's been trouble in the canteens and some of the second levy have been picking on some of the smaller boys in our levy. There's been a few punch-ups but nothing serious. What does happen is that when we have to work together they won't pull their weight.

I forgot to tell you I'm a corporal now. It doesn't change what I do but means a bit more pay. Just supervising loads to the front. A lot of these boys don't know one end of a mule from another but somehow they've got to lead them. Some learn, some don't. There are times when I think I'm leading twelve mules on my own. Can't learn, won't learn and I've clouted a couple round the ears which hasn't done'em much good, but it made me feel good for a moment.

The news came through we had ten thousand dead. Ten thousand dead and all for this bloody city. Is it worth it?

Love Jack

Chapter 21

It is early in 1856. Few troops are left in the Crimea and Jack finds himself discharged from the Land Transport Corps. Hardly anyone from the first levy remains. As the rumour mill stated, all those on half a crown a day have largely gone.

He and Ned are at the gates of the barracks having just been paid off. Jack has twenty-five pounds, Ned slightly less. There is an awkward silence between them. They know it's goodbye. Nothing has been said about 'us', each one talking about 'I'. Each one knows that they have no future together. Both of them will be returning to their roots; Jack to Pembrokeshire, Ned to Suffolk. The silence doesn't last long but in retrospect it will seem an age.

Ned, always the more talkative says, 'We've been through a lot together, Jack.'

'We have that.'

'What you going to do?'

'See Rosie first. Then get home.'

'How many years since you left?'

'Four.'

'Be a lot of changes.'

'A lot. Tommy the old boss drover is dead. I know that,' Jack said sadly.

'And a few more, no doubt.'

'The long droves'll be finished now, with the coming of the railway. I'll have to try the farms. It's early spring now and they'll need men on the big farms.'

'Going back to the farms then?' asked Ned

'There's nothing else.'

'Course there is. Mines and the iron works down your way.'

'Not that. See what the country has. What you doing?'

'Tell you what I'm not doing. Not back to the farms. Try my luck in London. I understand horses. There'll be plenty of jobs,' Ned declared confidently.

'Do you think so? I couldn't settle there.'

'We're different Jack. Very different. You know that.'

'I know.'

'Perhaps that's why we got on.'

'Yes'. There was a pause. 'Well Ned, got to be going.' They shook hands and looked one another in the face. It was goodbye. They knew they wouldn't see one another again.

'Got all your gear?'

'Yes.'

'And the cape?'

Jack smiled. 'And the cape. Won't be any use to the dead dragoon now. Goodbye Ned.'

'Goodbye Jack.'

Jack walked up the road and round the corner without looking back. Ned watched him go. They never saw one another again.

It was a cold February morning with frost on the ground and a mist which was just beginning to clear. Everyone on the street was cold, some people clapping their hands together, some stamping their feet and all, man and horse, discharging visible breath as a result of the cold. Once out of the city, Jack made for the ferry over the Severn, which would take him back into Wales. He had crossed that way several times before. He felt for the money in his pocket, was reassured as he walked briskly onwards to whatever fate had in store for him. He felt confident.

By midday he was on the ferry crossing the silent fog-laden river. It was impossible to see more than fifty yards ahead and the ferryman crossed the slightly rippling river current from habit rather than by sight. There was an eerie silence made all the more so by the invisibility of the bank on the other side and the quietness of both crew and passengers. The journey lasted for only a few minutes and then they landed. Jack knew his way even in this mist, taking the road to Abergavenny at a brisk pace.

Just before dusk and three miles short of his immediate destination, he put up for the night at a tavern, planning to leave at first light. If he pushed himself he would be at Llanduesant the following night. He was looking forward to seeing Rosie but it was not the feeling of physical and desperate urgency he had experienced in the past. It was just Rosie; the only person he had ever confided in, trusted and felt totally at home with. Her house was his only home.

The day had been a strenuous one. There was a heavy mist and a frost made all the harder and colder by the rising ground. He knew every inch of the way, though visibility was very limited. Even as he walked into the village there wasn't a soul around. Somehow everything had changed. The village looked smaller. The buildings looked smaller. A sudden thought came to him; he hadn't brought Rosie a present. 'You forgetful fool,' he told himself, 'you thoughtless man.' There was nothing he could do but carry on. Walking up to the door he saw it exactly as it was. Nothing had changed, absolutely nothing. Just a little bit shabbier. Hearing children inside, he knocked at the door. One of the children said, 'Someone at the door mum.'

Rosie opened the door with the two children looking silently from behind at the visitor. 'Jack!' she said, her voice, but much more her look, full of surprise. 'Jack,' she repeated, hugging him, with tears in her eyes. Slowly he put his arms round her, 'Rosie, good to see you.' He looked at her fondly, 'very good to see you.' He noticed she looked older. Shorter he thought and a little darker under the eyes which had deeper lines around them now which seemed to make her smile all the more attractive.

'Come in then. Cold it is.' He walked in, glad of the warmth from the fire. 'I got your letters,' Rosie said. 'Still in the army then?'

'No, I got paid off earlier in the week.'

'Sit down then,' she told him. He felt he was home again, but somehow it was different. The two children had grown up and were almost unrecognisable. 'You've grown Jack. My, you've grown.' She glanced at his wounded hand, holding it up to look at the missing finger. 'Does it hurt now?'

'No. Makes no difference at all.'

She looked thoughtful, 'Sit down there a moment. I've got something to show you.' She went into the bedroom, returning with a bundle wrapped in a blanket; a little boy with fair curly hair rubbing his eyes from the unwelcome interruption to his sleep. Handing the boy to him, she said with a smile of pride and expectation, 'He's yours.'

He grasped the boy with the blanket around him, feeling almost shell-shocked with surprise. 'Mine?'

'Yes, yours.' The boy lashed out at the unexpected visitor, crying loudly and persistently. Rosie roared with laughter. Holding the boy further away from him all the time, he invited Rosie to take the child back. He quietened down as she took him in her arms. 'Like father, like son.'

'What do you call him, Rosie?'

'Jack of course. What else?'

'How old is he?'

'Three and a half.'

Jack counted the months, realising that Rosie must have been three months pregnant when he had left. 'Did you know before I went away?'

'Course I did'

'Why didn't you tell me?'

She gave a knowing smile, 'You were a boy then. You had enough on your plate without this.'

Jack made a move to hold him again but received the same aggressive rejection. Rosie sat in the chair cuddling young Jack in her arms. He continued to look morosely and suspiciously at his father, the newcomer, while clinging to his mother. Jack smiled; somehow he would get his trust. They sat together for a while. Silence prevailed but there was an unspoken rapport between them. Rosie lent over and grasped his damaged hand, saying, 'Good to see you Jack.' He nodded in agreement through a mist of emotion, feeling that he had found his soul mate and was really home. The peace didn't last long, the children making demands on her, particularly the youngest.

'Well Jack, what're you going to do then?'

'It'll have to be farm work again.'

'There'll be nothing around here you know.'

'Back to Narberth then, bound to be work on the big farms at this time. Ploughing, sowing, you know.'

'When will you go?' she asked.

'Soon.' He knew he shouldn't have said it, feeling that he would be deserting Rosie and his son. She knew how he felt but said nothing. 'What do you do for money?' he continued.

'I manage somehow. They're good at the Drovers but it's not easy.'

He understood what her position was, having known little else himself.

'Rosie, I'll only stay a day or two. Got to get work.'

'I know,' she replied, shrugging in acceptance. 'When will you go?'

'In a few days.' By now he was warm, starting to doze off before the fire but only for a moment. His mind wandered. 'How long did Tommy last after we went?'

'Only a few days. He died here but they took him away for the funeral.'

'Tommy was good you know. Best man I ever worked for.' She didn't reply, not wanting to hear about the drovers or what had happened to them four years before. 'Straight as a line he was. Do they still come through?'

'Yes, but not as many, the Drovers' tavern takes less money now.'

'Seen Eddie since?'

'I don't know him really. I knew Tommy. Was there when he died,' she said sadly.

'Did he suffer much?'

'No, just slipped away. It happens to us all.'

'Don't I know it. Seen enough dead in the Crimea, at the siege of Sevastopol.

'A few hundred dead there,' Rosie declared.

214

'A few hundred!!! A few thousand you mean. Perhaps twenty thousand at the end. Us and the Russians.'

'All that number!' She sounded stunned.

'Piled high in places. The dying were worse than the dead. Crying in pain. Crying for water. Crying for God. Crying for their Mother. Terrible, never want to see that again.'

'You lost your finger.'

'That's nothing. Nothing at all.' She reached for the damaged hand but he snatched it away. 'Don't fuss over that.' She couldn't feel offended; he was back in the Crimea. A silence overcame them both. Even the children became quiet with young Jack asleep again, but still clutching his mother tightly. The entire household drifted into a heat-induced listlessness.

They were roused by a knock. The elder children woke up first. 'Mam, someone's there.'

She got up, still holding Jack. The landlady of the tavern, Rosie's employer was standing on the doorstep. Looking past Rosie, she could see her visitor. 'Oh he's back, is he? Are you coming to work?'

'I'll be down soon,' Rosie assured her.

'Jack, you'll have to look after the children,' she announced when she went back into the room.

'Alright,' he replied, having been woken by the sound of voices, 'leave'em with me.'

Within a minute or two she was out in the cold frosty air, running down the road to work.

'You've got him there, have you?' commented the landlady upon her arrival. Rosie did not reply. 'Hope he doesn't leave you again with something that wants a bonnet.' Rosie still said nothing but continued with her sweeping. The bar was still untidy from the previous night. Glasses and plates remained on the tables and rubbish on the floor. All that remained of the large, open fire was a small pile of grey and white ash and the dry unconsumed logs on the left. The walls were of whitewashed stone, the only addition to them being the smoke stains that had built up over the years. There was a flag-stoned floor and oak

215

tables, old and much damaged from years of use. The seats were also of oak, in the same condition as the tables. The room was cold, depressing and much in need of attention.

Mistress and servant had an uneasy relationship, made evident by the bitter remarks she periodically addressed to Rosie. Rarely did she receive a reply and then only a mild one. They were mutually dependant on one another. Rosie did much of the domestic work and served in the bar. Her presence brought in custom; probably half the beer sold was due to Rosie. She was entirely dependant on the work for any sort of income. The landlady was a large, bitter woman with a husband perhaps twenty years older than herself. Her husband played little part in running the business but was much occupied with a few cattle and sheep he kept on the thirty acres nearby. They had no children, which was a great disappointment to her. She resented her servant's fertility but was fond of her children, particularly young Jack.

Rosie worked relentlessly at cleaning the bar and the adjoining room. Her employer appeared periodically and without comment for no particular reason other than to see how she was working.

There was a sharp knocking on the door. 'Mam, mam,' was heard. The landlady, who was hovering nearby, said, 'I'll go.' Young Jack rushed in and into his mother's arms. 'I hate him, mam, I hate him.' The front door remained open and the already cold room became even colder with the blast of frosty air. With Jack in one arm, she closed the door with the other.

'Now, now Jack. Don't be like that. He's your father.'

'I hate him.'

Stroking his curly fair hair with her right hand and clutching him tightly with the other, she calmed him down, his tears gradually ceasing as she continued to reassure him. Putting him down, she then continued with her work.

The landlady looked on with a gleam of self-satisfied relish. 'Doesn't like your new visitor, does he?'

Jack clung to his mother's leg. 'Here, come to me,' said the landlady. He wouldn't go to her but clung to his mother even more tightly. Gradually he calmed down, accepting a small bite of food on the landlady's knee. They were interrupted by a sharp knock on the door, followed by Jack's entrance. Seeing his son on her knee, he said, 'You've got him, then. He don't like me.'

'Of course, he hasn't seen you before, has he?' He ignored her self-satisfied tone and look, turning away. She hugged the boy to reinforce her point. 'Nice little boy he is. Aren't you Jack?' He could feel his temper rising but managed to control it.

'Jack, I'll look after the boy, you get back to the others,' said Rosie.

They gave one another a look, which said "ignore that bloody woman". He left, slamming the door after him. 'That wasn't very nice was it?' said the landlady, hugging the child even more tightly and kissing him on the forehead. Again Rosie didn't reply. Gradually the work was done. Within two hours the fire was laid, lit and the room warm. She went home through the cold frosty afternoon, holding Jack's hand and wondering what was in store when she got there.

Jack, who was sitting in the chair when she entered, gave her a cold aggressive look. 'That boy's getting ruined by women and I'm not going to have it.' The lad clung to her leg. Jack went to grab him but Rosie got there before him, holding him close to her. 'Don't you dare!' she said, looking him straight in the eye with a degree of aggression he had never known from her before. He calmed down a little. 'Don't you ever hit me or this boy. Not ever.'

'This boy is being spoiled, you know that.'

'Where have you been then? Only met him this morning, but already everything is wrong.'

'I didn't know about him till this morning.'

'And you'll soon be off because there's no work here. And you call yourself a father.'

'But I am his father.'

'Well, behave like it then.'

'He's being spoilt by women.'

217

'Where are the men then? You've just arrived and are going off tomorrow.'

'I won't be off tomorrow. I'll be here a few more days.'

'Then you'll be off?'

'I suppose.'

'Three days in three and a half years. What do you call that?'

'I've got to get work so that I can give you some money.'

'Haven't seen much of it so far.' He reached in his pocket and offered her twenty pounds. She was surprised by the amount but did not show it. 'I don't want it if I have to put a pistol to your head. Sooner go on slaving at the Drovers than accept that sort of money.'

'Go on, take it Rosie. You need it.'

'No. I've told you. No.' He felt quite stunned by her remarks, and didn't know what to say. He would sooner face the Russian guns at the siege of Sevastopol than her anger and devastating logic. An awkward silence ensued, her steely look confirming his suspicion that she was not going to give him any respite. He could stand it no longer, so put on his cape and walked out into the failing light, leaving the money behind on the table. Into the frosty dusk he walked, along the old familiar track. A ball of torment and indecision, he didn't know what to say or what to do. After walking around for an hour, he returned, without coming to any decision about how to proceed. Once again, he knocked at her door. She answered. 'What do you want, then?'

'To come in.'

'Come in then, if you want to,' she invited him reluctantly.

Walking in, almost shamefaced he noticed the £20 where he had left it. He had hoped that she would have accepted it. What should he say? She seemed completely in charge of the relationship and intended to remain so. Jack had little experience of women and it showed. After some minutes, during which time she had continued with her chores, she said 'Aren't you going to sit down then?' He felt like an infantry soldier in the sights of a

218

Russian sharpshooter. Where was the next volley going to come from?

As the evening wore on, the two elder children gradually became accustomed to his presence and came towards him, the elder one taking his damaged hand and looking at it. Rosie noticed and scolded them, 'Put that down, he doesn't like talking about it.' They obeyed. Young Jack was as far away in the room as he could get. He smiled at him, to which the child responded by frowning and grasping his mother.

The children having been put to bed, the boy in his mother's bed, as Jack thought, he plucked up the courage to ask, 'Where am I sleeping, Rosie?'

'With me, that's if you want to.'

'Oh yes,' he said gratefully. She smiled to herself but took pains to hide it, giving him her severe look.

'Well, get into bed then.'

'Jack, where's he?'

'I've put him in with his sisters. Go on, get in bed. Do you still want to?'

He almost rushed into the bedroom before she changed her mind. Taking his clothes off, he got into the warmth of the space recently vacated by his son. For a quarter of an hour, then half an hour, then an hour he waited. Eventually Rosie appeared, clad in a heavy nightdress. 'You still awake? Thought you'd be asleep.' She got into bed; he moved over to give her the warmest space. Lying down, she made sure there was no contact between them. He snuggled up to her. She became aware of his erection. 'You can put that away. It's my time of the month,' she lied. He moved away from her. 'Turn over and go to sleep.' He knew he couldn't argue.

Waking up in the morning he didn't know what to expect. She was awake already. 'Sleep alright?' he enquired tentatively.

'Always do,' she replied tartly.

He felt there was no future here. He didn't know how to handle this woman or her moods. He felt mortified, as though he couldn't do anything right. Whatever he tried seemed to fail. In a

219

last desperate gesture he put his arm over her. She took it off immediately. 'None of that. Time you were up.' He got up, putting his clothes on in seconds and moving towards the door. She remained in bed with her back to him.

'I'm off,' he said.

'Thought you would be. Eat before you go.'

He went to the living room where the two elder children were already up. He heard Jack move into his mother's bed. Impotent with rage, he did nothing. The money remained where he had left it on the table. Eventually mother and son emerged. 'Haven't you eaten?' He shook his head. She ordered the eldest one to make breakfast. He didn't feel hungry, just wanting to speak to her before he left.

'Rosie, I want a word with you before I go.'

'You do, do you?' She commanded the children to fetch water and to take young Jack. They left the house.

'Well Jack, what is it?' He didn't know quite what to say. She gave him a soft look.

'I can't do anything right, can I?'

'Come here Jack.' She grasped him by the upper arms and drew him towards her, giving him an almost tender look. 'You don't understand women, do you Jack?'

'Suppose I don't, Rosie.'

'You're a lovely boy. You know that.' She hugged and kissed him, her emotion coming to the surface at last. He could feel the tears wet on her cheeks. She stood back, tearfully looking at him, then kissed him again. 'Go now before the children get back.' He pointed at the money on the table before he left. She watched him go, standing by the window clutching the brooch to her. He walked down the track towards Llandeilo, at a brisk pace. He didn't look back.

Chapter 22

It was August 1856. Jack, Caleb and Isaac were working for Griff, on a two-hundred acre farm south of the Preseli mountains. They did not live in the farmhouse but in a cottage used as servants' quarters a hundred yards from the main residence and just away from the farm buildings. It was hardly even a cottage, consisting of only one room with an earthen floor and a fireplace. The fire was rarely alight and the draught down the chimney blew cold air into the single room and through the dilapidated door, which hung at an angle and was no defence against the south-west wind. When the fire was lit, it frequently filled the room with smoke. In the roof of the hovel was a loft approached by a steep-angled ladder, which held the sleeping quarters, no more than some sacks filled with straw and covered with blankets. Even in the loft there was no respite from the wind. Slates were loose and the gap between roof and wall showed daylight. Everything about the place was shabby, neglected and dirty. No attention had been given to it for years. No man having a horse that he valued would have kept it in such a building.

In the winter, they worked from seven o'clock till five. In summer they started at the same time and finished when they could work no longer. Isaac and Caleb had worked there since leaving school, and felt that they were fortunate to have work, accepting their lot with fatalism and humility. Though young, they were painfully thin from the cold, the burden of work and the meagre diet. Their diet itself was boring and repetitive in the extreme; bread, cheese, buttermilk, rabbit-pie, potatoes and sometimes a little fat bacon. The routine was always the same. The serving girl brought the food into the back kitchen for them at ten o'clock, one o'clock and seven o'clock. Day-in, day-out, the time never altered and neither did the diet. The only variation was at harvest time, when the meals were eaten outside with

Griff. Marion, his wife, didn't go near the men, never even being in the same room with them. Griff was much more genial, particularly when he was working with them. He seemed to need their company, frequently prolonging the day to avoid going indoors. This did not go unnoticed by his servants.

On that August evening, when work was finished, they talked before they made ready to go to bed. The talk of the two younger ones was always about the food and the missus. Jack rarely got involved in the conversation; being older and more experienced than the others he felt somewhat set apart from them. He had no intention of staying longer than the next November's hiring fair.

'There was even less to eat tonight,' said Caleb.

'I saw. And the bread got two days ago,' replied Isaac.

'I know, once a week she bakes.'

'On the last day it's like rock.'

'Have to dip it in the buttermilk.'

'Did you see it tonight? Some of mine was mouldy, and not much of it either.'

Jack was only half listening to this conversation, his mind on other things, but he heard enough to make him decide to act. 'You want me to do something about it?' he asked the others.

'Yes,' replied one.

'But how?' asked the other.

'I'll deal with Griff and her. You do nothing.'

'Nothing?'

'You just refuse to work or I'll thump you good and hard. Understand?' They didn't reply but knew there was no way out. He gave them a cunning and knowing smile. 'At breakfast tomorrow I'll do it. The bread will be even mouldier by then. Leave it to me.' They gave him silent agreement. 'Remember we don't work till we are properly fed. Griff needs us now for harvest. He can't do without us.'

'Will we win?'

'You'll see, boys.' They knew they would have to obey him. 'I'll deal with Griff and Lady Muck. Not a stroke of work till we are properly fed. Not a stroke till she has baked fresh bread. I'll beat them.' Jack left them and went to bed.

'I don't think we're doing right. Do you?' asked Isaac.

'Got to do it now. No way out,' said Caleb.

'We could be in trouble you know'.

'He'll do it. He's tough. Anyway we haven't got to do anything.'

'Yes, we have to stop work.'

'Stopping work isn't doing anything.'

'It is.'

'Have it your own way then. Anyway, we're not going back.' They went off to bed.

The following morning, when their early tasks were finished, they made their way together towards the back kitchen. Isaac's stomach was fluttering as he was the last to enter the house. 'Leave it all to me,' were Jack's last words as he sat down. They waited several minutes for the servant girl to bring breakfast.

Click, click, click, she walked down the passage leading to the men. Bread, butter, cheese and buttermilk were put on the table. They heard her walk back. Isaac and Caleb's hearts were beating wildly as they waited for the action to start. Jack took his time, savouring the moment as he waited a few seconds but which seemed minutes to the two observers. He picked up the bread slowly, looked it all over and smiled, saying, 'This loaf seems to be dying.' The boys could hardly contain their nervous laughter. 'I must see the bread doctor.' Again he looked at the mouldy loaf. 'I believe her surgery is in the next room.' The boys again laughed till they were fit to burst but contained it, which made the pressure all the more intense. Slowly and deliberately he gathered the butter, cheese and bread in one arm and the buttermilk in the other, walking to the kitchen at a slow pace such as would be reserved for military funerals. Left, right, left, right, began the slow march, which ceased in the kitchen. Even Griff and his wife heard the sound, feeling something ominous about it. Jack stood before them, towering over them, not saying a word for almost a minute. He was determined not to be the first to speak. Griff was about to speak but was restrained by his wife. The silence could not continue and he blurted out nervously, 'What is it, Jack?'

Slowly and deliberately, Jack put the buttermilk down on the table then the butter and cheese. Holding the loaf, he pushed it into the face of Griff and then his wife. 'Mould!' he shouted which gave them both a start and was also heard by the boys in the back kitchen. 'Mould!' he shouted even louder. He gave his employers a look of suppressed rage, which alarmed them both.

Nervously Griff said, 'We'll get you another loaf.'

Jack laughed silently to himself. Boy, you don't know who you're dealing with, he reflected. Slowly, deliberately and to give the maximum impact, he threw the bread on to the fire as he ripped the loaf apart piece by piece. This was followed by the butter and cheese, which sizzled in the fire. 'The bread is a week old and mouldy!'

Griff was looking at him in submission and fear. 'I'll get a good one.' He moved to go to the pantry. Jack grabbed him and pushed him back in the chair.

'Sit down.' He did so, mesmerised. She went to get up. 'Sit down, you,' he said in a threatening voice, going to push her. She sat down quickly, before he could make her do so. 'Listen to me. From now on we're having proper food.'

'Yes,' Griff muttered almost inaudibly.

The boys had now got off their seats and were listening to every word. The maid was behind a door on the other side of the room in a state of extreme excitement.

'Proper bread baked three times a week.' He was interrupted for a moment.

'You can't do......'

'Shut up woman. You'll do what I say.' She went to leave the room but was pushed back in her chair. 'Fresh bread, understand? And more of it. Not that stuff.' He pointed to the remains on the fire. He waited a while to make sure his demands had the maximum impact. 'Butter. Not this rancid stuff that you have finished with. Fresh butter.' Again he left a silence. They did not reply. 'Meat. We get nothing but rabbit and small bits of fat bacon. Proper meat.' Again they did not reply. 'That hovel we sleep in. You wouldn't keep a horse in that draught, would you?'

Griff gaped at the onslaught but said nothing. Jack continued, 'The door doesn't fit and the roof leaks and it's not windproof. Not fit for a dog. You know that.' Griff could give him no argument. 'Then why are we in it?'

'Don't have money to do everything.'

'You've got money for her airs and graces haven't you?'

'That's not your business,' Griff's wife responded. She attempted to leave at this point but was pushed down yet again.

'It is our business. His money is enough for you to play Lady Muck while we starve on mouldy bread and rubbish food.'

Griff wanted the confrontation to end and wished to negotiate. 'Well what do you want then?'

'Proper food and plenty of it, and proper living quarters.'

'Well, I think we can do that.' He saw his means of escape.

'When?'

'Now, right away.'

'Alright then. We'll start with a proper breakfast. Now. No mouldy bread or rubbish food.'

'We'll start tomorrow. We've got to get the things in,' pleaded Griff.

'I agree. When you feed us properly we'll return to work. We're not doing a thing till you feed us properly.'

'But we've got to get the oats in. Weather could break. Be fair, Jack. We could lose the lot.'

'We've got a problem too. Haven't been properly fed for six months. Can't work on your food. You feed and stable your horses better then us. All we ask is the same treatment as the horses. It's not asking a lot is it?'

'You're pointing a gun at me?'

'You've been pointing one at me for six months. We're near starving. You know that. Tell you what we'll do; we'll make a start on the hovel. Make it a bit less draughty. Can't be fairer than that, can I?' Jack smiled to himself, relishing the advantage he had extracted. 'Call us when you're ready to feed us.'

All three walked off towards their home. The two younger men were all excitement as they walked away.

'Jack, we heard you go at her.' They smiled at one another.

'We're going to mend this hovel and we'll start on the roof,' instructed Jack, 'and don't mention any of this to a living soul. Understand?'

'Do you think you'll get your way, Jack?'

'Course I will, they have no option. Remember they won't want this to get out. Remember that.'

'They won't keep that quiet.'

'If we don't say anything, I'm damn sure they won't. They'd lose face.'

The boys agreed without saying a word.

'They don't work with the neighbours, he does it all himself. Though there'll be some talk that he isn't harvesting today. Anyway, you two shut up.' Soon they were on the roof, making good the missing slates.

In the house there was conflict between husband and wife. 'You gave way to those men. You're afraid of that Jack, you are.'

'They have a point. When I was a servant, twenty years back, I was fed better than they are.'

'They can't expect better. Who do they think they are? That Jack's getting too big for his boots. And threatening me! And you didn't defend me. Call yourself a man!'

'That's over now, what're we going to do? Feed'em better or let the oats rot?'

'I'd sooner let the crop rot than give in to those men.'

'If we did, we'd be bankrupt by the spring.'

'Haven't you got any self-respect? Don't give in to them.'

The argument went on for more than half an hour, with neither giving way. Griff, in exasperation, ceased to argue, went to the stable to harness the pony and then drove to town.

Jack saw him go. 'I think we're going to win this battle,' he said with an air of satisfaction.

Griff returned before dusk with more food than the family had bought in years. The weather had remained fine. He thought to himself with some anxiety how much of the crop he could have harvested had they made a start that day. He carried the provisions into the house, urging his wife to get on with the baking.

'That can wait till tomorrow. They can wait. We're not going to give them all their own way.'

'They'll not work till they're fed.'

'They'll start work at seven tomorrow and have breakfast at ten as usual.' She was trying to stand firm. 'You'll go down there and tell them exactly what I said.'

'I'll do it but mark my words, they won't budge.' Reluctantly and with a heavy heart he went to the hovel and repeated his wife's words.

Jack's reply was spoken in a mild voice as he was feeling some sympathy towards his employer. 'We haven't eaten since last night and now you're offering food tomorrow. You'd have mutiny in the army under these conditions. Tell her where to go for once in your life.' They looked one another in the eye with almost a smile.

For the first time ever, Griff confronted his wife; shouted her down, called her Lady Muck and a mean-minded skinflint. He went on and on till even she was lost for words. Knowing she was beaten, she stoked up the fire and mixed the dough. The bread was baked and, by dark, the men were fed adequately for the first time.

Griff and his wife kept their mouths shut. Jack and the boys remained silent. The servant girl did not. By the following evening, news of the incident was known by everyone within a ten-mile radius. It was talked about far and wide. Every known fact was chewed over and, where they did not learn fact, substituted fiction. It was the battle of Jack and Griff's missus. Almost everyone chuckled. Someone had confronted the old skinflint at last.

The year wore on. Jack and the two boys worked in an atmosphere of heavy silence with their employers. She kept an even greater distance from the men and Griff gave them their instructions in a cold and awkward manner. Time did not relieve the tension. Each knew they would move on when they were paid off.

'You going in November, Jack?'

'Yes, but not with you two.'

'Where to, though?' He didn't answer and they pursued it no further.

The last day of October came. Jack left early in the morning with his wages in his   pocket, without saying goodbye to anyone. The boys stayed on. Cardigan was his destination It was twenty miles, almost due north. The day was cold with the wind blowing in from the southwest, seeming like an invisible force driving him away from his old life to a fresh one. He could feel himself shedding his old life as a snake sheds its skin. A feeling of relief dominated his thoughts, and blinded him to the hunger he should have felt as he walked briskly along. He covered many miles, places came and went: Clunderwen, Llandissilio and Efailwen (scene of the first Rebecca attack on a tollgate). With the Preselis on his left he walked on, passing Crymmych and Frenni Fawr on his right and down to Blaenffos. Now the going became easier, although the wind still blew in from the same direction. Before dark, Cardigan was in sight. Crossing the bridge, he could see two boats tied up at the wharf, unloading cargo. Up into the town he walked, looking for cheap lodgings.

Over a bowl of cawl that night, he talked to others also waiting for the hiring fair. One had returned from the Crimea, another having been paid off from a boat and the last a pale, thin man with little to say for himself. Each man assessed the chances of the others and what competition they faced. The soldier was well on the way to becoming drunk, the sailor also. The last man would have been if he'd had any money. What sensible conversation there was deteriorated as the evening wore on. Jack went to bed.

In the morning he walked round hoping to find employment. There was always a centre of activity in any town. In Narberth it was the Saddler's. In London he had joined the army in the Wellington Arms. Even in Hereford there was a drovers' tavern. Not here. In desperation he moved from one pub to another, sometimes having to drink a glass, but mostly moving on without a purchase. His enquiries always met with the same reply, 'Wait for the fair.'

The day or two he spent in the town seemed like an age. Driven mad by idleness, the days seemed like years as he paced the streets in an impotent rage. When would the fair come? The rage drifted into depression, sometimes despair. This was a bad start. There seemed to be no future for him here but he had to try. He had always been a loner but now he felt lonely in a way he had never done before.

The fair did eventually arrive. Livestock were sold. Market hucksters peddled their wares in their time-honoured fashion. Gradually the town filled up. He moved around the town eventually finding himself with a group of young men some way away from the cattle sales. So this was where it happened.

Looking around furtively into the faces of prospective employers there was a look of anxiety on many of the faces. There were perhaps fifteen there. A farmer would walk towards the group, asking questions. 'Who employed you last? How long were you there? Why did you leave? What are you asking?' It was a horse sale, or even worse than that as the workers could be discarded at the end of one year.

Jack waited there for perhaps two hours. He began to despair. Then, without him being aware of his approach, a well-dressed middle-aged man asked, 'What's your name?' Jack told him. The man looked more prosperous than most there.

'Where were you last?'

'Pembrokeshire.'

'Farm?'

'Yes.'

'Why did you leave?'

229

'Too small a farm,' he lied.

'How long were you there?'

'A year.'

'Before that?'

'Crimea.' He showed his damaged hand.

He seemed impressed by Jack's apparent honesty. Jack added, 'I can shoe as well.'

'Can you plough?' Jack nodded. 'You look strong enough. I'll take you on at seven pounds a year all found. You won't get a better offer.' He agreed to this and they shook hands. 'Wait here. I'll take you home in half an hour.'

Half an hour passed. Then another half an hour. Finally his employer walked towards him with what looked like a farm worker several paces behind and obviously in his shadow. He came straight to the point. 'Jack Lloyd, you have not been straightforward with me. You haven't told me the true reason why you left your last job. Have you?'

'No, I haven't. I needed the work.'

The man seemed impressed by his direct admission, but still said, 'I can't employ you. You understand that, don't you?'

'I do.' It was all over.

The farm worker had heard every word.

Jack walked off. So, I've got to run a little further, he thought. Rain was starting to fall quite heavily. He took shelter, pulling his cape around his shoulders. When he had been there some minutes, deciding what to do next, he became aware of someone drawing near to him.

'Everyone knows about you, Jack Lloyd. Everyone!' He looked at him, recognising the face of the man who had been with his prospective employer. 'You're a troublemaker, you are.' The small rat-like face looked at him with a sadistic glee made all the more objectionable by a mouthful of very bad teeth. 'You'll never get work here. I'll see to that.'

Jack started to get irritated. 'Get away, you bloody little rat,' he cried out, pushing him away.

'Don't you hit me, I could have you for this.'

'Hop it.' Jack pushed him and kicked him in the behind.
His adversary now came back aggressively. 'Don't you kick me.'

Something in Jack snapped. The pressure had built up over a period of months; the quarrel with Griff, the disappointment at not getting work and now this irritant. Within three seconds, he had given him two blows under the jaw and he was unconscious on the ground. Whether anyone had seen, he had no idea. He had to get out. He knew that the blows had been far too hard for a man of his size. Had he killed him? Had he given him permanent brain damage? Would he ever work again? Everything had gone wrong in Cardigan. He had known it the moment he walked into the town. There was only one thing to do and that was to get out. Wrapping the cape around him, he walked into the rain at a fast pace on the road to Newcastle Emlyn.

Chapter 23

A lot had happened in the year he had been in Swansea. Within a day or two he found work with a building company working on the dock construction. Almost as soon, he found lodgings with the O'Haras, one of only two Irish families on Frog Street. Early the next year the eldest daughter Molly became pregnant. She and Jack married soon afterwards.

His life appeared on the surface to be settled. Probably as settled as it ever would be. He was in regular work and reasonably well paid. A great deal better paid than in his Narberth days. A baby expected soon and a good-looking wife.

Underneath, it was a different story. The household was in constant uproar for one reason or another. Old man O'Hara worked hard and regularly. He also drank hard and regularly. There were fights in the house and fights in the street. Jack had a moderating effect on him but only when he was around. Gradually the trouble started to irritate Jack beyond measure.

'Molly, we're going to have to move out, and soon.'

'But why Jack? Why?'

'The noise, the drink, your bloody father.'

'Ach, he's alright. He just has a few now and then.'

'Has a few? He's drinking all night, every night.'

'He's harmless enough, Jack.'

'He's a drunk. We've a baby due.'

'He'll quieten down when the baby comes, for sure. He's a heart of gold, you know that.'

'Heart of gold? A mighty thirst, you mean.'

'He's always liked a drink. He's a loveable man.'

'It's my wages as is keeping this house afloat. He drinks all his.'

'Jack, that's not fair, it's not the truth.'

'He works for beer. Don't fool yourself. We're moving.

Not far, but moving.'

'We can't move. I can't leave mother alone, Jack.'

'Why not?'

'She needs me. She can't manage dad.'

'Why not?'

'You know, now and then he drinks a bit.'

'Drinks all the time. If he was on his own, he'd be in the gutter.'

'Don't put it like that, Jack. He is my father. We'll have to talk to them tonight.'

'He'll go straight from work to the tavern and come home late, drunk. I'm not talking to a drunk.'

'What'll we do, then?'

'Sunday morning when he's sober. We'll see him then.'

'Alright Jack. I don't think you'll win this one.'

'I will win it if I have to beat him to a pulp.' He raised his clenched fist to emphasise the point.

'You're not being fair Jack. This family has to stick together.'

'I agree, but it's being pulled apart by a drunk.'

'There's six of us here. The two girls don't earn much but they help.'

'Soon there'll be seven. We've got to have a place of our own. Don't let's row any more. We'll see them on Sunday.'

'On Sunday without fail. I've got to get to work now.'

He looked at her directly as they ceased talking. She saw that he wouldn't forget Sunday morning. He walked out of the house and down the street. Greeted by several of his neighbours, as he walked deep in thought, he mumbled a reply without glancing up.

He was employed as a blacksmith with two others. Much of his work was with horses. The only one of them country trained, it was the work he liked best. The forge, entirely black inside, was lit only by the fire. The blows of hammer on metal continued without respite as the men bent over the anvil, hour after hour, broken now and then by the wait for the shoes to turn red in the fire as they pumped the bellows. The sizzling of the hot shoes being quenched in water came next and finally the nailing of the shoe into place. Day after day it continued. He loved the work, and loved the horses. In spite of the noise, he found it a respite from family life. Occasionally during the day old man O'Hara came into his mind but not for long. The work took all his concentration. When not shoeing the horses, he was making the shoes, only now and then doing other, industrial work.

His working day over, it took perhaps fifteen minutes to get home. With a sense of unpleasant expectation, he walked slowly, in no hurry to get to Frog Street. Why was he working all day to come home to this? Constant noise, constant conflict, constant drunkenness. He passed the windows of the terraced houses in the street, getting fleeting glimpses of family life inside. Walking in, he saw the old man unusually home early, but as usual drunk and making a noise. His temper began to rise. He looked at his father-in-law intensely, searchingly and aggressively. There were the beginnings of a throb in his temples. Could he control himself or would he let fly with both fists? Before he got to the kitchen, Molly spoke to him and also halted his progress. His wife was trying to placate him through her tears and a look of distinct despair on her face.

'Jack. Here,' she said, beckoning to him. He stopped to listen to her. There was a look of foreboding on her face. 'Don't go mad at what I'm going to tell you Jack. You won't will you? He tacitly agreed without saying a word. His by now calm composure reassured her he would agree to her wishes. 'Father's been sacked.'

'What for? Drunk on the job, I suppose.'

'You said you wouldn't get mad, Jack. You said.'

'I'm not getting mad, Molly. Just a bit annoyed. No good asking him what happened till he's sober. Then he probably won't know.'

'Don't be like that Jack. He's our father.'

'Drunk father, for sure.'

'Don't use that word "drunk" again. We've got enough to

234

put up with without you making things worse.'

'Get him to bed and I'll see him before I go to work in the morning.'

They tried to get him to bed without success. He wanted to talk and continued spouting his usual rubbish. The daughters gave into him, allowing him to continue. Jack again became annoyed. 'Molly, I'm hungry. I want food now. I mean now!'

'Something's ready but we got to sort father out.'

'I'll sort him out.' His eyes flashed.

Then they all heard the father say, 'Get me another pint of beer and I'll be alright.' One of the younger girls went into her purse to get the price of a pint.

Jack strode the three paces into the kitchen. 'Oh no, you don't. That you don't.' He thrust the purse back into the girl's hand. The father even quietened down after this outburst but couldn't help himself from saying in a quiet voice, 'It was only a pint I wanted Jack. Only a pint.'

'Oh no you don't, you bloody old drunken fool!' He kicked the chair and the old man fell slowly to the floor, only partially aware what had happened. 'No you don't. Get up to bed like they told you. Now. Go on. Now!' He stood over him glowering. 'Get up. Get to bed.'

The old man sobered up. Never in his own home had his authority been challenged. He got up unsteadily, looked his son-in-law in the face and with every ounce of willpower grasped whatever sober resources he had left, saying, 'Don't you order me about in my own home, you.' He raised his fists and struck out at Jack, first with the right and then the left hand. His intentions were so obvious that Jack got out of the way. Jack pushed him. He fell onto the floor once more. It was such a shock to him that he burst into tears, sobbing at the degree of humiliation he had suffered in the last hour or two. This went on for perhaps a quarter of an hour. Jack looked away then walked into the passage. Returning, he said to the family in dismissive exasperation, 'Get him up to bed.' This time, his father-in-law went quietly, still sobbing for a while till sleep overtook him.

Eventually they sat down and ate. Molly looked at Jack with some degree of reproach, 'You'd no need to be so hard Jack.'

'If he'd been drunk on duty in the army on active service they could have put him before a firing squad.'

'This isn't the army, Jack.'

'He's a drunk and he's buggering up this family. I've given him gentle treatment.'

'Jack, he's our father and he's always liked a drink.'

'What'll he do now then? He won't get another job. Not a decent paying one anyway.'

'He'll get something. He's a worker, is father. Always worked.'

'He'll need a good wage to pay for his beer.'

'Don't start that again Jack.'

'I shan't be buying his beer, for sure.'

'Jack shut up'.

'Beer's caused nearly every problem I've ever seen. The farm, drovers, army and now here.'

'Jack, shut up. We've had enough for one day.' It was her final attempt to shut him up. He knew it and kept quiet.

The evening continued in a heavy silence. Each one felt awkward. None wanted to speak yet they were all thinking of the same thing. What would happen tomorrow? They all went to bed. Jack lay next to Molly, stroking her stomach. She relaxed. The baby kicked. Under his breath he said, 'Feels like a rough customer to me.'

She laughed. 'I don't want another day like this again.' He wanted to say "it will get worse before it gets better" but didn't.

Mother and the two single daughters slept in the same bed, lying awake for some time. She said to them, 'Your father's really in trouble now. Will he ever get out of it?

'Course he will, mother. He always has done.'

'He's not as young as he used to be. It's Jack who's the man in this house now.'

'He won't take it that easy. I know father.'

'He has drunk too much, you know. It's finally caught up

236

with him.'

It was almost dawn and the family stirred. Jack and Molly, first to get up, lit the fire. It was cold in the house and the ashes from the fire spread perhaps a foot into the room. The room was in disorder. There was a sofa with a dirty cover over it which had been a deep pink but which now looked grey, two broken upright chairs and a small table on which were the remains of the previous evening's supper. Like the family, the house was in chaos. The walls had at one time been painted but only in odd corners gave any indication of the original yellow. The ceiling was a smoky grey from the oil lamps. The room smelt of unwashed human occupation, which to a newcomer would be as nauseous as it was instant. Almost without thought, the fire was lit, water heated and breakfast made which was consumed in silence.

Like many a drunk before him, the father got up early, only vaguely aware what had gone on the previous afternoon. As he had been put to bed early, the effect of the alcohol had worn off. Getting out of bed with all his clothes on, he walked into the kitchen looking like the unmade bed he had just left. His uncut but thinning hair pointing in all directions, his round drunken face only half awake, he rubbed his eyes as he entered. A grubby flannel shirt without a collar and missing several buttons, revealed a large white stomach. One of his braces was over his shoulder, the other hung down beside his holed and patched trousers. His feet were bare, dirty and the nails hadn't been cut for a long time.

Rubbing his eyes with both hands, he looked at his daughter. 'Got a cup of tea there, Molly?' He was about to pick it up, 'Have you put two sugars in?' She did so. While still standing, he drank it as fast as the temperature would allow. 'That's better,' he said, breathing heavily in satisfaction.

'You're coming with me to see the ganger to get your job back,' Jack told him.

It suddenly dawned on him that he had lost his job. The facts came flooding into his mind. He was aware he had been sacked but not the full details. 'It wasn't right what they did.'

'You'd been drinking on the job.'

'Not on the job.'

'Course not. No tavern on the site.'

'Sure I'd had a couple, but I wasn't drunk.'

'Get ready, we're leaving soon.'

'I'll do it tomorrow. I'll feel better by then. I'm not feeling well.'

'I'm going in a few minutes and I'm taking you to the ganger,' Jack said in a determined voice.

'That you're not,' he replied.

Jack walked the two paces to confront him, standing inches away from his face, looking at him with overpowering and scarcely suppressed anger. 'You are going. You stupid old drunk. I am not keeping this family myself when you can work. Swallow your pride, you stupid drunk.'

His mind then recollected Jack pushing him over last night and his own childlike sobbing in bed. 'I won't get it back, you know. The ganger's new. Been on the sites in America. Got it in for me. Thinks he knows everything.'

'Awkward or not, we're going to see him.' He pushed him in the small of the back to urge haste. Slowly and with a calculated lack of speed, he got ready. 'Don't get cocky. Understand?' said Jack. He didn't reply. Jack did not repeat himself. The women in the house stood back listening and gave furtive glances at the two men. The old man felt broken. How much more personal pride would he have to lose. Jack became aware of this and moderated his attitude towards him. 'Ready? See what we can do. What's his name?'

'Ben.'

'Ben what?'

'Ben Letworthy.'

'Funny name. Remember, don't get cocky. You'll have to say you won't get drunk again.'

'Alright. Do what you can for me. I know I do drink a bit.'

They walked the fifteen-minute journey at a moderate speed,

neither dawdling along in hopelessness nor striding ahead with confidence. 'You don't have to grovel, just say it won't happen again.'

'Alright.'

They walked the rest of the distance in silence, broken only by the sound of their boots on the metalled road. Entering the site, they made for the ganger's office, a small hut perhaps seven feet square. Inside were a stool and a desk with the top set at an angle with plans on top. The office was unoccupied. They waited outside in the dawn light for someone to appear. They didn't wait long before they heard a shout from behind, 'Get off this site, I sacked you yesterday. Get off, I tell you. Get off.' He waved his arms in anger.

They turned and saw a tall, florid man whose temper was nearly out of control. He repeated himself in an even angrier manner.

In a whisper, Jack said to his father in law, 'Don't move.' He moved in front to get between the old man and his adversary and looked the ganger straight in the face without saying a word. It reduced his anger to some degree. The ganger had fair curly hair, which was beginning to go thin on top. He looked at Jack and could not take his eyes off him. Slowly the anger began to flow from him as his look became more curious. Not to be distracted for long, he returned to what he knew was their original purpose.

'What do you want? Anyway, who are you?'

'His son-in-law. We know he was a bit drunk. Give him another chance, otherwise the family'll suffer'.

'You must be joking. Fell down drunk in front of a steam navvy. He's been warned.'

'How many times?'

'I've only been here a week and this is the second time. He's out.'

'The family'll suffer.'

'He's out. No arguing. Get out now, the pair of you!'

He told the old man to leave the site which he did, believing his position to be hopeless.

'I want to see you,' Jack told the ganger, who did not answer but looked uneasy. 'I've met you before.'

'You haven't.'

'O yes, I have.'

The ganger turned paler and couldn't look Jack in the face for more than a second or two. He was almost mumbling to himself, awaiting the next remark. 'Never met you before in my life,' he said.

'Yes, I've met you before,' continued Jack, 'I recognised your voice.'

'Where?'

'Long way from here.'

The man tried to use bravado to extract himself from this corner. 'Where? I said where?'

'You know as well as I do.'

'I don't know anything. Where?' His voice got louder. Two men approached him for instructions and also from curiosity; he brushed them aside with orders to come back later. He became agitated, wanting to find out how much his adversary really did know. Self-control was something he had little of and it was as much as he could do to keep his impatience under control. He felt threatened physically and mentally. If only this man would come out with what he knew.

'But I do know about you, Leftie,' Jack declared.

'Leftie! What do you mean, Leftie?'

'You were known as Leftie in Narberth.'

'Leftie? Narberth? Never heard of Leftie. Never been to Narberth.' His remarks rang hollow and his eyes were beginning to show signs of defeat. Even his voice lacked conviction. Jack could see and feel the man's world crumbling around him. It gave him a sense of righteous power he had never experienced before. He wanted it to continue but knew he would have to bargain hard to get his way.

'Come in the office.'

They both went inside, out of earshot of everyone. The man

knew he couldn't bargain any more. 'What d'you know?' he asked Jack.

'I was in the bedroom when you robbed the money.'

'You win. How did you know it was me?'

'The voice. I'd know it to my dying day. The other fella got transportation.'

'I heard about that a year or two after.'

'I went to the trial in Carmarthen. They didn't call me.'

'How long ago was it?'

'Fourteen or fifteen years. I was about nine then.'

The ganger, once he had admitted the matter, wanted to talk. Wanting to ask questions, something told him not to do so.

Jack was curious about him but wanted to conclude the matter in hand. 'You give the old man a start again and nothing'll be said. My word.'

'You give me your word?'

'I give you my word.' He offered him his hand, which was shaken with vigour.

'What you doing?'

'Blacksmith on the dock site. Farrier really.'

'Come here if you want a change.'

'No, not me. Stay where I am. Got to get back to work. The old man can start tomorrow?'

'Yes, but remember, if he's drunk on the job again there'll be no more favours.'

'I know that.' They shook hands again.

'Have a drink one night?'

'No, I don't drink.' It would be no good asking again.

His absence from work was unnoticed and the day went by as usual. Walking home, he thought about how he would deal with the old man. Would he be drunk or sober? If he was drunk, was he really worth bothering with? If he was sober, he would try once again.

'Where's the old man?'

'Upstairs, asleep.'

'Drunk or sober?'

241

'Jack, don't start again.'

'Shut up woman, I've got his job back.'

'How did you do that?'

'I've ways and means.'

'Go up and see him. He's only had a couple.'

He walked up the narrow stairs to the room where his father-in-law was dozing. 'Got your job back. Start tomorrow.'

'I don't believe it.'

'It's true.'

'Start tomorrow. Listen, if you drink at all on site again, you're out. Understand?'

'Don't know if I want the job back.'

'You'll go back, like it or not. Drunk again and you're out.'

'Sure, Jack, I can do it.'

Three days later he was sacked again for drunkenness. This time it was for good.

Chapter 24

Old man O'Hara's sacking and the circumstances surrounding it were all over Frog Street within minutes of it happening. Animated gossip about this incident was the sole subject of discussion for days. It was interrupted only when a member of the family passed down the street and then only for seconds. Furtive looks were cast in their direction as the gossips hoped to glean any further scrap of information. When fact was not available, then guesswork would do. The subject most discussed was how he had been taken on again after the first incident of drunkenness. There was not a charitable thought in the street.

'They'll come to no good, that lot. What do you expect from the Irish?' 'Up to Greenhill is where they should go.' 'The sooner they go the better.' 'That family'll come to no good, mark my words.' All these were remarks exchanged on the street, but so far not overheard by the O'Haras till one fateful Friday evening.

Bridget, the elder of the two girls, was walking home for the night having finished work as a barmaid in a tavern. The street was empty but for two women talking, unaware of their neighbour's approach. The talk was animated, their voices loud. 'O'Hara scum is what they are and scum they'll remain,' was the first remark that Bridget heard. After a hard day's work and feeling on edge, this remark was the straw that broke the donkey's back. She flew at them both; kicking, shouting, pulling hair and punching. In a moment the street was in uproar as a number of spectators appeared, drawn outside by the sound of fighting. No one intervened. It probably went on for less than two minutes but in that time there was hair in the gutter, cut faces and bruised noses. Bridget's temper was ferocious but there was soon more shouting than direct physical violence, with the two gossips getting the worst of it. The spectators and protagonists, totally absorbed in the uproar, were only aware of the constables' arrival when they broke into the circle with some force.

Grasping Bridget, who seemed the most aggressive of the three, the elder constable said, 'That'll be enough of that.' She quietened down immediately.

The younger and less experienced constable opened both arms in order to herd the other two girls away from Bridget. They were in full retreat and did as he wanted. They now started to shout accusations at one another, and would have resumed fighting if they had not been held back. What was apparent to the constables was that Bridget was unmarked but the two other girls were much the worse for wear.

Gradually the atmosphere cooled down but the crowd had increased. Enthusiastic gossip could be heard all around. Within ten minutes, Bridget was taken off to the police station by the constables, followed by her mother. The other two girls' names had been taken, and they were told to clean themselves up and be available if the police wished to speak to them again. The crowd gradually thinned out and dispersed into the night. The sporting event was over. The families of Frog Street talked of little else for the next day or two. Old man O'Hara's sacking was no longer front page news. He'd been replaced by his daughter.

The constables had questioned Bridget without getting too much sense out of her. She was to appear before the magistrates in the morning, having been charged with assault. The family discussed the matter. The old man, in his usual hopeless manner, asked the question, 'What'll we do?'

'They'll bind her over. That's what they always do in these neighbour's quarrels.'

'Anyway, she was tormented by those two. Who wouldn't lash out? You would, wouldn't you?'

'Course I would, both of them had it coming.'

244

'She was provoked, she was only defending herself.'

'Provoked beyond measure.'

'What do we do, then? They've got it in for us Irish.'

'Have to get a lawyer.'

'That'll cost money.'

'Whatever it costs, I'll pay,' put in Jack, who had so far only been a listener.

'Could be five guineas, you know.'

'I'll cover it, don't worry.'

'Who do we go to then?'

'There's only one to go to. Dan the devil.'

'Where's he?'

'I know his office. Walter Road.'

'How do you see him?'

'Go to his office of course.'

'When do we go?'

'Tomorrow first thing, you bloody fool.'

'Jack and Mother will go. That's best.'

'What do we do now?'

'Nothing. Get to bed and see him in the morning.'

After breakfast they made their way to Walter Road, arriving half an hour before the office was open. They huddled together like a large bundle of old clothes with the exception of Jack who stood apart, not taking part in the conversation. Eventually the front door opened and the whole family crowded in, led by the mother. Within a minute, the whole office took on a different odour which made the clerk speak to them from several feet away. They talked to him all at once without him understanding a word. Jack eventually talked over them all. 'We want to speak to Mr Daniel. Now. This morning.'

'I'll see if Mr Daniel is available. He has a court hearing this morning.'

The clerk, a hump-shouldered and razor thin man in his fifties, had been with the firm almost since childhood. He looked at them disdainfully over his wire-rimmed glasses. He would have liked to have delayed their discussion with Mr Daniel or

245

better still directed them to another firm but reluctantly did as he was asked. What remained of his thinning hair was plastered to his skull. Everything about him was white, except the suit and tie he wore which was black and the backs of his hands, which were streaked with blue from the prominent veins. Walking out of the room and up the stairs with short nervous steps, his shoulders became even more humped. He knocked, waiting till he heard, 'Come in.' Entering the office, he waited till Mr Daniel looked up.

'What is it, Percy?'

'There's a family of Irish down there to see you Mr Daniel. Court matter this morning.'

'How many are there?'

'A lot. Six or seven.'

'Send two up only. Understand? Two only.' He smiled to himself.

Walking downstairs even more slowly than he had walked up, the clerk directed Jack and his mother-in-law towards Dan's room.

They knocked, waited and entered. He didn't invite them to sit down.

'What's the trouble? Quarrelling with the neighbours?'

Mother started what had the potential to become a very long story but was stopped. 'Don't want to hear it.'

'But you……'

'Don't want to hear it. Is she in the cells?'

'Yes.'

'First we get her out.' He was a red-faced jovial man with a twinkle in his eye, able to communicate with anyone at any level. With a smile he asked, 'What's her name?'

'Bridget O'Hara.'

Smiling again, he replied, 'Good welsh name.' It broke the ice between them. 'You leave Bridget to me.'

'What will you charge?' inquired Jack.

'To you, three to five guineas. Go now. Court starts at ten to eleven.'

246

He walked to the court, nodded to the O'Hara family in a humorous and assured manner as he entered the court building, sitting down within the court on a seat reserved for solicitors. The court clerk was going through various papers, unaware of his presence. Eventually looking up he then said, 'Good morning Mr Daniel. Which case do you have an interest in?'

'Bridget O'Hara.'

'There are a few applications, then we can hear her.'

'Very well.'

The magistrates entered, everyone bowed to everyone else, the solicitor doing so in a grave and respectful manner which hid a mind full of confidence and good humour. He thought to himself, today is going to be a good day.

The applications completed, the prisoner was then produced. She looked a sorry sight. There was mud over her face, her hair was dishevelled and her clothes ripped. What with the hair over her face and the dirt on it, she could hardly see in front of her. Bridget might have been in another world. Confirming her name and address, she listened to the charge.

'That you Bridget O'Hara on the 24th day of February 1859 between the hours of 7pm and 8pm did assault Mary Jones and Edith Jenkins contrary to common law. How do you plead?'

Dan the devil leaned over to Bridget and said, 'Plead not guilty.'

'But the constables told me to plead guilty,' she replied in a perplexed voice.

'I'm representing you and you should plead not guilty.'

The clerk to the court was starting to become irritated. 'How much longer will this be Mr Daniel?'

'A minute please, learned clerk,' he replied good humouredly. Again addressing Bridget, he said, 'Plead not guilty.'

'Plead not guilty,' she blurted out to the court.

'How long do you want?' asked the irritated clerk.

'Seven days. Would the bench also agree?'

'Can the constables be here?'
They nodded from the back of the court.
'Will the bench release her in her own recognisance?'
'The bench is agreeable.'
'How long will this take?'
'About an hour.'

Bridget was released and told to come to his office alone that afternoon. She went home with her family, and Jack, now the only wage earner, went back to work.

'You pleaded not guilty,' Bridget's mother said to her.

'He told me to. Wonder how he's going to get me off? The constables told me to plead guilty.'

'Don't listen to the constables, stupid!'

'He wants to see me this afternoon.'

Bridget walked the short way to the office, arriving as it opened in the afternoon.

'Mr Daniel wants to see me,' she announced. She followed the clerk up on this occasion, being shown into the room as he departed.

'Sit down Bridget.' He gave her a smile. It made her feel good. There was something confident and intimate about him; she could trust this man. He was on her side, she knew that.

'Have you a walking stick at home?'

'Yes.'

'Have you an old-fashioned dirty dress worn by your grandmother, and an old shawl.'

'We don't have anything else in our house.'

'When you go to court, I want you to look as old as possible.'

'I can do that alright.'

'Bridget, when you come to court next week I want you to look old. Old hair.'

'Shall I put some ash in it?'

'Excellent,' he responded, 'and wrapped in an old shawl.'

'Bent over? Old walk?'

'Bridget, you've got it. Practice it. You won't have to

248

speak.'

'You're a good'un, Mr Daniel. You know they call you Dan the devil.'

He roared with laughter. 'You're corrupting me, Bridget. Now go home and come back to court early next week.' She walked to the door, already practising her aged condition. He smiled to himself. We've got a good one here. 'Bridget, come back'. She did so. He motioned her to stand before him. 'You say nothing to anybody. Nothing, do you hear.'

'I'll not say a word to anyone.'

'Not even your own family.'

'Not even my own family?'

'Absolutely no one,' he reiterated, 'that's very important.'

'Yes.' It had sunk in. 'You're a good'un, Mr Daniel.'

'A week today, outside the court. Come early.'

She hobbled to the door in an aged manner. At the door she looked back at him with a trusting, innocent smile. Holy Mary Mother of God, I do love that man. He knew the thoughts going through her mind.

The week bore heavily on Bridget's shoulders. Her family constantly questioned her but she put them off with bland replies. The mother's curiosity knew no limits.

'What did he say in that room of his, girl?'

'It was nothing mother. Told me I wouldn't be asked anything.'

'Girl, you can't go on like this, he must have said something. What was it?'

'Just said what it would be like in court.'

'That's all?'

'That's all. Now will you give it a rest, mother.'

So it went on all week but she never breathed a word to anyone till the day before the case. She couldn't contain it any longer and she had to tell someone, preferably someone who would keep their mouth shut. There was only one who could do that: Jack.

'Jack, a word with you.'

249

'Yes?' he answered quietly.

'A word with you away from this bloody family of mine. They're like cackling hens.'

They walked to the backyard which was out of hearing.

'Jack, you won't say a word to a soul will ye? At court tomorrow, Dan the devil wants me to dress up like an old woman.'

'Well, do it then.'

'Everything; walking stick, shawl, old clothes, grey hair and walking like a cripple.'

'Do as he says'.

'I haven't told them. How'll I get out of the house without them knowing?'

'Leave it to me'.

'He wants me in court early. I don't have to say a word.'

'Do as he says. Have you got all the clothes?'

'Yes and the ash to put in my hair.' He laughed.

'Ash in your hair?'

'To make it look grey.'

'What time do you want to go?'

'Soon after nine.'

'I'll get rid of them,' Jack reassured her.

She knew she could trust him to keep his mouth shut and to get rid of the family.

Sleeping fitfully, she woke up early. The court appearance weighed heavily on her mind. Tossing and turning, she knew she wouldn't be able to go to sleep again and got up to find Jack already dressed and ready. 'What you going to tell them?'

'Leave it to me, Bridget.'

She was excited. Couldn't eat or drink, and couldn't keep still. Time hung heavy on her hands. Eight o'clock became half-past then a quarter to nine. The family were all now up.

'Why aren't you in work Jack?'

'Given two hours off to see the Mayor and Sir Toby Herbert visit the town.'

'When'll that be, Jack?'

'In five minutes they pass the top of the road.'

'Why didn't you tell us?'

'If you want to see him, you'd better go now.'

'What about you, Bridget?'

'You go. I've got to get ready for court.'

The family trooped to the end of the road leaving Bridget alone.

Within two minutes she was dressed as an old woman, had ash in her hair, walking stick in her hand, a shawl round her shoulders and was running to the magistrates' court in an athletic manner. Within a hundred yards of the building she had stopped, breathless. Waiting for Mr Daniel to arrive, she kept the entrance constantly under observation. Dressed like an old woman, she had to walk and act like one. Groping round in the recesses of her mind, she hobbled a few yards. Having mastered the walk, she tried palsy shaking, visibly but not vigorously. She walked a few more yards, hobbling and shaking, becoming almost mentally an old woman. There was a sharp step behind her. 'Bridget, come with me.' He took her into the court, told her to sit in the dock and do nothing.

'Stand up when I tell you to. Answer to your name when asked by the court clerk. Do nothing else.'

'Right, Mr Daniel.' He left. It was cold in the dock and she started to shiver naturally. People came in and out, and looked at her. Some tried to speak but she gave no answer. Disappearing deeper and deeper into her shawl, she was now hardly visible, but with her eyes watching everything. The wait seemed to go on and on and her stomach constantly fluttered. Eventually the Clerk to the Justices entered the court. 'Is everyone ready?' He looked around for Mr Daniel. Not seeing him, he commanded the usher to find him. When he arrived, he gave the clerk a theatrical bow.

'You ready, Mr Daniel?'

'Of course, learned clerk.' The subtle mockery was not lost on the clerk, who frowned, or the few others in court including Bridget. She wanted to laugh but had to be satisfied with inner amusement.

251

The clerk entered the door adjacent to the raised bench. Returning immediately, he shouted, 'Be upstanding in court.' The magistrates entered. Dan, who was sitting in front of the dock, looked behind saying, 'Stand up Bridget.' She wasn't sure whether he gave a wink or not. Everyone sat down except her.

'Sit down,' the clerk instructed her. 'Are the defence ready to proceed?'

'Yes, learned clerk'. Bridget again restrained a laugh but with even greater effort. She was also aware that the whole of her family were now trooping into the court and making a lot of noise doing so. Also on the public seats were her two alleged victims. Allowing them to quieten, the clerk again spoke, 'Are you quite settled in the back of the court?' There was no answer. 'Then we can proceed. Prisoner in the dock, stand up. Are you Bridget O'Hara?'

'Yes sir.'

'Where do you live?'

'Frog Street, Sir.'

He read out the charge to which she pleaded not guilty. She sat down. Constable Jones was called to the witness box. He took the oath and gave his evidence in a self important and wooden manner. His chest puffed out, his red cheeks shouting out his liking for beer even more loudly than usual, he gave his evidence.

'I was proceeding with Constable Morgan at the end of Frog Street at around seven o'clock in the evening on February 24th when I heard a disturbance. Walking to the scene, I saw three women fighting in the street. There was a crowd around the fighting women. It was the Irish girl fighting the other two. The other two were getting the worst of it. They had bruised eyes, cuts on their faces and some of their hair was pulled out. Constable Morgan and I waded into this disturbance and grabbed the woman we now know to be Bridget O'Hara. The women continued to shout but we prevented any more fighting. We took Bridget O'Hara to the police station, questioned her and charged her. That's what happened sir.'

'Have you any questions Mr Daniel?'

'Yes.'

'Constable Jones, do you recognise the two women who were assaulted in this court?'

'I do sir,' he replied, pointing them out.

'They're in a sorry state, aren't they constable?'

'Indeed they are, sir. Very sorry state indeed.'

'They're quite strong girls, aren't they constable? Both of them.'

'Indeed they are sir.' His sense of self-importance became inflated before everyone present.

'It must have been someone very strong to injure those two girls so badly. And one person, was it constable?'

'Very strong, sir.'

'Look at the defendant in the dock, constable, is she capable of doing all that damage? This poor old woman.'

He looked at her for the first time. He deflated visibly before the eyes of the court.

'Is this old woman capable of inflicting such harm to two such young, strong women?'

He felt like someone who had been pole-axed and was lost for words. Without knowing what he was saying, 'Doesn't look like her,' slipped out.

'Constable, could this old woman have done this harm?'

He was lost for words, shaking his head.

The court remained silent for a moment or two then there was a shout from the public benches, 'She's putting it....' Before she could get a further word out the clerk shouted out, 'Quiet in the back of the court or you'll be put in the cells. Do you hear?' Again there was silence. It was as though the whole court had been pole-axed. Again there was the same interruption from the back of the court, 'She's putting....' The clerk was now extremely annoyed. 'Usher, take the woman making a noise out. This instant!' The usher took her by the arm and pulled her out, still muttering, while the court waited. The usher then returned to his place by the door.

There is always a time to pursue a matter and a time to keep quiet. Mr Daniel decided that the prosecution's case had been undermined sufficiently for the bench to throw the case out. The court settled down again.

'Has the defence any more questions?' asked the clerk.

'Not of this witness. Do the prosecution intend to call another witness?'

'No.'

Mr Daniel summed up briefly, dwelling almost entirely on the matter of identification and the unlikelihood of the defendant being able to inflict such harm on two young, strong girls. She was found not guilty.

'The court will adjourn,' said the clerk. The court emptied.

Dan the devil's achievement on that day further reinforced his near legendary reputation.

Chapter 25

Jack walked home one cold Thursday evening, tired and aching from bending over shoeing horses all day. Along the street he walked, dodging pools of water, piles of rubbish and those talking in the street. Ignoring the lights in the windows of the houses, he walked on deep in thought. Once he missed his step and almost fell into a particularly deep pool of stagnant water that had been there for weeks. Even familiarity with the general smell in the street did not make him immune from the effect of this pool. Even those talking in the street stopped talking as he passed. He arrived home.

No sooner had he entered than they all wanted to talk to him at once. 'Shut up, I'm tired, I want to sit down,' he said, but on they pressed him with their chatter. Raising his voice in suppressed temper, 'Shut up, I said, all of you'. They knew better than to press him further. Controlling his temper left him silently stressed and he could not relax as he had hoped. Gradually he did relax as the members of the family walked silently past him, looking and keeping conspicuously quiet which caused a heavy silence in the house. Unusually, he dropped into a heavy sleep which continued for perhaps two hours. Eventually he woke, realising how tired he must have been. He thought of what had happened during the day, and also of the walk home. Did the street have to be in this stinking mess? Water, shit and ashes everywhere? Not even in his poverty stricken childhood did he ever have to endure this mess. At least in the Preselis there had been fresh air, fresh water from the streams and the water in the wells was clean. Here, everyone had to get water from the same stream. Where did the shit go? Where could anyone find a place to dump it? There was no respite; it was stinking everywhere.

Family life at best irritated him, at worst caused him to lose his temper. They talked from morning till night, most of it rubbish. It just kept their tongues busy. The old man was as bad as any of the women. He could talk Irish blarney all day long. He hadn't found work and was unlikely to do so. Jack was now the sole earner. He didn't mind supporting the women in the family but he objected to keeping the old man. No longer the head of the house, no longer an earner, no longer having access to money to fund his heavy drinking, he had become a shadowy figure and more so by the day. He did what Jack told him to do. Now and then, one of the women gave him the price of a pint, which propelled him out of the house to the cheapest tavern. It was only the price of one pint. Perhaps his, now rarely seen, friends would buy him a couple more. He would return home reasonably sober but unfulfilled. He knew he would have to face Jack if he was drunk. O'Hara was an old and broken man and everyone knew it.

Jack got up, rubbed his eyes and washed his face in the bucket of water recently brought in from the stream. It was not clear.

Molly edged up to him. 'Jack, I've got to see you.' She was the only one who could persuade him. Brushing her conspicuous pregnancy against his side, she said   'Jack, my time's coming and soon.'

'I know, girl. What do we do?'

'Got to get a midwife.'

'Where do you get one?'

'There's one in Greenhill. Mother always used her.'

'What's her name?'

'Maggie Pollock.'

'Get her then.'

'Mother'll go up for her. It'll cost money, Jack.'

'That's what I work for, Molly. Send for her. How much longer, Molly?' He put his arm around her and stroked her stomach.

'A few days only.'

'A week?'

'Less. Day or two. That's all Jack.'

'How do you know, Molly?'

256

'Us women know these things.'

'Better get this woman quick then.'

'Tomorrow morning'll do.'

'Sure not tonight?'

'I'll be alright tonight, Jack.' He stroked her stomach again and they looked into one another's eyes. 'What do you think, a boy or a girl Jack?'

'Boy of course.'

'What'll we call it?'

'Jack, of course.' They smiled at one another. It was one of Jack's few moments of softness. 'Better get to bed, Molly. What have I got tonight?'

'Potatoes and a bit of bacon. Mother'll get it for you.'

The whole household now treated Jack with a degree of deference he had never experienced before, watching him eat as they silently stood back around the walls of the room.

Finishing his meal, he looked up at them. 'You're going to Maggie Pollock in the morning, mother.' The old man had slipped out of the room to an upright chair in the back kitchen.

'I am that, Jack. She saw me through'em all. All still living. She's a good'un, is Maggie.'

'Well, get her first thing.'

'I will that. A great woman and none of her own. Never married, said she'd seen enough of men not to make a fool of herself with one.'

He laughed and thought of the old man. He felt sorry for him but he had to make his domination of the family felt, otherwise they would be out of control again. Perhaps he would try and get him an easy job somewhere. But where? He was a rough and ready character, not a candidate for gentle tasks.

'You'll like her, Jack. Delivered all mine alive which is more than you can say for many,' Mrs O'Hara continued.

'Mother. Get her in the morning.'

She had a liking and respect for Jack and sometimes a little fear. How did he escape the drink? Not many did that. She knew he'd had a hard life though he never mentioned it to anyone, not even Molly. She knew little about him; he was a closed book. He rarely expressed emotion but was always there when there was a crisis. You could feel safe with him but never know him.

Mother went to Greenhill, coming back late in the morning with Maggie Pollock. Known to all in the area, she was short, broad and always dressed in black; a black dress which reached almost to the ground, black shoes, black hat and black umbrella. She had a round face and rosy cheeks, in spite of being in her late fifties, exuding calm to all. She rarely visited Frog Street, and then only to assist with a confinement for an Irish family and they were rare on the street.

'Well, how are the O'Hara girls?'

'Well enough, Maggie. Well enough. This'll be the first grandchild.'

'Something to celebrate.'

'Perhaps. There's been a bit too much celebrating over the years in this house already.'

'Perhaps you'll celebrate in the church at Greenhill.'

'We'll do that alright, Maggie.'

'A good priest they have too. Never do better than father. A good Irishman.'

'We haven't been for years.'

'You'd better start going again then. A good Irish family can't leave the church.'

'Aye, we must do that, for sure.'

'If we lived up there we'd probably be going. It's no Garden of Eden here Maggie, for sure.'

'Molly. When are you due?' the midwife asked.

'This week. I'm sure.'

'No idea of the date?'

'No.'

She felt her stomach for perhaps a minute while she stood up, without her having to remove clothes. 'Molly, which room you having the baby in?'

'Upstairs.'

'Clean the bed clothes, all of them. Understand, Molly?'

258

'Yes.'

'Clean boiled water. Understand. Boiled and clean.'

'Yes, but we get it from the stream. Sometimes it's not clear.'

'Get clean water from wherever you can find it. You do it.'

'It won't be easy.'

'Having a baby won't be easy, either. You have men in the house; get them to fetch clean water. I know it's not easy. Get it.'

'We'll get it, Maggie.'

'Are the men working?'

'Jack, my husband is. My father lost his job.'

'Get him to get clean water. You can't have enough of it. And boil it. All of it.'

'Yes, Maggie.'

'We will need soap too.'

'Yes, Maggie.'

'Soap and get it now, a big piece.' Maggie took charge of the situation which the family found reassuring.

'I'm not coming again till I hear it has started. Call me then, night or day.'

'How will I know?'

'You'll know alright, girl.' She smiled and walked back to Greenhill, her rotund figure dodging the obstacles in the street, first the pool of water then the small piles of rubbish, finally a large stone was avoided before she disappeared from sight.

Life continued in the O'Hara household, though it was rarely called by that name now, the neighbours calling them the Lloyds. Two in the family were now called by that name; it would soon be three. Jack continued to work and the old man seemed to be visibly failing by the day. The women, full of expectation, had a new interest in life with the first grandchild in the family and the first birth for very many years.

Ben Letworthy had made two approaches to Jack to work for him, without success. Why he made these approaches he did not know. He was afraid of his knowledge, wanted to get nearer to him but wasn't quite sure why. Having him in his charge would give him some control over him. Jack made him uneasy. He had knowledge of the robbery but Ben was sure he would never make a complaint against him. What was it that made him uncertain about Jack? If it came to a punch-up he thought Jack would get the better of him but it would be a hard fight. He was used to power and for others to try and ingratiate themselves with him. Jack did not do so. In fact, Ben felt he was ingratiating himself with him.

He saw himself in Jack twenty-five years before. So that was it. Was he the son of the woman he made pregnant in the Preselis so many years ago? He couldn't remember her name; didn't remember whether she had ever told him her name. He could remember her: slim, dark, worn out with poverty, overwork and child-bearing, but with a real spark of humour and sensuality. Knowing he had used her, used her harshly for his own pleasure, then moving on, he felt a real twinge of regret, an emotion which rarely touched him. What would have happened if he had settled with her? He'd have moved on eventually. Had he ever done anything else?

Was this Jack his son? Of course he was. He saw himself in everything about him. The fair hair, robust build, capacity for hard work. Those around them looked up to them both. Yet they were different. He was bad tempered and a drinker. Yes, he was that alright. Jack, he didn't like drink and was quiet. He reflected on the silent demand he had made upon him and it sent a shiver down his spine. Yes, he would have to be wary in his dealings with him. Never would he give a threat he could not carry out. There was no doubt about that. Not only was he wary of him, he was also a little frightened of him. For the first time in his life he had to admit this fact. Yes, Ben Letworthy was a frightened man.

He wanted to get near him but didn't know how. Did this Jack also suspect that Ben was his father? He would be a fool if he didn't and Jack wasn't a fool. Ben reflected on how he could make the approach. Would he be welcomed with open arms or would he get the brush off?

Jack was aware of this man's need to ingratiate himself,

intending to use it to the limit. Ben spoke to him when it was not necessary, feeling a need to please, to strike up conversation, to be thought of favourably. All these overtures placed Ben in an ever more despised position and Jack in a superior one. These approaches, which Jack always answered with a monosyllabic reply, gave him a sense of ever-increasing power. Jack was almost certain he was his father and despised him for it, waiting for an opportunity to destroy him. The moment would come. Jack was certain of that. Yes, the moment would come.

Jack sat in his shabby surroundings, in the only comfortable armchair in the house. Thoughts raced through his mind. The baby was due shortly. It was none of his business really; that was women's work. He had no power over what would happen, but it would happen here.

His mind wandered to Llandeusant, the Drovers, Rosie and young Jack. He hadn't thought of them for months, far too many months. His emotions softened. He smiled to himself. It was a small, private smile. What the hell am I doing here, he thought to himself. His face changed, as did his mood. His eyes filled with tears as he thought of Rosie and Jack. Why did I leave them? Why? A silent anger shook him. Why had he found himself here at the age of twenty-six with a wife to whom he was indifferent, a family who were at best irksome, at worst intolerable, driving him frequently to the verge of murderous rage with their noise and useless chatter. Did life have to be like this?

Jack's only real satisfaction in life was his work. He'd worked since he was a small boy; worked to the best of his ability. It had gained him respect even at an early age. He'd earned good money, particularly in the Crimea. Work was where things went well for him, where he was happiest. Was there nothing else to life? It seemed that everyone except him drank to gain satisfaction. He didn't feel that this was happiness, just drowning your sorrows. Perhaps some people had no stability at home or in work and had to drown their sorrows. What a pointless life they led.

His thoughts returned to Rosie, and the all too short time they had spent together. It was only days. There had never been one like her before or since. That dark hair, that cheeky way she had but above all that smell. Yes, the smell of her. He was almost consumed with a desire to walk out of the house and to Llandeusant. He could do it in a day. If he went, perhaps he would never come back. He certainly wouldn't get work up there, that was certain, but to be in her arms once more would be bliss, he thought.

'Molly.' Jack looked at her directly. 'The baby's due. This is women's work, isn't it?'

'Yes Jack, women's work.'

'I'll be in the way, won't I?'

'You'll be in work, I should think.'

'But I'd be in the way here?'

'Yes, leave it to us women.'

He thought to himself, of Rosie, of young Jack. How old would he be now? Seized by an almost compulsive desire to get away, he made up his mind. It seemed an urge to travel over which he had no control. Like the birds who migrate. His mind was made up. He had to go now.

'Molly, your time is near. I'm leaving you all to it. Your mother, sister and Maggie, all to it.'

'Jack, where you going?'

'Away for a day or two. Leave you all to it.'

'Where to, Jack?'

'Away for a couple of days, that's all.'

She accepted his answer. It wasn't the first time a man had walked away at the time of a confinement. Somehow she knew he would be back.

'When you going?'

'Now,' he replied. Picking up his old cavalry cloak, he left some of his money with Molly and walked out before any of the family was aware of his departure. Up towards Greenhill, Pontardawe, and the road over the Black Mountains. At the summit he turned off the road in a north-easterly direction, arriving at dusk to find Llandeusant just the same.

Walking to the door, he knocked twice quite hard, to be heard above the chatter inside. Jack came to the door in shabby clothes and with a dirty face. 'Man at the door, mam.'

Jack smiled at him, wanting to pick him up but somehow knowing he would be rejected. There was no look of recognition on young Jack's face. Jack smiled at his son but gained no favourable response. 'Man at the door, mam,' he repeated.

Rosie eventually came to the door. Her face lit up, she wiped her flour-covered hands on her apron, put her arms round him and hugged him. He responded with equal enthusiasm. Standing back, a benign smile enveloped his face as he looked at her. 'Good to see you Rosie.'

'And you Jack.' She smiled back as she looked him in the face. He knew the smile so well but had seen it so infrequently. He softened all over. 'Say hello to your father, Jack,' she said encouragingly to her son. He stood back looking sullenly at the intrusive male who had just entered the house. 'Say hello to your father,' she repeated but he still responded in a similar manner.

'Sit down Jack,' she said, clearing the chair for him. He did so, feeling a degree of comfort and familiarity he never had at home.

'What you been doing, Jack? Must be four years now.'

'Working.'

'What at?'

'Shoeing horses, bit of other blacksmith work as well.'

'Are you married?'

'Yes'.

'Children?'

'First one due now.'

'Now? At this moment?'

'At this very moment.'

'Are you going back?'

'Got to do that.'

'How long you staying?'

'Couple of days.'

There was silence between them. He looked at her, seeing she was older but still the same Rosie. When he hugged her, she still smelt the same. What was it about her which made him so at home in her company? It was everything about her, of course it was. Yet he knew in a couple of days he would go home.

'You're a right one, running out now.'

'I'm going back, you know.'

'No, you're not a runner, Jack. I'll say that for you.'

'Didn't stay with you, did I?'

'You couldn't, could you? No work here.'

'Suppose so.'

'What's family life like?'

'Difficult. Yacking all day. Irish family. Blarney non-stop.'

'That wouldn't suit you.'

'No.' He smiled and reflected to himself, yes, Rosie knows me.

'You the only man in the house?'

'The only earner. The old man's a drunk and got sacked a month or two back.'

'You keeping the lot of them, are you?'

'Yes. I don't mind that but they won't drink my money. That's for sure.'

She laughed; it was the same old Jack. 'You happy, Jack?'

'Sort of. Settled I suppose. You happy, Rosie?'

'I've got the children. Got no money, but I've got them. It's hard work and struggle but the children are as good as gold. I've got young Jack. Don't forget that.'

'Good boy, is he Rosie?'

'He's a handful sometimes but a good boy. A real grafter he is. Not much of a scholar.'

'His mother and father aren't either, are they?' They both smiled.

'Fed up with family life, Jack?'

'Does get to me. Had to be out of the house when the baby was arriving.'

'Leave it to the women, is it?'

'That's about it.'

'Do they know about us?'

'Not a thing. Nor will they know.'

'You always had a mind like a rat-trap, didn't you?' He smiled a cynical smile to himself.

'If that's the way you put it.'

'I know you, Jack Lloyd.'

'I know that Rosie. No-one else does.'

'I think you're right there, Jack.'

'I think I know you too, Rosie.'

'A bit of me, perhaps. More than most.'

'Still at the Drovers?'

'Yes, still there. The cattle trade's gone down since you were here.'

'Tommy's gone and I saw Eddie a few years back in Carmarthen. Drunk and looked like a tramp.'

'Haven't thought of Eddie for years. Is he alive?'

'I doubt it. He'll end up in the union for sure, if he isn't there already.'

'Tommy was his wet nurse and, when he went, so did Eddie'.

The light was failing and their conversation ceased. Jack sat down reflecting on the last few years, while Rosie was preparing the children for bed. Jack watched his son, who kept as much distance from his father as he could, but looking at him all the while. He would have liked an emotional response but knew it was not within the capability of either of them.

'Jack, off to bed now. Say goodnight to your father.' He retreated into the corner, his eyes never leaving his father. 'Go on, Jack, say goodnight.' The boy seemed immovable as he sucked a finger, continuing to stare at him. She dragged the boy reluctantly to him, wanting them to kiss one another. The father felt awkward and didn't know how to respond but offered a hand to shake. The boy retreated almost into his mother's skirt. The boy did not offer a hand but the mother forced him to do so. They shook hands, the father hopefully and the boy reluctantly.

Releasing their grip, young Jack ran into the bedroom.

'Not a warm welcome.'

'Give him time and he'll be alright.'

'I haven't got that much time.'

'How much time have you?'

'Couple of days at the most. Got to get back to work.'

A few tears fell down her cheeks. She looked at him. He saw the tears, feeling them in his own eyes as well. 'Rosie, why isn't life more straightforward?'

'I'm the last one you should ask.'

'Never seem to get what you want.'

'You get what you want and you don't hang on to it.'

'We know that, don't we Rosie.'

'We'd better drop this subject.'

'Perhaps we should.'

They both drifted off into their thoughts for some minutes, each aware of the presence of the other, exchanging occasional glances which said more than any words. It was an atmosphere of pathos, what might have been and what would never be. The peace was broken only by her putting more wood on the fire. By now the children were asleep in bed. Jack and Rosie had their supper of rabbit pie, swede and potatoes and became drowsy before the fire.

'Perhaps I shouldn't have come, Rosie.'

'Course you should. We always want to see you here. Anytime. You know that.'

'Course I do.'

'Well, don't be so bloody sorry for yourself then. Come here.' He walked the few feet over to her, and into her arms. It was the old familiar Rosie once again. Why the hell did I ever leave? Her softness, the smell of her and her understanding of him overwhelmed him once more. He wanted to stay there for ever. Even a word would break the spell. For half an hour they remained in one another's arms. 'Cwching Rosie, you like that don't you Jack?'

'I do that, girl.'

266

'Stay here then.'

'Long as I can.'

'Must get to bed now, Jack.'

'Can't we stop here, then,' he mumbled sleepily.

'More comfortable in bed.'

'I was comfortable here.'

'Come on.' In his drowsy condition, he put one foot in front of the other into the bedroom, then lay down and fell soundly asleep. It had been a long day and he had walked very many miles. His sleep continued even when the dawn was flooding through the window. Waking quickly to an empty bed, he heard the children and Rosie all talking. Almost automatically he got up, walking into the kitchen where the children were being made ready for school.

'I slept well, Rosie.'

'I know that.'

'What time is it?'

'School time. They'll be off in a few minutes.'

'Do you like school, Jack?' he asked the boy. He didn't answer, moving into the corner again, giving his father the same constant stare he had done the previous night. Accepting he would get no answer from his son, he did not persist but felt annoyed that his only child was hostile to him. They ate breakfast; bread, butter and milk before leaving for school in their shabby clothes, the girls appearing more cheerful at going than their younger brother, who kicked stones around with the other boys. Do anything rather than school, Jack thought, watching them through the window. He saw the girls almost running to classes while their brother played with his friends. Yes, he knew how he felt. Would he ever learn to read, he wondered?

'When you going to the Drovers, Rosie?'

'Soon.' There was an ominous silence between them, each knowing the next question. 'When you going back, Jack?'

'Soon, Rosie.'

'I knew you would. When?'

'When you leave for the Drovers.' They looked at one another for a minute or two without saying a word. 'Good to see you, Rosie.'

'And you Jack. Come back anytime. You're always welcome, you know that.'

'I know that, Rosie.' They hugged long and hard without saying a word. Releasing their grasp of one another, he said, 'I'm going to be off.'

He walked through the door and, without looking back, retraced his steps to Swansea.

Chapter 26

In the early hours of the following morning Jack arrived home. Wet through and exhausted after walking more than sixty miles in two days, he did not want to go in. He didn't know why. Every house in the street was dark, except his own. Looking through the window before going in, he could see no one. There was a light upstairs and the hum of conversation in the house. Before going in, he stopped to think; will I go in and carry on with life as before or will I walk away and start a new life somewhere else? There'd always be plenty of work for someone with his skills. Not thinking of the consequences of his departure, he fantasised about a new start. Get rid of the old life and start afresh. No responsibilities. Few possessions. Freedom. Where would he be in an hour if he walked out at this moment? Back to Rosie and Llandeusant? That would not be a fresh start. Begin again where no one knew him? His pondering lasted for no more than two or three minutes before he walked in to resume his old life once again. The die was cast.

Hearing the conversation upstairs he walked towards the front bedroom, finding all the family there.

'Where you been Jack?' asked Molly who was lying in bed with the baby asleep beside her. She looked exhausted and vulnerable. He didn't answer right away. 'Jack, where've you been? You said nothing. Jack, tell me.' She looked imploringly at him, expecting an answer. 'Jack, you're soaked. Tell me where you've been.''.

He didn't know what to say. Didn't want to tell a lie. Didn't want to answer her question.

'Boy or a girl?' he asked, looking at the baby by her side.

'Boy.' He moved to kiss Molly and pick up the baby. 'Jack, where've you been? Jack, tell me.'

'Went away. This is for women. Don't want me around, do you?'

'Why didn't you say, Jack?' He ignored her question and picked up his baby boy as gently as he knew how. The lad had a good head of fair hair and a lined face, and was oblivious to anything going on around him. Drifting in and out of sleep as Jack held him, the new father stared at his son with a sense of proud wonder. A vulnerable, warm smile came over his face. Everyone in the family noticed it, seeing a softer side to him they had never seen before. He continued to hold young Jack, mesmerised.

'He's a great little fella, Molly. You've done a good job there. Did you have a hard time, girl?'

'Very hard. He's ten pounds and I'm stitched.'

He looked at Molly in pity, lost for words. He resumed looking at his son. No one spoke. Putting him back down beside Molly he said, 'When was he born?'

'Yesterday afternoon.'

He didn't reply. Standing there, his thoughts drifted to where he had been when young Jack was born. Walking towards Llanduesant and into the arms of Rosie. This boy wouldn't reject him. He'd do everything with him. They would be partners. He'd be a real father to him. He'd tolerate this bloody family now he had someone to really take an interest in and love. A reason for living. Not knowing how to put his feelings into words, he remained silent. It wasn't long before the family started chattering again as they always did. Hardly aware of the conversation, he looked at the baby, still mesmerised. Only Molly fully took in the depth of his feelings. A fresh step had been taken in their marriage. Would it remain so?

The spell was soon broken. He thought of the next morning. 'Well Molly. Got to get some sleep before work tomorrow.' He looked at her, then the baby with a fondness they had never seen before. 'You've done a good job there, Molly.' She knew she had found a vulnerable side to him. It reassured her that she might have some degree of control over him, which she had never expected before. It made her feel safe. He bent down and kissed her gently. Before going to bed, he gently pinched the baby's cheek and smiled. He was asleep as soon as his head touched the pillow. It had been an eventful few days.

The next day followed the usual pattern as it had on hundreds of occasions before. Walking up the dirty street, avoiding the rubbish and puddles of stale water, arriving at the forge where a string of horses always needed to be shod, or shoes had to be made. The weather was overcast with an intermittent drizzle. It was good to get away from it, inside the forge. This day was different, there was not that suspicion and frequent suppressed anger in him or the black thoughts which were part of his everyday life. There was a spring in his step, joy in his thoughts and sometimes a smile on his face. Everyone noticed it.

Three of them worked the forge. Jack was the unpaid charge hand. All of them had heard the news of the baby's birth.

'Well, Jack. The baby's arrived.'

'It has. A boy.'

'What's his name?'

'Jack, of course.'

'Congratulations, boy.' They slapped him on the back, one after the other. He smiled a modest smile but laughed heartily within himself. He'd never felt so good.

'Wife alright, Jack?' He nodded, resuming work again.

'Heard the news, Jack?'

'What news?'

'Changing the ganger here.'

'What happened to Isaac?'

'He had a pull. Won't be coming back.'

'What's wrong with him?'

'All of a sudden, on the site, he got breathless. Been at home these two days.'

'He won't come back.'

'How do you know?'

'Everyone says he's bad. Real bad. His wife says he's been short of breath ever since. Can't walk up the stairs.'

'Who's got the job then?'

'Nobody knows yet, but the word is Ben Letworthy.'

'Him?'

'Nobody likes him. He's a bully. A real bosses' man.'

'Is he?'

'Let's see what he's like when he comes.'

'They say you know him Jack. That right?'

'No. Only spoken to him once.'

'Everyone says you got something on him.'

He smiled to himself. 'Don't listen to gossip.'

'You got something on him. What is it?'

'Nothing, good boy. Nothing.' He laughed to himself. If only they knew.

'How did you get your father-in-law old man O'Hara his job back?'

Jack smiled to himself but didn't immediately answer.

'Letworthy had never taken a man back after he'd sacked him before.'

Jack was surprised this matter had become public. If these boys knew, everyone knew.

'How'd you do it Jack? How'd you do it?'

'Asked him to give him another chance, that's all.'

'Come on Jack, there's more to it than that. There must be.'

They realised he was in a better humour than they had ever seen him before. Never before would they have been able to question him so personally. In spite of their probing, his mood did not change. His answers deflected all their inquiries. Eventually they gave up.

The midday break arrived. Jack walked quickly home as it was only a few minutes away. The two others sat down to bread, cheese and cold tea.

The talkative one returned to the subject. 'He's got something on him, you know.'

'I know.'

'He nearly talked, you know. I got him going. Nearly got there.'

'You won't get it out of him.'

'I will. Got to wait my time.'

'Letworthy and Jack look alike you know.'

'That's what they say.'

'Are they father and son?'

'Shouldn't think so. He's from Devon. Only been here a year or two.'

'Perhaps not. Though you never know.'

'They do look alike. Both as strong as horses. Jack doesn't drink though. Letworthy lives on it.'

'He's a deep one, is Jack. From the Preselis and speaks Welsh.'

'Then marries an Irish girl.'

'Gets her father another chance.'

'We'll never get to the bottom of it, will we?'

Jack's return brought their conversation to an end. Looking at his face, they knew that further inquiry was not an avenue they could pursue.

'Been home to see the boy, Jack?'

He only smiled in reply, returning immediately to his shoeing. So it continued till the end of the day. A dozen workers left the site at the same time who all lived around the same area of town. They walked home together in a group. One spoke up. 'It's Letworthy then, so they say.'

'That's what they say. Letworthy, unless they get someone from outside,' said another.

'They won't bring an outsider in,' put in another.

'Why not?'

'Never done it before.'

'There's always a first time.'

'No, he'll get the job.'

'What do you think, Jack?'

'Wait and see,' Jack replied.

'There'll be some sackings for sure.'

'There will, that,' agreed another.

'And some hungry kids.'

This last remark made Jack think. Mine won't go hungry. I'll make sure of that. He'll push his luck with me, but I can deal with him, no doubt about it. It gave him a quiet confidence. I'm looking forward to the challenge, he thought. Challenge there would be, there was no doubt about that. They all walked on.

'Letworthy's on another site,' the conversation continued.

'A smaller one.'

'They may not know about him.'

'They know about him, good boy. They know about him.'

'All these contractors are as thick as thieves.'

'Not much goes on which they don't know about.' The conversation went on, ending only when they broke off to go to their homes.

Walking in the house to the usual chattering, Jack went to the cot to pick up young Jack who was sleeping soundly. The family, hearing him come in, stopped talking. Not wanting to wake the baby, he did not pick him up but bent over and kissed him. Molly came into the room, walking for the first time after her confinement. She looked pale and a little unsteady on her feet. He put his arm around her. Their cheeks rubbed together. 'You alright, Molly?'

'A bit weak, Jack. It took a lot out of me.'

'I know that. But he's a fine lad, alright.'

'He is that. A chip off the old block.' She smiled a wan smile and looked at him.

'You sure you're alright, Molly?'

'I'll be alright but it did take it out of me. Got to give me some time.'

He gently stroked her back and then her stomach. She relaxed. 'Sure you'll be alright Molly?' She nodded, looked at him and then away. 'Just give me some time, that's all.' Sitting down, she looked up at him wanting to talk.

'What is it, Molly'?

'They're talking.'

'Who?'

'Everyone.' He wanted to ask who everyone was but didn't pursue the matter.

'What they saying, girl?'

'They talk about you and that Ben Letworthy.'

'What do they say?'

'You've got something on him. You know him?'

'Don't listen to gossip.'

'I've only seen him once. He looks just like you.' He smiled to himself, while looking at her. 'Don't listen to old women's tales.'

'It's not just old women who are talking. The men are as well.'

'Men who are old women.' Again he gave an amused smile.

'Jack, what is it? Tell me.'

'It's nothing, Molly.'

'I don't believe you Jack. What is it?' He was in a rare soft mood since the birth of Jack, and she pursued the questions without getting an answer. If I told her, it would be all over the town in an hour, he thought. He continued to smile in his enigmatic way.

'He looks like you. Is he your father Jack?'

'Could be, but Letworthy's a Devon man.'

'Did you know your father, Jack?'

'No. Never seen him. Never knew his name.'

'Did your mother never mention him?'

'Never.'

'Why not?' asked Molly.

'She was dead when I was six.'

'Who looked after you then?'

'My sister, Megan.'

'Didn't she mention your father?'

'Only once. We had different fathers, me and the girls. There were three girls. Megan died when I was only eight or nine.'

'What did you do when she died?'

275

'Got a job.'

'Working since eight or nine?'

'Why not, what else is there to do? Work never did me any harm. It kept me going.'

She asked herself, 'What else was there to do?' An orphan twice over at the age of six. No wonder he is so tough; he had to be to survive. She was now lost for words. She had learnt more about him in the last twenty minutes than she had since meeting him first. Wanting to know more, she didn't know what to ask next. Jack would never come out with it. There was more to know, she could tell.

'You're a deep one, Jack.'

'Same as hundreds of others, Molly. Plenty fought worse battles than me and survived.'

'A few perhaps.'

'What about the famines in Ireland? Many had it worse than me. Always had work. Always had food. Many worse than me Molly.'

'You had no family, Jack.'

'Made my own family as I went along. In a family now, aren't I?'

'What happened to your sisters? They alive?'

'I think so. They went into service, in the local big house.'

'Don't you want to see them, Jack?'

'I suppose so.'

He hadn't seen them for years and never thought of them. Did he want to see them? Not really. What was the point? It made him feel funny after all these years to even think about them; what they looked like now, whether they were married. It made him reflect on his youth, school, work, his mother (who he was hardly able to visualise now) and his sisters, Tommy and Eddie on the droves. How did he find himself here at twenty-six? Seemed it was just grabbing opportunity as it came along.

'We could go and see them Jack'.

'No, I don't think so.' It was enough to deal with the day to day matters. The burdens were enough at the moment. Their

276

talk had dug up old memories and made him feel curious but also made him feel the distance between now and his early years.

He looked out of the front door at the mess in the street. Rubbish which was dumped and allowed to rot away and puddles of water. Preseli wasn't like that. The wages were poor but the water was clean and the air fresh. It was what he noticed when he went to see Rosie. Some of the past was good but you can't go back. Why not? That's life I suppose. The past became shrouded in mist as he thought of the future. The future at the moment was Ben Letworthy. Ben would push his luck sooner or later, and Jack would be ready for him. It was going to be fun and there would be only one winner. He smiled a confident smile to himself. Yes, there would be only one winner. Would he do it in public or would he do it in private? That was the question he asked himself. Soon he would know.

'You look worried, Jack,' Molly said as she crept up silently behind him. He turned round to face her. 'What is it? Ben Letworthy?'

'No. I was just thinking Molly.'

'What about Jack?'

'Just us. That's all.'

'It's Ben Letworthy, isn't it Jack?'

'Partly, Molly. Don't worry.'

'I do worry, Jack. What is it about him? Is he your father?'

'If he is, he hasn't told me.'

'What is it about you and Letworthy? There is something, isn't there Jack?'

'Molly, shut up. This is between me and Letworthy.'

She asked no more, walking away from him with tears in her eyes. As she did so, she heard him say softly, 'Molly, this is for me and me alone to deal with.' He wanted to say he was sorry but felt unable to do so. It was the nearest he could get to an apology.

She felt hurt and again very vulnerable at his aggressive reaction. Within the last couple of days, she had given birth to

277

young Jack and was still exhausted. He was obviously very attached to the new arrival yet he had disappeared into his old secret self. Why wouldn't he confide in her? She was his wife. He had no one else. But where had he been for the last two days? It had been a long way and he was tired and a bit thinner when he returned. Also he seemed further away than usual. There was that distant look in his eyes. Perhaps she would have to accept the fact that he would never confide in her. He certainly confided in no-one else. There was something between him and Letworthy. If they were father and son, then that was quite simple. Nothing to hide really. There must be more than that. Everyone knew he had only had two minutes with Letworthy and father had his job back. What had he said to him? She accepted the fact that if he told her, she would tell her mother then it would be all over the town in minutes. In spite of that, she wanted to know. It was like a thirst she knew would never be slaked.

He retraced his steps to her, put his hands on her upper arms and looked into her face with a small smile, 'Molly, this is something I can't tell you. I never will tell you. It will go to the grave with me. I have to deal with it in my own way. You couldn't possibly imagine what it is in your wildest dreams. Not in your wildest dreams. Let me tell you this, I won't lose on this one.'

She knew it was no good pursuing this conversation. He saw acceptance in her eyes and smiled a warmer smile.

'Molly. Leave Letworthy to me.' She nodded

'Alright, Jack. You win, you always do.'

He put his arms around her. She felt the warmth and the protection of them and felt safe. He lingered, inhaling the smell of her, acknowledging to himself that it was quite similar to that of Rosie. He felt closer to her than he had ever done before. He had done the right thing by remaining in Frog Street.

'Molly. You and Jack will come to no harm. Leave it to me.' He released her, looked into her eyes and smiled a more intimate smile than he had ever done before.

Chapter 27

Sir Lionel Lambert sat in his office, which was a room off the hall in his imposing mansion. It had a view over Swansea bay and was large, perhaps twenty-five feet square. In spite of its southern aspect, high windows and tall ceiling it was dark within. Every aspect of the room spoke volumes about its owner. Dark walls, painted a colour which it was difficult to define, were overlaid with portraits in oil and two townscapes of Swansea. His desk faced the sea and to the right was a plan of the docks, part of which was being extended. On his desk was a small-scale version of the same plan.

A large imposing man, dressed almost entirely in black, he was every inch the Victorian industrialist. He looked intensely at the plan, periodically making short notes in a book on the right hand side of the desk, the only area not occupied. He made pencil marks on the plan, covering one area then another. He made further notes in his book relating to dates and the corresponding numbered areas on the plan. He applied himself to this matter for perhaps an hour. Not once did he look up nor did his intense concentration flag. Had someone been in the room and put him under scrutiny, then they would have been aware that here was a man under pressure. Perhaps it was the intensity alone that gave this impression; certainly there was no indication of impatience or anxiety. Here was a man who devoted himself entirely to the task in hand with few outside interests. He had a quiet authority which few challenged. Humour was a characteristic which was singularly absent from his personality.

There was a knock on the door of his office. Hearing it, he completed the drawings and notes before answering. It was as if he had emerged from a deep sleep and in the matter of a few seconds had to concentrate on another matter immediately.

'Come in,' he boomed in his loud, resonant voice.

The site manager walked two paces into the room, removing his hat, 'You wanted me sir?'

Sir Lionel carried the plan and his notes over to a large table, round which there were a dozen chairs, sitting down in the only one which had arms. 'Here!' he commanded Jackson the site manager, reinforcing the word with a gesture of his right hand. Jackson stood perhaps three feet from him. He was not asked to sit down. Spreading the map out before him, he put the notebook within easy reach. Silence prevailed as Sir Lionel mustered his thoughts. Jackson kept his master's face within his sight but his eyes wandered towards the map and notebook. It was probably no more than a second to two, but long enough to tell him Sir Lionel was under pressure over time. It always gave Jackson a slight feeling of alarm, waiting for his master to speak, but today the feeling was more acute. Watching him, he could almost feel his thought processes.

At last he spoke, 'We've lost the ganger, Jackson.'

'Yes sir.'

'Seen him since he left?'

'Yes sir.'

'Will he come back?'

'No sir.'

'Why not, Jackson?'

'I've seen him twice since he got took ill. Last time last night. He's still breathless. Can't get up the stairs.'

'Well, if he won't come back, who will replace him and quickly?'

'The only man is Ben Letworthy. He's the ganger on the other site. I've heard of him. They'll let us have him'.

'Is there anyone else, Jackson?'

'No one as good as Letworthy, sir.'

'Are you sure Letworthy is good, Jackson?'

'Very good, sir.'

There was a pause as Sir Lionel thought, then he looked him in the face and said, 'Jackson, we are under time pressure to complete this contract. We aren't behind but we are not ahead

280

either.' He then paused and thought for a moment or two. 'Will this ganger control the men and the pace of work there?'

'Oh yes sir. He's tough, is Letworthy.'

'Does he keep their goodwill as well as keeping them at work?'

'He keeps 'em working but they don't like him.' Jackson didn't want to admit that the men didn't like Letworthy but it was no good telling lies to Sir Lionel.

'Why don't they like him?'

'He can be a bully, sir. The men don't like that, sir.'

'No, I suppose they don't. Who else is there?'

'No one, sir.' Jackson badly wanted Letworthy to defend his own position, yet he disliked him.

'Are you sure, Jackson?' Does this Letworthy drink?'

'He does, sir.' He knew it was no good telling him anything but the truth.

'How heavily?'

'Heavily, sir.'

'During the day, Jackson?'

'Not during the day, sir. Not as I know sir.'

'Are you sure, Jackson?'

'If he drank in the day, I'd know it sir. There is one other man, sir. A blacksmith, Jack Lloyd, much younger than Letworthy. A big man, and he can certainly command respect. Looks like Letworthy. There is talk.'

'What about?'

'That they may be father and son, sir.'

'Never mind that. Has he been a foreman?'

'Never in Swansea, so far as I know, sir.'

'No, if he's untried we can't consider him. Never been a foreman. We can't consider him for a ganger. Letworthy it is. Go and get him now and have him there tomorrow morning.'

'Yes sir.'

'Jackson. This Jack Lloyd; consider him for a foreman's job when one comes up.'

'Yes sir.'

'Does he drink?'

'No sir, never.'

'Never. Are you sure?'

'Yes sir, never ever.'

'Remember, we can't take any chances with this time penalty hanging over us.'

'No sir.'

'Get on with it then, Jackson.'

'Yes sir.' He walked to the door, bowing as he went through it. Closing it behind him, he put on his hat, breathing a sigh of relief as he went.

Hardly had he gone two steps out of the front door, when he heard Sir Lionel's voice call, 'Jackson.' It was like a foghorn, making him immediately uneasy. He returned, removed his hat and stood at the door of the office.

'Jackson, I will visit the site at nine o'clock on Thursday next, the day after tomorrow. Also, see me tomorrow at this time after Letworthy has been installed.'

'Yes sir.'

Sir Lionel turned round to give the plans further study, thereby dismissing Jackson. Relieved to get out of the company of his employer, Jackson walked towards the town. He had much to accomplish that day.

Jackson's office was only two rooms, one leading out of the other. The first room was occupied by an ageing male clerk who had worked for Sir Lionel for very many years and whose loyalty to his employer was legendary. Not known for his imagination or initiative, he nonetheless had a formidable memory and could be relied upon to carry out any instructions given to him.

Jackson walked through the first office, ignored its occupant and sat down behind his desk. 'Peck,' he shouted much louder than was necessary in two such small rooms. Peck walked in. There was no love lost between them. Jackson would like to have dismissed him but knew it was impossible with Sir Lionel alive. There was a bond, built up over long years of them being master and servant, which was unbreakable. Jackson, a relative newcomer, could never invade this relationship and it made him resentful. He made life difficult for Peck as far as he felt able but pursued his resentment no further.

'Peck. Do you know Letworthy, the ganger?'

'Yes Mr Jackson.'

'Tell him to come and see me here immediately.'

Peck never questioned any order that was given but replied hesitantly, 'Yes, Mr Jackson,' more from age and infirmity than a reluctance to undertake the task.

'Well, get on with it.' Peck left the office, walking the relatively short distance to Letworthy's place of work.

Letworthy was in his small office, which was no more than a cabin six feet square. It was unusual to find him there, but he was expecting the call as the news had flashed around the town at the speed of sound.

Peck walked slowly, but as fast as his aged legs would carry him. He was observed by all who were within sight and those who weren't in sight moved to a place of vantage.

When Peck entered the cramped office, Letworthy gave him a grin of delight. The grin was all encompassing, almost obscene. A mixture of delight, power realised and an addiction for alcohol were evident in his face. Normally he would be dismissive to all who he had power over and he certainly had power over Peck, but within that grin was an ingratiating dimension as he deferred to Peck for this brief moment. Getting up from the only chair, he offered Peck the seat, which he took. Peck was breathless and waited a minute or two to regain his breath.

'Want a cup of tea?' Letworthy asked him.

Peck shook his head. His breathing gradually returned to normal. 'See Jackson now,' he eventually managed to say.

'Now?'

'Yes. Now.'

'You mean right away?'

'Yes. Right away. Now.' Peck needed a further minute or two to be fit to walk back. 'You go on. I'll follow.' He took an instant dislike to Letworthy. Never before had he seen a look on anybody's face of such obscene greed for power. 'Go on. I'll follow,' he repeated. 'You walk faster than me'. He wanted to get out of his company as soon as possible. But now he would have to work more closely with him. The prospect offended. How could he put enough distance between himself and this man? How could he undermine him? He had liked Isaac and knew he would never come back. Isaac had led by persuasion and example. Liked by many, even loved by a few. A non-drinker. Letworthy was a drinker, there was no doubt about that. He had beer branded on his forehead. His red face advertised the fact. Sir Lionel did not like drinkers. A teetotaller himself, he would not tolerate drunkenness in those in responsible positions in his companies. Once or twice he had had to employ foremen who drank, but he was very reluctant to do so. Everyone knew his views.

Though the bond between Peck and his master was a long-standing and close one, they were rarely alone in one another's company more than once or twice a year. Even then the communication was formal. A feeling of dislike, made all the more intense by his powerless position, went through and remained in Peck's mind for some time. I will undermine Letworthy and drink will be my ammunition, he vowed.

Walking back slowly, he arrived at the office to hear the hum of the two men talking in the next room. The conversation was coming to an end. 'You will take the position then?' asked Jackson.

'Yes. Of course. When do I start?' replied Letworthy.

'Tomorrow morning at seven o'clock. Prompt.'

'What happens if Isaac gets better?'

'He won't.'

'So I get the job till the contract is completed?'

'As long as you do the job properly.' Jackson was mildly condescending towards him, which Letworthy absorbed, felt irritated by but hoped he had not visibly reacted to.

'What about the company I'm with now?'

284

'Sir Lionel will deal with that.'

'You sure?'

'I'm sure he's dealt with it already.' Jackson took a deep breath and looked Letworthy in the face. 'Sir Lionel doesn't like drinkers. You drink?'

'Only at night and then not much.'

He intensified his look, leaving a long pause to underline his point. 'You are a heavy drinker, Letworthy. Don't argue. You won't fool Sir Lionel. He knows you drink. If he smells it on you during working hours, you'll be out, neck and crop. Be warned.'

'But I....'

'Don't argue, Letworthy. You won't get another warning from me or him.'

'Very well,' he answered, almost crestfallen.

'The day after tomorrow Sir Lionel inspects the progress here. He'll be here at nine o'clock. Be warned; have everything in order, and know the plans from top to bottom by then.'

'Yes, I will.'

'Remember one more thing. Peck in the office has known Sir Lionel for thirty years and has his ear. Remember that. Start tomorrow morning at seven o'clock.'

Jackson directed him out of the office with just a flick of the right hand. As he rose to go, he lingered, giving Jackson an enquiring look.

'Yes, Letworthy?'

'What will the pay be, Mr Jackson?'

'The same as Isaac.'

'What did he get?'

'I've told you, the same as Isaac.' Jackson was determined not to answer the question and thereby put Letworthy on the defensive. Letworthy knew better than to pursue the matter but felt annoyed. Would this attitude continue and how could he overcome this barrier? He walked through the outer office, giving a searching glance at Peck who did not look up, although he was aware of his scrutiny. Peck smiled to himself.

Jackson did not like Peck or Letworthy. Peck did not like

Jackson and detested Letworthy. Letworthy was beginning to see that bullying and bluster would not work with these two. Would he be able to defend himself and further his position here, and how would he deal with Sir Lionel? As he walked back to his cabin for the last time, he began to have reservations about developing these new skills. Jack Lloyd flashed into his mind. If he could deal with him, and do it publicly, he would establish his power. It was a high risk strategy. Would he try it or not? His first day would be very important. Caution was not one of his characteristics. Impulsiveness was and he knew it. All eyes were on him. None wanted him to succeed. Lost in his own thoughts, he only became aware of it as he locked up for the last time. Walking back to his lodgings, no one spoke to him.

He went to bed early, without visiting his regular tavern, but he could not get to sleep. Jackson and Peck flashed through his mind. Fists and bluster were no good there; he would be out in a minute. How could he get access to Sir Lionel and so bypass his two adversaries. For hours he thought about it without coming to any conclusions. An old saying occurred to him, 'You don't get a second chance to make a first impression'. That first impression was important. Everything hung on it. He would have to get the site in order in less than a day. He knew there had been slackness in the short time since Isaac left. He also knew that to get respect he would have to dominate Jack Lloyd. That would have to wait. Surely Sir Lionel would not want to see the blacksmiths' shop. He ruled it out of his mind. What he would do was to get everything up to date and read the plans, but he hadn't been given a copy of the plans. That would be his first task in the morning. Would Jackson be obstructive? Possibly, but if he was he would not inform Sir Lionel. Would he ever get sole access to him? Jackson would certainly not let that happen if he could help it. In these matters he knew that opportunity frequently presented itself when you least expected it. When that happened he would drive a coach and horses through it. A momentary surge of power went through him at the prospect but he decided that on the first day he would take it quietly.

He slept for perhaps two hours and then only lightly, getting up earlier than was usual. It was not yet six. He didn't eat but drank two cups of tea and thought. A need for a pint of beer came over him. Why, he didn't know. Had he been on the smaller site he would have given in to his craving. Last night he had done without alcohol. Was the need so strong after such a brief time without? It was many months since he had had a dry evening. The need didn't last long. The new challenge beckoned as he made his way to the site, arriving before seven.

Standing in the site cabin which was little bigger than the one he had left, Letworthy summoned the four foremen directly in charge of the navvies. He particularly ordered that Jack Lloyd, the blacksmith charge hand, not be called. Jack received the news within a minute or two of the order being given and knew he had won the first round. He continued to work, taking particular trouble to hide his feelings of elation.

Letworthy and the four foremen were cramped in the office, all apprehensive as to what would happen next.

'I'm the chief here now and you obey my orders and mine only. You all understand?' They mumbled in reply. 'You understand?' he said, much louder. He could feel his face go red. It was a high risk strategy. They mumbled again. He demanded their obedience individually now. 'I didn't hear you. You'd better answer me one by one.' Reluctantly, they gave him their word, which was extracted with difficulty. He hadn't received the fearful co-operation he had hoped for, though it was a start.

'I'm going to see each section this morning. Each of you men will show me everything that you are responsible for. I will give you work targets which will be kept. We'll start at the nearest one and end at the furthest one. Get back to work, apart from the foreman of the nearest section. Who's that?'

'Me.' He put up his hand.

'What's your name?'

'Arthur James.'

'The rest of you get back to the site. James and I will go to his section. Go on. Get back to work.' The three returned to their places of work, mumbling to themselves that things would change. Christian names, which Isaac had used to everyone, were now not to be used. Immediately creating an atmosphere of hostility, everyone was against the new ganger and all looked for ways to compromise him. He knew he would have this effect but his new-found power gave him a confidence which thrived on their hatred for him and invested him with a boldness which he had not possessed earlier that morning.

'James, to your section.' James didn't reply. They walked over planks, round wheelbarrows and in between piles of bricks. Before they had even reached his section, Letworthy commented 'This place is going to be tidied up straight away. It's a bloody mess, that's what it is. How did it get in this state?'

James did not comment but every word registered in his mind. Rapidly they got to the site. The steam navvy was working and horses were pulling loads up the short but steep incline. Not saying a word to a single labourer, Letworthy looked at the work in hand, giving brief glances towards the men who continued working. He spent half an hour there, asking one question then another of the foreman, with never a word to the men. Not making a note, he took all the details in. So it went on with all the foremen who at the end of his visit were directed to report to him in his office at noon.

At the appointed time the four men, all in a huddle, walked into his office. Looking them all in the eye, they responded with furtive looks which reassured him. Launching into them with confidence, they didn't reply unless directed to answer and then only meekly.

'This site is a mess. You know and I know it. Everything is untidy. Even before I get to the proper work I find things just thrown down. Wheelbarrows left where they were last used. Wood dumped far away from where it is needed. Same with bricks. This will stop and stop now. Do you understand?'

They didn't reply.

'Do you understand?' He demanded their reply which was given in a reluctant and quiet tone. He had wanted a louder reply which would have reassured him more but time was against him and the site must be tidied up before tomorrow.

'Each of you will have half your strongest labourers spend the rest of the day cleaning this place up. You will also have half your horses doing the same. This site will be tidied up by tonight. Sir Lionel is coming tomorrow at nine o'clock.'

'We know,' James remarked.

'How do you know?'

'Everyone knows.'

Wanting to find out how they knew, he accepted he would not get a straight reply.

'In one hour we start.'

Men were driven hard and horses even harder to get matters completed. By the end of the day the worst of the disorder had been corrected but resentment had been built up which would not be forgotten. The horses, if they had been able to complain, would have done so more vigorously than the men.

Jack was not part of this but heard everything and built up an antagonism perhaps even more venomous than the rest of the men. He felt the time was near for him to settle an old score.

Chapter 28

Sir Lionel Lambert was as dominating in his own house as he was in the world in which he worked. Dinner was served at eight o'clock prompt and woe betide any member of the family who was not present. No alcohol was ever served nor was there any in the house. There were always five members of the family round the table and frequently more. He sat at the head of the table and his wife at the other end. The fare was varied and the portions generous. Conversation was limited and almost always initiated by the master. The subject matter was invariably formal. It was an ordeal the family had to suffer. Though never commented upon openly, there was a silent and mutual understanding between the other four members of the family that this was a burden to be carried but to keep it as short as possible. This was expressed by the raising of an eyebrow, a fleeting glance or a shrug of the shoulders. Silence was the unspoken weapon to shorten the cheerless and dominating hour.

Lady Lambert, a cowed and thin figure, rarely, if ever, spoke at these times. Her husband only had to glance at her for everyone to see the crushed look in her grey watery eyes. Worn out and defeated, she invariably wore faded old clothes, much washed, which she had had for years. Every aspect of her demeanour was submissive.

Charles, the eldest son, sat at the right hand of the father. He held a post of limited responsibility in the family business, handling the accounts, but was under the domination of the father. He had considerable abilities but was never really allowed to use them. He replied to questions from his father in monosyllables and never looked him in the face. Any answers which went further and suggested an alternative line of action were dismissed in a crushing and destructive manner before the whole family.

Albert, the youngest, a humorous and light-hearted young man, had no feel for business, but pursued a superficial career as a poet and supporter of the arts. In fact he was just a social animal who lived for personal enjoyment and the social life which went with it. The organisations supporting the arts in which he had an interest had occasionally received money from his father. Sir Lionel had, on a very limited number of occasions, visited these venues principally to see the money had been spent as promised. Taken there by his son, he had been ill at ease in such places and was totally dismissive of the patrons. Albert had propelled him along on a tide of bonhomie before depositing him back in his carriage, all the while having a superficial smirk on his face, which was lost on no one except his father.

On several occasions he had got into scrapes, principally as a result of gambling, when his father had had to bail him out. Sir Lionel hated doing it, and resented it for days, constantly reminding his wayward son that this was the last time. It never was. Albert was a lover of low life; ladies of the town, seedy drinking haunts and any form of gambling which presented itself.

Lucy, the second child and only daughter was the apple of Sir Lionel's eye. Nineteen years old, she was educated to a modest level and since leaving school had done little. Urgings by her father to do something constructive met with no response on her part. In fact the last thing she had any intention of doing was to engage in anything constructive. In spite of considerable vitality, her life had no direction. There was little social life that the family engaged in and her circle was limited in the extreme. She despised without reservation the few who did come within her social circle. She made disparaging remarks about them and was not reticent in expressing them at considerable length. Her father adored her, a fact of which she was abundantly aware as were the rest of the household. She answered him back and challenged his suggestions. He never seemed to be able to muster an adequate reply. His bluster was no match for her quickness of mind. The verbal fencing between them was so one-sided that he became irritated in the extreme, an irritation which he initially suppressed but soon was vented on the more defenceless members of the family.

Looking at his daughter, he was mesmerised by her. Adored her. Couldn't help himself. Lucy was perhaps two inches over five feet with a good head of curly black hair and humorous blue eyes with more than a streak of insolence in them. She looked everyone straight in the eye, had a reply for any remark and treated everyone the same, whatever their social class. Gardener, visiting industrialist or kitchen maid; all were treated alike. Few could resist her outgoing manner. Her figure could best be described as well nourished and she had a large bust of which she was inordinately proud. Always dressed largely in black, she wore a white lace blouse which exposed as much of her splendid assets as the times she lived in would allow. Men were drawn to her; she turned heads by the hundred as she rode, infrequently around the town and more often in the surrounding countryside Had anyone ventured beyond her confident exterior, they would have found a woman tossed in a sea of emotional passion. Her riding trips into the country alone always found her at her most troubled. Men were easy to get, anyone she set her eyes on, but the one she desired was to be extraordinary, not ordinary. When he arrived, she would know. Yes, she would know and he would not escape. Never losing hope that he would eventually come, she went through moods when she became impatient in the extreme.

The silence weighed heavier than usual in the dining room that night. Even Sir Lionel felt it.

'What have you been doing today, Lucy?'

'Riding, father. Just riding.'

'Who with?'

'On my own, father.'

'Why on your own, Lucy?'

'Who is there to go with, father?'

'What about the eldest Lamb boy?'

'Little Dickie Lamb. Why would I want to go out with him?'

Sir Lionel knew that he was getting into one of those arguments he could not win. The family winced and looked at

292

Lucy in anguish, silently imploring her to shut up. Lucy knew that they wanted her to stop and did not return their stares but continued looking only at her father.

'He's one of us. A suitable person for you to ride with,' Sir Lionel continued.

'Father, you know and I know that Dickie Lamb is a boring little mouse.'

'It's not right to be out on your own, Lucy.'

'Why not father? I've never come to any harm.'

'Lucy, it is neither proper or right, and you know it.'

'Who do you suggest I go with, then?'

'A suitable escort.'

'Who? Please father, don't suggest Dickie Lamb again.'

'There are other young men.'

'Dickie Lamb's friends I suppose? All idle butterflies.'

He shut up, annoyed that he had been hurt by such devastating logic and unable to reply. Anger festered within him which everyone picked up immediately. They all looked at their plates as the dinner was eaten. That is, except Lucy, who looked round in an almost triumphant manner pleased with her performance and victory. She glowed with pleasure. His wife and two sons were wondering which one of them would be the butt of his anger. It certainly would not be Lucy. Each at one time had thought to themselves, how does Lucy get away with this? She is not intimidated by him. I am. Why?

The master said final grace, thanking almighty God for the meal. In the same breath the father spat in anger at Charles as they got up from the table, 'I want to see you in the office.'

Cowed by the demand, he followed his father. Sir Lionel demanded that he produce accounts for the preceding three months which the son searched for and rapidly found. Charles did routine book-keeping which, with even a moderate degree of competence, left little room for error. The father went over the accounts looking for trouble which he had difficulty in finding. As he searched, the son became more nervous and fearful by the minute. The silence was even more difficult to bear than the

293

destructive criticism when it came. Over and over the accounts he looked. In copper plate hand writing, they were a fine exercise in craftsmanship. Up to date and accurate in every detail; they were faultless. On he searched, becoming more irritable by the moment.

'What are you looking for father?'

'When you address me, you do so as sir. Do you understand?'

'Yes, sir.'

'That's better.'

At last he found something to criticise. The pressure visibly reduced, and an ever so slight look of satisfaction crossed his face. 'Where have you recorded depreciation?'

'I haven't, sir.'

'Why not?'

'You never requested it, sir.'

'Can't you act on your own initiative. Do I have to spell everything out to you? You fool.'

'I suggested it three months ago, sir.'

'No you didn't.'

'I did sir.'

The conversation three months before flashed through his mind but only for a moment. He could not change direction now. Never would he give away. Never would he admit error. On he had to go. All the more aggressively because inwardly he knew he was wrong.

'You did not, young man, don't argue with me.' The deception he was pursuing and the need to hide the fact made his anger even more violent.

'Very well father, what do you want done?'

'Record the depreciation, you fool.'

'Yes sir, at what rate of depreciation do you want the capital goods written off.'

'Use your initiative, man. Your initiative. This.' He tapped the side of his head with his right forefinger. 'With this. Understand, with this.' He looked at his son, his face full of

294

anger and maintained the penetrating gaze for several seconds. He seemed exhausted by the effort of his temper, and was quite breathless as his large frame subsided in the chair. He remained still until his regular breathing returned. He emerged almost benign after his two or three minutes of rest and recovery. The breathing did not return to normal immediately, but the anger ceased. Always in fear of his father, Charles saw him for the first time to have a vulnerable side. Never had he expressed anger in this violent child-like manner. He remained in the chair longer than he would usually have done.

'Charles, get on with the accounts. Consider the correct level of depreciation. We'll talk about it in the next week.'

Sir Lionel knew he had gone too far, but he could never admit this to anyone, only in fleeting moments to himself. Wanting to put the clock back half an hour, he knew he couldn't. Turning to look at his son, a look of pathos crossed his face which Charles picked up immediately. He knew his father's moods even more correctly than he did himself. For the first time he felt almost sorry for his father. The vulnerable side had exhibited itself to him directly for the first time.

'Is that all father?' He was not corrected for using the more familiar form of address. In fact he did not know he had used it till he heard the word.

'Yes my boy. That's all. Get back to your mother.' He remained in the chair while his son left the room.

Sir Lionel needed to rest now. The repressed aggression within him had always been largely under control, vented only when it was really needed. For serious matters, not for invented trivia of this nature. What am I doing? Am I losing control, he thought. His breathlessness returned which he tried to control by attempts to relax but to no avail. There was pressure in his head and a beating movement as he became aware of his blood circulating. It had happened before but not at this pressure. Almost losing consciousness, a reddish haze apppeared before his eyes. Was this the end? So much done, but so much more to do. The site to finish. Only I can guide that through to its conclusion. Only I can do that. I must survive. Gradually the mist receded. The pressure in his head subsided. Full consciousness gradually returned.

Had anyone else been in the room, they would have seen his face almost drained of blood and eyes facing towards the wall but seeing nothing. His eyes focused on his future and the direction his life might take. Never before had he considered the matter of death. Now he had been confronted with it for the first time. He knew he was mortal for the first time in his life. The funerals he had attended came into his mind, those of lesser and greater men. Never had he in any way identified with their inevitable fate. Now he did. He was mortal and might live a shorter life than many he knew. Much of his life flashed through his mind. His father and mother who he hadn't thought about for years. His brothers and sisters, where were they? Where were they living? Were they even still alive? Sitting down for a further hour, he reflected on everything. The construction project would have to be completed. There was no option. What then? Take on more work or devote the rest of his life to charitable matters? He was comfortably off but not as well off as everyone thought. Life could continue in the present house but he would have to be careful. No more rescuing Albert from his worst acts of folly. Could anything be done about him? Lucy would get married. It was not a case of whether she would but when. Charles, what would happen to him? He could make his way in the world but he had no drive. Sir Lionel had now totally calmed down, continuing to reflect in a state of near paralysis.

Charles had been talking to his mother in the kitchen for some time now. The housekeeper had completed her tasks and gone home, together with the scullery maid. It was somewhere where Sir Lionel never ventured and they were all able to talk without an audience.

'He's never been like this before, Charles. Shouting and screaming.'

'I know Mother. It's not like him to shout like that.'

'Is something wrong?'

296

'I don't know Mother. I don't know.'

'What was it about?'

'Accounts, depreciation, that's all.'

'What's that?'

'When something is bought, they write it off over a period of time.'

'Write off what?'

'Say a steam shovel lasts for ten years. They write it off over five years.'

'I see.'

'It's about controlling costs.'

'Is he in financial trouble, Charles?'

'Not really. The construction has to be completed on time otherwise there will be penalty clauses.'

'Will he do it on time?'

'He should do, though he will run it very near. We don't need any delays.'

'Will there be delays?'

'I don't think so. There could be labour troubles.'

'Will it make money?'

'Some, but not a lot. I don't think he'll lose on it.'

'Why's he gone roaring mad like this, Charles?'

'Perhaps it's his age. How old is he Mother? He'll never tell anyone.'

'He's sixty two this July.'

'Didn't know he was as much as that.'

'He's getting on and he can't take all this workload.'

'You know him. Thinks only he knows how to do it. He's got a meeting on the site at nine tomorrow.'Is he worried, Mother?'

'No more then usual.'

'Mother?' He left a long pause before continuing, didn't know how to phrase it. He could say almost anything to his mother but never directly condemn his father. It was a sort of mutual loyalty. 'Mother. You heard father shouting in the office at me?'

'Everyone heard it, Charles. Everyone.'

He still didn't know how to say it. Not wanting to make direct destructive remarks about his father he nonetheless wanted to get across what had happened.

'You know, Mother.' She remained silent and alert to his every word. 'He's never blown up like that before. Never lost control before. It's always been cold and threatening.' Again he paused. She watched, listened and waited. 'You know how he is.' She nodded, not speaking a word. 'When he blew up, he seemed almost childlike. I was sorry for him. Honestly. I was sorry for him.' He looked at her and she again nodded to him which established a mutual understanding. 'You know mother, he was just looking for something to shout about.' He paused again. 'When he lost his temper, he went really mad, but his eyes weren't properly focused on me. I almost laughed out. You know that's not like me.'

'I know Charles. It was Lucy who really started him off.'

'I know that. It's always her.'

'She likes annoying him. He'll never take it out on her. Always you and me.'

'Never takes it out on Albert.'

'He's given up on him. Albert knows it.'

'We're soft targets, Charles. That's what we are.'

'You're right Mother, we are.' They looked in agreement.

Charles continued, 'Then, Mother, when he stopped, he seemed to lose all sense of me being in the room. All during his outburst he didn't know I was there. Then he became sort of calm and friendly as though there had been no outburst. He wasn't talking to me. It could have been anybody. When he eventually said to me "Get back to your mother", it was the only time when I felt he knew me.' He shook his head, puzzled at what had happened.

'I worry, Charles.'

'I know you do, Mother, but there's nothing we can do.'

'Nothing at all?' she asked questioningly.

'Nothing at all, but I do feel sorry for him though.'

'I don't think he'd want to hear you say that.'

'I know he wouldn't.' They both gave a chilly smile in agreement as their glances briefly met.

Perhaps an hour and a half had passed as they had talked in the kitchen. 'Haven't heard him go to bed yet. Must be still in the office. You'd better go and see. Quietly,' she suggested, putting her forefinger to her lips in a conspiratorial manner.

Walking out of the kitchen towards the office, he trod slowly and quietly. The door, slightly ajar, was pushed open and Charles ever so slowly looked in. His father was sitting in the armchair with his head against the upright, not having moved an inch since he had left the room. He was asleep with a look of peace on his face and breathing quite normally. Not knowing what to do, he returned to his mother who was hovering outside the office door. They returned down the hall to the kitchen.

'What'll we do, Mother?'

'Wake him and get him upstairs.'

'You sure mother?'

'Yes. We'll do it now.' She walked resolutely into the office, followed by Charles. Shaking him gently, her husband's eyes opened immediately but it took him some seconds to recall where he was.

'Where am I, girl?' He hadn't called her 'girl' for years.

'In the office, Leo.'

'How did I get here?'

'On your two feet, Leo. Time you got to bed.'

'How long have I been here?'

'About two hours.'

'That long?' He knew he had been pulled out of a very deep sleep. 'What did I come in here for?'

'Accounts. Look there on the table.'

'I don't remember them.'

'Come on to bed, Leo. Think about them in the morning.'

They both got him to his feet, walking each side of him as he made his way upstairs, just able to do so unaided. No sooner did he lie down than he was asleep.

Chapter 29

It was perhaps seven o'clock on the day of Sir Lionel's visit to the site. Ben Letworthy had been in work an hour, inspecting the site, giving orders and making the project presentable. In spite of some passive but nonetheless calculated hindrance from the engineer, he had taken the trouble to see the work was up to date. He was confident the visit would go well but that did not remove any of the anxiety that such a visit always engendered. With everything ready, it was now just a wait till his arrival. The lack of activity on his part now that matters were in order made him all the more nervous. Would he want to inspect an area he had not thought likely? His anxiety continued.

Jack Lloyd had an unusually large number of horses to be shod. He knew this the previous night and had made an early start, as had his two fellow workers. No area was a more intense scene of activity than the blacksmith's forge. The sound of the hammers was heard all over the site. Nearer to the forge could be heard the hissing of hot shoes quenched in water interspersed with the brief but commanding shouting at a horse who moved at a vital time when the shoes were being fitted. This shouting could result in very bad temper and swearing with a particularly irritable horse. Jack, as the unpaid charge hand but armed with physical strength and long experience, always shod these difficult horses. Such horses were known individually and came to him directly. He enjoyed the challenges, knowing he could manage reasonably easily where others would have difficulties.

'Percy's cob is coming in today,' said one of his assistants.

'Why isn't he here?'

'He had a few last night. Might be in late.'

'He has a few every night.'

'I know.'

'He's going to get the bullet one of these days, and not before time.' Jack wasn't a boss's man and never would be but he hated idleness and despised drunkenness. He'd seen enough drunkenness in his time. It was a plague. Why hadn't he been affected by it? He didn't like the taste, and liked the effect even less but most of all because it made fools out of men.

For the first time in years he thought of Tommy and what he had taught him so many years before. He'd never had an employer like him since and never would. Didn't drink. Kept his cards close to his chest. You couldn't fool Tommy no matter how hard you tried. This passed through his mind in a second or two as he took a breather before changing to the other rear leg of a placid horse. Wiping his sweating forehead with a dirty rag whose original colour was no longer visible, he resumed his work, much of it spent bending over nearly double and frequently under mental and physical strain. So it went on for perhaps a further two hours, when he broke to drink water, stretch himself and again wipe his brow. As he did so, he saw Percy leading the temperamental horse in. Already it was starting to get frisky, giving out a very slight neigh as it shook its head. The horse's behaviour became all the stronger as it came nearer the forge. Finally it raised both feet in the air before coming to a halt.

'Why didn't you bring her in first?'
'Got in a bit late you know, Jack.'
'Drinking again, Percy?'
'Don't say that man.'
'You'll get the bullet one of these days, good boy.'
'Never.'
'You will. Letworthy'll have you for sure.'
'Never.'
'He will. He isn't Isaac, you know.'
'I do a good job.'
'When you're here. Give me the reins.' He did. The firm grasp Jack took of the reins had a calming effect on the horse. Perhaps horses with such a very long association with man know

301

who they can antagonise and who they can't. Certainly, any outside observer would have immediately recognised how this spirited and intractable horse became malleable when under his control. Grasping both reins as near the bit as was possible, he pulled the horse's head down to the level of his own. With their heads only an inch or two apart, he said slowly, 'Woo, boy.' Continuing to hold the horse firmly, he waited again to make the horse feel his firm presence. Then he tied her up outside. 'Come back in two hours, Percy.' Dismissing him with a wave of the hand, he returned to the fire.

'You know Sir Lionel is coming round this time?' his assistant said.

'Yes.'

'Do we have to do anything?'

'Probably won't come here.'

'What if he does?'

'If he comes, he comes.'

'Do we have to do anything, though?'

'What's your job?'

'Shoeing horses.'

'Carry on shoeing horses then, you fool. What else do we have to do? Put out the red carpet?'

The assistant laughed to himself. Jack always knew what to say, always hit the nail on the head. You always felt safe with Jack, he did everything right. Most of all he was a genius with horses. Everyone knew it. There were a lot of farm boys here. Even they said they'd seen nothing like him. Who could have calmed down that spirited horse? Not Percy. Probably not me, he thought. How would it be shod if Jack wasn't here? One or two knew him from Preseli. They all said he was a dark horse. No one really knew him.

The spirited horse was led to the door of the forge and tied again with no spare rein to move its head. The old shoes were taken off without trouble. It should have been shod some weeks before. It was typical of Percy to leave the matter undone. Jack trimmed the hooves then heated the first shoe. Holding the rear

302

nearside foot, he saw that the shoe was too large, and returned it to the fire. Waiting a minute or two for it to reheat, he removed it and hammered it to the correct size. He returned to the horse. Now came the most difficult part of fitting the shoe. Holding the rear hoof with his left hand, he burnt the hot shoe into the hoof with his right hand. It was a particularly important time in fitting a shoe which needed all his concentration. It was also the moment when a spirited horse would kick. The shoe hissed as it touched the hoof. Pressing it in further to get the correct fit, he was oblivious to all the noise which was going on around him. In the space of a few seconds the noise became louder, one man's voice rapidly dominating all the others. Eventually he heard his surname called. Still he carried on, ignoring all that was going on around him. Knowing this horse needed his undivided attention, he would not be distracted by others. This horse could give him a severe kick.

Suddenly he felt a severe kick from behind, but it wasn't from the horse. Slowly he put the horse's foot down while still holding the hot shoe in his right hand, and looked round. There was the red, animated face of Letworthy who was shouting, 'Lloyd, you drop everything when I order you.'

Jack looked him in the face in a cold, concentrated manner. His look was for Letworthy alone. Those who saw the incident, and several did, said that Letworthy wilted before his stare. It continued for perhaps a few seconds more as Jack continued to hold the shoe in the tongs in his right hand. Sir Lionel was standing by Letworthy, a fact which Jack was totally oblivious to. Slowly he walked back into the forge, passing Letworthy as he went and brushing against him as he did so. A cold anger consumed him as he slowly and deliberately put the shoe near the fire and the tongs onto the bench. Even more slowly, he walked out of the forge, turning to face his assailant some three feet away. No one except Jack had moved in the last minute. Perhaps a dozen persons saw the incident.

Letworthy began to shake inwardly and with a nervous shout ordered all those nearby to get on with their work. They moved reluctantly but kept their eyes on the two men. Continuing to look at him hard, Jack could see his adversary weaken before his eyes. Now he felt like a cat with a mouse; he would have fun but not for long. Just a breath of a smile came over his face which made Letworthy feel even more defeated. Jack knew if he pursued this he might apologise which was the last thing he wanted him to do.

'What you want?' he asked with quiet ice in his tone, continuing to fix him with his gaze.

'Sir Lionel...' He was unable to complete the sentence before Jack hit him under the jaw which sent him falling against the lengths of iron leaning on the outside wall of the forge. He was stunned but not knocked out. Jack stepped forward and gave him another similar blow which rendered him unconscious. Falling from an inclined position to a horizontal one, Letworthy fell across the forge entrance. Jack gave him a kick of contempt as he lay on the ground. It was all over. The whole incident lasted less than a minute.

There was an outburst of chatter and shouting immediately Letworthy fell to the ground but not for long. The roar of Sir Lionel quietened them all down. 'Get back to your work, all of you.' They seemed reluctant to move. 'Now!' He shook his silver handled ebony walking stick in everyone's direction to which they gradually responded. The rage on his face was frightening. It became a deep crimson as his eyes flashed in uncontrollable anger. 'Get back to work, all of you. Now,' he repeated.

Nobody, not even Jack, knew what to do next and remained still and silent. Never before had anyone seen Sir Lionel in a mood of such uncontrolled anger. He had frequently taken someone to task when a fault had been discovered but his remarks would be brief. Every word hit the target and his authority was absolute. No one within hearing would challenge him. This was different; he'd lost control. As the men returned to work there were mutterings and ill-concealed smirks as they moved slowly away.

'He's gone mad, he has,' remarked one.

'Jack'll go and soon,' commented another.

'And Letworthy soon after him,' put in a third.

'Could be a strike,' was said by one of the workers, in expectation and hope.

News of the incident was all over the site within minutes. Work did not come to a standstill put the pace was reduced as the talk increased. What had happened? What would happen? Above all, what would happen to Letworthy?

Sir Lionel had cooled down. His face was no longer florid but now appeared drained of blood. He felt confused, unable to think clearly. He wanted to sit down but knew he couldn't. His recollection of what had happened was not altogether clear. The blacksmith being kicked, then coming out of the forge and pole-axing the ganger gradually came back to him. Long experience had taught him that he had to make accurate decisions and carry them out resolutely and quickly. Those around him were silent and watching his every move, even Jack.

Letworthy soon regained consciousness, rising to his feet unsteadily, watched by all, including Sir Lionel. The facts came back to him more clearly now. Knowing he couldn't lose control again, he spoke to the engineer by his side quietly, 'Get rid of the blacksmith. Now.'

'Now?'

'Now. Right away.' The tone of his words and his quiet courtesy were quite at odds with his outburst only minutes earlier.

The engineer walked up to Jack, touched his upper arm and gently guided him into the forge. 'Jack, you know you've got to go, don't you?'

'I know. I'll go now.' Picking up his coat, he gave the forge a last glance before leaving it, walking past the unshod temperamental horse as he went. He gave her an affectionate stroke as he left the site for good. Through the gate he walked, turning to close it as he went, giving a wink to the engineer who had now returned to Sir Lionel's side. It wasn't even half past

305

nine and much had happened already. What would the rest of the day hold?

Jack walked back towards home, feeling almost light-hearted. There was a spring in his step and a smile on his face as he covered the short distance to his home. Walking in through the open door, he sat down. No one was aware of his arrival for some minutes. There was a buzz of conversation somewhere but he couldn't hear what was being said and didn't want to.

Silently he went over what had happened that morning. He laughed and laughed to himself. What would be Letworthy's next move? Would he get the sack? Who would bring Jack his wages, which were due? It should be the ganger but would he get someone else? Would they try and withhold his wages? There'd be a strike if they did that. He didn't want a strike, all the men losing time and then wages. He had a hold over Letworthy. How could he use it to maximum advantage? Jack would never make a complaint to the police but he'd never reassure Letworthy on that point; always keep him hanging in suspense, was Jack's plan. Would Letworthy even keep his job, he wondered, because he'd been involved in a serious incident in his first week as a ganger. Lost in his thoughts, Jack smiled to himself.

Molly walked into the room in bare feet without Jack hearing.

'Jack, what you home for at this time?'

'Got the sack, girl.'

'Why Jack, why?'

'I hit Letworthy.'

'Just hit him? Just like that?'

'He kicked me when my back was turned.'

'Why would he do that, Jack?'

'Had the big boss with him and wanted to look big himself.'

'Won't get back then?'

'No chance. I'm out. Have to look for something else.'

'What'll we do, Jack? You're the only earner.'

'I'll get money, girl, have no fear of that.'

'How Jack?'

'Never been without a job. Raven doesn't change his colour, girl.' He put his arm around her and gave her a comforting hug. 'Trust me, girl.' Sitting on his knee, she was reassured by his arm around her waist and a smile of endearment. 'We'll be alright. Have no fear.' It would be as near as he would ever get to confiding in her. She felt safe.

However, had she gained a glimpse into his mind she would have found a sea of uncertainty with storm clouds looming. A storm that would come sooner rather than later. Would he go to prison for hitting Letworthy? Would he get work again? He would be blacked on any big job, but hopefully his skills as a blacksmith would enable him to survive.

She remained on his knee while he said, 'Molly, I'm going to be home till night. If Letworthy calls, I'll see him. Understand, girl?'

'Very well, Jack. Will he call?'

'Someone will. Got to give me my wages.'

'Have they?'

'Got to. There'd be a strike if they didn't.'

'Never.'

'Letworthy'll want to know how he stands with me.'

'What d'you mean, where he stands?'

'He knows and I know. Sure he'll come.'

For the first time in Sir Lionel's life, he was uncertain what action to take and drove home in his carriage alone to think matters over. Jackson was ordered to visit him in an hour and Letworthy resumed his duties in a very crestfallen manner, spending the entire morning in his cramped office. The work resumed but on a slower basis as chatter proved more attractive an option.

At the appointed time, Jackson arrived at the Hall and was shown directly into the office. 'Jackson, this matter must be dealt with today. Not a moment later.' He looked at Jackson directly as he spoke, 'Letworthy was a fool to kick him. You know that.'

'I do sir. Very foolish indeed, he was.'

307

'What are we to do, Jackson?'

'Sack them both. Letworthy has lost face and in public. His authority has been undermined.'

'You think he should go?' asked Sir Lionel

'Only if we have someone better to replace him.'

'Have we?'

'No sir,' admitted Jackson.'

'Then he stays. We can't afford trouble now. We can't lose a day. The blacksmith will have to go to court; we can't overlook his behaviour.'

'That could be difficult, sir.'

'Why, Jackson?'

'It's rumour. Only rumour, sir.'

'Well, out with it, man.'

'They say they're father and son.'

'Got the same surname, Jackson?'

'No sir. He's Lloyd.'

'That doesn't make any difference, Jackson.'

'There's something else.'

'More rumour?'

'Yes sir. Lloyd has some sort of hold on him.'

'It doesn't affect this matter, Jackson.'

'It might, sir.'

'How?'

'Letworthy was the ganger on the adjoining site. Jack Lloyd's father-in-law was sacked for persistent drunkenness by Letworthy. Jack Lloyd got him restarted.'

'You're saying Letworthy can't be trusted?'

'I'm saying what happened sir.'

'I see.'

'Sir, Lloyd would be a far better ganger than Letworthy.'

'Why didn't you suggest him before we appointed Letworthy?'

'I did sir, but you ruled him out for lack of experience.'

'I remember. He doesn't drink, does he?'

'That's him.'

'Is he a good blacksmith, Jackson?'

'First class. Never seen a better.'

'I was one myself once, you know.'

'I didn't know, sir.'

'Not as good as Lloyd. If I had been that good, I might not have been here.' He smiled to himself. He allowed the matter of assault to drift from his mind. 'Letworthy stays.'

'Sir, do you want Lloyd paid for the part of the week he worked?'

'Yes. Today, without fail. There could be trouble if we don't.'

Jackson left. It was still not noon. He rode back, deep in thought. The day had turned out better than he had expected with him having a firm grasp of Letworthy, one he would not relinquish. If he stepped out of line, failed to reach an objective or lost control of matters in any way, he would flog him and flog him hard. He wasn't as physically strong or aggressive as Letworthy but he knew he had total power over him.

As he walked into the office, he said to Peck, 'Get Letworthy in right away.' Seating himself in the chair, he waited but only for a minute or two. Letworthy arrived, knocked and waited some time for an answer before hearing the command, 'Enter.'

He was not asked to sit and Jackson hardly looked at him before speaking. 'Letworthy, much against my recommendation to Sir Lionel, you will remain in your post. I will watch you like a hawk. If there are any more mistakes, you will be out. It comes with the strong suggestion that you don't go around kicking the more competent members of staff.' The sarcasm of his final remark was not lost on the recipient. 'Also, you will deliver what wages are owed to Jack Lloyd, tonight. Collect them from Peck. You will also look around for a skilled blacksmith, preferably a non-drinker.' Letworthy's face went red with embarrassment. He began to speak but heard, 'Letworthy, I don't want to hear from you. Get out.'

At seven o'clock that evening, Letworthy walked down

Frog Street with the wages which were due. He was seen by many as he walked towards the house, and by everyone as he walked away. He knocked. Jack came to the door.

'Got your wages.' He held them out with a shaking hand. Jack took what was due to him. 'Can I see you a minute, Jack?' Jack looked at him, without replying. Letworthy went red in the face. 'I want to see you alone. Just a minute or two, that's all'. Jack looked at him again. Letworthy maintained his red face as perhaps a second or two passed. 'Just a minute or two. It won't take long. Got to talk to you.' Jack could tell that he had got him on the defensive. He shook his head slowly and deliberately, without saying a word. Letworthy turned and walked back the way he had come. It was only a hundred yards but felt like the longest walk he had ever taken. All eyes were on him except for Jack's. He had returned to his chair.

Chapter 30

Ben Letworthy had left the street with all eyes on him. He could feel them. The rays of ill-will penetrated every square inch of his person. A man fuelled by power and authority, this was one of the lowest points in his life. Had he been an observer on the street, he would have seen his head begin to hang and his shoulders become more hunched. There was a cowed, almost frightened look on his face. He wanted to run out of the street but carefully maintained his usual pace.

He would hold onto his job by a thread no stronger than a spider's web. All were now against him; everyone on the site from top to bottom; the workers, the foremen and, most dangerous of all, Jackson. He was the one who would do the most damage, against whom he was least defended. He would have to fight him with logic. Jackson had the ear of Sir Lionel. What was going on in Sir Lionel's mind? Only God knew and possibly Jackson. Above all, he wondered whether there would be a strike. He'd be out if that happened unless he and he alone could settle it. Probably he'd be out anyway, as he'd be identified as the cause of it.

Letworthy had fifteen pounds in his pocket, a room in a tavern and a slate he paid at the end of the week, not much to show for his life. This Jack Lloyd was certainly his son by that woman in the Preselis. He couldn't even remember her name. This son of mine knows I've been involved in a robbery. Would he shop me, and what would be the consequences? It was fifteen or twenty years ago, and I had all that money in solid gold sovereigns, almost a thousand. Where did they all go? Now I'm here alone, with everyone against me. Everyone.

All these thoughts went through his mind as he walked back to his bed at the tavern. Some of the workers he passed walked around him or crossed the road, not wanting to acknowledge him. He walked into the bar and sat alone for almost three hours, drinking pint after pint of beer. A few looked at him, muttered to themselves, and then looked away. When senseless with drink and unable to drink another drop, he made for bed. Falling on the floor, he couldn't get up.

'Leave him there.' said one patron.

'Give'im a kicking. He's big enough to take it.'

The landlady called her husband to carry him upstairs. Whatever those in the bar thought, he was a good customer, spending most of his wages there. Grabbing him by one arm, they lifted him up sufficiently to be able to hold the other. Husband and wife carried him up the stairs, a dead weight which they eased on to the bed, laying him on his side.

'He'll be as sick as a dog.'

'So long as he doesn't choke himself. Don't want a dead body here. Or lose a good customer.' She gave him a cynical smile.

An hour after Letworthy had left Frog Street, three men called at Jack's home. The two blacksmiths he worked with and one other. He called them into the front room.

'Come in, boys.'

'You alright, Jack?'

'Yes, I'm alright.' He smiled to himself.

'Got your wages?'

'Letworthy brought 'em round an hour back.'

'What did he say?'

'Nothing.'

'Nothing at all, Jack?'

'Nothing. He wanted to talk. I didn't.' He smiled to himself, relishing his victory.

'The boys have been talking. Want your job back?'

'No.'

'Sure? Some of the boys would strike you know.'

'Leave it alone, boys.'

'They would, you know. Might get'em all out.'

'No. No.' He raised his hands in disbelief.

'Why not, Jack?'

312

'Listen boys. I can fight my own battles. Don't need anyone to fight them for me.'

'They could do this to one of the others.'

'Well go out for him then. Not me.'

'I think they'd do it.'

'No, boys. Don't go out for me. There's always casualties in strikes. I'm not one of them and never will be.' He laughed quietly to himself. His visitors saw this and pressed him no further.

'What you doing for money Jack?'

'Got some for this week. I'll find work alright.'

'They'll black you. You know that?'

'I'm twenty-six. I've worked twenty years. The workhouse isn't in sight yet. Or ever will be.' They all laughed. They all knew he'd always get work.

'What happened to Percy's horse?' Jack enquired.

The blacksmiths laughed, raising their hands. 'Don't talk to us about Percy's horse.'

'Did you get the shoes on?'

'Took about two hours. Had to work late to finish the rest.' They all laughed together. 'We'll get you back to shoe Percy's horse.' They laughed again.

They moved to go. 'You don't want the job back then?'

'No. Wouldn't take it if it was offered me. Wouldn't take it.'

'Sure Jack?'

'Sure, boys.' They left, talking as they walked up the road.

'He's a great fella.'

'Say that again.'

'What'll he do?'

'He'll get by. Nothing'll stop Jack.'

'Too true.'

As the men were leaving Frog Street, Jackson was facing Sir Lionel in his office.

'Well Jackson, have matters settled down?'

'So far as I can see, sir.'

313

'Any unrest, Jackson?'

'None so far. If there is any, it will be in the next twenty four hours.'

'I don't like that man Letworthy holding the ganger's job. He's a drinker if ever I've seen one. He should never have kicked that blacksmith. If that happened again we'd have a strike. You know that. I know that. Look round for someone else.'

'I will sir.' Jackson smiled to himself. It was the ammunition he needed. How would he twist the knife into Letworthy's chest? He relished the thought of the look on his face. Letworthy was never able to hide his feelings, whatever they were. Jackson would create the opportunity. Finding a replacement had to be his first priority. It would not be easy but he would find him. Letworthy looked just like Jackson's drunken, brutal grandfather who had fortunately died when he was twelve years old. It would be like settling an old score. He recalled his grandfather's drunken violence. He would hit out at the children under any excuse. If he couldn't find an excuse, he would invent one. Jackson's early years had been plagued by him.

Leaving the office, he felt warm all over. Arriving home in the failing light, he reflected on the day. It had certainly been eventful and he had gained a little more of his master's confidence. Sitting back in his most comfortable armchair, he drank a glass of whisky, something he rarely did and then only sparingly. It had been a good day.

Jackson had his sources of intelligence. On this site it was Joshua. A colourless bricklayer with few if any friends on the site, Joshua had once given him a trivial piece of information when he was out of sight of the rest of the men. Why he did it, Jackson didn't know. He was not paid. Perhaps he wanted to get close to those with the real power. Perhaps his natural inclination was to fawn, to be servile. Royal palaces were full of them. Surely there were positions the world over where no other characteristics were needed. In any event, Joshua had given him, over a period of time, pieces of information of varying relevance.

314

Twice he'd given him a sovereign. Joshua seemed to have a sixth sense as to what was useful and what wasn't.

Jackson had a second large glass of whisky. The curtains were drawn. The fire was blazing. He became drowsy. He was roused by the maid announcing, 'There's a man at the door, Sir.'

'Who is it, Daisy?'

'Don't know his name. Been here once before. From the site.'

Jackson thought it might be Joshua. 'I'll be out in a minute. Don't ask him in, Daisy.' She nodded.

He didn't want to look as though he'd just woken up. Walking to the bathroom, he combed his hair, washed his face and walked to the back door. 'Yes Joshua?' At that moment he disliked this little 'snake in the grass'. Everything about him was repellent. Holding his cap in both hands, he gave a little bow and an obsequious smile. Joshua looked at Jackson, trying to read his thoughts. Like all such men he was able to pick up any little nuance in another's thoughts. His first glance recorded a certain hostility towards him. Giving an ingratiating smile, he waited for Jackson to speak first. Jackson did not do so. Joshua, like all such men in these circumstances, could not handle the silence. He had to speak. 'There won't be a strike, sir'. Jackson nodded, giving a look of expectation which silently asked, 'Is that all?' Again Joshua could not handle the silence. Jackson was being difficult by not speaking. He saw the patronising smile begin to appear on his face as he looked down on him from his position of advantage on the top step. This made Joshua's manner all the more submissive.

He spoke quietly, looking at his employer. 'Letworthy's blind drunk in his lodgings. Had to be put to bed.'

Jackson now felt mildly sympathetic towards him. Why, he didn't know. He reached in his pocket, found a sovereign, gave it to him and returned to the fireside. He hardly said a word. He thought of Joshua. Poor, weak, treacherous little man who would sell his fellow man for a couple of sovereigns and a chance to rub shoulders with the management. He'd probably do it for nothing.

What Jackson couldn't understand was the risk he was running for such trivial reward. If he was found out, he'd be beaten to a pulp. The firm wouldn't help him. That was certain. Why did he do it? It would never get him a foreman's job. He wasn't even much of a bricklayer, much less a leader. Perhaps the role of spy appealed to him, so that he could stab in the back those with power over him who he disliked. The information was useful, very useful. He had a sixth sense about that. Sitting in his chair, he smiled to himself. Yes, events were going his way. He would be up early.

Jack was also up early the next day, before anyone else. The prospect of the lack of work unsettled him. What would he do? He settled down to breakfast; bread, cheese and tea eaten alone at a dirty wooden table. He thought, not about what he intended to do in the future, but what he would do that day. Get out of the house for the whole day, and find some fresh air. He remembered his life with the drovers. How he missed the fresh air, constant change of scene, friendship and loyalty to your group. It had been similar to being part of a troop in the army. Thrown on your own resources, you could act as you thought best. The site was different. It was the same job day after day, bosses around all the time, then home to the family. It rotted brains and killed initiative. He loved Jack and Molly was good to him, but what did family life mean apart from constant yacking? What were the challenges anymore? Shoeing Percy's horse and he didn't even finish that. He was made for better things.

Molly appeared with the baby on her arm, as Jack was finishing his breakfast.

'How long you been up, Jack?'

'An hour.'

'What you doing today?'

'Getting out.'

'When will you be back?'

'Before dark.'

'What you going to do, Jack?'

'Just get out. I got to get out.'

316

'Going to look for work Jack?'

'Not yet, girl. Something'll turn up. Have no fear.'

She looked worried as she held young Jack more firmly, but said no more.

'I'm off, girl.' She didn't reply. Where was he going and what would he be doing? She had no idea.

Letworthy had got up at the usual time, drank tea provided by his landlady but ate none of the cawl provided.

'You had a load on last night,' she accused, looking him directly in the eye.

He smiled and shrugged his shoulders. His face was red, his eyes bloodshot and his breath smelt very strongly of the previous night's excesses. The grubby unmade bed he had just vacated had the same dishevelled appearance.

'Wash your bloody self, man. You look awful.'

He knew he did and went to wash in the back yard. The cold water he pumped into a bucket got his circulation moving again. Repeatedly splashing his face with the cold water woke him up. Shaving with the icy water was painful but in fifteen minutes he was looking more presentable. 'Do I look alright, missus?'

'A bit better but you smell like a small brewery.' He was off. Walking the short distance to the site, the difficulties he had to face yet again came into his mind. His thoughts were defensive. How will I keep out of the way of Jackson with this smell on my breath? In the past he had always been confident about defending his own corner. Somehow he had always had an ally he could trust and who would work in his interests. Now there was no one. All were against him.

Jackson went directly to Letworthy's cabin. Even from a hundred yards he could see that the door was open and the cabin occupied. He smiled to himself; a smile of expectation. He could feel a flutter of excitement in his stomach. It was something to be relished slowly, like good food. His pace slackened as he got nearer and nearer. When he was within twenty yards, Letworthy noticed him. He came out of the cabin, walking towards Jackson holding his hand out in expectation with an enquiring look on his

317

face. The handshake was returned as briefly as possible.

'Into the cabin, Letworthy.' They walked in, Jackson going first. Letworthy turned away from his adversary as far as was possible, holding a dirty handkerchief in front of his mouth. 'Are we keeping up with the targets, Letworthy?'

'Sir. The excavations are up to date but we're a day or two behind on the retaining walls, sir.'

'Why man, why?'

'They were a day or two behind when I took over a week ago. I think we've gained a day, Sir.'

'You'll catch up?'

'Yes sir, I will.' He had dreaded Jackson's visit but his mind was put at rest by the first few questions. This made him lower his guard. He felt more secure, relaxing the grip on his handkerchief and looking Jackson in the face.

Jackson continued with questions of minor relevance to the running of the site. Some of the ganger's old confidence returned. He replied to the questions in a more animated manner. His questioner encouraged this.

'You now have matters under control Letworthy? Ship shape?'

'Yes sir.' He now almost glowed with pride. The worst had not happened.

'Everything, Letworthy?'

'Yes sir.' Now he became slightly uneasy. A look passed over his adversary's face, which he did not like. If he had been asked, he could never have put it into words. It wasn't directly hostile, yet it engendered unease. He could almost register a change of breathing as the look took effect. It took no more than a second. Jackson immediately knew his change of attitude had not been lost on the ganger.

'Replaced the blacksmith, Letworthy?'

'No sir.'

'Why not?'

'Good ones are not easy to find.'

'They aren't, are they? What do you propose doing about

replacing him?'

'Keep looking. Putting the word out.'

'He was a good blacksmith, Letworthy.'

'Very good, sir.'

'If I'd been Sir Lionel, I'd have sacked you and not him.' He didn't have an answer. 'I mean that, Letworthy.' Still he didn't have an answer. Jackson stood and looked at him, then bent over towards him until he was no more than six inches away.

'Had you been drinking when you kicked him?'

'Oh no, sir.'

'Are you sure, Letworthy?' The ganger wanted to run and hide but there was nowhere to go. 'You are stinking of beer. Stinking. Did you drink a barrel of it last night?'

'I had only a few sir.'

'A few? Your breath is rotten with alcohol. Your eyes are bloodshot. Your face is scarlet. You are sodden with drink. Don't....tell....me....lies.'

Letworthy didn't know what to say. Tears were beginning to form in his eyes. Jackson could not let go. He had all the power. He was fighting him with words, his favoured weapons. He'd caught him at his lowest ebb. Jackson had all the cards.

'If I'd been that blacksmith, I'd have beaten you to a pulp.' Letworthy backed into a corner. It crossed his mind that he could take a punch at his enemy, but he felt too defeated. Neither did he feel able to speak. He'd just have to take all the punches.

'What did you kick him for? You fool.'

'Sir Lionel was there. He wouldn't stand up when he came. Wouldn't show respect.'

'Sir Lionel likes workers, not those who stand about. He was a blacksmith once himself.' Letworthy expressed surprise but not in words. 'Let me tell you, he's got your measure. Any more trouble from you and it's out.'

Walking back through his office door, Jackson said, 'Morning, Peck.' without looking at him. He was more cheerful than he had been for a long time. He felt on more intimate terms with Sir Lionel. There had been a change in his employer. As Jackson sat at his desk doing nothing in particular, he tried to work out what it was. In the past, Sir Lionel would never have reacted with such anger to an incident of this sort. He had shown anger before but it had never been out of control. There were moments when he did not appear to be mentally functioning at all. There was a look in his eye that was not quite focused, and he had slow reactions to questions he had been asked. What was the problem? Jackson felt that there was no one with whom he dare discuss this matter.

Chapter 31

Jack left the house and began walking towards Kilvey Hill. Slowly he walked, over the Tawe and past various taverns he had heard mentioned. Some of the people he passed knew him, many more since the incident. He climbed up the hill for the first time. Never, since his first day in the town, had he had such a view. The harbour was full of ships with hardly a square yard of water visible, some were arriving, others setting sail. Further up the river, the air was full of grey-green smoke which tingled the nostrils, and was all-enveloping. There was the constant, inescapable noise of industrial activity. Jack thought of the Preseli mountains. What was he doing here?

The day was fine but cold, with the wind coming in strongly from the south west. There were clear views to the North Devon coast, but less so up the Swansea Valley where much of the industrial smoke was being blown. As he looked in that direction and over the town itself all he saw were chimneys, all belching smoke over the town on still days or up towards Clydach and Pontardawe when the prevailing south west wind was blowing.

On top of Kilvey Hill, he imagined himself as a seagull for a brief moment, with a view of it all; this ravaged vitality which nothing and nobody could stop. It had a will of its own, like a crowd out of control. Would it ever stop growing? Could the docks take any more ships? Would they be able to build any more metal works? Could any more houses be crammed into the terraces already covering every available piece of land? Then he looked at the dock where he had worked till a day or two before. Steam navvies were blowing steam. He could see the forge but there were no horses outside. It seemed like another world now.

He shivered with the cold as he had not brought his old military cape with him. This turned his thoughts towards his service in the Crimea. The battles had much in common with the present prospect. The men and horses running here and there, all under pressure to get things done, all under orders. The noise, the smell, and above all the piles of waste. On the battlefields, it was the waste of life.

Here it was the same. Not the loss of life; that was a longer term outcome. At least the battles came to an end; this life of toil was unending. Twenty four hours a day, seven days a week. Did God really intend us to live like this? His mind went back even further to the stories from the old testament he had heard in chapel. Abraham didn't live like this with his flocks. Why should I?

He got up, walking slowly east to wherever this track would take him. Turning round occasionally to see where he lived, he could hardly believe what he saw. No one was up on the hill. Perhaps no one ever came up there. They were too busy in the town working, struggling and getting by as best they could. Opening a gate, and then closing it behind him, he continued on the track which bore very few signs of use.

It was not a made road, only a track through the rough grass, heather and gorse. A brown line which meandered through the upland landscape like a stream sprung from the earth. He walked on, with the sea always to his right and the upper Swansea Valley to his left. Gradually the industrial sprawl became less visible but the smoke remained.

He thought about how he had lost his job. He felt almost pleased. In the back of his mind he had always resented having to work to the orders of another. It wasn't oppressive at the forge but he always felt under the whip. Isaac left him alone which made it easier to bear. Letworthy, his own father, had caused him to reach breaking point. He was on the street and without work yet, in a strange way, he felt he had got the best of it. He would never acknowledge Letworthy as his father, or even speak to him again. Deep down he wished that misfortune would befall him. Even deeper down he was sure that this would happen. He didn't know why, he was just convinced of it. He had feelings not of hatred, more an amused contempt. Yes, Letworthy would come to a sticky end. Jack was also sure that Letworthy would feel the

322

same. He knew it from the defeated look on his face. Letworthy's gold had done him no good. A fool and his money are soon parted.

It got a little warmer as the day went on and he sat down in the grass facing the Bristol Channel. He couldn't take his eyes off the harbour, wondering how they got the ships in so closely. Not wanting to go home, he walked on slowly along the high ground till it descended then turned around. He had not seen a soul all day.

For nearly twenty years he had not thought much about his family. Now he had time to reflect. His mother's funeral came back to him: the cold, the wet, the crying, Picton Jenkins's preaching. He recalled the feeling of being an outsider, ignored by everyone, even his sisters. The only attention and that unwelcome, came from his uncles. Were they even still alive? He had little recollection of his mother apart from her lying in bed, coughing. Then came her death. He had not known what to do, felt numb. What were you supposed to do?

Meg came into his mind. He didn't remember much of her, only her sharp temper and even sharper remarks. 'Mother was stupid about him. A real wrong'un, he was. Left before you were born. Back to Devon with the law on his tail. She had a terrible time having you.' That was all he had ever learned about his family. Then Letworthy came into his life. He'd done the right thing, keeping him at a distance. Shit on him if I get the chance, he vowed to himself. That's all I know about my mother and father. A bit different from the O'Haras. God knows I feel an outsider there, but perhaps that's the way I want it. It's easier. Don't tell anyone anything, be my own master, live life on my terms. Deeds not words.

Slowly he walked back. Very slowly. He was oblivious to everything except his thoughts. Did he want to get back to work in the town or did he want to find some other method of making a living. He'd be blacked for certain in Swansea. He thought he could overcome that as his reputation was widely known and second to none. How would he make a living otherwise? He could never run a tavern; the drunks would drive him mad. Old man O'Hara would be a burden he couldn't always control. Could he move? No, he couldn't move the family. That was impossible.

Gradually the sound of muffled steps on grass entered his consciousness. Then he heard the sound of harness metal clinking followed by a short snort. He looked up to see, perhaps forty yards away, a very fine light chestnut horse coming towards him. His first glance was at the horse. Never had he seen such a fine one in Swansea. His mind had to go back to the Crimea to recall such quality. It looked like a general's horse, spirited, well-groomed and arrogant. This horse knew he was superior: the swing of the head held high, the walk and the sense of power which could be unleashed with the slightest order. This one was a winner.

He noticed all this in the space of a second or two. Then he looked at who the rider could be on such a splendid horse. He saw a young woman as arrogant as her mount. Her clothes were smart and the bowler hat worn with the confidence of a monarch wearing a crown. The look in her eyes commanded authority. Here was a woman used to having her own way. Jack stepped one pace from the path to let this rider pass. He looked her in the eye. His gaze was returned with confidence but for only a moment. She couldn't maintain eye contact with him. She looked away, then looked at him again but still was unable to hold his gaze. She urged the horse into a trot to pass out of his way quickly, without another glance.

He smiled to himself. She had everything in her favour: horse, clothes, good looks, youth, breeding. He was a man in shabby clothes, looking little better than an unemployed industrial worker, which was his present position. Yet he had this woman at a disadvantage. Who was she, he wondered. He supposed that she was the daughter of a local landowner or industrialist. She was, without doubt, from a rich background. He hadn't seen such a fine horse for many years. He had only shod a few like that and none in Swansea. Then he thought of her. She was a cracker, no doubt about that. She can have her way with me anytime, he thought. He couldn't get her out of his mind. She was good looking and, like the horse she rode, spirited and arrogant. She'd be a challenge. He thought of nothing else as he walked back. That black curly hair (he loved black hair), that commanding tilt to her head as she looked at him, the eyes which said everything. What is it about eyes? No more than a couple of square inches and you see them for no more than a second or two, yet they say more than any gesture. A relationship could be established by one glance. He was determined to find out who she was. He was now well on the way back, with the high point of Kilvey Hill only a short distance away. Not wanting to go home, he slackened his pace.

Lucy Lambert had ridden past Jack at a trot, then reverted to a walk. Her reaction to this man, who was no more than a workman and an insolent one at that, annoyed her. She wanted to get off the horse and kick herself, to feel able to go back and confront him. Knowing she couldn't, she rode on at a slow walk. She always looked her father in the face and challenged him where necessary. What was it about this man who had visually confronted her and won? This had never happened to her before. It felt like defeat, a thing she had never experienced before. Something told her that if she went back and confronted him he would still emerge the winner.

His look had also sent other feelings through her; a sense of excitement, danger and risk. Yes, there was risk in that look. Never before had she felt this way about any man. Why him? He would be trouble, she knew that. She had looked at him for no more than a few seconds but she had taken him all in. He had fair curly hair on his chest as well as his head. He was tall, a bit less than six feet. He looked as strong as a horse. She couldn't get him out of her mind, yet she still felt a sense of pride. Why should I be obsessed with this man? Why wasn't he in work? Was he up to no good? But what would he be up to here? There was little to gain, nothing to steal or poach apart from a few rabbits and he didn't have a dog or a ferret with him. He had nothing with him. He appeared to be just idling his time away up here with nothing to do. She'd find out who he was. She didn't know how but she'd definitely find out.

It was time to turn back. Would he still be on the road? If he was, how would she pass him? At the gallop without looking at him, or trotting past and acknowledging him? She would prefer the latter. She walked the horse back, still undecided. There was a troubled feeling in her stomach which would not go away, and was entirely unfamiliar to her. Well on the way back, she saw her man ahead. He was walking slowly but still on the highest part of the hill. She urged the horse to a gentle trot. Yes, she would look him in the eye and say, 'Good afternoon,' trotting on at the same pace. She came nearer and nearer. The feelings in her stomach troubled her even more intensely.

Hearing the horse, he stood a pace to one side to let the horse and rider pass, looking her in the eye as she approached. Her nerve left her when she was no more than twenty yards from him. Kicking the horse into a gallop, she rode by without returning his gaze. He smiled to himself. Round two to Jack Lloyd, he thought.

Riding past, she took the road down to the town. Knowing she had lost again, tears of annoyance fell down her face. 'You coward. You fool,' she reproached herself. Very gently trotting the horse the rest of the way home, she was lost in thought. How could she overcome this humiliation?

Jack turned to face the town and began walking downhill, the woman still on his mind. She was good looking, there was no doubt about that, and arrogant. Tried it with me, didn't she? She'd try again if she had a chance. Would she get another chance, though? That depends on whether I get some sort of job with money. What I've got will run out in a week. What'll I do without money? The family will have to live on rabbits and a bit of theft. I know a lot about rabbit catching, he thought, but I'll have to learn about thieving.

Down he walked into St Thomas, still thinking what his next move would be. The smell of the town returned. It had never really left him all day but now it became more intense. It irritated him. Past one tavern then another, he walked. He was acknowledged as he passed by people he knew slightly and others who he did not know at all. The road became more crowded as he passed the biggest tavern on the east side of the Tawe. There was a crowd outside including the landlord, a large middle aged man in a loud tweed suit and bowler hat. Overweight, red faced and possessed of a jocular personality, he was known all over this side of town as "Sporty Charlie". He was a true character, his irrepressible personality a magnet to customers, and his premises much frequented by those in need of his particular form of excitement. As a result, he was able to charge slightly more than others for his beer. He also traded as a bookie, which was his principle source of income. From time to time he ran his own sporting events, not officially recognised but generally known to all who were drawn to such things.

When Jack was still twenty yards from the group surrounding the landlord, he heard him shout out, 'Lloyd is here. The man who hammered Letworthy. Come here, boy. Let's see you.'

He walked towards them, mildly amused by the recognition he had gained. One or two were there from the site, remaining on the outside of the gathering, some of whom thrust forward to slap their hero on the back. Staying outside for twenty minutes, Jack said little, heard nothing of consequence but basked a little in his new found status and local fame. The crowd began to disperse until only Charlie and a couple of others remained. The landlord leaned towards Jack and said, 'In here. I want to talk to you.' Jack hesitated. 'Come on in, you,' he continued, directing Jack past the drinkers to a room at the back. 'Sit down.' He did so, not knowing what this unexpected intimacy entailed. 'Listen, Jack. They're all talking about you.'

'I know some are.'

'Some! Everyone knows about it. Everyone.'

Jack smiled. He wasn't immune to the regard in which he was now held.

'Listen, Jack. You got work?'

'No. I'll be blacked. I know that.'

'You have been blacked. Never work for the big contractors again here. You know that?'

'Course I do.'

'What you going to do for money then, good boy? You're a big strong man. What you going to do then?'

He shook his head. 'Don't know. Something'll turn up, I suppose.'

'Can't wait for something to turn up. Got to get up and find something. What you going to do then Jack? What you going to do?'

'Something'll come along. Never been without work.'

'Listen, I've got an offer for you. You're handy with your fists, aren't you?'

'Think I am.'

'You know I've got the yard at the back?'

'Yes. Big yard isn't it?'

'I run some fixtures at the back. You know, bare knuckle fighting. I could give you a start on Sunday afternoon. Ten pounds, win or lose.'

'I could do with the money. Who against?'

'A man from Merthyr. Paddy McGinty. Getting a bit old now and too fond of the beer. Won't be too hard for a first fight. I'm looking for someone young. I think you're the man I need.'

'Alright, then. What time on Sunday?'

'It'll be at three but come at two. I'll have a word with you before. It's on then?'

'Yes, it's on.'

He reached in his pocket, giving him five guineas. 'The rest at the end of the fight. Don't drink beforehand.' They shook hands. Charlie winked at him. He assured himself that he had a new star. 'Want a drink?'

Jack shook his head. 'I don't.'

'Sunday at two, then.'

He walked home; glad he had found a source of income but

knowing it was the hardest trade he would ever follow. In the past he'd seen a few of these old battle scarred prize-fighters with their thirst for beer, their memories, and their scarred faces. He didn't want to end up like that. One or two and he'd get out. That's what he would do. He wouldn't end up like one of those old fools. He'd never do that.

Over the river and following the coastline, he came to the site on his left then the approach to Frog Street. The stench in the street hit him; he'd forgotten how bad it was. He hadn't thought of the street or his family all day. Walking through the door, and grasping the gold in his pocket, he heard the usual chatter from inside. His temper rose, but by an act of will, he overcame it. Comforted by the feel of gold, he gradually relaxed. It was the first time he had ever been paid in advance in his life. It made him feel very uncertain and slightly suspicious. There must be a catch somewhere.

Chapter 32

He hadn't slept all night. He wasn't tired because he hadn't worked for days. The fight on Sunday was on his mind, and the memory of that woman. He tossed and turned most of the night. Molly slept, woken only now and then by Jack's movements. 'Can't you sleep Jack? What's wrong?'

'Never mind girl, I'll get off before long.'

'You haven't slept, have you?'

'Not much. You turn over, I'll get off.'

She did so and was asleep as she turned. Not a deep sleep, but the sleep of a mother who has to be aware of a child's cry. Young Jack was in a cot in the room.

His thoughts went from one problem to another but most of all he considered that woman. She had got right under his skin. He was irritated by this. All the more so because she was so obviously well off.

What was he letting himself in for with this fight? That was a loser's trade. Never met an ageing fighter yet who wasn't penniless and married to the beer barrel. Not that he'd met many; perhaps they didn't live that long. He distrusted Charlie. He was always on the right end of the money and absent when things got tough. Tough they surely would be, thought Jack, if he followed this trade.

It was well after four. He couldn't stay in bed any longer and got up while it was still dark. He made the fire, boiled the kettle, looked for tea but there was none so he used the tea leaves in the rubbish to make a weak brew. Sitting and sipping the tea, he drank three cups, each the same pauper's liquid. Tasteless, but warm and wet. Were they so poor they couldn't afford tea? He became annoyed, but there was no one with whom to quarrel.

Walking down the street, he took in the smell which annoyed him further. The houses were starting to stir as the first

330

signs of dawn crept in from the east. What was he to do that day? Get out of this bloody street and soon as he could. He felt in his pocket for the five guineas which made him feel uneasy. Money in advance; he'd never known it before. It put him on trust. Bosses don't trust you. They don't trust anyone. Why had Charlie? He suspected that Charlie was as crooked as a corkscrew, and only doing this for personal gain. Why the money up front?

He walked past the site. There was a watchman in the cabin, more asleep than awake. One or two workers were starting to arrive. It was too dark for him to recognise any of them. He walked on. That place where he had worked so hard seemed somehow distant. It was only days since he was sacked but it seemed an age. It was part of his former life. He didn't want to know about it.

The sun had taken its first step over the horizon. He'd take a walk today, the same as yesterday. Would he see that woman? He wanted to ask someone who she was. Charlie would know. He knew everything. Getting back to the house, he saw only old man O'Hara, who was sitting down warming himself by the fire. He was about to start talking. Jack had seen the signs a hundred times before. His temper rose as he saw the first signs. He'd got to shut him up, the bloody old windbag. Jack looked at him, very annoyed. 'Where's the tea? Have you and the women drunk the bloody lot? Where's the tea?' His temper increased as he spoke. The demand was heard all over the house.

'Tis the women who know, Jack my boy. Tis the women who know,' he answered in a pacifying tone.

Jack let out a heavy breath of exasperation and frustration which said much more than words. This bloody old man could manipulate any situation. Grasping him was like grasping an eel. Jack looked at him. It was a look of annoyance but also one of resignation. He didn't want any tea, just to know why there wasn't any in the house. He looked at the old man. It was only a week or two since he had been sacked. He'd lost weight; he spent too much time around the house. There was a defeated look on

331

his face. Work and beer had been his life. They'd been taken away from him, and nothing had come to replace them. Jack felt some sympathy, even pity, for him. There was nothing he could do. He certainly wouldn't give him any beer money. In two years he would probably be dead. Had he thrown in the towel already? It looked like it.

The unexpected noise had woken Molly who came into the kitchen with the baby. It was obvious she had been roused from a deep sleep. 'What you shouting about, Jack?'

'No tea. Why are we out of it?'

'Just out of it, Jack.'

'Why, woman? Have you no money? Is it all spent?'

The old man moved back, reluctant to get involved in the quarrel. Jack grasped his wife by the arm. His eyes flashed but only for a moment, 'Woman, why are we out of tea?'

She cried out in pain and protest, 'Take yer hands off me, man Take yer hands off me and me with the baby.' She cried out again, tears in her eyes. He released his grasp of her but the imprint of his hand could be seen on her arm. Putting his face in his hands, he breathed a sigh of remorse.

'I didn't mean it, Molly. I didn't. Really.'

The old man shrank further into the corner. He would have left the room but there was no door nearby to use. Jack wanted to reassure Molly. He put his arm around her to show remorse. All he could say was, 'I'm sorry girl. I'll never do it again. Never. Honest.' He stood in front of her, feeling awkward. He put his hands in his pockets and felt the guineas. Taking them out, he said to her, 'Sorry, girl. Have these.' He gave her all five.

She took them but didn't look at what they were, just held young Jack close to her. She lifted him up and kissed him. He seemed to wake up. She kissed him again. Jack looked at the scene, feeling remorse going right through him. She put the baby down on the table to rearrange his clothes. At the same time she put the coins on the table. She was surprised and a little alarmed by the amount. 'Jack, five guineas. Where'd you get them?'

'Don't worry where they came from, girl.'

'Jack, tell me where you got it from?'

'Don't worry, it's honest. Least, I think it is.'

'Haven't been thieving, have you?'

He smiled to himself, thinking it was a real joke. Then he laughed a bit more, saying, 'Know me better than that. You're a one, you are. Worry for the family, you do. Anyway, what about some breakfast now?'

'Let me sort Jack out, and then you'll have a good one with this money. Just wait a bit.'

He sat back in the chair, more settled than he had been since he got in last night. Again he thought of that woman. He wanted to ask someone but didn't wish to make his interest public. There were no secrets in this town.

Nearly an hour later, he had finished a breakfast fit for a king. Bacon, egg, bread and tea. Yes, tea; nearly two pints of it. He smiled with satisfaction. Then reality returned. How many punches would he trade for that breakfast? The clouds gathered. What was in store for him?

Getting up, and wiping his mouth with his sleeve, he stretched his arms. 'That was good, Molly. I'm off now, girl.'

'Where to, Jack?'

'Get some fresh air. Look for work.'

'Back to get some more of that money?'

'Never mind, girl. We'll be alright.'

'Go on, then.'

He took his cape, put it over his shoulders and walked directly to Kilvey Hill, but avoiding Charlie's tavern. It was good to get up there. The day was warmer. A warm breeze from the south-west blew the cape into the back of his legs. It felt good to be alive. How he wished he was with the drovers again. This walk was a boy's walk, not real exercise. He couldn't walk up and down here all day. He went through the gate and, after closing it, leaned against the upright post to look over the harbour. It was crowded as always with every type of ship, as beautiful in its way as the country. He remembered his journey to the Crimea, sailing from a harbour such as this, recalling the cramped conditions, the variety of people and the chaos of unloading. He had loved the horses, every one of them different, like people. He'd met a few like Percy's horse. Perhaps Letworthy was a bit like him. He'd like to have got those shoes on; he felt it was a job unfinished.

He lay down on his cape, letting the sun shine on him. He hadn't slept all night and felt he could fall asleep at any time. He dozed off and then awakened several times. He lost track of the time but a glance at the sun told him it had not been long; it was not even midday yet. Suddenly he heard the slow but regular footfall of a horse. His heart missed a beat which fully awakened him. Looking in the direction the sound was coming from, he saw the woman on the horse. Without thinking, he got up and resumed leaning against the post. His heart began to pound. What would he do? She was fifty yards away. The slow walk of the horse did not alter. Yes, it was her alright, on the same horse and in the same clothes. His heart continued to beat rapidly. He felt a pain in his stomach; a pang of uncertainty. On she came, nearer and nearer, at the same steady pace. He knew she would have to get through the gate.

Lucy saw Jack even before he saw her. Her heart raced, she could hardly get her breath and almost stopped the horse to regain it. Now shaking, she could hardly control herself. What was she to do? She would never retreat. She must go on whatever happened. Somehow she controlled herself outwardly. Inwardly, she was jelly. Could she look this man in the face? Nearer and nearer to him, the horse plodded on. With the crop in her right hand and gripping the reins with both, she held them tighter than she had ever held anything.

Now she was within twenty yards of the gate and had to look him in the face. She felt a momentary confidence but couldn't maintain it and had to look away. His look was unflinching but had an element of confident humour in it too. It was the look of someone who had already won. Jack stood by the post, not moving an inch. On she came, one step after another. Covering the last few paces, she stopped at the gate. He didn't

334

hinder her progress but neither did he assist her. He looked at her, amused. What's your next move, Lady, he thought. Hardly had the thought entered his mind, than he heard the command.

Holding the riding crop in her right hand, she ordered, 'Open the gate.' She raised her riding crop for emphasis.

For one fleeting moment he was affected by the tone of her voice; the sound of authority; the bark of command. Here was a woman used to having her own way. He knew a great deal about men who gave orders in this manner, but had no experience of it from a woman. After a moment's hesitation, he regained his confidence.

'I said, open the gate, man.' She brought the riding crop down on the side of Jack's head.

'Don't do that again, woman.' He spoke slowly but was boiling inside. The look he gave her was malevolent, angry but above all determined.

Somehow she knew she was losing but on she went. 'I said, open the gate. Do you hear me?'

Again she aimed the riding crop towards the side of his head. He grabbed it in a grip of iron. She wouldn't let go. He pulled the weapon towards himself. Still she wouldn't let go. It was a battle of wills. She had never known what it was like to give way. Gradually she was pulled off the horse, her feet came out of the stirrups then, with a sudden thud, she was on the ground. Without knowing it, they had both let go of the riding crop. He grasped her by the arm; a grip which paralysed her from head to toe. Yet the look in his eyes was not entirely destructive. She looked at him, her mouth open, her eyes taking everything in.

'You take a crop to me. You little devil.' He brushed his hand to the left side of his face then looked at the palm on which there was blood. 'You little devil,' he repeated, smiling the smile of one who holds the trump card. He would take his time.

'You came up here to see me, didn't you?'

'You're....'

He didn't allow her to reply. 'Didn't you?' he repeated more urgently.

'I came up here to ride,' she spluttered, almost incoherently. She tried to escape but knew it was hopeless. His grip on her was one of iron.

Jack guessed her background was rich and powerful. It made him want to linger over his moment of power. He was also excited by her magnetic attraction for him and the spell he had cast on her.

'I know what you want.' With his free right hand and in no longer than it took to take a breath, the buttons on her coat and blouse were torn open. She held her breath, wanting to shout but unable to. With a second tear, her skirt came off. The horse stood nearby, remaining unmoved by the happenings around him. In an even briefer time, Jack loosened his trousers and gripped her by the waist with both hands; a grip from which there was no escape. Utterly powerless, she had to leave herself in the hands of Jack Lloyd. Slowly he moved, consumed by passion yet gripped by iron self-control. He would control every aspect of this encounter. His movements were more urgent now; he had never felt more powerful in his life.

He looked into her eyes. She no longer seemed alarmed, but had a faraway look; she was looking towards him but not at him. Had she looked into his eyes, she would have seen a softening, and the beginning of a smile. Almost like a bolt from the blue, her arms were around him, clinging to him as if hanging on to life itself. This seemed to make him all the more controlled as he raced with the speed of a thoroughbred to the finishing post. He seemed inexhaustible.

As he maintained this murderous pace with the self-administered spurs and crop whipping him to even more speed, he heard the roll of thunder nearby, very slight at first then louder and louder. There was lightning but only felt and seen by the lady. On and on he galloped, not slackening his speed. Then she felt an explosion and shouted out. She no longer had any control over herself. Again she roared, louder and louder. Gradually she subsided as did Jack who still exercised an iron control over himself. They remained as they were. Not knowing whether she

336

was in the real world, she looked around to confirm she was there, her arms no longer round him.

He looked her in the eye, smiled a broad smile, and thrust into her, saying 'That better girl?'

Without warning, she put her arms round his neck and clung to him, crying, 'I've never been so happy. Never. Ever.' She clung to him for several minutes, eventually releasing herself.

Amused, fascinated and mesmerised by her, he smiled in a warm intimate manner. 'Want some more?'

'Not now.' They released their hold on one another and put their clothes on. The horse continued to look on, unconcerned.

Sitting down facing one another, she asked, 'What's your name?'

'Jack Lloyd. Who are you, owner of this good horse?'

'Lucy.'

'Lucy who?'

'Lucy Lambert.'

'Sir Lionel's daughter?'

'Yes.'

'Live at the big house?'

'Yes.'

He held his face in his hands and laughed to himself. What's going to be the end of this, he thought to himself.

'What do you do?' she asked him.

'Nothing at the moment.'

'Not working?'

'No.'

'You don't look like an idler.'

'I'm not. Got sacked a week back.'

'Where?'

'The big site your father runs. Never mind about that.'

'How often do you come up here?'

'Only the second time. Wouldn't have come today except I thought I might meet you. I got lucky didn't I?'

'You're an old devil, you are.'

'Not so much of the old, now.' They looked one another in

337

the face and smiled with a mutual understanding.

He moved nearer and put his arm around her waist, feeling an intimacy he had never felt before, not even with Rosie. Rosie had been a sort of mother to him. He'd never quarrelled with her. She was always the same. He was always welcome. This one was different; she was going to be trouble. But I'm Jack and I can handle her, he thought, enjoy the challenge like Percy's horse. He'd never get bored with Lucy.

'Coming up here tomorrow, Lucy?'

'Only if you are.'

'I'll be here then, Lucy. Start from home after breakfast. I'm going to be off now.' He pulled her closer, kissed her and then got up. 'Tomorrow.'

She nodded, 'Tomorrow. Don't be late.' She drew him to her and kissed him again. She knew she had been awakened. Pushed over the Rubicon. Life could never be the same again. Jack knew it too.

They parted at the gate; she went on ahead. One would have expected elation but they both felt that there was an ominous side to this encounter. Each knew what the other was feeling. Their minds thought of little else as they returned home.

Chapter 33

Lucy reflected on the events of the day, managing to arrive home with her damaged clothes unnoticed. She handed the horse to the groom and ran upstairs with indecent haste. Ripping her clothes off as fast as she could, she put similar ones on from an overloaded wardrobe. Her breathing eased. Lying on the bed with her legs and arms apart, she felt as if she was welcoming her new found life. She felt she was floating on air. So this is what love is like. If it is then I want more of it, she decided. It was not like the thrill of giving orders which were obeyed, though she did enjoy that. She was taking orders for the first time in her life and was thrilled by it. Jack certainly knew how to give orders. But who was he? How did he earn his money? Why was he idling up on Kilvey Hill in the middle of the day? She was determined to find that out and soon. Drifting off into a dream state, she was awakened by the parlour maid speaking, 'You alright, Miss Lucy?'

'Yes Jane, yes' she replied, slightly disconcerted by the question 'I'm alright.' She knew that domestic servants knew everything that was going on in a house. They missed nothing, absolutely nothing. What would she do about the torn clothes?

'Anything I can do, Miss Lucy?'

'No Jane, nothing. Nothing at all.' She became almost flustered but somehow contained it. Had Jane seen her coming in? Jane was a mainstay in the home, never a gossip but she missed nothing. She'd have to do something about those clothes, but what? She wanted to change the conversation.

'Is Sir Lionel in, Jane?'

'Yes, Miss Lucy. He's with Mr Jackson in the office.'

'You can leave, Jane.' The maid left but not without giving the room a further brief but all-encompassing glance, which Lucy could not fail to notice.

339

Getting up, she grabbed the clothes in a bundle from under the bed. Standing on a chair, she put them on top of the wardrobe, folding them roughly and pushing them down behind the surround at the top. They would not be seen from the floor, not even by the tallest person in the household. Now she must see Jackson. Stepping down the stairs at a calculated, measured pace she walked through the front door and down the drive, stopping at the first place where she could not be observed from the house.

She didn't have to wait long till she heard the sound of shod horses' hooves and iron-clad wheels grinding on the gravel. Jackson came towards her. She raised one finger for him to stop. 'Jackson. I want to speak to you for a moment.'

'Yes Miss Lucy.' He raised his bowler hat in a respectful manner. It amused her that she'd never get this treatment from Jack Lloyd.

'A word in your ear, Jackson.'

'Yes, Miss Lucy.'

'In the strictest confidence.'

'Of course, Miss Lucy.' He gave her a deferential bow.

'The very strictest confidence, Jackson. Not even to anyone in the Hall.'

'No Miss Lucy, not even to anyone in the Hall.'

'What do you know about Jack Lloyd?'

'I know him. What do you want to know about him?'

'Everything.' Her cheeks took on a cherry red glow and her manner an eagerness which Jackson noticed.

Jackson felt he had to be cautious. 'What do you mean, everything?'

'Did he work for you?'

'For your father. He was sacked a few days ago.'

'Why?'

'He hit the ganger in front of your father.'

'In front of father? Why did he hit him?'

'It was about giving orders and taking them. That's all.' Jackson didn't want to say any more but Lucy would not allow him to go.

'What sort of a man is he?'

'A good blacksmith and a rough character. Very rough indeed.'

'Has he a family?'

'Married into an Irish family. May have a child or two, I don't know. Miss Lucy, I don't think I should be answering any more of these questions. Certainly not on a confidential basis. You're putting me in a very difficult position.'

'One more question, Jackson. Just one.'

'Go on, then.' He grasped the reins, preparing to drive the horse on.

'What's he doing for work now?'

'I don't know, but you can take it from me that he'll get by. No doubt about that. Now Miss Lucy, I must go.' He shook the reins for the horses to move on and he raised his hat in a perfunctory manner.

She knew a little more about Jack but it was not enough. She returned to her bedroom and lay back down, spread-eagled on the bed and looking up at the ceiling at nothing in particular. Consumed with emotion to the point of obsession, she could not get him out of her mind. "A blacksmith and a rough character" Yes, he was certainly that. She could feel his callused hands, as tough as leather, in hers. No, much tougher than leather. Again she felt those hands on her waist. She removed enough clothes to see where he had handled her. She was heavily bruised on either side. Looking at the marks, she was thrilled to view the legacy of that morning's encounter. She carefully locked the door before looking at herself all over. Looking at herself admiringly in the mirror, she stroked her hips and smiled self-indulgently. You're a fine looking girl, she told herself; no, you're a fine looking woman and I'm not the only one who thinks so. Putting her clothes back on, she unlocked the door and sat on the chair. It was not where she had last placed it. Hardly had she realised this, than there was a knock on the door. 'Yes,' she responded.

Jane walked in with the torn clothes on her arm. 'Miss Lucy,

341

I found these on top of the wardrobe.'

Lucy flushed but composed herself as far as she was able.
Jane noticed.

'What shall I do with them Miss Lucy'. She looked
directly into her eyes.

'I came off the horse yesterday, Jane. They'll have to be
destroyed'. She flushed even more intensely.

'They could be mended, Miss Lucy.' Her look was
piercing. She knew that Lucy was lying, that was obvious. 'Such
a pity to throw away such good clothes, Miss Lucy, but if you
say so, I'll take them downstairs.'

'No, leave them here, Jane. I'll get rid of them.' She
moved towards her and took the clothes, throwing them on top of
the wardrobe.

'Hope you weren't hurt in the fall, Miss Lucy. That's a
good horse usually, Miss.' Jane had the advantage and couldn't
help driving the point home. 'You're bound to be a bit bruised,
Miss Lucy. Will you go to the doctor's?'

'No, I shall be alright Jane. Now leave me.' She ushered
her towards the door which she closed. Breathing a sigh of relief,
she threw herself back onto the bed. So Jane knows, she thought,
but she'll keep it to herself unless her knowledge proves
dangerous to her. It was impossible to keep any secrets from
domestic servants.

Next morning, soon after breakfast and having ordered the
groom to make the horse ready, she was on her way up Kilvey
Hill. Jack was waiting for her at the gate where they had met on
the previous day. Dismounting, she threw herself into his arms
but he did not respond in like measure. He held her gently at
arm's length, smiling a warm, inviting smile. 'Good to see you,
Lucy Lambert.'

'And you, Jack Lloyd.' She thrust towards him again, then
hugged and kissed him which he responded to in similar
measure. He'd never known this sort of passionate enthusiasm
before. Were these sort of women different? She certainly smelt
differently. Perfume, I suppose. They looked, smiled and hugged

but Jack felt awkward in this new world. He liked it but needed time to get used to it.

'Let's go and sit down, Lucy.' They walked towards some gorse bushes. He took off his cloak and laid it on the ground.

'The red carpet treatment'.

'No, the grey'.

They repeated what had occurred yesterday though with less vigour. Lying together afterwards, he looked at her waist. 'Girl, you're bruised. That wasn't me, was it?'

'Entirely your work, Jack.'

'It isn't, is it?'

'You've got to plead guilty to that. Look what you've done to me, you masterful brute.'

'I think you had a hand in it, Lucy Lambert.' They both laughed.

She looked at him mischievously. He laughed back at her and blushed a little. They wrestled in a gentle, playful manner like puppies in a litter; not the violent, dynamic clash of their first encounter but more intimate, more humorous, more established. It was as though they had known one another for years. Each caught the other's thoughts, laughing intimately. So it went on, for how long, neither knew.

The wind from the south west became a little cooler. They dressed. Neither Lucy nor Jack had ever felt like this before. They lay back and talked. Lucy knew there were vast aspects of her lover's life which she did not know. Perhaps she didn't want to know but she had to ask. All she knew was what she had learned from Jackson. A rough character who had been sacked for violence which occurred in front of her father. He was a rough character, alright. Don't I know it? What was he doing for money? No job. A family to keep. These people lived from hand to mouth. How would he survive? She was captivated by him yet knew there was a social gulf which could never be bridged. For all that, she'd hang on to him. She'd hang on to him whatever the cost. He'd never get away.

'Jack, what are you doing for money?'

'I'm getting by.'

'Doing what?'

'Got something on the go. A one-off.'

'Doing what, Jack?'

'Nothing that would interest you.' He became slightly irritated by her persistence.

'Everything about you interests me. What is it?'

'Don't go on, Lucy.'

'What is it, Jack. You're hiding something from me. What is it?'

He was unable to resist her persistence. 'Just a bit of a punch-up, that's all.'

'What do you mean, a punch up, Jack?'

'Sort of boxing, that's all.'

'For money, Jack?'

'Yes. Wouldn't do it for free, would I?'

'How much, Jack?'

'Ten guineas, win or lose.'

'But you might get hurt, Jack.' Her brow furrowed in anxiety.

'Don't think so. Never happened yet. Got to have the money.'

'You have to do that to get money and with that damaged arm?'

'That won't hold me up. Never has done yet.'

'Jack, you could get hurt. You know that.'

'Could get hurt drinking the water here, or you riding back on that horse.'

'I could give you money.'

'I don't want your money, Lucy. I'm twenty six. I've been working twenty years one way and another. I've never taken a penny from a woman and I'm not going to start now.'

'But Jack....'

His voice became louder and his manner visibly annoyed. 'Listen, you've heard me, shut up! No more or we'll quarrel. Understand?'

344

She was silenced, finding it difficult to hold back tears at his aggression. Was this their first quarrel? The silence between them could only be cut with a sharp knife. It lasted for some minutes, but eventually they looked at one another. A slight smile appeared on her face, which broke the ice. He then responded with a broader one. They hugged again.

'What you thinking about, Jack?'

'How things will turn out in the next day or two.'

'What things?'

'Just things.'

'Money for the family, Jack?'

'That's part of it.'

'What about this boxing Jack, and your damaged arm. How did it happen?'

'In the Crimea.'

'That's bad, Jack.' She took hold of his arm and looked at it, stroking the scar with her other hand. 'How did it happen?'

'Don't go on, woman. Many didn't come back. They bought it. Some lost arms and legs. I was lucky. This is nothing.'

'But Jack......'

'I said, don't go on about it woman. Shut up, woman. Shut up'. His manner was aggressive, his face became flushed and his eyes flashed. She knew better than to pursue the conversation.

He became irritated again and lapsed into a brooding silence. He lay down with his back on the cape looking at the sky and becoming aware of the drop in temperature which sent a brief shiver through him. Where am I going from here, he asked himself. I've got a wife, a child, a family, no work and a fight in two days which will lead me nowhere. Now I've got Lucy. What the bloody hell am I doing up here on this mountain with this woman? Why the hell am I not in work shoeing horses? There isn't a better farrier in Swansea. I know that and everyone who works with horses in Swansea knows that.

He wanted to get up, discard this woman, walk back into town and look for work. There must be work somewhere. He didn't get up but lay there thinking, with the occasional drift of

345

her perfume a reminder that she was beside him. For an hour or two it was a refuge but sooner rather than later he would have to face the world. This lazing on the hilltop was sort of cowardly. I, Jack Lloyd, have never retreated from the world for the simple reason I have never been afraid of it. Marie Jenkins, the Russian Army or Ben Letworthy; I faced them all as best I could. If I could face Marie Jenkins and get by, I can face anything. For perhaps half an hour he lay reflecting on his life during which time Lucy remained silent.

Mentally shaking himself, he raised himself on his elbow feeling as if he had come out of a long sleep. 'Lucy, I'm getting up.'

'Jack, you've been asleep.'

'Have I?'

'Yes'.

The horse, some thirty yards away, was becoming unsettled as he kept the two improbable lovers under observation.

'Lucy, your horse is getting anxious about you. Two men in your life.' He laughed heartily to himself. They both laughed and then kissed.

'What's his name?'

'Lancer.'

'Good name. He's a fine horse. Haven't seen one as good as him since I've been in Swansea. He's a general's horse.' Jack got up to look at the horse, leaving Lucy sitting up on his cloak. Walking towards him, he took hold of the reins lightly, patted his flanks then stood back and looked at him, saying quietly, 'You're a fine horse Lancer, my boy. Haven't seen one like you for many a day.' Then out loud to Lucy, he said, 'How old is he, five?'

'Nearly right Jack, almost six.' She watched him handling the horse, admiring his familiarity and knowledge. There was nothing he didn't know about horses. Even the wicked and troublesome would become manageable in his hands. She could see it with every move he made. Understated and confident, he didn't have to plead his case.

He continued admiring the horse for a long time. Admiration

346

for her man now drifted into mild jealousy but still she would not speak to him. He was mesmerised by Lancer. He hadn't seen one like him since the Crimea and there weren't many as good as him there. Stroking him now and then, he almost felt love for this horse. Her jealousy now became more acute. She rose and silently walked towards them, remaining only a few feet from them for quite some time before Jack became aware of her presence. He smiled at her. She did not respond. 'You're in love with that horse,' she remarked with some force.

'It's a fine horse. Won't see better than him in Swansea.' He became almost dewy eyed as he patted the horse admiringly yet again. Picking up her disapproval, he would not respond.

'You're ignoring me,' she challenged.

Bloody stupid woman, he thought, continuing to admire the animal. He became annoyed at her; would he have to put up with such irrational remarks? Putting herself on a level with this horse. They are different, he thought, not in competition for his affection. Perhaps these bloody upper class women were all like that. He became acutely annoyed but kept it to himself. These feelings quickly evaporated to be replaced by ones of sympathy, but hardly understanding. He turned from the horse, put his arm round her shoulder, pulled her to him and kissed her on the cheek. 'What's wrong, girl? Jealous of this horse? Pull yourself together girl.'

She grabbed him round the neck, putting her face into his chest. She became aware for the first time of the smell of his chest; musky and sweaty. A slight sob escaped from her and, unseen by her lover, tears ran down her cheeks. She pulled him down to the ground again. They lay in one another's arms for several minutes.

He wanted to release himself and made to do so. 'You don't have to go yet, Jack.' She hung on to him more tightly. He released his hold on her, finding her clinging irksome.

'We got to go, girl.'

'Why Jack. We've got nothing to do, have we?'

Suppose we haven't, he thought to himself, but I want to go. It was now becoming tedious. His mind drifted back towards Rosie. She was so different, so busy, so understanding. None of this clinging. He wanted to be out and quickly.

'Listen, Lucy. I've got plenty to do. Can't wait.' He didn't know what he had to do. He just wanted to go.

'I'm going,' he said, removing himself from her grasp and getting up. All the while Lancer looked at them both, unaware of the emotional furnace beneath him. She got up and straightened her clothes, protesting at her lover by looks rather than words.

'No good looking at me like that. I'm going.' She continued to look at him with a mixture of resentment and disappointment. While he retrieved his cloak, she untied the horse, waiting for his return.

She evaded his attempt to kiss her, saying, 'When will I see you again?'
Looking at her, he again realised how attractive she was. 'Tomorrow, then.'

'You sure,' she replied eagerly, wanting to see him but trying to put him in the position of being more ardent. She was not disappointed.

'Course I'm sure. Tomorrow.'

'I don't want to press you if you don't want to come.'

'Course I'll come tomorrow.'

'Don't come if you're getting fed up with me.'

'Course I'm not getting fed up with you. Same time, same place then.'

'Only if you want to.' For the first time she was putting him on the defensive. He didn't like it one little bit. 'Do you want to come or don't you?' It was brinkmanship and they both knew it.

'Tomorrow. Same time, same place,' were his final words.

'Very well'.

She mounted the horse and rode off. He followed on foot. They parted without any further show of affection.

They had only been together twice but, with the exception of Sir Lionel and his wife and the O'Haras, most who knew them

348

were aware that there was a relationship between them.

Jack walked down the hill, across the river and towards his home. He was accosted by Charlie on the way. 'Sunday then, Jack Lloyd?' They exchanged a few words. A humorous, suggestive look appeared in Charlie's eye. 'Been up Kilvey Hill, Jack?' He nodded. 'Training for the match then?' His look became even more inquiring and suggestive. Jack smiled but did not reply. So it was all out. Nothing he could do about it. Inevitable.

Chapter 34

It was early on the Saturday morning. Molly had just heard the news in the street. She ran into the house looking alarmed, wiping her hands on her apron as she did so. She shouted out, 'Jack, what's this about you in a fight at Charlie's tomorrow. Is this true, Jack. Tell me.'

He didn't want to reply, having hoped that the encounter would be over before his family knew. Lost for an answer, he said nothing for a moment or two.

'Jack, is this true? Tell me,' she persisted. 'What's happening Jack? I've got to know.'

'Molly, it's nothing. I'll just be gone an hour or two and then I'll be back.'

'You could be hurt and where would we all be, Jack?'

'I shan't be hurt, girl. Don't worry about me. I can look after myself.'

'I don't like it. You know that.'

He stepped towards her, put his arm around her waist and smiled reassuringly. 'Don't worry Molly, I'll be alright. Honest.'

'Jack, I never know where I am with you. You know that. Why don't you tell me, Jack?'

'Don't want to worry you, that's all, Molly.' With his arm still round her, he squeezed her waist. 'I'll be alright, girl. Nothing's going to happen to me.'

She breathed a heavy sigh, not of relief but of resignation. 'Well Jack, I know I can't alter you. You'll have to get on with it and the sooner the better. Don't do anything stupid. Remember there's me and young Jack here.'

'Don't worry Molly. Don't worry.'

The whole family knew by now. Old man O'Hara felt some reflected glory at having a bare knuckle fighter in the house, distantly smiling at his son-in-law but remaining silent. He'd now been almost entirely silent since being sacked. His voice, when he did speak, was much quieter and his appearance now aged, especially as he had lost a good deal of weight.

The women in the family now viewed Jack with some awe, unconsciously sitting apart from him or as far apart as the cramped house allowed. The noise, always apparent in the home was now reduced to little more than a whisper. Jack noticed it but wished it had occurred for other reasons. As usual he got out of the house as soon as possible, this time walking to see Charlie.

Along Frog Street he walked. Even at this hour there were men and women on the street. They acknowledged him with a quiet deference but made no further efforts at conversation. Walking parallel to the coast but a good way from it he crossed the Tawe bridge and made his way to Charlie's tavern.

Receiving no answer at the front door, he went round to the back, found it open and saw a woman who he presumed was Charlie's wife in the scullery washing up. Thin and harassed looking, she directed him into the kitchen but continued working.

'Where's Charlie?'

Continuing to wash up, she replied in a flat voice, 'Still in bed.'

'When does he get up?'

'Not yet. In an hour or two I suppose.'

'Tell him I'm here.'

'Who are you?'

'Jack Lloyd.'

'I've heard of you. You're against the Merthyr man on Sunday.'

'Tell him I'm here, will you?'

'He don't like being called as early as this and he'd had a few last night.'

'It's after seven. He can't grumble at that, can he?'

'Leave it a while and I'll go up then. Want some tea?'

'I'll have the tea but go up and get him down then, won't you?'

She didn't reply but soon gave him the tea. He drank it slowly, looking around the rooms. The place was as dirty as his

351

own home, probably more so. The stone walls were dripping in grease. Everything about the two rooms was depressing. They faced north and looked out upon a high wall surrounding the large yard at the back in which there were a number of barrels stacked in an orderly manner. It was the only expression of tidiness he had seen so far.

Finishing his tea, he asked, 'Can you go for Charlie now?'

'He won't like it you know. Leave it another half an hour. Have a beer.' She moved to get a glass.

'No, not for me.' raising both hands in refusal. 'No, honest. I don't drink.'

'Sure you won't?'

'No, I really don't drink.'

'Not many like you.'

'No, not many.'

'Your man from Merthyr likes a few.'

'Does he?'

'More than a few.'

'Go up and get Charlie down. I'm not waiting here any longer.'

Feeling she was between the hammer and the anvil, she took the line of least resistance. Rousing Charlie out of a hangover seemed a preferable option to dealing with this impatient prize-fighter. Reluctantly she made her way up the creaking stairs and opened the door to the bedroom. Even to her insensitive nose the initial smell was a shock. The window was closed, the heavy curtains drawn and the occupant burrowed deep under a feather quilt, snoring. The room was pervaded by the smell of stale alcohol, made all the more unbearable by the overpowering warmth in the room.

Shaking him then stepping away, she said, 'Charlie, Charlie, someone for you.' Twice she repeated this, drawing back the curtains as she waited for any response. He turned towards her, just conscious, with his eyes narrowed as the light from the now clear window shone on his face.

'What is it?'

'Someone to see you, Charlie.'

'What time is it?'

'After seven.'

'Who is it?'

'Jack Lloyd, he calls himself. You know, he's against the man from Merthyr'.

'I know. What's he here at this hour for? I got to bed late.'

'Are you coming down, Charlie?'

'Suppose I'll have to.'

'How long then?'

'Give me ten minutes.'

'Sure you're not going off again?'

'No, I'll be up in ten minutes.' He raised himself up on his elbow and looked around the room, enduring his headache as he did so. Suppose I'll have to get up, he thought. He looked an awful mess. His hair, nearly white and thin, was pointing in all directions. Worst of all was his face; normally a jocular red, it was now a blotchy scarlet which even ventured above his eyebrows. His eyes were bloodshot and having difficulty focusing on his surroundings. He was still in his shirt, the collar only having been detached. He had gone to bed with his trousers still on. Gradually getting out of bed, he had to endure rapier-like thrusts of pain in his head with every movement he made. He slowly put his clothes on and wondered how he could wash and perhaps shave to make himself presentable to Jack Lloyd. He had to go through the kitchen to wash. Would he just let Jack see him as he was and damn the image he had built up of Sporty Charlie?

He dressed in the clothes that had fallen by the bed, combed his hair and made his way down the stairs and into the kitchen. Jack looked at his promoter first in shock then in amusement, which he tried to conceal. A brief silence followed as Charlie sat down, wiping his eyes as he did so.

'What you want at this time, boy?'

It mildly annoyed him to be called boy but he did not show it. 'What time is it tomorrow, Charlie?'

'Three.'

353

'What time do you want me here?'

'Two.'

'Who's the man from Merthyr?'

'Billy, he is.'

'How old?'

'Older than you. Quite a bit older. You'll finish him easy. You've got to make it last. Understand?' Jack didn't reply; he didn't know what to say. How would he fake a fight? Everyone would know. 'Listen, if it doesn't last a good few minutes you won't get the other half of the money. Understand?'

Jack could hardly believe what he had just heard. 'Say that again.'

'You heard.'

'Listen, Charlie boy, ten hours or ten seconds, win or lose, if I don't get the other half your mother won't know you when I've finished with you, boy.' He shook a fist at him.

Charlie was shocked by this response. Never had he faced such a determined character. He thought that he owned his fighters, at least during the period when the contests took place. They were his men, did what he said and fought as he directed. Strong in the arm and weak in the head, they were. Knowing that he couldn't continue with his hectoring, he took a milder approach.

'No need to be like that, Lloyd. I was only joking,' he said unconvincingly.   'That's it then. I'll go. See you tomorrow at two.'

'Remember, make it last.' Charlie couldn't help driving his point home but did so in a far from convincing manner.

Jack didn't reply, left by the back door and went home. It was now a matter of waiting. He became irritable, almost jumpy. 'Molly, some breakfast,' he demanded. She was dressing young Jack and didn't immediately reply. Raising his voice, he said again, 'Molly, do you hear me? Some breakfast.'

'Wait Jack, I'm dressing the baby.' She resented being spoken to in this manner.

He waited but became more anxious inside. Thinking about

the confrontation, he speculated as to the outcome. Was his opponent going to be a walkover as Charlie had stated. He couldn't be believed. Not a word that came out of his mouth could be relied upon. What was Billy from Merthyr like? The woman he assumed was Charlie's wife had said he was a drinker. It was the uncertainty that made him restless. Getting up, he went to the kitchen. 'Molly, I want some breakfast.' Hardly had he said it than he saw that she was washing Jack and he regretted his impatience.

'Wait a minute and I'll see to you,' she said without looking up.

'I can't wait Molly, I'm off.' She tried to urge him to have some patience but without success. He walked out of the house without another word and set off towards Kilvey Hill. His mind was in turmoil with thoughts of every description flying in and out, without respite: the fight on Sunday; Rosie and their son Jack; Molly and baby Jack. He considered Lucy as well, he didn't doubt she'd be pregnant before long. At the moment she was the least of his worries. He walked on past the gate where they had encountered each other. Grinning to himself briefly, he walked on. By now it was noon and he had seen no one. Why was he irritated with Molly, he wondered. He came to the conclusion that he was anxious for Sunday at four o'clock to arrive and to have the remaining half of the money in his pocket. He wouldn't do this again, not ever. He'd get it behind him and then find real work. This hadn't happened to him before. He'd never been a day out of work apart from when he was discharged from the Crimea. It began to fill him with some alarm, even overtaking thoughts of tomorrow's battle. They were surely missing him at the forge, but he'd never be taken back on there. He'd never get those wages again in Swansea

Continuing to walk until the incline became steeper, he returned even more slowly. Thinking about tomorrow, he became resigned to whatever would happen. You couldn't plan the future but only grab opportunities when you saw them. It was all luck. His pace quickened till he came to the high point overlooking the city. He sat down and laughed; a quiet cynical laugh. It was all chance. Why try and do anything? Why not sit back and let it all happen. Lady luck was sometimes on your side and sometimes she wasn't.

He hadn't had much luck with Marie Jenkins. The cane on the back of his knuckles every hour of every day, it seemed to him. 'How did I get out of that dark tunnel?' he asked himself. 'I dodged school as much as I could to work for money to keep the family. I said "Yes miss" to Marie Jenkins when what I meant was no, no, no. I had a murderous determination not to be ground down when my enemy had all the power.' He now knew that his determination made him refuse to learn to read. He'd got the better of her. A faint smile crossed his face. Life's like that. If he could best Marie Jenkins, he could best anybody. How long he had sat there thinking, he didn't know. Getting up, he slowly made his way home avoiding Charlie's tavern.

Arriving home, he felt more settled and now found himself ravenously hungry. He waited for more than half an hour for Molly to appear.

Arriving with Jack in a shawl and loaded with shopping, she was quite breathless. 'How long you been back, Jack?'

'Half an hour.'

'Where you been?'

'For a walk.'

'Where?'

'Kilvey Hill.'

'You're always going up there, Jack. Why?'

'Fresh air, girl. Remember, I'm a country boy, always have been and always will be, you know that.'

'Suppose you are.'

'Got some bacon in there?'

'And potatoes and leeks.'

'Sounds good. How long?'

'An hour if someone'll hold Jack.'

'Give him to me.'

She did so. He was asleep and remained so for half an hour.

356

Getting the fire alight, she prepared the meal. First the bacon (salted, fat and home cured) followed by the potatoes then leeks cooked in the bacon juice.

'Fit for a king Molly.'

By now she was juggling with the baby who had woken up, the fire and serving the meal. 'Don't know whether you'll be a king this time tomorrow. I hope so.'

'So do I girl, so do I,' he replied, eating what was before him with gusto. He hadn't realised how hungry he was.

Sitting down after the meal, an unusual silence came over the family which remained all evening. Occasionally old man O'Hara chipped in with remarks about the following day which received hardly a reply, only disapproving looks from the rest of the family which rapidly silenced him. It would have been easier for them to have talked but somehow Jack quietly dominated the atmosphere and silence prevailed. A heavy burden of possible tragedy hung over all, not least over Jack. He slumped lower in the only armchair as his brow became more furrowed. He was reassured by the fact that it would be over the next day but what would be the outcome?

Jack went up to bed even earlier than usual, going up alone, lying down but not sleeping. Molly joined him an hour or two later.

'You awake, Jack?'

'Yes.'

'You going to be alright tomorrow?'

'Of course.'

'You going to be able to sleep?'

'I'll get off soon enough.'

'I'm worried, Jack.'

'Don't worry girl, I'll be alright.'

She put her hand on his arm, the damaged one. He put it round her neck, pulling her to him and kissing her lightly. 'Don't worry Molly, I'll be alright.' She didn't reply again but drifted off into sleep. He remained awake till the early hours of the morning, eventually drifting off into a heavy sleep from which he was awakened soon after nine o'clock.

Getting up, he washed in the backyard observed by the family then returned to the kitchen.

'Breakfast. What you want Jack?

'Usual, bread and cheese. Not much.' He sat at the table, again deep in thought, eating what was in front of him without being aware of it or the presence of the family looking at him.

'I'm off,' he indicated, moving towards the door.

'You had enough?'

'Won't eat any more till it's over.'

Walking towards the coast to get some fresh air, he would have liked to have gone up the hill but would have had to pass Charlie's Tavern. This was something he wished to avoid, disliking his jocular duplicity. He'd seen plenty like him selling quack medicines at the fair in the Preselis, always there when the money was being taken but never there in the action. Perhaps war was a bit like that.

Walking along the beach, he could see Mumbles. The fresh sea air put new life into him. It was like being on the farm again. Walking quicker, the thoughts of the event to come drifted in and out of his mind. Getting nearer to the tavern, he could hear the hum of voices. When his approaching figure was identified, Charlie and a few others almost ran towards him. Jack took an instant dislike, almost hatred, towards the promoter. If he could generate this kind of hatred against his opponent the outcome would never be in doubt. Slapping him on the back, Charlie never stopped talking. This continued till they got to the bar, hardly stopping when they got in.

'Charlie, shut up for God's sake.'

Charlie stepped back a little, shocked by the words of the man who he thought he was doing a favour. He seemed lost for words for a moment then said, 'Have a drink Jack.'

'Not likely.'

'Billy's had one. A whisky.'

Charlie indicated to the barmaid with his finger and thumb. He took hold of the glass, put it to Jack's lips and tried to pour it into his mouth. Jack brushed it away, the whisky falling onto the ground and the glass smashing.

'Take it away, you bloody idiot.' His eyes flashed and he wanted to hit Charlie but knew he couldn't. Hate welled inside him, much more venomous hate than he had ever known before. Everyone in the bar noticed it. Even Charlie was now lost for words. All eyes were upon him. Silence prevailed. You could hear a leaf fall.

Never at a loss for words, Charlie murdered the silence with more manufactured enthusiasm. Jack looked at him now more with irritation and resignation than anger. The end was in sight. But where was his opponent?

'Charlie, shut up for a moment. Where's this Billy?'

'Never mind him, Jack lad, you'll see him just before you start.'

The atmosphere was getting more excited and the talk more rapid. Beer was going down in large quantities. They were starting to drift into the back yard, which would hold about two hundred and still leave the protagonists room to move, but only just. Everyone would be crushed together. It added to the excitement. The atmosphere was one of near hysteria, being whipped up by Charlie who always needed to be the centre of attention.

The two protagonists had still not seen one another. This had been engineered by Charlie. Jack was still in the bar and Billy in another room. Charlie worked on the crowd; bets were taken with much money changing hands. On he continued, knowing he would have to start the contest sooner rather than later. Eventually and now in a more hushed voice, he announced, 'Gentlemen, I present to you those who we have all been waiting for.' There was a long pause.

In the bar, Jack was now taking off his shirt and was being manhandled by several men he did not know. He disliked it and swung his elbows around him in an irritated manner, saying, 'Keep your bloody hands off me.' They did so. He was now very tense, listening for Charlie to introduce him. He warmed up a little, punching the air in front of him with his clenched fists. Then he heard the words, 'From my left, the local man, Jack Lloyd.' He walked in with his fists still clenched. 'Give him a cheer.' He received three cheers. 'The local man is fighting for the first time.' Charlie kept the patter up before introducing his opponent. Jack was slapped on the back, and encouraged with shouts of admiration and support.

Then he heard the words, 'From the right, Billy from Merthyr.' Billy danced in with a flourish, punching the air with his left hand then the right. Looking at Jack, he hesitated for no more then a fraction of a second. That fraction of a second was noticed by all, but he danced on as he had done dozens of times before. He was many years older than Jack, probably more than ten. His face bore the marks of many contests and his dark hair was now limited to a short fringe around the outside. Shorter and perhaps broader than Jack, it was the width of middle-age rather than youthful muscle. On he danced, almost afraid to stop.

Finally Charlie's voice was heard. The two men stood face to face. 'Now, boys, a fair fight to the finish.' Billy gave Jack a punch towards the jaw as Charlie spoke. Jack dodged the full force of it but it just glanced off his chin.

Charlie stood back. Annoyed by the first blow which Jack regarded as a foul, he now sized Billy up knowing the outcome was never in doubt. They sparred for what appeared a long while but which was no more than seconds. There were no blows landed, just fists touching. Jack, by this time, knew his opponent lacked speed of reaction.

Twice he moved to hit the other man, but twice he held back. The third time he landed a blow under the jaw. Billy went down for good. Charlie counted out one to ten. He could have counted to a hundred before Billy would show any signs of life.

The crowd milled around the victim, then hugged the winner and slapped him on the back, shouting encouragement. The fight had hardly lasted a minute. The excitement was over. Billy was taken into the bar to revive. Though beginning to wake up, he was hardly rational. The crowd thinned out. Those that remained discussed the outcome. Some even speculated about Jack's next fight.

All Jack wanted to do was collect the money and go home. It was the easiest ten guineas he had ever earned. Then he thought of Billy and hoped he hadn't done him too much damage. He went down easily, too easily. At his age he shouldn't be fighting. He'd done too much of it. His face spoke volumes. Walking into the bar to collect his shirt and speak to Billy, a way was cleared for him. Billy was now more or less conscious, sitting on the floor and leaning against the bar. Grabbing his shirt, Jack walked the three steps to Billy and bent down to shake his hand.

'You going to be alright, Billy?' he asked. His opponent nodded.

'I'll be alright,' he said in resignation, then looked towards the floor. Billy knew it was the end of the road for him, as did Jack. The others didn't have any idea what was going through the minds of the two fighters. Jack felt sympathy for Billy and almost wanted to cry, but he held back the tears while he made a fast exit. Putting his shirt on, the tears flooded into his eyes. No one saw them.

Chapter 35

'Jack, thank God you're alright. The good lord answered my prayers.' Molly hugged him in relief. He did not respond, tolerating her gesture. It had been a non- event really. He hardly had a feeling of victory, though victory it had been. In the background, old man O'Hara mumbled his congratulations, now even more shrunken than the day before.

'Were you hurt Jack? Were you hit?' asked his wife.

'Didn't touch me at all. Over in a minute.'

'What you going to do now, Jack?'

'Sit down here.'

'Then what?

'Collect the money from Charlie.'

'Haven't you got it?'

'He'll give it to me.'

'You sure? They say he's a rogue, you know.'

'He'll pay up girl, don't you worry about that.'

'I hope so.'

'I'd better look for work tomorrow.'

'Where you going to look, Jack?'

'The big contractors won't look at me.'

'What you going to do then?'

'Something'll turn up. I'll worry about that tomorrow morning. We got food in the house for a few days. When I get the rest of the money from Charlie, we'll have food for a few more.'

'I'm worried what you're going to do, Jack.'

'So am I, girl. That makes two of us.' He settled into the chair and closed his eyes, signalling that the conversation was over. He remained dozing there for more than three hours, sometimes just awake, at other times asleep. Thoughts came to the surface of the past and the future. What would happen in the future? That was the important one. He was out of work and likely to remain so. If he did get work, it would be for a back street forge and low pay. He had reached a watershed in his life and he knew it. He couldn't keep his family on this back-street money. As he sat there with his eyes closed, his thoughts raced. Never before had he faced a life without work. Am I going to end up like the old man, only twenty years sooner? His thoughts alarmed him.

He considered the options. Charlie would surely want another contest but ten pounds now and again was not a job. Where would that lead? In a year or two he would look like the old fighters he had met in the past. It was a short life. Sooner or later you had a bad fight, and then it was downhill all the way. The more he thought, the further he found himself away from a solution. It annoyed him. Unable to sit still any longer, he got up to go and see his promoter.

It wasn't a long way to his tavern but, as he walked, he was greeted by almost all who passed him. He acknowledged this without even looking at most of them. He was a celebrity now but he wasn't sure whether he liked the attention. He walked reluctantly into the bar which now contained only the heavy drinkers, addicted to Charlie's dubious bonhomie.   The conversation stopped as he entered but only for a moment.

'Jack, my boy, come inside. We've been talking about nothing else since the fight. Have a whisky, my boy.' He declined with a shake of the head. 'Go on lad, just this once.' Again he shook his head, 'No.' He stood there, not knowing what to say. The talking resumed, mostly directed towards Jack.

'Jack, Swansea's proud of you. Saw him off quick sharp.'

'Never saw anything like it.'

They bombarded him with praise but what he wanted was Charlie's money. His admirers drew closer, not slapping him on the back but wanting to. Not many of them were sober. Even Charlie had an excited redness about his face. Jack just waited for the moment to ask to speak to him alone. The moment came sooner than he expected. Looking him in the eye, he leant

363

forward to within an inch or two of his face, not to dominate or intimidate but to obtain his attention without observers.

'A word in the back room, Charlie?' Nodding in reply, he led Jack into the back room.

'The rest of the money, Charlie.' Jack could see that Charlie was reluctant but didn't know quite how to put his point.

'Jack lad, I shouldn't really be paying you the rest of this money.'

'Why not?'

'I lost money on the fight.' Jack knew this was a lie and positioned himself between Charlie and the only exit out of the room.

'I don't believe you. Don't believe it.' Jack could feel his gorge rise, having some difficulty in suppressing his temper. 'Lose money, how?'

'It didn't last. You didn't give the boys a good run for their money.'

'You didn't find much of an opponent.'

'You could have made it last longer.'

'What is it? A match or play acting?'

'I'm saying you didn't give the boys a good run for their money.'

'You going to pay me or not?'

'I'll have to see. Haven't seen how much I've lost. Won't know till tomorrow. Come back then lad. I'll probably have it for you then. Alright?'

'No. You pay now or I'll take it out on your hide, Charlie boy.'

'There's no need to be like that, Jack.'

'Come on, cough up, Charlie.'

He didn't want to pay up but didn't know for how much longer he could keep him at bay. 'Listen Jack, I've got to count my money.'

'Do it here then, on the window sill.' Jack closed the exit door. 'I'll see it don't get stolen, Charlie. Jack'll look after you and your money.' He laughed to himself. Charlie knew he could delay no longer. He took the three steps towards the window. Searching his pockets for loose coins, he could find none. He would have to take the hessian bag out with the sovereigns in.

'Haven't got it on me Jack. I've left it somewhere,' he lied.

Jack looked at him long and hard 'Lying again. I heard the coins clink.' With one rapid movement he plunged his hand into Charlie's pocket, grasped the bag and threw it onto the windowsill. 'Now pay up!' he demanded.

Grasping the bag, Charlie opened the drawstring and tipped out the contents. Some spilled on the floor. He went grovelling on the dark floor to recover his wealth. Jack gave him a slight kick in the behind.

'Here, Mr Money Bags. Pay me first and grovel for your profits after.'

He rose from the floor, face flushed, with some of the spilt money in his hands. 'Alright then, I'll give you the five pounds,' he said, handing it to him.

'Guineas, not pounds,' Jack reminded him. He handed over the correct money at last. Jack grasped his ear and twisted it, saying, 'You never give up, do you?'

Not wanting to miss a further business opportunity and still flushed, he said 'Jack, another contest. A proper one this time. What about it lad?' he enthused.

'I'll see, Charlie, I'll see.'

'A proper one this time, Jack, not one of these backyard jobs. On Kilvey. A real show.' Charlie visibly swelled with pride and self importance as he thought of promoting this event. Yes, he'd have it on Kilvey Hill with a thousand spectators. He thought of all the money he'd make.

'Who against, Charlie?'

'Barty, that's who I'd get.'

'Who's Barty?'

'Haven't heard of him? Barty from Brecon.'

'Never heard of him.'

'Never heard of Barty the Brecon Bruiser?'

'No, never.'

'You're on then, Jack?'

'I suppose so.'

'A deal then.'

'Wait a bit, Charlie.'

'What's wrong then, Jack?'

'What's the money?'

'All you think about is money. Never seen one like you before. We'll fix something up. You know I wouldn't let you down.'

Jack smiled, knowing he had the advantage. 'Charlie, the only person you wouldn't let down would be Charlie. What's the money? Come on, out with it.'

'Twenty guineas. Can't be fairer than that.'

Jack laughed long and loud. 'You never give up, do you Charlie? Twice the money, ten times the crowd.'

'I'm risking my money though Jack. You understand that, don't you?'

'I'm risking my life. You understand that Charlie, don't you?' He looked him in the eye, not being sure whether to laugh or not.

'You'll come to no harm Jack, you know that don't you?'

'Every fighter comes to harm. Ever seen one who hasn't?'

'What money d'you want then, lad?'

'One hundred guineas, cash in hand, up front before the contest.' He held his open right hand before him

'You're not serious?'

'I'm always serious, Charlie'. His mind went back more than a decade. On the back of a pony, he was less than a length behind Tommy up in the Preselis. Although long dead, he now came alive before him. Tommy always used silence in negotiating a deal. Always get the other side to talk first. Examine the other side's desire to close the deal. Did they want to agree or were they desperate. Knowing Charlie wanted this contest badly, he remained silent.

Charlie's face became even more flushed, and his breathing became heavy. Jack was beating him in two ways, in his pocket

366

and his pride if the prospective fight did not take place. Jack broke the silence at last. Playing Tommy's old trick he said, 'That's my last offer.'

Charlie did not know how to reply. He didn't realise he had been victim to the tricks of one of the shrewdest cattle dealers alive. He wasn't used to these tactics. It was as though he'd been hit between the eyes.

'Be reasonable, Jack. Be reasonable.'

'Think about it, Charlie. I might get work in the meantime. These fights are a sport for fools.'

Charlie was still shocked by the sum demanded but hadn't put the matter out of his mind. In fact he was juggling with figures and contemplating ways he might be able to manipulate Jack into accepting less. The notion of "winner takes all" went through his mind.

'Come back tomorrow, Jack and we'll talk a bit more.'

'I'll come back but remember it'll be a hundred guineas there.' He opened his palm to him again. 'I'm off then,' he said, going to take his leave.

'Up Kilvey, is it Jack?' Charlie said, giving him a knowing look. 'Wrestling in the gorse with the big man's daughter.' He gave a knowing lewd chuckle as his adversary departed east.

Jack was annoyed that it had become public knowledge. If Charlie knew, everyone else would also. He gave a sigh of resignation as yet again he went to meet Lucy. He walked wearily up the hill. He wasn't exhausted, just lost without work. There was a vacuum in his life. It was tiring having to live on your wits, because you had to have your wits about you when dealing with Charlie. He didn't have an ounce of honesty in his whole body. Did he ever think about anything but Charlie and where the next sovereign was coming from?

Leaning on the gate, feeling breathless, he saw her coming. Their meetings were now following a pattern. It had become routine. Had she been closer to those she passed as she rode up the hill she would have heard comments such as: 'Going up to see her man', 'The duchess and the blacksmith', 'That'll end in trouble' or 'Mark my words, they'll come to grief.'

Their greetings had become subdued, their need for one another more patient though the ardour was certainly there in abundance. He helped her off the horse and they kissed. After tying Lancer loosely to the gatepost, they walked towards the gorse bushes. They lay down on his cape; it was now almost routine. Hugging for a minute or two, he then released himself.

'Jack, what happened to you in the fight?'

'I won.'

'Were you hurt?'

'No, only lasted a minute.'

'Why so short, Jack?'

'He was old. Should never have matched us.'

'Why not?'

'Too old he was. It was cruelty on him, it was. I put him out of his misery as quick as I could.'

'How?'

'Gave him a quick one under the jaw.'

She grasped him again, clinging to him. 'I'm glad you're not hurt. You haven't got to do this again, have you Jack?'

'Just one more, Lucy. That'll be it.'

'Why have you got to do it?'

'No work girl. No work.'

They lay together, not speaking but both thinking about the future. Uncertainty lay ahead for both of them. They wouldn't live happily ever after. They knew it but never mentioned it. Lucy became restless. He knew she had something to say but didn't encourage her to speak.

'Jack, I've got something to tell you.'

He was giving her his total attention. 'Jack listen, I've got something to tell you. Do you hear me?'

'Course I hear you. What is it?' He was mildly irritated.

'This is important, Jack.'

'What is it?'

She didn't want to tell him in the mood he was in, but had no option. 'I'm sure I'm pregnant.'

368

He sat up, breathed heavily and put his head in his hands, totally at a loss for words. Eventually he looked up and into her eyes. 'Are you sure?'

'Yes Jack, sure.'

'How are you sure?'

'We women know these things.'

He put his face in his hands again, shaking his head as he did so.

'What's wrong Jack, aren't you pleased?'

'I suppose I am.'

'Suppose you are?' Tears filled her eyes. 'What does that mean?'

'Listen Lucy, I've got a lot on at the moment.'

'A lot on. What about me and the baby?'

'What can I do?'

'Aren't you pleased?' she asked, imploringly.

'Course I'm pleased but what can I do about it? It's too much.' He remained with his head in his hands for a few minutes.

'Listen, Lucy.' He grasped her by her upper arms. 'It's getting on top of me. I've a son in Llanduesant, a wife, a son and her family to support in Swansea and I'm out of a job. Any money I get is from fighting and there's no future in that. Now you're having a baby. Before long Molly'll be having another. I can't do anything for you, Lucy.'

'I know that Jack. I just wanted you to be pleased.'

'Listen Lucy, I am pleased but I can't do anything. What you going to do anyway?'

'I'm going to have it.'

'Course you are. You've got no choice.'

'I could do something but I'm not going to.'

'What you going to do then, Lucy? Can't have children through the bush if you live in the big house. I can't marry you, can I?'

'I know that.'

'What you going to do then?'

'Don't worry, I'll find a way out. Leave it to me. You'll find out when it's over.'

'How'll you do it, Lucy? I know you're a determined little devil.'

'Don't you worry Jack, you'll find out when it's over but I'll rear the baby. Have no fear of that.'

'I'll wait and see then, girl.'

'Who's this woman in Llanduesant?'

'A woman I knew when I was much younger, that's all.'

'What's her name?'

'Rosie.'

'Rosie what?'

'I don't know. Never thought to ask her.' It then occurred to him that it was strange he didn't know her surname. She was just Rosie. Everyone called her Rosie.

'Funny you didn't know her name. How long were you with her?'

'A year or two. Saw her when we went through with the cattle. Drovers we were.'

'You've been a drover?'

'Yes.'

'How long for, Jack?'

'Years.'

'Why did you finish?'

'Railways took over.'

'I shouldn't have asked such a stupid question. What did you do then?'

'The Crimea then.'

'You've been to war?'

'Yes.'

'Is that where you got that scar?' She touched it.

'Didn't get it eating bread and cheese, did I?' She was lost in admiration, her feelings becoming even stronger as he divulged more of his past. Waiting for a moment or two for all the facts to sink in, she became even more curious.

'This Rosie, what was she like?'

'She was lovely. Rosie was lovely.' A faraway look came into his eyes, and his voice became softer. The words had escaped his lips without him knowing. He was about to say it again but didn't.

Lucy, for the first time in her life, became jealous. She was consumed with jealousy. She was in an alien country and a hostile one. Jealousy was something felt by those who couldn't get their own way. It was the fate of the weak and the humble and she wasn't weak or humble. Who was this bloody Rosie? He'd had a child by her but didn't even know her damned name. She was probably living in a hovel on charity, not knowing where her next meal was coming from.

'Jack, who is this bloody Rosie?'

'Lucy, I knew her when you were in school.'

'Lovely? What's lovely about her?'

'Lucy, she was my first girlfriend. It happened a few years ago.'

'Do you still see her?'

'Now and then.'

'What's now and then? Have you seen her this year?' Her questioning became angry and penetrating. Becoming really consumed with jealousy, her anger grew as she confronted the first moment in her life when she couldn't have her own way.

'Yes, of course I have.'

'While you've been with me?'

'No.'

'When then?'

'Earlier in the year.'

'You're not to go there again. Do you hear?'

'You won't stop me.'

'I will. You won't go up there, do you hear me?'

He laughed at her, then pinched her left cheek with his right hand hard and vigorously which made her all the madder, only letting go when he had drawn tears from her eyes. She kicked out at him. 'You bloody bastard, you won't go up there again, do you hear?' He laughed at her which made her feel impotent with

371

rage. She kicked out again.

He mockingly said to her. 'You jealous little vixen.'

Now at her wit's end, she shouted, 'Let me go, you brute, let me go.' He did so momentarily, but leapt on her, ripped her clothes off with more rapidity than before, and quickly shed his own. Their congress was violent, active and longer lasting than ever before. Her climax created such violent convulsions that she wondered if she would explode. It was like being thrown over a cliff; falling through space from which there was no end. How long it lasted, she didn't know. Eventually it ceased and she found herself looking into Jack's eyes, whilst his hands continued to massage her waist. He released his grasp without moving his position, smiling at her gently. She was breathless and powerless but for a moment didn't know what to do. Almost as though launched from a cannon, she hit him round the face with both hands. 'You bastard! You bastard!' she shouted. Trying to move, she was helpless. Closing her eyes, she gave up the struggle, and was visibly exhausted. They remained there for perhaps three or four minutes. He moved slightly. 'Is that better?'

She nodded, giving a final heavy discharge of breath as a final act of submission.

Lying beside her, he held her close to him. 'What you going to tell the sewing ladies in the Hall, girl?'

'Shut up. I just want to go to sleep here until dawn.'

'What'll we use for blankets?'

'You.'

He laughed, wanting to say something in return but was lost for words. She could feel his mental struggle. Giving his waist a slight pinch, she said, 'Shut up. I want to sleep.' She slept for perhaps three hours until the declining sun and cold awakened her. He remained awake, thinking of the future. With every day the problems increased. No day added to them more than this one.

Snuggling a little nearer to him, she hoped to delay the need to get up but it was for minutes only. The cold got to her. She

roused herself first on her elbow, looking at her man. 'Jack?'
    'Yes Lucy,' he replied almost formally.
    'You're never going to get rid of me.'

Chapter 36

It was a Sunday all would remember. It was early and a heavy mist hung over the town and the bay leaving a damp weave on everything out of doors. No one stopped outside longer than was necessary. Those obliged to had damp faces freshened to a deep pink by the moisture. The streets were damp but with an absence of running water. Jack was running along the beach in the direction of Mumbles. It was to be his big pay day.

Thoughts were crowding through his mind at alarming speed. Who was this man, Barty? He'd heard a lot of comments about him. Nothing he had gleaned so far gave a full picture of him. Was he Goliath or just a mere mortal? No one seemed to know. If they did then they gave no accurate description.

His train of thought altered direction towards money. He wasn't in this business to fight the world, but just to look after his family. To keep the wolf from the door. Charlie could be trusted no further than you could throw him; perhaps not even that far. When would he strike him? It would be no good unless he did it in public. Only shame would extract that sum of money from him. Could he get together with Barty? Would he be hostile till the end of the fight? If he managed to get the money before the fight, who would he give it to? Lucy seemed the only one who had the sense, ability and integrity to safeguard such a sum. That was impossible. Molly would be hopeless. The old man would drink it in the first tavern he passed and be robbed by the time he'd had his second pint. What would he do? In the past he'd always found a way to solve these problems, but now he was uncertain. He'd always been alone and wanted it that way but now he could do with a friend he could trust. Ned, that's who he wanted now, the only real friend he'd ever had. Good friends were made in the army; they were essential. They'd share their last crumb with you. Then you parted. He hadn't thought of Ned since they went their separate ways. Funny, isn't it?

Again he returned to thinking about Barty. He must be in Swansea by now. Where could he find him? Charlie'd got him hidden away somewhere, maybe at the tavern. These thoughts rumbled through his mind without solutions being found. It worried him. He became anxious but speeded up to try and clear them from his mind. Turning round, he ran back at a faster speed.

On the way home, he decided not to go to Charlie's. He was resigned to letting matters run their course; there was nothing he could do. It would all be over in eight hours. Running into Frog Street, he was covered from head to foot in the mist which left an opaque film of water all over him. His face was already bright red from the exertion of running.

Only Molly was up, nursing young Jack. 'He's growing Molly. Growing by the day. A fine lad. Got to give you credit for that.'

'Never mind young Jack. What's going to happen to old Jack?'

'I'll be alright Molly. This'll be the last, have no fear. It'll be all over tonight. I'll get work soon.'

'That's what you say. If anything happened, what would we do?'

'Nothing's going to happen to me, girl. Have faith in me, Molly. Have I ever let you down?' She hadn't an answer.

'Molly, I'm tired. Haven't slept much. I'm going to bed. Wake me up at twelve if I haven't woken up, girl.' She didn't reply but went on nursing young Jack.

Jack slept heavily, much more so than he expected. For several nights he had slept fitfully but was now making up for lost time.

Roused out of his sleep by knocking at the door, he heard several men loudly asking for him. It was apparent that Charlie had sent them. They had come to take him up to Kilvey Hill. The match was at least two to three hours away. He certainly had no intention of leaving till the last moment.

375

Molly came through the bedroom door, wiping her hands. 'They're here from Charlie. Jack, I don't like this. Have you got to do it? We could get by somehow. I've got a bad feeling. Nothing good'll come of this. I don't like it.'

'I'll get up, girl. Go down and give'em some tea. Have they had a few?'

'Some of them, more than a few.'

'How many are there?'

'Six, I think. All lit up, they are.'

'Go down and give'em tea, nothing more. Understand, nothing more.'

She descended the stairs, asking, 'Who wants tea?' There wasn't an answer, only a mumble of disappointment. She repeated the question, only louder. The eldest one there lowered his voice, looked Molly in the face and with as much charm as he could muster asked, 'Have you got anything stronger?'

With a degree of strength and aggression she didn't know she possessed, she answered, 'There's no drink in this house. Do you want tea or not?'

'We'll have the tea, missus,' he agreed. This quietened the men down, almost sobered them up. When the tea eventually arrived, they drank it like chastised school boys. All they could do now was wait. Jack came down the stairs, hardly acknowledging his callers, and went to wash in the backyard, taking his time about it.

Molly came outside. 'Jack, do you want something to eat or drink?'

'Nothing to eat, but I'll have half a cup of tea.'

Slowly he dressed and joined his visitors. He was irritated by their presence in the house. What were these ageing drunks doing here? Didn't Charlie trust him to come for the match? Were these men part of Charlie's fairground act? Certainly this huckster's shouting would last longer than the match. How he disliked, even hated all this playacting, just to line Charlie's pockets. Would he get any money from him before the fight? He certainly wouldn't get it afterwards. He was on a carousel he couldn't get off.

Something told him his position was hopeless. He thought of all the old fighters he had met, all hard up. Broken faces and broken men with not a shilling to their names; he didn't want to end up like them.

Anger seized him. 'You lot, get out.' They hardly moved, not seeming to register what was in his mind. 'I said "get out" the bloody lot of you.' The anger now got through to them and they all left. 'I'll be up there, have no fear,' he called after them. He followed them along the road, waving them away in anger. They moved along the street but only a short distance so as to be out of the orbit of his anger. More people were now in the street than usual. All eyes were on Jack. Knowing that there was nothing to gain from this unwanted attention, he went back inside, intending to ignore all those around him. His anger must be directed at Barty, he reminded himself.

Once inside again, he became unsettled and could not focus on the matter in hand. He became irritated by his family and could not avoid snapping at them. The family kept their distance. Time marched on; he planned to leave one hour before the start of the match.

Ignoring them all, he left the house walking at a brisk pace and by the most direct route to Kilvey. Speaking to no one, he was cheered on the way. Surrounded by a climate of suppressed hysteria, he walked on. Charlie's sidekicks could not keep up the pace. On he went, over the bridge and up the hill. As he walked up, he passed through the ranks of the spectators who made way for him and shouted out words of encouragement. Not responding, his pace did not slacken. The crowd behind him now was quite large, with most of them having difficulty keeping up. Reaching the top, he found that a large crowd had already gathered. Most of the men were in bowler hats and a handful mounted on horses. On he walked to the far side of the crowd where Charlie could be heard but so far not seen. The crowd had gathered into a circle around him but kept their distance.

Charlie came to meet him. He was in his element; shaking hands with the new arrival and talking constantly, working the crowd up as he continued.

Jack looked the promoter in the face and demanded, 'Money now, Charlie.'

Charlie ignored the demand and continued shouting at the crowd. Jack ordered those immediately around him to get out of the way. They backed away like frightened curs.

'Charlie, the money,' Jack repeated.

Again he continued with his patter although he had heard the aggressive demand.

'Charlie!' he shouted for all to hear. He pointed to the spot in front of him. 'Come here!' Charlie obeyed almost automatically.

'Jack, my boy,' he whispered, 'have no fear, you'll get the money. Couldn't bring it up here. I might get robbed.' Raising his voice with the last few words, so that those nearby could hear, he gave Jack a wink full of cunning duplicity. 'You'll get your money, have no fear Jack lad. Trust me. Have I ever let you down? Trust Charlie.' The crowd were inclined to believe him.

Jack was lost for words, not finding the resources to reply. Charlie'd won again. He couldn't back out now and it seemed likely he would not get his money. An impotent rage seized him. Consumed with such anger, he knew it could only be directed towards his opponent.

Charlie put as much distance between himself and Jack as possible. His cohorts had now caught up with their prize, surrounding him with platitudes of encouragement. They didn't know what else to do as they could detect a silent rage within him which made them wary. They kept a yard or two's distance but did a good job of keeping the crowd away.

The crowd was now perhaps four to five hundred and would get no bigger. At the rear and with an excellent view over the whole scene were Albert Lambert and Dickie Lamb, both mounted on fine horses. 'This is fun Dickie, isn't it? First time in twelve months I've been up here. Who have you bet on?'

'The Swansea man.'

'How much?'

'Ten guineas.'

'Is that all? Couldn't you manage more? Is the old man keeping you short?'

'Very short of late. Who have you bet on?'

'Same as you.'

'What's your wager?'

'Fifty pounds.'

'That much?'

'The old man doesn't know yet. Did it on credit with boozy Charlie. Knows I'll pay up or rather the old man'll pay up.' He laughed a cynical laugh. 'A real card, Charlie. Making a bloody fortune on this match, I wouldn't wonder.'

'How do you get your old man to cough up all the time, Albert?'

'Shame Dickie, shame. If you're lord of all you survey, you can't take shame, believe me Dickie.'

'Who is this Swansea man?'

'Jack Lloyd. Father sacked him a while back. Hit the ganger in front of father. That's insolence for you.' They both laughed. 'If he can do that, he can destroy the opposition. My money's on Jack Lloyd.'

Anger continued to consume Jack. He couldn't take it out on Charlie. One whack and he'd go pop. Sooner or later he'd go pop without a whack. He visualised Charlie's eyes which were nearly popping out of his head already, because of the booze he drank and the weight he carried. The thought of Charlie going pop amused him, but not for long. The anger returned.

Now the crowd was getting more animated. They wanted action. Surely they couldn't keep them waiting much longer. A group of ten or more made their way towards him in the middle of which was Charlie. He directed the others away from him. 'I've got to have a quiet word with Jack,' he said.

Everyone was now perhaps four to five yards away from them. 'Jack, a word,' he whispered in his ear. 'Won't have to wait long now lad, but listen, I've taken a lot of bets on you and I'm top heavy. Know what I mean?'

379

'Yes.'

'I want you to do me a favour?'

'What favour?'

'Make it last a few minutes then take a dive. I'll make it one hundred and ten in your hand after the fight.'

Jack could hardly believe what he was hearing. 'Me take a dive? Lose in front of all these people? You must be joking.'

'You won't do it then, Jack? I done you all these favours, put you on the map, and that's how you treat the hand that feeds you. I'm ashamed of you.'

'Course I won't do it. I got some pride you know. You ought to know that by now.'

'I'm going to lose a lot of money cos of you. You know that, lad?'

'Shouldn't have taken the bets.'

Charlie's mind was working at great speed, looking for ways of escape, so far without success.

'Jack lad, it'll have to be winner takes all then.'

'Does Barty know?'

Charlie, for once, was lost for words. He and his hangers-on went to speak to Jack's opponent. Jack could hardly believe what he had heard. Charlie was devious but he had never realised to what extent. He felt shocked as well as angry. He would do nothing more till he was called. Time hung heavy on his hands; seconds felt like minutes; minutes felt like hours. When would the call come? Please God, he prayed, call me and get this over with.

He felt in limbo. Too many thoughts were going through his mind. Words of encouragement were coming from those around him which made the confusion even more acute. What was his opponent like? "Barty the Brecon Bruiser", people called him. One thing was certain, he was older than Jack. Then the call finally came.

Responding to Charlie's call, Jack and his supporters walked slowly towards the centre of the crowd where a space had been made. It was a small round space already occupied by the more excited spectators. From the opposite direction came the other party. Walking slowly, both groups drew nearer. The atmosphere became more ominous with every step. Slowly they moved, both the same distance from the centre of conflict. They both had shouts and words of encouragement thrown at them. It seemed a long time but within a minute or two they were facing one another, shirts off and with Charlie between them. Even he was quieter than usual. The crowd became silent with expectation.

The protagonists looked at one another. Charlie faced the opposition and the undiluted glare of Barty. Shorter, older and heavier than Jack, he was not lacking in confidence. Jack was momentarily rather shocked by his appearance. It was only for a moment. He was facing the greatest challenge of his life. Anger, determination and confidence infected his whole being. A strange quiet came over the scene. To his right side he heard a shout from a voice he knew. 'Give it to him Jack and come home.' It was old man O'Hara. He smiled to himself, knowing he had something to fight for. The shouting was over. Charlie spoke to the contestants then stood back. The fight began.

For perhaps a minute they sized one another up and exchanged only minor blows. The crowd expected more, shouting words of encouragement and hoping for blood, carnage and destruction. The crowd moved in on them. There was hardly room for action. The shouting continued. Punches of modest force were exchanged with no one emerging as the stronger. They moved nearer one another and into a clinch from which they seemed unable to extract themselves. Barty gave his opponent a kick between the legs.

The effect on Jack was instant. A shock went through his whole being. It was as if he had been pole-axed yet still remained conscious. Then he felt a second blow, exactly the same. He fell into the crowd for a second or two, unavailable for more punishment. Getting himself up, partly being pushed to his feet by others, it took several seconds for him to do so. Unaware that the crowd were baying for blood, he faced the challenge of his life. Could he fight this pain and carry on or would he give up?

Never had he experienced such pain. Even when the pain eased, he wanted to be sick. He couldn't be sick; it wasn't an option. Somehow he struggled to his feet, hindered more than helped by the crowd. Again Barty aimed a kick between his legs but somehow Jack dodged out of the way. The blows he had suffered had temporarily reduced his strength. Things didn't look good. Keeping his enemy at bay for a few more seconds gave him time to recover. If he was to win he would have to do something quickly. With a determination to fight the pain he didn't know he possessed, he addressed himself to his opponent. His murderous desire to destroy Barty reduced the pain and propelled him forward.

The circle had become so small that they hardly had room to manoeuvre. Jack launched himself at his enemy who fell back at an angle into the crowd. Struggling to get up and becoming unbalanced by the efforts of the crowd to get him to rise, his guard was lowered. Jack gave him two blows to the jaw, causing him to lose consciousness. The centre of the circle moved back, leaving Barty on his side on the floor. He was defeated in probably less than two minutes.

Without knowing why, Jack stood two paces back then propelled himself forward, kicking his opponent in the back of the neck. The snap of bone breaking was heard. An ominous quiet descended over the crowd but not for long. The chatter of a hundred voices broke out. No one knew what to do.

Barty's whole body shook with a spasm for a moment or two before becoming permanently inert. Within a second or two, all the onlookers knew they had witnessed a violent death. The mood of the crowd had changed. Those within the inner circle wanted to get away and those further out were straining for a glimpse of the victim.

While this was happening, Jack stood looking down at Barty, just another member of the crowd distinguished only by being without a shirt. Mesmerised by what had happened, he stood still while all about him was movement. Some of the crowd had dispersed but most of the spectators had merely stepped back a few yards. A few kept looking at the body. Jack stood back, ignored by all.

Charlie, for once lost for words, wore a frightened look. How was he going to get out of this one? The consequences flashed though his mind. What would happen to him? The crowd started to talk amongst themselves.

'What happens to him now?'

'Got to get him from here.'

'He's dead.'

'Dead as mutton, he is.'

'We haven't heard the last of this.'

'They'll have to take him away.'

'They'll not just bury him, you know.'

'They'll ask a few questions about this.'

'Who will?'

'Be a post mortem.'

'What's that?'

'Questions how he died.'

'Someone'll have to take him down.'

Jack continued looking at the body, spoken to by no one. Everyone was frightened to approach him. He still seemed mesmerised; he was in this world yet not part of it. He half listened to the conversations going on around him.

At last he reacted. 'Here,' he said to one man's request, 'take him down on that. Isn't the first dead body to be carried on that' He pointed at his cavalry cloak. I shan't need that where I'm going, he thought. A mood of impending doom overcame him. He walked down the hill alone, unaware of anyone around him. He was walking the last few hundred yards he would ever walk as a free man.

Up ahead were Albert and Dickie riding close together on their horses.

'It really has been a jolly day, hasn't it Dickie, and a profitable one' Albert commented, hitting his pocket full of coins.

'A day I could have done without, Albert.'

'Don't be a spoilsport, Dickie. These blood sports are so jolly,' he replied as he laughed a cynical smile.

It was a Sunday all would remember.

Chapter 37

Jack was arrested within an hour of leaving Kilvey Hill and had remained in the police cells ever since. Not allowed any communication with anyone, he was fed and watered by the police but received no other human contact. The cell was small, dark and cold even on the warmest day. Quite deliberately, his captors ignored him.

The police were making inquiries as to who had been at the match. The names Albert Lambert and Dickie Lamb kept coming up. There would be a trial, there was no doubt about that. These two witnesses would be more convincing before a jury than many of the others.

With some trepidation, the officer in charge visited the Hall. He was ushered into a side room and kept waiting for twenty minutes before Albert arrived, still in his dressing gown, having obviously just got out of bed. Speaking to him for an hour, he made notes then departed. Feeling he had done a good morning's work, he left by the front door. One more witness statement like that and that thug Jack Lloyd would be going for a short walk at eight o'clock one morning in the not too distant future.

The family sat down to lunch. Sir Lionel as always dominated the gathering. Silent at first, he waded through the first course of the very substantial meal. He paused a while before ordering the second course.

Addressing the whole family, he enquired, 'What was that policeman doing here this morning?' No one answered. Waiting for the effect of his question to sink in, he looked around the table, particularly at Albert who was looking down at his plate. The silence continued. All felt the weight of the master's demand. 'Albert, have they been to see you?' He didn't answer. Raising his voice to the level of thunder, he demanded, 'Have they been talking to you?'

He couldn't put his father off anymore. 'Yes, father.'

'What about?'

'Just a small matter, that's all father.'

'Small matter. He was here an hour and a half.'

'It isn't important, father. A small matter I saw yesterday.'

'What small matter? I want to know now.'

'There was a crowd and someone got hurt, that's all father.'

'Where was this crowd? Albert, I want to know.'

'On Kilvey Hill, father.'

'Why were you up there? You've never been there before. You're hiding something from me.'

'No father, I'm hiding nothing.'

'You're hiding something boy. What is it? Are you in another of your scrapes? What is it? Tell me. I want to know.'

All the family were fascinated but fearful observers of this battle of words. Lucy appeared amused by Albert's predicament. Father was at last nailing his foot to the floor. Not before time.

'Albert, if you don't tell me, I shall find out. I suggest you come clean for once. What were you doing up there?'

'It's like this father, if you must know. Dickie Lamb and I were riding on the top there. We saw this big crowd and didn't know what they were up there for. So we looked and what do you think we saw? These two low-lifes fighting.'

'Then what happened?'

'We didn't see what happened. We were just riding. One of them got killed. The man from Merthyr got killed; the Swansea man survived.'

Lucy's look of amusement turned to shock. Tears filled her eyes and, reaching for her handkerchief, she left the room sobbing conspicuously for all to see. Running upstairs, she locked the door of the bedroom and threw herself on the bed crying long and loud. She was left there for at least two hours before anyone approached her.

'You'd better come in the office, my boy,' Sir Lionel

directed. Ignoring the second course, he hustled his son out of the room so they could be alone.

'Sit down you fool.' Albert did so. 'What were you doing up there and I don't want any of your lies?'

'Just riding father, Dickie and I.'

'Don't tell me lies.' He got up, his eyes flashing, physically intimidating his wayward son. 'I want the truth and I will have the truth. Do you hear?'

Even Albert knew there was now no escape. He would have to come clean.

'Well father, there was this match up on the hill. Dickie and I went up to see it.'

'What sort of a match?'

'A boxing match, father.'

'Why are you going to these low life events? Why man, why?'

'Well, we went, Dickie and I. The match didn't last long. The man from Merthyr went down, got kicked and had his neck broken.'

'Who was the other man?'

'The local man, Jack Lloyd.'

'What name did you say?'

'Jack Lloyd.'

'Big and fair, is he?'

'Yes, that's him.'

Sir Lionel sat back, wiping his brow with his hand in an attitude of surprise and disbelief. 'How much more are you going to tell me? How much more?'

'What's wrong, father? Do you know him?' Albert asked, feigning ignorance.

'Know him. I sacked him a while ago.'

'You employed him?'

'Yes. How many more shocks am I going to have today?' His anger had subsided. Now he seemed bewildered by the turn of events.

'Where's this Jack Lloyd now?'

'In the police cells, I believe.'

'Where's the man from Merthyr?'

'In the mortuary.'

'They won't get into any more trouble. We have something to be thankful for at least.' He sighed, reflecting on the recent turn of events. Had he known that Lucy was carrying Jack's child it would probably have killed him. He was never to know. 'Have you any more shocks for me Albert?'

'No father, honestly I haven't.'

'You sure? Honesty rarely surfaces in your relationship with me.'

'I do try to be a good son, father.'

'So far you haven't been very successful, have you? While you're here, I'd better discuss your future with you.'

'Have you got plans for me, father?'

'Yes.'

'What are they?'

'I'm thinking of sending you abroad, Albert.'

'That sounds jolly, father. Where?'

'Where would you like to go?'

'America. Sounds such a colourful place.'

'Well, you decide where you want to go and I'll give you an allowance.'

'You don't want to get rid of me, do you father?'

'Yes I do. My patience is exhausted.'

'How long do you want me to go for?'

'Permanently. A single ticket. Where do you want to go, son?'

'I'm not that bad, am I father?'

'Not bad! Name one positive contribution you have made to this family in the last year?'

There was silence while Albert tried to find an answer.

'You can't, can you?'

'Not at the moment, father. I'll think of something.'

'You'd better think quickly.'

'Father, you're going to make me into one of those

388

remittance men aren't you?'

'Yes I am and soon too.'

'How much are you going to give me, father?'

'Fifteen pounds a month.'

'Could you make it twenty, father?'

'That's my last offer, Albert. Decide where you want to go and I'll order a single ticket there. The sooner, the better.'

'Yes father'. Albert knew better than to argue at this stage and left the room. It was a shock to him, a great shock but he did not show his feelings of uncertainty about the new direction his life must take. He's heard about these remittance men. They departed these shores and were rarely heard of again. Occasionally you heard of one years afterwards but only to record a death, the details having been sent by some nun who looked after him in his final destitute days in South Africa, or was it some Pacific Island?

Lucy remained behind her locked door, tormented initially by uncontrollable grief and despair. Now it had become gentle weeping. She lay on top of the bed sucking her handkerchief and reflecting on the future. There was a gentle knock on the door to which Lucy did not respond, followed by another which she still did not answer. The third was louder, much louder. 'Lucy, are you alright?' asked Jane. There was still no reply but Jane heard some movement behind the door.

Softly Lucy asked, 'Is that you Jane?'

'Yes Miss Lucy.'

'Are you alone?'

'Yes Miss.'

'Who sent you up?'

'Your mother, Miss Lucy.'

Slowly the door opened. All Jane saw was a red face, ravaged by weeping, with no sign of any moderating of her grief.

'Come in, Jane.' She entered the room, relocking the door after her.

Hardly able to put one foot in front of another, Lucy eventually got to the bed and virtually collapsed onto it. 'Sit down here, Jane,' she said, indicating that she should sit beside her.

Jane took her hand, stroking it comfortingly. 'What's wrong, Miss Lucy?'

'Something dreadful has happened.'

'Do you want to tell me about it, Miss?' Lucy shook her head.

'It must be something dreadful, Miss Lucy,' she said, inviting revelation. 'You can tell me if you want, Miss.'

'It's nothing you would understand, Jane.'

'I might, Miss Lucy. It's a man, isn't it?'

Like a frightened animal, she raised her head from her handkerchief and looked directly at Jane. There was a look of alarm and shock on her face.

'Do you know something, Jane?'

'Nothing, Miss Lucy. I'm putting two and two together and making it ten which I expect is the right answer. I'm right, aren't I Miss Lucy?'

'How do you know? Have they been talking?'

'Don't worry, Miss Lucy. "They" don't know anything.'

'How long have you known, Jane?'

'When you came in with the ripped dress and the flush on your cheek, I knew there was a man in your life.'

'You noticed that, Jane?'

'I couldn't miss it.' You must realise that whatever goes on in this house is picked up by the domestic staff. Absolutely everything. We may be just staff on five pounds a year but we are not fools you know.'

'I know that Jane. I know that.'

'Who is the man, Miss?'

'I can't tell you that, Jane.'

'Could you marry him, Miss Lucy? You'd make a fine wife and mother.'

'That's out of the question.'

'Why, Miss Lucy?' she asked gently and cunningly.

'It would be impossible, Jane. Impossible.'

'Why, Miss?' she asked, seeing Lucy becoming more open and confiding.

'Well Jane, you'd better know. I've no one else to talk to.' Her defences were coming down. Never had they come further down, apart from during her relationship with Jack.

'He's Jack Lloyd, married and used to be a blacksmith with the firm until he was sacked.'

'I had heard, Lucy.' She took her hand again.

'You've heard, Jane? Who from?'

'Lucy, you've got to know, it's common knowledge.'

'Common knowledge, Jane?'

'Yes, Miss. You can't hide it. Everyone knows.'

Lucy looked up, acutely alarmed. 'Everyone knows?'

'Yes, you've got to accept this fact, Lucy. You used to go to Kilvey Hill and meet up there.'

'But we didn't go together.'

'Lucy, you must accept it. People know'.

'Jane, there's one more thing.' She paused, and then admitted, 'I'm pregnant.'

'I guessed you would be. What are you going to do?'

'I don't know. But you can be sure of one thing, I shall rear it. Make no mistake about that. I shall rear it.'

'It won't be easy. What will you do, Miss Lucy?'

'Jack Lloyd is married already so I can't marry him. That's out. It would have been out anyway.'

'He's in trouble, you know. Most likely he'll be charged with murder.'

'A man dies in a boxing match and the other one is charged with murder? Jane, it gets worse by the minute.'

Lucy returned to despair again, sucking her handkerchief and staring into space. Jane remained with her for a silent hour, broken only by weeping. Eventually Jane suggested, 'Lucy, don't think the worst. It may never happen. It probably won't happen.'

Lucy sat up. 'Why does all this happen to me? All this at once.'

'Everyone gets problems you know, Lucy. Everyone, even me.'

'You? What problems, Jane? Not you.'

'Yes, me. I was in love with someone once. The son of the house I was in. It didn't work out. We had a baby but it was reared by my sister. Even me, plain Jane, has had her problems. You're not alone, believe me.'

'You had a baby, Jane?'

'Yes, a boy. Colour sergeant in the Welsh Guards now. Married with two children.'

'Do you see him at all?'

'Not for five years. I always think about him though.'

'Well well, Jane.'

'Every penny I earned went to keep him, every penny.' Her eyes filled with tears. 'Life isn't easy for most of us. You have it better than most you know, Lucy.'

'You can't say it's easy for me now, Jane. Can you?'

'In life, you always have problems. Some folk have problems all the time. Jack Lloyd's life hasn't been easy. You know that better than anyone.'

Lucy reflected on what Jane had said then on her own position. 'Jane, you make it sound as though my problems are normal, ordinary, happen to everybody.'

'Troubles happen to everyone, Lucy. Everyone. Who hasn't had difficulties to face?'

'But Jane, mine are different, you know that.'

'Not really. You're going to have a baby and you're not going to get married to the father. How many women have had to face that tragedy? Hundreds and hundreds. Some of them poor, not knowing where the next shilling is coming from. Your family's got money. Plenty of money.' The last three words were expressed with some bitterness.

'Money isn't everything, Jane.'

'It is if you haven't got it, Miss Lucy. You've never been without.'

The sergeant was in work early. The previous day had been fruitful. He had obtained statements from Albert Lambert and

Richard Lamb. Now all he needed was a statement from Sporty Charlie and Lloyd could be charged with murder. Everything sewn up in two days. His employers would be proud of him. He had every reason to feel good. The best time to hit Charlie was first thing in the morning when he would be getting out of bed with a thick head, probably an acute hangover as he would be worried, perhaps terrified at the outcome of the match he had arranged.

Looking as smart as he knew how, he walked toward Charlie's Tavern. Walking slowly and confidently, he took the direct route to his destination. The walk almost became a swagger as he drew nearer. It was still not eight o'clock but the streets were busy. All noticed him, many guessing the reason for his journey.

Knocking on the front door, he received no answer. He knocked again with his cane, louder than before but with a similar result. Going to the back, he found the scullery maid washing up. She let him in without him having to knock.

Looking down at her from as great a height as he could manage, he asked condescendingly, 'Where's Charlie?'

'In bed at this hour. Can't you come back a bit later?'

'No, it has to be now. Get him out of bed.'

'He won't like it, you know.'

'I won't like it if you don't get him out.'

'Sure you can't come back later?'

'This matter can't wait. Get him out now.'

'Alright then, but don't blame me if he's a bit mad.'

'You get him out and leave him to me.'

She left the room and made her way upstairs. Gone for no more than a minute or two, he heard a muffled protest from upstairs which went on for some time. She returned to tell the sergeant, 'He says can you come back later in the morning? He'll be ready for you then.'

'Go upstairs and tell him I won't wait. If he doesn't come down, I'll go up to get him.' Feeling she was between the hammer and the anvil, she reluctantly went to Charlie's bedroom

393

again. More muffled grumbling was followed by her return.

'He's coming down. Don't blame me if he's in a bad mood.'

'I shan't do that, woman. I'll take the blame.'

'Sure, I'm glad of that.'

'I'll just wait. Get on with your work. It looks as though there's enough of it. Just ignore me.' She pressed on with her work, at the same time keeping an eye on the policeman.

Eventually Charlie stumbled down into the scullery in a dishevelled state, looking even worse than usual. His visitor knew he'd called at the right time.

'Come into the kitchen,' he beckoned, pulling a chair out. 'Tea for the man here, girl,' he shouted with a husky voice. Charlie was frightened sick. His eyes revealed his feelings which his visitor noticed immediately. They sat down facing one another on either side of the table.

'Well Charlie, a man got murdered at the match you organised. What have you to say?'

'Holy Mary, Mother of God, I've murdered no one. You know that. I'm not even capable of it.'

'We don't think you killed him but you organised the event, didn't you? If you hadn't organised it, a man wouldn't be in the mortuary and another in the police cells. Would they, Charlie?' He didn't answer. 'Would they, Charlie?' He looked him in the face as he asked this question. Charlie was disintegrating before his eyes. Again he pressed his point home, 'Would they, Charlie?'

'Suppose not. But I didn't murder them. You know that.'

'We know that, Charlie. But you organised a match, without official approval, where someone got killed. Remember that. What have you got to say Charlie?'

In the past, Charlie had always had the confidence to talk his way out of any scrape he had got himself into. Now, for the first time in his life, he seemed to have lost his way. He was internally grasping at straws which floated away before he closed his fist. There was a long gap during which he seemed lost for words.

394

He'd never felt so defenceless before. He could see no escape route. The sergeant had seen men in this dilemma before but never seen anyone so utterly defeated. It made him feel powerful, confident and controlling. He also knew that he could charge him only with a public order offence.

'Well Charlie, what have you got to say?'

'What do you want me to say?'

'I don't want you to say anything. You must tell me how you organised this contest?'

'It wasn't me who totally organised this. It sort of happened you know.'

'Sort of happened? Who was the other person who helped you organise it?'

'It got sort of arranged, you know. These things aren't always straightforward, you know.'

'You were organising it, weren't you Charlie? It was you who did it all, wasn't it?'

'Not really. The crowd just went up there for the contest.'

'Happened just like that, Charlie?'

'Yes, that's right. On the spur of the moment.'

'Rubbish. It had been planned weeks before. You know it. I know it. You organised the whole thing.'

'Not me entirely.'

'You and who else, Charlie? Father Christmas?'

Even Charlie saw the joke, giving his questioner a bleak smile.

'Alright, I'll tell you it all.'

'Now listen, Charlie. I have questioned Albert Lambert, Richard Lamb and Jack Lloyd. They tell virtually the same story. I'm going to question you and I don't want a pack of lies. See?'

'What'll happen to me?'

'I don't know. It'll be out of my hands. All I want is the truth from you. If you tell me the truth, then I will tell the court you have made a full disclosure of what happened. It's simple. If you help me, you'll help yourself. Understand?' Charlie stopped and thought for a while.

'Alright Sergeant, I'll tell you it all.' He went through the details, omitting nothing.

'That's better, Charlie. Your story's more or less similar to the other three.'

'What'll happen now, sergeant?'

'I don't know. We've got to deal with the serious matter first.'

'Serious matter?'

'Yes, murder is serious you know.' It suddenly dawned on him how serious the whole matter had become. 'Someone could be hanged, you know. Probably will be. Don't think it's going to happen to you.' The policeman gave him a mocking laugh. Leaving by the back door of the tavern, the sergeant felt even more satisfied with his inquiries in this matter.

Within a month Jack had been committed to the next Assizes by the magistrates' court and was lodged in Swansea prison awaiting his fate. Lucy had married Dickie Lamb and was now beginning to show signs of pregnancy. She had made several visits to the prison to see Jack but he refused to see her. Barty had been buried in Merthyr following a finding of unlawful killing by the coroner's court. It was a large funeral. Charlie had not paid Jack his hundred guineas in spite of frequent requests to do so. The O'Hara family were only weeks away from the gates of the workhouse. It had been an eventful month.

Chapter 38

It was the first day of the Assizes. The trumpeters heralded the arrival of Justice William Bradwell. He limped slowly from the carriage and up the steps, apparently oblivious to what was going on around him. His leg had been damaged many years before in a hunting accident. All of the crowd were looking at what he was holding in his left hand; a piece of black cloth which was now quite tattered with age. Well known on this circuit, he was familiar with the way to his chambers. Followed by the Lord Lieutenant of the county, they were soon out of sight of the crowd which always gathered to witness his arrival.

There was only one case of significance at the Assizes and that was Jack's. He was already in the dock with warders on each side. In front sat the prosecuting counsel. Sir Waterloo Jones, now a Queen's Counsel, was there for the defence. Behind them were solicitors and other supporting staff. The court was a gloomy room full of oak panels fitted many decades before. It was a place of foreboding, devoid of any form of direct sunshine and perhaps even devoid of hope. Nothing could flourish there.

Conference with counsel was now over. No more preparation could be undertaken. It was like waiting for a battle to begin. Jack felt like a soldier tied to a tree during a battle. Others would have to defend him. It was alien to him and made him feel defenceless. He had always defended himself in his own way and had confidence in his own ability. Now he was a defenceless child in the hands of others. He couldn't even give evidence on his own behalf. While these thoughts were going through his mind, he heard a loud voice shout, 'Be upstanding in court.'

The Judge limped in and stood in front of his chair. He was followed by the Lord Lieutenant and then his Marshal who did the same. The Bench bowed to the court. The court bowed to the Bench and to the Royal Coat of Arms. They sat down and commenced business immediately.

The Judge gave Jack a cursory glance. For one brief instant they looked one another in the eye. At that moment Jack knew his days were numbered. What he saw were the palest blue eyes he had ever seen; they were cold, penetrating and as sharp and unforgiving as a cutlass. He had an old, lined face, blue-veined and angry. Jack was sunk and he knew it. The jury were sworn in and the trial began.

Before the charge was put to him, Waterloo walked up to the dock and beckoned Jack towards him, saying, 'Plead not guilty.'

A hopeless fatalism gripped him as he drew in on himself, becoming progressively more detached from all that was going on around him. He looked around but did not focus on anything. The warders on each side of him gave a nudge and said, 'Stand up quick.' He stood up, still in a daze. The charge was read out to him but he failed to hear what was said. All eyes were on him, noticing his listless condition.

'Read it again,' the Judge ordered the clerk.

He heard Waterloo's voice say in a stage whisper, 'Plead not guilty.'

'Not guilty,' he said in a vague tone.

Gradually he became more conscious of what was going on, listening to the witnesses' evidence then drifting off again. Whenever he looked at the jury, one man was always staring at him. It was a look of anger and vindictiveness. He never seemed to move. Large and overweight, he was well into middle age with thinning hair but had an air of prosperity about him. He looked as though he had a need to dominate, judging by the way he was determined to stare Jack out.

The witnesses were all heard on the first day. Jack returned to his cell and Waterloo came to see him. They stood facing each other but with Jack looking towards the floor. What Waterloo said to him, he had no idea. Jack stood there without hearing or seeing anything.

'Well Lloyd, it will all happen tomorrow. It doesn't depend on whether you killed him or not by kicking him; you can't dispute that. It all hangs on whether you deliberately intended to kill him. The pleadings will all be concluded tomorrow morning. How long the jury will take is anyone's guess. Goodbye.' He left the cell, walking as quickly as possible, relieved to be in the fresh air once more.

Jack sat down without knowing he had done so. The face of that juror came back into his mind. I don't know him, he thought, but he seems to know me. Why is he so obsessed with me? Is he just plain viciously minded? That must be it. I'm not going to get much of a chance with him in the jury room. It's strange that I haven't looked at the others.

He went back to prison, now in a cell of his own. He lay down on the wooden bench remaining there till morning. Hardly sleeping, he refused the food offered him but drank the tea. It was with a bleak expectation that he waited for the approaching dawn and the sun to rise. It had been the longest night of his life.

Back to court in the morning, he faced the same routine. Standing up as the judge entered, he sat down again to hear the prosecution sum up which was quite brief. This was followed by Waterloo who seemed to speak at very great length. The words, 'The victim died from the blow administered by the defendant but did he intend to kill him? Of this you must be certain,' were repeated by the barrister. These remarks kept ringing in his ears. Jack looked at the jury who were all engrossed in listening to Waterloo, except for the one juror who had been looking at Jack all along. He was still in the same clothes and looking at him in the same immovable manner. Was he a plaster man? Had he been there since yesterday? Jack felt a mild fatalistic amusement. The Judge briefly summed-up. Jack heard little of what he had said, only remembering the words, 'Here is a man engaged in a savage and brutal trade. Of that there is no doubt. A man was killed.'

The words kept ringing in his ears. Savage and brutal trade. Savage and brutal trade. He smiled inwardly. Dear Lord, a great deal less savage than the battles in the Crimea. He shook his head in a hopeless, accepting gesture observed by none, not even Mr

Illwill on the jury. Savage and brutal trade? Had he been in a battle with thousands of bodies lying scattered around? For days there were only looters turning over dead bodies for anything of value; carrion crows in human form. Many of them were women. I can't open my mouth, he thought, and if I could it wouldn't make a scrap of difference.

The jury retired to make their decision. The room to which they retired was as dark and depressing as the court. It contained just a dozen upright chairs and a table. They didn't know one another and all but one had never sat on a jury before. There were awkward looks at one another. They were unfamiliar with one another and even more unfamiliar with their present surroundings and the heavy degree of responsibility resting on their shoulders. Whether the defendant lived or died was their decision. While most of them were still becoming accustomed to their new surroundings, they heard a loud demanding voice saying, 'You must elect a foreman. Do you hear? Elect a foreman before we do another thing.' He waited for a reply which was not forthcoming. 'Any of you been on a jury before?' Still he received no reply. 'Well, I've been on a jury before and been the foreman,' he lied. 'Does anyone else want to be the foreman?' Again there was no reply. 'Right, I'm the foreman then. Let's get this matter done quick sharp.'

A quiet voice from the corner of the room spoke. 'Hadn't we better sit down to discuss this matter?'

'We don't need to sit down. We can get this matter decided in a minute or two.'

The little man who had spoken out sat down but the self-appointed foreman would not remain silent. 'Sit down then, if you must but I want this matter cleared up. We all know what the truth of the matter is. Don't we?'They all sat down with the foreman sitting at the head of the table. There was an initial silence. The foreman didn't like silences. 'Come on, all of you, get this matter decided. He killed him deliberately. You know that and I know that. Don't you? All of you.'

The little man spoke up. 'We should all give our views on

400

this matter. A man's life depends on it.'

The foreman was impatient to get a quick conviction. 'We want a quick decision, not a lot of time-wasting. He's guilty. You know it and I know it.' He went round the table asking everyone individually, receiving eight replies indicating a conviction.

The little man smiled to himself, asking quietly, 'I seem to remember that whenever I looked at you during the trial, Mr Foreman, you were always looking at the prisoner. Did you hear any evidence?'

The foreman, unused to having his commands challenged, wanted to explode with anger and frustration but knew he couldn't. He also seemed lost for words, eventually lying in his own defence. 'Course I did. I heard every word.'

'I'm glad to hear that, Mr Foreman. Did you hear what the judge said about how certain we have to be that he intended to kill the other man?'

'Course I did.'

'Then it has to be discussed, Mr Foreman. You understand that? This isn't a cut and dried matter.'

The foreman had to accept the fact that it would have to be discussed, all because of this bloody little cocky sparrow. 'Well, get on and discuss it then. Eight of us think he's guilty. What have you got to say then? Go on then. What you got to say?'

'The point is: did he mean to kill him when, in that period of no more than a second or two, he kicked him in the back of the neck. It was certainly not premeditated.'

'Premeditated? What does that mean?'

'You obviously were not listening to the judge's summing up, were you?'

'Course I was. I heard every word.'

'What does it mean then?'

'Course I know what it means.'

'Premeditated, as you quite clearly don't know the meaning of the word, means he intended to kill him. Made up his mind beforehand. Came to a decision to kill him.'

'I know what you mean. Course I do.'

401

'It's not what I mean; it's what the word means.'

The argument continued for two hours, with the foreman becoming increasingly annoyed and frustrated and the little man getting pleasure from irritating this stupid bully. Whatever the foreman said, the little man always gave a winning reply.

The foreman's natural reply under other circumstances would be to shout the opposition down and if necessary hit him. These options were not available on this occasion. First he became annoyed, an emotion over which he normally had little control. He had to contain this fury as time and time again he was made to look a fool.

The little man made what he hoped would be his final remark, 'In the space of less than a second this man could not have decided to kill his opponent and carried it out. It was not premeditated. He is not guilty. That is my decision and it will remain so.'

Hardly had the little man ceased speaking than there was a knock on the jury room door. The foreman, hoping the little man would not speak again, almost immediately returned to his bombastic, bullying manner. Always needing to be in control, he answered the door.

The court clerk asked 'Are you anywhere near coming to a unanimous decision?'

'Yes, we're quite near.'

'No, we are not,' spoke up the little man. 'A unanimous decision is as far away as ever.'

'If you can't come to a unanimous verdict within an hour you must return to court for fresh directions from the judge. I will call again in an hour.'

The foreman nodded. He now became frightened. He had to get a decision before the hour was up. So certain was he that the judge would take action against him that he made an immediate calculation. Nine for conviction, one against. The two who were undecided must be confronted. 'You.' He pointed at the youngest juror. 'What do you say? He's guilty isn't he?'

'I'm not sure'

'Well, make up your mind then. We've only got an hour.'

The little man could not hold back his opinion. 'We haven't got an hour. We've got all the time in the world.'

The undecided juror remained undecided. 'Did he mean to kill him? It all happened in a second or two. He'll hang if we find him guilty. We all know that.'

'Course he's guilty. I know it. You all know it. All except him.' The foreman gestured towards the little man. 'It's not about long words. It's about common sense. Common sense, that's what it is.'

'Did he mean to kill him? That's what we've got to decide. I'm not sure. If I had to vote at the moment it would be for "not guilty". I'm just not sure.'

The foreman eyed the next undecided juror. Got to work on him, he thought, otherwise I'll never get a conviction at all. He was an old man, the oldest there. He looked benignly, almost humorously at the foreman.

He decided that bluster would work on this little man. 'You. Not going soft on this murderer are you?'

The old man didn't answer straight away. The foreman was impatient to get a quick decision. A unanimous verdict was now out of the question.

He didn't answer immediately but continued to look at him. Eventually he said. 'We're not in a hurry, are we?' He said it to annoy the foreman who had this pressing need to get the man convicted as quickly as possible. 'Haven't decided yet. We could take a week over this you know.'

Alarm gripped the foreman. He was worried that he would be seen as incompetent; that he would be accused of a failure to deliver. The face of the judge came into his mind. He'd have no second thoughts about dealing with him. What would he do? Almost before the eyes of the other eleven, he seemed to diminish in size. His shoulders became more humped but above all defeat showed in his eyes. All of them saw it. The bully had become the bullied.

The old man, still smiling in his own quiet way said, 'The

judge said we could take as long as we like, didn't he?'

'That doesn't mean a week. He's got other things to do, you know,' he replied with less desperation.

The old man felt that Jack had committed the murder, didn't want to say so but only wished to torment the foreman, to whom he had taken a real dislike. Feeling like a cat with a mouse, he continued to torment him, always bringing up the need to take time. After more than half an hour of this, he had had his fun and was also feeling tired.

There was a knock on the door. Again the foreman answered. 'Please will you all return to court,' was heard. The order hit him like a body blow. His stomach fluttered with fear, his face was dominated by it. What would he say if asked why they hadn't come to a decision? It had to be faced. They followed the clerk back into court.

'Would the foreman stand up' He did so. 'Answer yes or know to these questions.'

'Have you come or are you near to coming to a unanimous decision?'

'No sir'.

'Then you will retire again to consider a majority verdict.'

Justice William Bradwell looked at the jury showing neither pleasure nor displeasure as he dismissed them. They trooped back to their room. The foreman felt some relief that he hadn't been punished. A majority decision; ten to two. All he had to do was change the mind of one waverer. Just one. There was one undecided juror who hadn't spoken except to lodge his opinion.

'You haven't said yet, have you?'

'I haven't spoken yet. It's a difficult one, isn't it? If he didn't want to kill him why did he kick him in the back of the neck? That's what I ask myself. A kick like that would kill anybody. Everyone here.'

'Most of us say that. You go for conviction then?' Again the foreman wanted to get matters over with and deliver a guilty verdict. He could see the end in sight.

'I think so. I'll go for that. Guilty.'

Gesturing to the old man, he asked, 'What about you?'

He'd angered and worried the foreman but, no longer having the energy or desire to pursue it further, he said, 'Guilty.' It was what he truly felt.

'You,' he demanded, looking at the little man who didn't answer immediately. Was he on the verge of producing a unanimous verdict?

'I told you at the start that my decision was "Not guilty". It is still the same. Can you all live with this decision which will send a man to the gallows?' They all remained silent, even the foreman. None were able to return his gaze.   'Be it on your own heads.'

The foreman knocked on the door. The court clerk sitting outside opened it immediately.

'Got an eleven to one verdict.'

'Stay where you are.'

It was perhaps ten minutes before they were directed back to court. The wait to be called seemed full of overpowering and impending doom. Even the foreman was overcome by it. There was no way out now.   Back to court they walked, none looking at the defendant.

'Will the foreman of the jury stand up.' He did so. 'Answer yes or no to these questions.'

'Have you come to a unanimous decision?'

'No.'

'Have you come to a majority verdict?'

'Yes.'

'Is the prisoner guilty or not guilty?'

'Guilty.'

The silence which had prevailed till this point was now broken by an outpouring of pent up emotion. The jury still had not looked at the prisoner. For only the second time during the trial, the judge looked at the prisoner. What he had to say was a forgone conclusion.

Walking down to the cells, Jack stole a look at the foreman. Their eyes met. What Jack saw was a look of furtive guilt as he quickly looked away.

In the warders' eyes he had become a different person. They treated him more cautiously, looking at him in a more searching manner. They took their time and listened to what he had to say. Back in prison, he was in a cell of his own.

'Anything you want, Jack?'

'Tea.'

In ten minutes they were back with his request. Standing over him, they did not know what to say.

'How long have I got?'

'Three Sundays.'

'That long?' They didn't answer immediately.

'Want the preacher, Jack?'

'Don't think he'll do me much good now.' He laughed cynically to himself. 'Do you?' They didn't answer. Soon they were gone, leaving him alone.

The jurors went home to their families and Justice William Bradwell to his lodgings to spend the evening with the Lord Lieutenant of the County and one or two senior magistrates before beginning his journey to the Assize Court in Chester. Local matters were discussed: the industrial development in the town; law and order and the local police force; the weather, water supply and health problems in the town. The matters of the preceding two days were not mentioned at all.

Jack lay on the hard wooden bench which would be his bed for the last few days remaining to him. Molly and young Jack came into his mind. What would happen to them? Would it be the workhouse or would they survive by their own efforts. One hundred guineas from Sporty Charlie; there was small chance of getting that now. Waves of hopelessness broke over him. Having to accept the inevitable, he was no longer in charge of his own destiny. He had thought he was in charge of that at the age of six; that was the hardest part of all.

Chapter 39

It was a misty, overcast day as Joe the railway carter made his way from the station to the bottom of Wind Street then along Oystermouth Road. He was grey- haired now but had had the job since the railway opened. Thin and generally with a happy contented look on his face, he had few if any enemies and numerous friends. On this day there was a troubled look on his face. The numerous and warm greetings he always received fell on deaf ears that day. He seemed unaware of anyone else's presence as he went about his duties.

The four wheeled wagon he drove was low to the ground, straight on the sides and drawn by a well-fed and well-groomed black shire horse. She clip-clopped along at a stately pace. Maisie was his pride and joy. The brasses were always polished, the harness well maintained and the cart always clean, well painted and never overloaded. Just behind the seat was a nosebag full of oats. When they stopped, Maisie was a magnet to children. Every child in the town must have stroked her at some time and not a few adults. She stood more than eighteen hands high so many of them could not reach her head, having to be content with stroking her sides. For the smaller ones even this was an effort. Joe was a kindly man who had never married, finding a relationship with his charge less troubled and more fruitful than anything anyone else could offer. He was frequently ribbed about Maisie being 'the wife' or 'your favourite daughter'.

On this day his mind was not on the road ahead, the misty weather or his horse but on the packet for delivery in the back of the wagon. Along the seafront he travelled. It would be his first stop. When he arrived at the front of the prison he turned into the cobbled area in front of the main gate and got out with a heavy heart, patting Maisie automatically as he got down. Walking to

407

the rear, he opened the tailgate and with one movement lifted the small piece of cargo out, and then carried it to the door in the prison gate. He got out his book and opened it, taking a pencil from behind his ear and with that hand knocked at the door with two strikes. It was opened by a prison warder almost as soon as he had knocked. Joe picked up the parcel and gave it to the warder, releasing his hold as soon as he could

'Those bloody ropes,' he said.

With calculated disinterest and calm it was taken and placed inside.

'Sign here.' The warder did so without saying a word. Joe got back in the seat, giving a quiet word to Maisie who resumed her walk. He heard the door of the prison shut loudly then the rebound of the knocker. He breathed a sigh of relief as he travelled as fast as Maisie could walk away from this place of doom. Though he could get away from the place, the feeling remained with him all day, broken only by having to think where he was going and what he had to take where.

It was later in the day; the weather remained the same with a little more rain falling though not heavily. On the pavement leading to the prison gate an observer would have seen what appeared to be a large bundle of rags moving towards the main gate of the prison. The two women moved slowly, stopped then continued to move. Closer observation revealed that one of them was holding a young child; young Jack. They were crying and talking incoherently as they walked, aware that they would be seeing Jack for the last time. They were consumed with despair, holding one another, crying then mumbling their grief to one another. By stops and starts they arrived at the main gate eventually summoning enough courage to knock. It was opened by the same prison warder who signed for the ropes but on this occasion he took a more reasonable approach.

'Come in. Sit over there,' he said in an almost conciliatory tone. He indicated a room to the left then disappeared into what seemed the bowels of the prison. They waited what seemed hours for his return. It was only five minutes.

He returned, addressing them almost apprehensively. 'Only the wife. Not the child and mother-in-law.' Again there was an outburst of sobbing from both women. They were in a situation which was unfamiliar. Neither of them was articulate and they just wanted to get it all over as soon as possible so they didn't protest. Molly gave the child to her mother and followed the warden meekly. Which way she went, she had no idea. All she saw were the stone walls and other warders all looking at her. Eventually she found herself sitting down in a dark room with bare walls, a small window with iron bars and a heavy door slammed behind her. She waited. No longer crying, she now seemed beyond even that. Never had she felt so powerless, so hopeless or so doomed.

Without her knowing it, a door had opened behind her and Jack walked in flanked by two warders. She got up, clinging to him in despair for a short while.

'Jack,' said the taller and older warder, 'we've got to be here but you just go ahead with Molly. Take no notice of us.'

She was shocked by his appearance. He'd lost weight and looked pale. There was a rounded look to his shoulders. No longer was there any fire in him. He had been a prisoner for too long.

They appeared awkward with one another; they hadn't led a domestic life for months. Neither of them knew what to say. Eventually Jack enquired, 'Well girl, how's the boy?'

'He's fine. Downstairs he is, with mother but they won't let him in.'

'Bastards they are. No good asking them.' The anger came back to him but only briefly. The fight had gone out of him; fatalism had now taken over. For the first time in his life he knew what the future held. Again there was silence between them. He felt he had to make conversation. 'How's the old man and your mother, girl?' She replied in brief platitudes. 'You're looking a bit fat girl. Eating well?' he asked almost humorously.

It was the last straw; she started sobbing. The warders felt

409

awkward and wanted to do something but didn't know what. He put his hands gently on each side of her waist then brushed her stomach with the back of his right hand. They both knew the answer to the question. 'How long, girl?'

'I'm five months, Jack.'

For the first time since he had administered that fateful kick, tears came in his eyes. Then he felt a brief rumble of despair before he controlled himself again. 'And me not around to keep them.' Tears filled his eyes again. 'How you managing, Molly?'

'We're getting by Jack, as best we can. We're Irish you know.'

He gave a wry smile, knowing he was yesterday's man. They would get by without him. They'd get by but not as easily, as comfortably nor as securely. But people did survive somehow or other. He could feel the life force ebbing away from him almost like a bleeding wound. Oh, that he could say farewell to Molly and face his end before she had left the building. A hopelessness came over him which was noticed and would be commented upon by the warders as long as they lived.

A mile away at the Hall, Lucy lay in bed, heavily pregnant and not having slept a wink all night. Her eyes were red. Her whole face was ravaged by despair. She shook with an impotent rage. It had been the first time in her life that she had felt the thunderbolt of passion and a magnetic attraction to a man and now it was being taken from her in the most cold and brutal manner. Jane had been nearby most of the time but she was weary and Lucy was past comforting. All in the house knew the reason for her despair apart from her father and Dickie, her husband.

Dickie and Lucy had married some six months before but in no way was it a real marriage. She had from the start treated him with contempt which began soon after the wedding breakfast. At first he was annoyed then he came to accept it and now he kept his distance, living much of his time at his family home and mentioning his attempts at marriage with some amusement. How he could acknowledge that the child Lucy was carrying was his

410

was never known. Was he completely innocent or had he blinded himself to the facts? It was certainly never mentioned to his face but behind his back he was frequently called a cuckold.

In the absence of anything else to do, Dickie had arrived at the Hall. Dismounting from his horse, he shook hands with Albert who looked at him quizzically. The handshake was a limp one.

'Well Dickie, my old friend, how are you?' Albert gave him a searching look. 'What are you doing today?' Albert, usually indiscreet and invariably communicating with a certain vulgar humour was this day quite the reverse.

'How's Lucy?' asked Dickie, almost without knowing he had spoken.

'Not well at all old boy. Don't go up there today. In a bad state. Leave her alone today, Dickie. She's a very troubled girl.' His informal words were not in unison with the look he gave his friend. It was searching, even slightly troubled. Dickie did not pick up these signs.   Wanting to get him off the premises as soon as possible he said, 'Dickie old boy, I'm riding out to Gower. We must go together.'

'Albert, I'd like to see Lucy before we go.'

'Dickie old boy, that can wait. She's in a bad state, very bad. Not a good time to go, old boy.'

'I only want to see her for a minute.'

'Dickie,' he spoke to him eye to eye and slowly, 'listen to Albert. Not a good time to see her. We're going out now. Listen to Albert for once.' He continued to look at him to reinforce the point. 'Wait till I get the mare out and we'll go to Gower.' He walked towards the stables round the corner.

Hardly had he turned into the stable than a pony and chaise drove over the yard, the iron-rimmed wheels and horse's hooves making a loud noise on the cobbled surface. Hardly had the horse stopped than Lucy ran out of the back door to get into the chaise. Unaware of Dickie's presence, she climbed in assisted by Jane. Her face well wrapped up but the upper part still visible, her grief had in no way diminished. Settling herself down, Jane moved to

411

shut the chaise door. Dickie ran towards them, reaching the vehicle before it could move off.

'Lucy, it's me,' he said with a look of expectancy on his face.

She looked up into his face. He was shocked by her look of despair. Once she had seen him, her feelings turned to anger. 'Get out of the way, you bloody fool,' she spat at him. 'Driver, quickly! Away!' she directed. He hesitated, having one family member holding the cart and another inside, but in conflict with each other. 'Driver, away I said!' He now didn't think twice but cracked the whip over the pony which responded immediately. Dickie was as bewildered as ever. Why such venom?

Pony, driver and passenger made their way to the prison at a fast trot. Arriving outside, she commanded the driver, 'Wait here.' She knew his name but had forgotten it in this time of crisis. She walked to the gate and knocked firmly twice. It was opened quickly.

'I've come to see Jack Lloyd,' she demanded of the warder before he could open his mouth.

'What are you then? Family?'

'I'm Lucy Lambert, daughter of Sir Lionel Lambert. I've come to see Jack Lloyd.' Her grief temporarily gone, her pride and arrogance were acutely visible.

'Are you his parent or his wife? They are the only ones who can visit the condemned man, you know,' said the warder mildly.

'I've told you who I am. Now take me to him,' she demanded.

'Listen. I can't let you in unless you're family. Mother, father or wife, you see.'

'I said take me to him. Now.'

'I can't make this decision. You'll have to see the governor.'

'I think I better had. Send him to me now.'

'Wait in there, Miss.' He pointed to a room on the right hand side. She walked up the steps and sat down on a bench in the stone-walled room. Her feeling of despair returned; there was no hope here but she was determined to see Jack one last time. She wanted him to see her as she was carrying his child. Not knowing how long she remained there, her feelings moved from hopelessness to anger then back again. She looked around the room. Everything about it was dark and depressing. Nothing could grow or prosper here. Somehow she managed to dismiss thoughts of the following day.

She heard the sound of someone approaching. Heavy boots clomped down the corridor then stopped outside the room she was in. The heavy door opened and the governor walked in with the warder following behind. She could tell by his bearing and manner that the governor was obviously a former military man but dressed in civilian clothes. He came straight to the point, looking her directly in the face with a look that was understanding and held a hint of compassion.

'You want to see Jack Lloyd, the condemned man?'

The last two words hit her and hit her hard. It was like a hard blow to the stomach. She had to struggle to control herself.

'Yes.' She rose to her feet.

'You're not family?'

'No, not quite. I have to talk to you alone.'

He turned to the warder. 'Leave us and close the door.'

She stood up, looked him in the face and said, 'I'm carrying his child.'

'I see. It's not usual for anyone other than parents and wives to visit on these occasions.'

'Would you make an exception in this case, Governor?' Her manner was full of pathos. She was almost pleading but mustering enough tragic charm for him to respond to her wishes.

'It depends if he wants to see you. If he does then you can have half an hour. If he doesn't then you cannot see him and must leave peaceably. You understand?'

'Yes,' she nodded.

'I must also warn you that condemned men don't always

behave as you would expect them to. You understand that? He could say no. Then you will not see him.'

'He'll see me, governor. I can assure you on that point,' she said with quiet conviction.

'Very well then. Sit down. I won't be long.'

She returned to the cold seat and waited but not for long. She heard the steps of his return only a moment before he appeared at the entrance to the room where she sat. He looked at her as he walked into the waiting area, almost closing the door behind him. She returned his gaze, already knowing the answer.

'It's not good news, Miss Lambert. He won't see you.'

It was all too much for her. She cried long and loud and pleaded for him to try again, to no avail. Sitting down, she drew in on herself to nurse her grief, anger and frustration. Could anyone in the world be in more despair than her? Her troubles were breaking over her like a stormy sea, each wave worse than the last.

The governor didn't know what to do but could only stand and look. He felt impotent in this situation. He'd never had to face a woman in this condition before. Her background made it all the more difficult to handle. The battle of Balaclava had been easier than this, a great deal easier.

Slowly she subsided, her grief almost spent. Slowly she got up without looking at him, went down the few steps, through the door in the main gate which was already open and into the chaise. 'Driver, home.' He trotted home gently. Lucy was hardly aware of the journey, lost in her own quiet despair. Not caring what she looked like or who she was seen by, she stared out into the bay with unseeing eyes. Several ships were at anchor and a mist beyond them no doubt enveloped many more. She was not even aware of the gentle drizzle which had been falling all day. In her thoughts she dwelt on Jack's fate. He could never be replaced. They could have had a life together, no matter about the differences between them. She would have seen to that. What awaited him now? Rotting in the ground in an unmarked prison grave, forgotten for ever.

She stroked her stomach which was eerily reassuring. They couldn't take Jack away from her entirely. The baby would be a constant reminder of him. It would be a boy, of that she was sure.

The journey wasn't a long one but it seemed to go on for hours. A calm came over her. The inevitable had to be accepted. Her eyes were still red but were now free from tears. Sitting upright now, she looked around her. The horse, chaise and passenger clattered into the back yard. Lucy got out unaided.

'No Jane, I can manage myself thank you.' Almost confidently she walked up the stairs to her room, followed by her confidant. Almost throwing herself into the chair she gave a loud and conclusive sigh. Jane walked in behind her mistress and waited for her to settle.

'Miss Lucy, do you want anything?'

'A very strong cup of tea.'

Twenty minutes later the tea was drunk and Jane was still standing there waiting for Lucy to speak. She wanted to be of assistance but more importantly to hear what had happened. She would hear all but only in Miss Lucy's good time; you could never hurry Lucy.

Without any forewarning Lucy ordered, 'Jane, shut the door.' She did. 'Has anything happened in my absence?'

'No Miss.'

'Good.'

Jane could wait no longer. 'I hope it wasn't too upsetting, Miss Lucy?'

Lucy seemed about to speak but no words emerged. Tears appeared in her eyes as thoughts were flashing through her mind. Speech eventually surfaced.

'Jane, it was hell. I could never go through that again. Nothing almighty God has to offer could be worse than that.'

'Was it as bad as that, Miss Lucy?'

'Worse. He wouldn't see me.'

'You never saw him?'

'No, and there he was only a few yards away.'

'How awful, Miss Lucy.'

'Jane, he's dead already. There's nothing I can do. I don't know what was going through his mind. Can't blame him. Thinking about his wife and children. They could end in the workhouse. They may be there now for all I know.'

'Must be funny to know when you're going to go.'

'And for those left behind Jane? Like me.'

'There's nothing else you can do Miss Lucy, is there?'

'Oh yes there is, Jane. I've got to safeguard him.' She pointed to her stomach. 'I've got to prepare for his future if I do nothing else.'

'Have you got long now, Miss?'

'A few days, that's all. Perhaps only a day or two. We'll be busy then Jane.'

Jane's eyes filled with tears of which Lucy was unaware.

'Jane, leave me now. I've got to have a rest. It's early in the day but I feel tired. Don't go far. I may need you in a hurry.' She stroked her stomach. Lying flat on her back, she felt the baby kicking inside her. He would be a handful, she thought. Soon she was asleep.

It was nine o'clock at night. The governor had been home for three hours. Sitting by the fire he considered with apprehension the arrangements for the following morning. Never before had he had to preside over such a ceremony. He drank more whisky than usual that night before retiring.

'You're going to bed early tonight,' commented his wife.

'Yes dear, I've got a busy day tomorrow. Have to be away before six.'

'Why so early, dear?'

'It's going to be very busy first thing. Have got to see it done properly.'

'So early?'

'Yes.' She didn't know. He wasn't going to tell her.

416

Jack had lain for an hour in his final resting place in an unmarked grave, alongside other felons who had met a similar fate. The soil was a little higher than the surrounding grass and still fresh. Within months the soil would be trodden down to the same level, leaving no trace of its occupant except in the memories of those who had known him. The atmosphere in the prison, always tense and full of foreboding on these occasions, was even now starting to evaporate. Locked in their cells when the execution had occurred, the prisoners had been let out and were now eating a late breakfast before returning to their usual tasks.

Lucy had howled like a wolf all night and now lay on her back totally spent with neither the emotional nor physical energy to grieve any more. Dickie had yet again come upstairs to see his wife but was dismissed with the last ounce of emotion she possessed. All she could do now was wait for the baby to be born. That was her task now, that and no other. Jane now slept in the next room and had done for the last four days. Hardly having had any sleep for two nights, she was still propelled forward by the sole and privileged access she had to Lucy. She was the fountainhead of information for those in immediate contact with the family. There was an unspoken level of embarrassment associated with the scandal of Lucy's situation.

'You alright, Miss Lucy?'

'Yes Jane, I'm alright.'

'Miss Lucy, I'm a bit tired. I'd like to get an hour or two's sleep.'

'Very well Jane. You're next door if I want you. Don't go to your usual room.'

'Very well, Miss Lucy. Can I go then?'

'Not before you've made the bed and replaced the water. It's been there all night. Then you can go.'

'Very well, Miss Lucy.' She did as she was told then asked

again, 'Can I go now, Miss.'

Ignoring her request, Lucy announced, 'Jane, my time has come. I know it.'

'Miss Lucy, you must get a doctor.'

'I suppose I'll have to.'

'You've got to get a doctor and a midwife. You've got to, you know. Now.'

'Go on then Jane. You get them.'

'Who do you want me to tell?'

'Go to mother, she'll get the doctor. Do whatever you think, Jane. Just get them. Go now?'

Jane walked down the stairs and knocked at Lady Lambert's door.

'Come in.' she called. She was sitting down in an upright chair, unoccupied and looking somewhat vacantly at Jane .

'Yes, Jane?'

'Lady Lambert. Lucy's time is near. She needs a doctor.'

'Well Jane, go out in the chaise and bring him back with you.'

'What about a midwife, Lady Lambert?'

'Do what the doctor suggests.'

'Shall I go now?'

'Of course.' She remained immobile, knowing that others would undertake what she should be part of herself. How would she explain to Sir Lionel a six month marriage and a nine month baby? Not knowing how to deal with the questions which would be asked, she returned to the vacant, dark world she spent much of her life inhabiting.

Jane ran up the few steps to Doctor McTavish's surgery, being let in by his wife. 'Miss Lucy, Sir Lionel's daughter. The baby's on the way,' she burst out breathlessly.

'Sit down, then.' She pointed to the waiting room. 'The doctor must finish his lunch.'

'I think her contractions may have started, madam.'

'Sit down and wait. A few minutes here or there won't matter. You don't want a bad tempered doctor, do you? You just

418

wait.'

She waited uncomfortably, constantly moving in her seat and wringing her hands with her eyes darting round the room looking at nothing in particular. How long she was there she had no idea. It seemed an age. Consumed with anxiety, she remained agitated till the doctor appeared in front of her without warning. He looked at her with a calm expression on his face and with the faintest of smiles and an enquiring look which said, 'Yes, what is the problem?'

'It's Miss Lucy, Doctor, her time has come,' she almost shouted out. He remained unruffled but his smile became more obvious.

'Well, I'll have to come and see her. In the meantime, you'll have to get the midwife. Do you know where Connie lives?'

'No,' she replied. He gave her directions.

'I'll be along in about an hour. Plenty of hot water, soap and towels. I don't have to tell you that, do I?' Still he looked at her with the same benign smile.

Had this man ever worried, she thought to herself. His mood did have a pacifying effect on her; she would feel safe with him. Nothing would alarm him, it appeared.

'Off you go now to get Connie. I'll be along in a while.'

Usually she didn't like taking orders from men. She did so when she had to but resented doing so. They frequently made such stupid decisions and had no idea what the effect of their decisions had on the lives of the women they dominated. They just didn't understand women. Somehow Doctor McTavish was different.

Jane pondered on her current situation; she had been unable to bring up her own child but would shortly be looking after the child of another.

Before long she was riding in the back of the chaise with Connie by her side. Connie wanted to talk, being aware of the gossip that had circulated in the town since the wedding of Lucy and Dickie. Jane was afraid that she might give something away.

'Has she started having contractions yet? 'Connie asked. She didn't know Jane's name.

'No not yet, but she won't be long.'

'It only seems yesterday that they got married.'

Jane would not be drawn. 'She's been upset recently and the baby could be premature.'

'Hope it's not too premature. She might lose it.' Connie gave Jane a knowing and questioning look. 'Sometimes you do get a very big premature baby. Had it once or twice in some of the better families. Better fed I suppose.' She maintained her gaze on Jane who was embarrassed and looked away but loyally said nothing. Connie knew it was no good pursuing the matter any more and remained silent for the rest of the journey.

The chaise rattled over the cobbles and stopped. The two women got out. Jane still did not want to look the midwife in the face.

'Well, take me up to the mother-to-be.'

'You'd better see her mother first.'

Jane knocked on Lady Lambert's door. 'Come in,' they heard from the tired voice within.

'This is Connie the midwife, Lady Lambert.' She hardly looked up.

'Well, go up and see Lucy. I always said a midwife was more help to me with the three births than any doctor. Go and see her. I may come up later. If you need to stay here then there's a bed for you. What's your name?'

'Connie, Lady Lambert.'

'Good to see you here, Connie.' Smiling at her guest in a languid manner her words came out almost automatically. She returned to her former state of inertia knowing that matters were in the hands of those more capable than her. It was really too much trouble and the effort too great to do anything or even to think about anything.

Jane and Connie made their way upstairs, the midwife looking at everything in the house which she had never entered before. It was only when she got to the top of the stairs that she realised

420

how breathless she was. Knocking at the bedroom door, there was a quick reply to come in. Connie gave Lucy a warm and enquiring look. Lucy appeared exhausted.

'I think it's started,' she said.

'When are you due, Miss Lucy?' asked Connie.

'When am I due or when am I supposed to be due?' She gave a laugh to herself which the midwife responded to more visibly than Jane. Connie had a relaxing effect on her which also released her inhibitions. Jane noticed this, becoming immediately and perceptibly jealous. Lucy responded to Connie's direct earthiness which seemed to be such a welcome change from the way Jane spoke to her which she only now saw was ingratiating. It had been cultivated by many years in domestic service where you knew your place.

'When are you due? Midwives don't rely on make believe.' She gave her a knowing and warm smile.

'Now. Forty weeks to the day. Not a day less or a day more.' All three smiled. Jane was beginning to see that Connie was no threat.

'To the day?' Connie smiled a familiar and intimate smile. 'So we won't have a premature baby then?'

'No. Definitely not. Forty weeks to the day.' Again they smiled at one another to which Jane was an observer only. Her jealousy resurfaced. She was impatient to get the baby born and the midwife off the premises. They had a relationship established in minutes which she had never had and never would. This midwife did not know her place.

'Well my girl, you're young, strong and well fed. I think everything's going to be all right. The doctor knows and he is only a few minutes down the road.' She smiled at her benignly, lingering for a minute or two. 'You'll be alright, girl. You'll make your husband into a father and your parents, grandparents. Nothing like a baby for bringing a family together.'

'I don't think that will happen here'.

'Just you see, my girl,' she reassured her. 'I'll stay upstairs here till the baby arrives.'

Molly and her family were consumed with grief. It was as though every support had been taken away from them in one fell swoop. Jack was irreplaceable in every respect. He could never come back. His physical and emotional absence was what had hit them at the moment. Nevertheless he was there in spirit and would remain so as long as Molly lived. The neighbours came in and out, always finding them in the same state of helplessness. The old man had been given some whisky which was rapidly coming to an end.

This went on for a day or two more but then, as always in such families, they had to face the future and it was the women who made the first move. The old man had slept in the armchair all night and remained so in the early morning. The previous day's wake and considerable consumption of whisky had left him looking ill and ravaged, probably shortening his life expectation. It didn't look very long anyway.

'Mother,' said Molly, 'we've got to get by as best we can. I've saved a few shillings from what the neighbours left. Not a lot but it'll buy us a few potatoes and something wet to put on them. I will call at the market at the end of the day; the prices may be down to clear the stock.'

'I'll come with you, girl. Two pairs of eyes are better than one. We'll get by. My Mother, God rest her soul, got us through the famine. How, only the good Lord knows. It killed her though. We got over here and she was dead within a twelve month. No one ever had a better mother.' Her eyes filled with tears which she wiped with her apron. 'A mother in a million, she was. She never saw you, more's the pity. She reared us all.'

'You've hardly ever mentioned her before, mother.'

'Perhaps not, but she's rarely far from my thoughts, Molly. I hope to God she is looking over us. We surely need her help now.'

They walked slowly,nay, almost shuffled towards the market stalls, their long skirts almost brushing the ground. Everything about them expressed poverty and hopelessness. Over the cobbled streets they walked without looking up, only occasionally speaking to one another. Without seeing, they knew they were the subject of comment and morbid curiosity. The odd word could be heard. 'That's the...', 'It's those...' then the rest of the sentence became hushed. Sometimes they looked up to find the speaker watching them with intensity then looking away in embarrassment. The bolder gazed at them, seeming unable to look away. It was new to them, having always lived a life of invisibility. They felt embarrassed and awkward but said nothing to each other, feeling secure in their mutual company.

Eventually getting to their usual stall, they looked at the potatoes, Molly searching for her last few shillings as she did so. They looked at one another then at the stallholder who knew them well. Even she was briefly lost for words, eventually uttering, 'Sorry about the bad news.'

Mother and daughter looked at her and saw a face both curious but also awkward and hesitant. They were lost for words, but just pointed at the potatoes. 'What'll ten pounds be?' They were told. 'We'll take'em and some parsley.' They paid and then walked on to the butcher.

There wasn't much left now, just a few of the poorer joints which did not look fresh. The butcher watched them, knowing of their tragedy but saying nothing. They looked slowly at what was there, eventually pointing to a large sheep's head.

'How much?'

'Thruppence to you, ladies,' he answered, trying to inject some improbable cheer into them. They nodded and he put it in the wicker basket they carried. 'Anything else, ladies?' They shook their heads, shuffling back home with hardly a word exchanged.

Sitting down with some relief, they started to make the meal. 'Well mother, it'll see us over for two or three days.'

'And then what, Molly?'

'Something'll turn up. It always has done.'

'Where from, girl? I'm not young any more. I've had too much of this.' She sobbed into her apron. Molly ignored her, continuing to prepare the meal.

'Sit down, mother. We've got three days food. Many haven't got that. We'll eat tonight, for sure. Many won't do that.'

The old man stirred in the chair. 'You've got something, Molly?'

'Yes, and no thanks to you. If you had your way it would all be down your throat in whisky. Shut up and wait for the meal. While you're sitting on your behind, think of some way of making a few shillings.'

'We're sure going to miss Jack.'

'He won't come back now and even the Good Lord can't work that miracle so don't put off some ways of making a few bob. Not talking, some action, you bloody old fool.'

'Don't be hard on me girl. I'm a feeble old man.'

'Feeble through the bottle, father. If you hadn't been a drinker, you'd still be in work. The wake of the last few days has done you no good.'

'But I had to pay my last respects to Jack. You know I did.'

'Shut up you old fool and go out and make a bob or two. Talking never got you anywhere.'

'Don't be hard on your old father, Molly.'

Lucy sat up in bed leaning against the pillows piled up behind her. The baby boy, two hours old, was in her arms. The confinement had not been an easy one and the mother had to be stitched. That was now over and she had eyes only for the baby. He was a full nine pounds. Round the bed were gathered all the members of the family including Lucy's husband. They were not so much round the bed as back against the walls. One would make a step forward to look at the baby more closely and hopefully hold it, only to be faced with a glare which would have done justice to a leopard. Not a word was spoken but she kept all at a distance and all silent.

The baby now started to feed vigorously, his mop of fair hair and round face moving up and down as he did so. Soon he fell

424

into a contented sleep. Still Lucy could not take her eyes off him.

Even the dominant Sir Lionel remained silent for some time but impatience eventually got the better of him. Still remaining against the wall and perhaps more than six feet from the bed he asked tentatively, 'Well Lucy, what's he going to be called?'

'Jack, of course.'

'Jack isn't a proper name. It's slang for John.'

'I think he should be called Richard,' said Dickie Lamb in a weak voice and from the furthest corner of the room. Albert, standing next to him, gave him a dig in the ribs and gestured to him to keep quiet. All but Sir Lionel and Lady Lambert looked surreptitiously at one another, some more boldly than others. Albert looked again at Dickie with a mixture of contempt and disbelief. He was sure the marriage has not been consummated. How the devil could he show his face, even less suggest his own name? Was he really as stupid and naïve as he appeared? Was he a complete innocent?

Lucy gave him a dismissive glare, 'You would, wouldn't you?'

Albert was unable to suppress a giggle which was heard by all.

'It's a suggestion, Lucy,' he replied.

Everyone kept quiet for a while, none wanting to break the silence or move forward, nearer to the mother and child. Mesmerised, none wanted to leave the room either. Each one was waiting for another to make a move.

Sir Lionel could take the silence no longer. 'Well Lucy, how much did he weigh?'

'Nine pounds,' she almost shouted in a tone of defiance, reinforcing the two words with a look which lingered.

He wanted to say something but the family around him and his daughter's venomous look restrained him. Figures were going through his mind. Married six months and has a nine pound baby. The shame and horror that flashed across his face was obvious to all in the room, particularly to his wife. His face coloured and he showed a suppressed anger. He said to himself, 'When I get that daughter of mine on her own some questions will have to be asked. That bloody little Dickie Lamb will have to answer a few questions.' Already he was juggling with plans to get them out of Swansea. He could not contain himself any longer.

'Well, what will this child be called?' He gestured in a dismissive manner as though to cast them from his life. There was no immediate reply. Again he asked the same question.

Lucy looked at him, clearly the only one in the room not intimidated. 'I've told you already father. He's my child, I made him and he will be called Jack.'

'Jack is slang for John. You know that as well as I do.'

'Well father, he can be christened John but he will be called Jack.'

'We'll see about that.'

'Yes we will, father, the decision has been made.'

Sir Lionel strode towards the door, making an immediate break in the atmosphere. The others now felt able to behave more naturally. The room gradually emptied.

'Jane, you stay,' Lucy requested.

Dickie lingered behind, hoping to hold the baby and taking a step nearer to the bed. He hovered, waiting for Lucy to make the first move.

'Get out,' she hissed at him. He did so.